A Taint in the Blood

S. M. STIRLING

A Taint in the Blood

A Novel of

THE SHADOWSPAWN

A ROC BOOK

ROC
Published by New American Library, a division of
Penguin Group (USA) Inc., 375 Hudson Street,
New York, New York 10014, USA
Penguin Group (Canada), 90 Eglinton Avenue East, Suite 700, Toronto,
Ontario M4P 2Y3, Canada (a division of Pearson Penguin Canada Inc.)
Penguin Books Ltd., 80 Strand, London WC2R 0RL, England
Penguin Ireland, 25 St. Stephen's Green, Dublin 2,
Ireland (a division of Penguin Books Ltd.)
Penguin Group (Australia), 250 Camberwell Road, Camberwell, Victoria 3124,
Australia (a division of Pearson Australia Group Pty. Ltd.)
Penguin Books India Pvt. Ltd., 11 Community Centre, Panchsheel Park,
New Delhi - 110 017, India
Penguin Group (NZ), 67 Apollo Drive, Rosedale, North Shore 0632,
New Zealand (a division of Pearson New Zealand Ltd.)
Penguin Books (South Africa) (Pty.) Ltd., 24 Sturdee Avenue,
Rosebank, Johannesburg 2196, South Africa

Penguin Books Ltd., Registered Offices:
80 Strand, London WC2R 0RL, England

First published by Roc, an imprint of New American Library,
a division of Penguin Group (USA) Inc.

First Printing, May 2010
10 9 8 7 6 5 4 3 2 1

 REGISTERED TRADEMARK—MARCA REGISTRADA

LIBRARY OF CONGRESS CATALOGING-IN-PUBLICATION DATA:

Stirling, S. M.
A taint in the blood: a novel of the Shadowspawn/S. M. Stirling.
p. cm.
"A ROC book."
ISBN 978-0-451-46341-8
I. Title.
PS3569.T543T35 2010
813'.54—dc22   2009049588

Set in Adobe Garamond
Designed by Alissa Amell

Printed in the United States of America

Acknowledgments

Thanks to Richard Foss, for help with the fine details of food, wine and restaurants.

To Kier Salmon, for *all sorts* of help! Including the name of "Rancho Sangre Sagrado," and other bits of idiomatic conversational Spanish, and useful discussions.

To Marino Panzanelli and Marco Pertoni for help with Italian, and also the other members of the Stirling listserve.

To Melinda Snodgrass, Daniel Abraham, Sage Walker, Emily Mah, Terry England, George R. R. Martin, Walter Jon Williams, Vic Milan, Jan Stirling and Ian Tregellis of Critical Mass, for constant help and advice as the book was under construction.

To Jack Williamson, Fred Pohl, Sprague de Camp and other Golden Agers for inspiration; and Roger Zelazny and Fred Saberhagen.

A Taint in the Blood

CHAPTER ONE

Ellen Tarnowski pulled over to the side of the road and turned off the engine; utter silence fell, save for the pinging sounds of hot metal contracting. With the car stopped, she could rest her forehead on the wheel and let the tears flow.

"I love him. I loved him. And he never let me in, he never told me the truth. Oh, shit, shit, *shit!*"

When she raised her eyes again the glow of the headlights broke in rainbows for a moment from the drops on her lashes.

"And I hope the flying gravel *ruined* his stupid Ferrari!"

The thought made her hiccup laughter and then choke on another sob. Then she rubbed a hand across her eyes and started at the sight of a human figure standing at the edge of the pool of light. Her foot hesitated over the gas pedal and her hand was on the shift when the half-seen shape walked towards the car—towards the passenger side. She turned her head to follow, and her left elbow slipped down on the lock and window controls.

Chunk. Whrrrrr.

The high-desert chill poured into the slightly steamy warmth of the car and the overhead light came on. Ellen felt a cleansing surge of anger as an infinitely familiar countenance stooped to look in at her.

"If you think you can talk me around again, you fucking—"

That's not Adrian, she realized an instant later. *It's not even a* man. *Get a grip, girl! Start separating and stop obsessing!*

But the resemblance was eerie. The same oval sharp-chinned face on a long skull, lobeless ears, the same wide forehead, the same yellow-flecked brown eyes and smooth olive complexion. The hair was raven-black and silky too, but far longer than Adrian's ear-length. And she was in her mid-twenties, like Adrian, like Ellen herself. Embarrassment gave her a little strength; she knew her face must be streaming tears.

"Excuse me," she managed, after clearing her throat and swallowing. "I thought you were someone else."

She couldn't see another car and this was a long way from anywhere, unless you were a coyote. The city-glow of Santa Fe was barely visible eastward through the high-desert night, the blaze of stars almost undimmed.

"Are you in trouble?"

"No, you are," the other said.

"What?" Ellen said, wiping at her tears with a wad of Kleenex.

"My, my," the woman went on, in a voice like warm velvet stretched over the edge of a knife. "How could Adrian bear to give up such sensitivity? Your emotions have a bouquet like steak tartare with a little chopped wild onion and a touch of horseradish. Marvelous!"

The words were English—with a slight trace of an accent and foreign diction; French-but-not-quite, she thought, like Adrian's except stronger. But they made no sense. Ellen felt as if she'd run down stairs and expected one more at the bottom that wasn't there. The stranger leaned forward through the window, with both her elbows on the upper edge of the door.

She's got the same sort of hands, too, Ellen realized suddenly. *Long fingers but the first three all the same length. Pianist's hands. Strangler's hands.*

Her teeth were white and even and a little disquieting as she smiled cheerfully.

"You're subject to muscle cramps, aren't you? Especially when you're under stress. High probability, at this point."

"I think you'd better go—"

The sick pain gave just enough warning for Ellen to grab at her neck and bend away from it to relax the knot. It felt as if the muscle were about to tear loose from the base of her skull and her shoulder at the same time. A breathy gasp escaped her. She could see the stranger open the door and slide into the other seat through a blurred gaze. Then her knee jerked up as another cramp knotted into the sole of her foot. But that was impossible; they *never* came more than one at a time.

The third hit in her thigh, just above the back of her knee. Her diaphragm locked on a retch and her eyes rolled up in her head as her hands locked and the fingers curled in spastic quivers. There was nothing in all the world but her flesh trying to writhe off her bones like snakes.

She never lost consciousness, not quite, but everything blurred away. When she came fully back to herself she was hunched across the wheel making small snuffling sounds. The humiliation of feeling strings of drool dangling from her lips made her wipe frantically with the Kleenex; there was nothing she could do about losing control of her bladder except get home. It had never been that bad before, or not since she was a child.

Even without the agony that had left her trembling and weak she wouldn't have been able to resist the hands that gripped her right arm at wrist and just below the shoulder, turned and locked it. The stranger's face bent towards the inside of her elbow, hidden by the fall of black hair, but dull curiosity was all she could feel. There was a sudden icy pain in the thin skin there, a mere flicker compared to what the cramps had done but *sharper* somehow.

The fog lifted from her mind, but the weakness remained; that gradually gave way to a glassy, almost pleasant calm where she didn't *want* to move. She slumped against the door, unable even to look away.

Someone is drinking my blood, she thought. Some remote objective part of her decided: *This is* gross.

"Marvelous," the other said when she sank back, licking her lips.

Her face was glowing with delight, as if lit from within. She touched a finger to the small wound, and it clotted with unnatural speed.

"Properly prepared, the right emotions give these *layers* of taste. I don't care what our biochemists say, it's not just pheromones and serotonins and analogues to MDMA. There's a deeply spiritual aspect. Don't you think so? Forgive me if I'm babbling, but to me that was like a really massive hit of snow. Or pure crystal meth."

"Who are you?" Ellen whispered; the calm was thinning, but it lay like melting ice across panic. Her breath came faster. "What are you?"

"Well, on the *what* front, I don't need to be afraid of perky cheerleaders with sharpened broom handles," she said. "And my name is Adrienne. Adrienne Brézé."

That gave her mind something to grasp at. "You're his *sister?*"

A peal of laughter. "I'm his evil twin!"

Adrian isn't a monster, she thought; the odd clarity still held her a little. *He's an asshole, but he's not a* monster.

"Do you mean he actually never . . . Oh, the poor boy is even more troubled than I thought!"

Ellen screamed and tore at the door handle. It snapped in her hand; that was enough to jar her to silence, staring at the little curved shape of metal. She released it, and it fell to the carpeting with an almost inaudible thud.

"There's always a possibility of that happening," Adrienne said. "Fatigue in the crystalline structure. And you *were* pulling very hard. Now drive us to your place. We have *so* much to talk about. After all, we both want what's best for Adrian, don't we?"

"No! Get out, get out—"

The other's hand gripped her jaw with brutal, astonishing strength and pulled their faces together until they almost touched. The velvet tone turned to a hiss:

"*Drive*, she-ape. Or I'll peel you like a tangerine!"

"Thank you, Herr Müller," Adrian Brézé said, in German. "Most comprehensive and detailed."

Thank you for making me do this with a hangover, he added mentally, blinking in the bright late-afternoon sunlight that poured through the great windows behind him and reflected off the pale stucco of the wall and the backs of the books.

One might argue it's my fault, but it's also far too painful for me to be fair, he went on to himself as he hit the button and the drapes swept across to put the room in shadow.

The man on the other side of the video call was square-faced, with thinning blond hair and an immaculate suit. If he found Adrian's bathrobe odd for what was technically a business meeting, he didn't say a word. The commissions probably ensured that, even for an anal-retentive German broker in Frankfurt.

"I believe the quarterly report is satisfactory," Müller went on. "Especially considering current market conditions."

"It will stay satisfactory as long as my instructions are followed precisely," Adrian said. "That was why I parted company with Willoughby's in London. They took time arguing with me in '09, and cost me a good deal."

"There will be no problems of that nature with us, Herr Brézé." A hesitation. "Although I would appreciate some idea of the procedure you use for your selections."

"I look at the listings and flip a coin," Adrian said succinctly. "It's a subconscious process."

A slight sour smile rewarded him. "As you wish, Herr Brézé."

When the screen on the wall returned to its drifting colors he rose and walked down the long corridor to the pool room. It wasn't large, but it did have a wave function that let you swim against an artificial current. And it was gratefully dim, which helped with his throbbing headache.

He'd tried to drown his sorrows in a bottle of Camus Cuvée 3.128. Getting drunk on that miracle of the Grande Champagne country was mildly blasphemous, and hadn't solved his problems. It didn't make the house less echoingly empty, or chase away the shadows of Ellen's presence that would haunt it now.

Cognac didn't make me feel less cold.

But at least the brandy had delayed having to think about it, and the pain did the same now.

I wouldn't have been good for her in the long run, anyway. You shouldn't be around real people, Adrian. You know that. You know why you didn't try harder to make it up. Keep that thought in mind. Ellen . . . deserves better. All you can do for her is let her go, and make it plain it's all your fault.

"Which evidently she does. Throwing a decanter at your head is a *hint*, Adrian."

He drank four glasses of water, did some stretches and slipped into the pool. Tylenol, rehydration and exercise made him feel—

"Halfway human," he said as he toweled off, laughed and swept back the drapes.

He was still hungry after scrambled eggs with chives, three rashers of Canadian bacon and pumpernickel-rye toast.

"But then, I'm always hungry," he murmured to himself, the habit of a man much alone.

The hunger never went away, but you could learn to act as if it had; just as he could put aside the ache that he'd never be seeing Ellen again.

"You have experience with enduring cravings that can never be satisfied, eh?"

His mood was mellow enough after the second cup of Blue Mountain coffee and first cigarette that he only cursed mildly when the doorbell rang. It was someone who knew the code, too.

There was a screen over the sink in the kitchen. He looked at the man standing outside his front door and sighed; medium-tall, tanned, cropped white-and-brown hair, very fit for sixty, dressed in jeans and boots and windcheater, and holding up an elevated middle finger to the should-have-been-invisible video pickup. Adrian sighed again and stacked the dishes in the washer.

"Harvey!" he said, opening the door without standing aside. "How not glad I am to see you again after so long!"

"You'd rather have a giant pink rabbit on your doorstep?"

"I can do that. You can't."

"Stop being an asshole and let me in, Adrian," Harvey said.

The gravelly voice held a hint of Texas, smoothed and overlain by a lifetime of travel. His eyes went up and down the younger man's form, from silk polo shirt to handmade kidskin shoes.

"Still dressing like an Italian pimp, I see."

"Like a very expensive French gigolo, actually. Come on in, and don't stay as long as you like. *Mi casa es mi casa.*"

Harvey Ledbetter walked through and stopped for a moment to look at a gold-and-umber-toned painting of a woman in a long dress, sitting with her back to the viewer and reading before a dresser.

"Souvenir from the London thing in '02?"

"They'd only take it again if I returned it to the museum," Adrian said.

Harvey grunted agreement, then went on into the glass-walled living-room.

"Still living in this silicon-birdcage piece of sub-Corbusier shit," he said. "I wouldn't, if I had your money."

Looking down his gaze swept over a steep tumbled wilderness of ravines and piñon and juniper and patches of old snow. In the middle distance two mule deer sprang out of bare cottonwoods along a creek, and a red-tailed hawk went by just below the retaining wall at the edge of the cliff. Beyond lay a ragged blue immensity, rising to the snow-capped Sangre del Cristo range.

"I send you a lot of my money. Besides, I'm a Shadowspawn, re-member, Harvey? I'm evil. Of course I like Modernist architecture."

"You bought it for the view. And you're not evil, you just have a lot of relatives who are," Harvey said.

A Taint in the Blood

A low table in rough-cast glass held a malachite box. Harvey opened it and took one of the slim brown-banded cigarettes within and lit it.

"And anyway," he went on, sinking into a leather-cushioned chair. "A lot of Shadowspawn *hate* Modernist stuff."

"That's the old Mustache Petes. Some of them still wear opera cloaks all the time. For God's sake, Brâncuși sleeps in a coffin!"

"You're not keeping up with the war news," Harvey grinned.

"No, I'm not. I told the Brotherhood I was resigning after that monumental cluster-fuck in Calcutta and made it stick when they threatened me."

"As I recall, I backed you up on that."

"You did. I thank you again. You're still not going to *talk* me into coming back. What part of *retired* don't you understand, Harv? We've had this argument before."

"Thought you might want to know about Brâncuși. He's dead."

Adrian raised an eyebrow. "He's been dead since 1942, and it hasn't slowed him down much."

"No, I mean *really* dead, not just his birth-body. I took a team in there and we got some plutonium wedges into his coffin. That'll teach him to use a mausoleum without an escape tunnel just because it's authentic."

Adrian froze for an instant. The ghost of a pain worse than silver shivered along his nerves.

"Christ. Now I'm impressed," he said. "It's been . . . a long time since the Brotherhood got one of the masters."

"Since *we* got one, Brézé and Ledbetter, best team in the business. Remember Zhuge Jin? Good times, right?"

Adrian remembered naked terror, the pain of knives slashing at his body, the rage that could not be contained and the face of a killer beast staring at him from his own mirror.

"Not exactly," he said dryly. "And it didn't accomplish anything. The bad guys won a long time ago. If you don't believe me, I can turn on CNN."

"You're even more optimistic than usual, Adrian. What happened, a truck run over your puppy?"

Adrian went to stand before the window, looking over the hills and letting smoke curl out of his nostrils as the sight soothed him.

"Well, my girlfriend left me last night."

"She throw a bottle of brandy at your head, or did you just crawl into one?" Harvey said, his nostrils dilating. "Smells like good stuff."

"Both."

"She's OK?" Harvey's voice was careful.

Adrian's mouth quirked up. "As far as I know, unless she went off a curve driving back to town. And the police would have contacted me if that happened. Call it a learning experience."

The other man relaxed. "And what did you learn?"

"That masochists don't really want to be treated badly. They just want to *play* at being treated badly. And that the more I knew Ellen, the more I liked her; and the more I liked her, the more I knew I was bad for her. It's . . . not a problem with any solution that's good for *me*. I hope she can be happy, but that meant letting her go. Driving her away."

The banter dropped out of the other man's voice. "You're part human, Adrian. Never forget it. You're not a bad person. You've got problems, but you try hard to work around them. Dammit, I raised you for ten years. I *know*."

"I killed my foster-parents, Harvey. My egg hatched and I know what came out."

Harvey shook his head. "I don't think you did kill them, Adrian.

I think that was your sister. And . . . she's back in town. That's what I came to tell you."

Adrian whirled. His cigarette fell from his fingers to the rough flagstone of the floor.

"You're sure?" he whispered. "Adrienne?"

"Pretty sure. We've got a hack on the face-recognition program Homeland Security is running on the surveillance cameras at Albuquerque Sunport. I can't think of anywhere else in New Mexico she'd be interested in. She's not one of their watchers at Los Alamos and they don't have anyone that high-powered working the State government. Their renfields handle that."

"Christ! I thought the Council were going to leave me alone if I stayed out of things!"

Harvey stared at him, his faded blue eyes steady. "Like, you *trust* them?"

"Well . . . no. More like trusted their self-interest in keeping me retired."

"The Brotherhood don't think she's here on an official errand for them, anyway. She still has a major jones for you."

"Tell me about it."

He picked up the cigarette, crushed it out, tried to light another. That fell from his hands onto the floor. He forced himself to breathe, in and out, in and out.

Fear is natural. Let it pass without feeding on itself.

"And she might not give a damn what the masters thought. Shadowspawn . . ."

"Aren't team players, yeah," Adrian said, keeping the raw terror out of his voice by main strength. "Especially not us concentrated pure-strain types."

He scrubbed his hands across his face, feeling his brains begin to work again.

I hate that deer-in-the-headlights feeling. Fuck, she hasn't killed or turned me yet, and it's not because she didn't try! The honors were about even in Calcutta.

A little voice whispered at the back of his mind:

But since then she's been practicing, growing stronger, and you've been trying to deny what you are. You both have the genes for the Power, but that only means so much. You were a warrior then. What are you now?

"I can't very well appeal to the Council to call her off, either," Adrian said. "Not if it's a family matter—and they'd think it was."

"She *is* your twin sister, biologically speaking," Harvey pointed out.

Adrian turned and shook his head slowly. "No. She's my anima. My own personal nightmare. She's the mirror I can't break. How long has she been here?"

"A little less than two days. Probably sniffing out the lay of the land."

Then Adrian's face went fluid; he could feel the blood draining from it, with a shock greater than fear for himself.

"Ellen!"

CHAPTER TWO

Adrienne Brézé liked the sun. Her Second Birth would come in less than a century, and then she wouldn't be seeing sunlight ever again, not if she outlived the planet. Now she sat relaxed with her face to the sky on the park bench, legs crossed at the ankle and hands in the pockets of her long duster-style astrakhan coat. Pigeons cooed; there was a slight murmur of traffic, but the narrow streets around Santa Fe's central plaza mostly held a pleasant smell of spicy local cooking from the restaurants.

People bustled around the little stretch of grass and cottonwoods centered on the Civil War memorial, parcels in their hands. More wandered down the long portico of the Palace of the Governors behind the pine-log pillars, looking at the jewelry the Indians in from the pueblos sold, or prowled the expensive shops on the other three sides; their emotions were almost as predatory as hers. Northward reared the towers of Bishop Lamy's cathedral, tall Norman Romanesque-Gothic in a low-slung and obsessively Southwestern town, and beyond that the snow-capped peaks of the Sangres.

What . . . do . . . you . . . seek . . . Daughter . . . of . . . the . . . Night?

She stiffened at the mental touch, then relaxed, closing her eyes and letting the world fade. The feel was unmistakable; like the smell of rock and dust, like watching sunset fading on a wall and eyes glittering in the gathering dusk. One of the Old Ones, a master.

An effort like a *push* behind the eyes.

I . . . hunt . . . our . . . enemies . . . Father . . . of . . . Darkness.

If . . . the . . . traitor . . . slays . . . you . . . we . . . will . . . not . . . aid . . . or . . . punish. He . . . knows . . . this. We . . . would . . . not . . . lose . . . the . . . children . . . of . . . your . . . children . . . or . . . his. Much . . . effort . . . many . . . years . . . and . . . much . . . magic . . . went . . . into . . . your . . . breeding. You . . . are . . . Shadowspawn . . . as . . . of . . . the . . . great . . . days . . . and . . . there . . . is . . . Power . . . in . . . your . . . very . . . blood.

This form of speech conveyed your true emotions unless you were *very* careful. She was, and kept it neutral as flowing water:

I . . . have . . . children.

Only . . . two . . . and . . . you . . . cannot . . . bear . . . after . . . your . . . body's . . . death. Their . . . blood . . . is . . . questionable . . . also.

I have deposited . . . many . . . ova . . . with . . . NewGen . . . Reproductive . . . Services . . . master.

Now *he* let emotion show: confusion. *Oh. Very . . . well. Slay . . . or . . . be . . . slain.*

Her eyes opened; she let out a breath of exasperation that flapped her lips and startled a pigeon at her feet.

"Nice to know I'm valued for more than my womb, you antique sexist pig!" she muttered.

A Taint in the Blood

A homeless man was approaching, ready to ask for a handout; leathery skin and rank scent and layers of tattered cloth. She glared at him and found the weakness—a blood-vessel in the brain ready to rupture, weakened by drugs, bad feeding, alcohol and stress from the untreated chemical imbalances that rode him more savagely than even her kind could do. She *pushed*. The world shifted slightly as might-be switched to *is*, like a breath of cold air up the spine and a tightness that went *click* and released around the brows. The man collapsed.

Adrienne rose and stepped by him; it would probably be minutes before someone noticed it was more than the usual unconsciousness. She'd planned on spending the afternoon at the O'Keeffe Museum, or possibly shopping for jewelry, but . . .

But I had to expend energy talking to Mthunzi, damn it! And now I should get back.

A little prickle urged her; now was the time, and no later. Now.

Ah, well, there goes the afternoon anyway.

She bought a burrito and ate it as she walked eastward, enjoying the whimsical wooden statues along the Santa Fe River—what they'd call a creek somewhere wetter. The tangy *carne adovada* was warm and bit at her tongue as she wandered up Canyon Road. Perhaps the earth-colored adobe and faux-adobe of the galleries could become monotonous in time, but for the present she liked it; it reminded her somehow of the uniformity of Umbrian hill towns in Italy. The sculpture ranged from cowboy-kitsch to weird. One attracted her eye, done in the pseudo-Hopi style; a stick-thin figure with antlers and a long blunt muzzle or mask, raising its arms to the sky.

A memory tugged at her; a recollection of early childhood, sitting on the sofa on a Sunday afternoon and watching—

"It's Bullwinkle!" she chuckled to herself. "Or close enough for government work. Bullwinkle the Shaman!"

That made her feel a little better as she reached the two-story apartment building and let herself in. Her nostrils expanded as she sprang up the stairs, taking in scents of blood and sweat and fluids; that triggered a delicious trickle of awareness as she opened the door. Pain, throttled rage, endless uncomprehending fear . . .

And is that a thread of desperate hope? Can't have that *disturbing the harmonies.*

"Sweetie! I'm back!" she called cheerfully, and gave a little skip at the shock of despair.

The apartment was small, but so was the building, and it occupied the whole of the second story; a kitchenette, a living-dining room, bedroom, bath and tiny balcony with a decorative string of chili peppers. Even so, it had probably been fairly expensive this close to the plaza and the gallery strip on Canyon Road, and there were a couple of excellent local landscapes on the walls. The telephone was on the divider between the kitchen counter and the living-room couch, and it was ringing as she came in. The bruised, naked form of the human was out of the closet where she'd left her and three-quarters of the way across the floor, wriggling desperately towards the telephone despite the gag and the wrist-to-ankle padded cuffs and chains.

Conveniently located in that remarkably *naughty collection of bits and pieces under her bed.*

The third ring, and then—

Click.

"I can't come to the phone right now—"

Adrian's voice broke in: "Ellen, *pick up*. I'm not playing head-games. You're in danger, your *life* is in danger. Remember I told you I have enemies? They're in town and they'll try to get me through you. If you won't call me, just get out of town. I'll square it with Giselle at the gallery and cover the tab, no strings, don't even tell me where you're going, just pick somewhere far away and *go*. Call me when you're across an ocean."

Click.

Ellen stopped her rolling wiggle and slumped. Tears tracked silently down her oval straight-nosed face, joining the marks of others. She snuffled again and again, struggling to breathe.

"Now the telephone," Adrienne said. "*That* is a civilized means of communication."

She checked; three messages from Adrian, the alarm increasing with each one. More left on the cell, and a quick check on the PC showed e-mail as well.

"And you would have gotten to it on the next call if I'd been any later. Impressive determination."

She threw her coat over a chair, grabbed the other by the slack in the chain and dragged her to the edge of the sofa. The haunted blue eyes stared at her as she sat and pulled her loose gray blouse over her head.

"You can *never* get blood out of silk, and this outfit is a Dominique Sirop original. Are you listening to me? I get upset when people don't. It's a weakness of mine."

A frantic nod, and she went on: "You know what I was doing, when I could have been in the O'Keeffe or shopping or back here torturing you? I was talking to Master Mthunzi, head of the Council's breeding program. He's in that ridiculous Zulu witch-doctor's shack he keeps in the Drakensberg. And how did we have our little intercontinental chat? Did he—"

She pulled an oblong object out of a clip on her belt and held it up before she tossed it onto the chair with the coat and blouse.

"—phone me or instant-message me or text me or send an e-mail on my very expensive fifth-generation everything-but-a-vibrator Black-Berry? No, he did not."

She unclipped the small holster and automatic from the small of her back, threw it on the chair and waggled a finger in the bound woman's face.

"Nooooo. We had our little conversation by long-distance *telepathy*. And . . . you . . . end . . . up . . . talking . . . like . . . this . . . and . . . do . . . you . . . know . . . why?"

Her voice rose. "Because . . . at . . . that . . . range . . . *telepathy has shit bandwidth!* So much for the lost Golden Age of the Dread Empire of Shadows."

She sighed. "Why, why, why do we have these relics, these fossils, these Pleistocene cave-painting wannabes running the Council of Shadows?"

Then she put a hand to her forehead and let her eyes widen in mock surprise.

"Oh. We're immortal. That's why. You would not *believe* what the low turnover does to middle-management career paths."

Ellen began sobbing again, low and quiet and desolate. Adrienne shut her eyes and shivered with a delight that made the tiny hairs down her spine stand as the skin crept and her breath came faster. Her tongue came out and touched her lower lip.

"Oh, now you're making me hungry, you flirt, you. Well, enough about politics and my working day. Time to have a snack."

The human began to squeal like a trapped rabbit as she was heaved effortlessly onto the sofa, shrill even through the rubber-ball gag. Adrienne knelt on the floor and slapped her face back and forth. When she was quiet again:

"Now, if you promise to scream *quietly*, I'll take that gag out and let you blow your nose before I feed on you. All right, *chérie?*"

A nod.

"You promise?"

Another. She unbuckled the leather strap and tossed it aside, ignoring the lung-stretching breath the other was taking.

"*HEL—*"

Only one syllable broke free before her hand clamped on the throat. Just a touch of thumb and little finger, but she could feel the nerve impulses running beneath the sweat-damp skin. *So* and *so.*

Ellen bucked and heaved. Her face turned dark with blood as the throat clenched, and her eyes began to bulge. Her heart hammered louder and louder as the awareness of death surged up from the hindbrain. Adrienne bent over her, lips parted.

Yes, oh God, yes . . . no, no, not yet. Was that Help *or* Hell? *But later, later. You can only kill them once.*

A whooping gasp as the muscles around the trachea relaxed. Adrienne waited until awareness returned, and then dabbed at the blond woman's face with a Kleenex from the end-table.

"Ellen! You *promised!*" she said. "Mutual trust and reciprocity are *very important* to a successful relationship! Now, you're not going to break any promises again, are you?"

"No."

A breathy whisper, but there was sincerity behind it.

"Then let's get these ridiculous chains off you. There, that's better, isn't it? Here. Blow. Your tears and blood are delicious, but I draw the line at snot."

She held out her hands over the human's body and wiggled her fingers, running them through the air from knees to chin and back.

"Where, where, *where* shall I bite? Yes, the neck is traditional but the marks might draw attention. I thought we'd go out to La Casa Sena on Palace afterwards, the *Insight Guide* recommends the food there highly. Fiber and bulk are important for me too and *you* should get plenty of protein to keep up your red-cell count. No, hands above your head. Stretch, that's it. My, you are in good condition. I do hate the way the obesity epidemic produces deeply buried veins and over-sweetened blood. It's like drinking secondhand McDonald's toadburgers. And you have such delicate skin. I can see your pulse all over."

"Please, please don't hurt me anymore. I'll be good, I promise, I'll do anything. Just don't hurt me, please."

"Oh, are you going to beg and plead? Why, you saucy minx! I absolutely *love* that! You know, we're not in a hurry . . . but there are those who argue that it's immature to play with your food. You don't think that, do you?"

A whisper: "No."

"Good."

She reached out a finger and touched the other's navel, tickling.

"Because to them I say . . . well, actually, I don't say anything to them. I just make their heads explode."

"God, that tastes like absolute shit," Adrian said, and spat into the sink to clear his mouth. "*Merde. Scheisse. Mierda. Shĭdàn.* There are no words."

"That never stopped you before," Harvey said. "You always were an articulate little bastard. Give it a try. I've only heard your bitching and moaning about blood-bank surplus a couple of hundred times."

The younger man nodded. "Like eating week-old roadkilled skunk on a hot day."

He threw the emptied blood-bag into the waste disposal and gripped the rough edge of the granite countertop, barring his teeth as he fought against a surge of nausea. The blood burned its way down his throat like the cheapest raw bathtub hooch ever made, edged with sandpaper, and coiled in his gut like a burning snake. His breath hissed out, and then the contents of his stomach stopped trying to climb back up his gullet.

"Glad to see you're not enjoying it," Harvey said dryly.

"It's dead, it's cold, and worst of all it's from someone who was calm and relaxed as they did their civic duty at the blood bank and listened to fucking New Age water music. But I need the oomph."

He laughed mirthlessly and reached for the glass of red wine. It cleared his mouth, but the effect of the blood was hitting his nerves now. He could *feel* them like a metallic web beneath his skin, more alive but jangled with a nails-on-slate quiver from the crown of his head to the tips of fingers and toes. The warning flutter of a migraine started at the back of his brain stem, telling him what the payment for the foul blood's sudden strength would be.

"Shadowspawn make a big thing of how we're like wolves and tigers and whatnot, head bull-goose top predators, but you know what we're really like? Mosquitoes."

Adrian looked through the open well in the kitchen wall and into the dining area. The horizon was darkening in the east, but it wasn't quite night yet. The coming of it thrilled along sharpened senses, an impulse to run through the sage and juniper, to hunt and howl and stalk. To leave the prisoning flesh behind. He snarled at the thought.

"Whoa, boy," Harvey said, and he realized it must have been a literal snarl as well.

"She's got Ellen," he said grimly.

"Not proven. The girl could just be so pissed off with you she won't return your calls. Remember, if she *hasn't* met your lovely sister, what you're saying sounds like conspiracy-theory rants."

"I know Adrienne. It's a taunt. She always stole my toys."

"Let's get ready. Sunset's coming."

"Hour travel time to Santa Fe. We could leave about now," Harvey said.

"No, too chancy. I'm not going outside my protections without full dark to work with—that'll equalize things. We should be able to get to Ellen's place by around seven thirty, and at least pick up the trail."

Harvey hesitated, then said: "She got you spooked?"

"Yes," Adrian said frankly. "It's not just the thought that I might lose. It's the way fighting her makes me more *similar* to her, inside my head. She knows that, too."

"Well, fightin's the only alternative we got, right now."

The older man opened his traveling case and dressed from it; boots and pants and belted high-collared tunic of loose black leather, with gloves and close-fitting hat. Adrian could feel the mesh of ultrathin silver wire within, like the sensation of having a tooth drilled when the painkiller didn't *quite* work.

"Christ, I don't know how you can stand that," he said. "Besides looking as if you're cruising for rough trade, or scouting for Ming the Merciless."

"In San Francisco, I look positively restrained. You do the Power stuff. I shoot."

He took a weapon out of the case. It was a double-barreled shotgun cut down to a massive pistol, an old-fashioned model simple as a stone ax with external hammers and all the metal parts silver-inlaid. Adrian winced and extended a hand towards it.

"Gelatin slugs?"

"Silver nitrate and a trace of radioactive waste in liquid silicone," Harvey said. "If there were Shadowspawn elephants, this would knock 'em down. It wouldn't do a renfield anything but harm, either."

He slid it into the loops inside the skirt of the leather coat, and added a box of shells to one pocket.

"Nasty. I notice you're not trying to use revolvers anymore."

Harvey shrugged. "Failure rate got too high, like the way it did with automatics back in the forties. The more probability gets warped—"

"—the easier it is to warp," Adrian finished.

"I've got the blades, too," the older man said, tapping the insides of his forearms. "They always work."

"Good. If I really had to do it and didn't care how much it hurt, I think I might be able to screw the action on that monster-truck coach gun. Or possibly the charge in the shells. And if I can do it, she can."

"Shit. We'll be back to crossbows, next."

"Yeah, only *they* will still be able to shoot *you* with machine-pistols. Now, what was that about them not really winning?"

Adrian was already in what he intended to wear; nearly-new hiking boots, jacket and trousers of charcoal-gray denim and roll-topped shirt, casual-smart enough for street wear but tough and nonbinding and giving reasonable protection to his skin if he had to move fast. He went to the Cassatt in the hallway and swung it back. The safe beneath the picture-frame had no handle, only a blank disk of steel in its center. He placed a palm against it, and let the rhythm of the circuits resonate. When they did, he thought a phrase in a language that had been long dead when Stonehenge was new.

Click-clunk.

The thick steel wedge swung open. The interior was bigger than you might expect. He reached in and took out a Glock, checked the magazine and snapped it home. There were bundles of various currencies inside the safe as well, passports in several different names, and a leather case that held ranked SD memory cards and small sealed vials. He took out a black nylon knapsack and checked the contents: colored chalks, artist-style markers, three steel hypodermics shaped to be used as daggers and loaded with a mixture much like the filling in the slugs of Harvey's coach gun. And a sheathed knife, with a curved nine-inch blade and a hilt of dimpled black bone, next to a rolled-up black right-hand glove of a heavy soft material. He set his hand to the knife, hissing slightly at the twinge of pain through the insulation.

"Like old times," Harvey said with a crooked smile.

Adrian put his arms through the straps of the knapsack and tucked the blade beneath the tail of his jacket.

"No. In the old days we'd have had more backup. And so would Adrienne. It would have been official, part of the war. There's something wrong here. She's left me alone for years, since I retired. Why now?"

"Crazed bloodlust and twisted sexual obsession? Hate? Monstrous cruelty?"

"Oh, sure, and backatcha, standard Shadowspawn family dynamics. But there's something happening here I can't put my finger on. The Council may not stop her but it isn't going to thank her for this."

"The Brotherhood isn't going to be all that happy with *me*, Adrian. They don't really like you all that much these days and we don't have resources to spare."

Adrian faced him and made a gesture—what would have been a fist against the shoulder, if he hadn't been wearing the silver-strung leather.

"I appreciate this, Harv. You always were stand-up."

A shrug. "If we're going to commit suicide, let's get it over with."

"—*tzin!*"

Ellen Tarnowski stood exactly where she'd been told. She swallowed and tried to make her legs stop shaking, and fought against the fog that threatened to roll in from the corners of her sight.

I thought I was as afraid as I could be. I was wrong. This feels . . . bigger. It's the way you'd be afraid of an avalanche.

Her apartment felt *wrong* now; somehow the whole world did, a sensation that the smell of stale sweat and blood and musk magnified.

All the furniture had been pushed back against the walls. Adrienne Brézé stood in the center of the living-room wearing only a black lace thong, legs and arms outstretched to make a chi-cross, an outline against the faint light leaking from the nearly-closed bathroom door. It caught on her eyes in an occasional glitter of golden-brown, or on a sheen of sweat against olive skin. Her fingers moved in small, intricately precise motions and her face had the blank intensity Ellen had seen before on artists lost in their work.

Now and then she spoke. At first it had been in Latin, and then in a language Ellen didn't even recognize much less understand, full of clicks and whines and buzzing sounds and restless sibilants. Several times she took a piece of colored chalk and marked a glyph on the floor, odd spiky shapes that made the insides of Ellen's eyes itch until she let her gaze fall out of focus. One last word, a sound that refused to render itself into syllables at all; she made herself stop trying when it began to circle around inside her head like a wasp.

What is that? she wondered. *It doesn't really sound like speech.*

The eyes swung her way, and she tried to freeze even her thoughts.

"It's Mhabrogast," the deadly velvet voice said. "According to legend, it's the language spoken in Hell. The native tongue of demons. Adrian really has been keeping you in the dark, eh?"

Ellen whimpered. Adrienne smiled with a catlike turn of the lips.

I didn't ask! Ellen cried silently. *I just thought it. Can she read my* mind? *Oh, God, can't I even* think?

Adrienne sighed and relaxed her stance.

"There, that will do it. Read your mind? Emotions, intentions, sensations, *oui*, easily. But for verbal thoughts, well, telepathy's a quantum entanglement process and it takes time."

"Quantum entanglement?" she said, bewildered.

"Do I *look* like a physicist? Damp towel, dry towel, my new clothes. Quickly! Soon this won't be a good place anymore, however happy the memories of it we share."

She obeyed. Adrienne's eyes remained abstracted, with none of the cat-playful malice of the past day. Somehow that was just as terrifying.

"Now, pick up the bags and walk *precisely* behind me until we're out on the road."

They went out into the cold of early evening. The moon was a thin-pared tilted sickle and Venus was bright in the east, but the dying sun still washed most of the stars out from the dark-blue arch of heaven. Ellen let the suitcases thump to the ground and hugged her fringed wrap around her shoulders, conscious of things *not* seen out of the corners of her eyes.

A faint gleam of light showed through the window that had been her home. Adrienne put her hands on her hips and grinned; her eyes seemed to follow patterns in the air above the two-story building.

"*Damn*, but I am good!" she said, the mad cheerfulness back in her voice. "Now, let's go before my brother shows up."

"He'll rescue me," Ellen said, then whimpered as she heard the words.

"He'll certainly try," Adrienne agreed. "It's not that I don't love you for yourself, *chérie*, but you make the most wonderful bait. How are you feeling?"

"Weak. Shaky. Sore all over. I don't think I can drive now. I'm sorry, but I couldn't. I'm afraid I'd wreck the car."

"Well, then," Adrienne said, putting an arm around her waist and helping her to the Prius. "Let's get you something to eat."

She sat curled shrimp-fashion, hugging herself in the passenger seat. The sun was declining in the implausible crimson-green-blue-gold glory that Santa Fe alone seemed to have. As Adrienne drove towards the bridge over the river she began to sing softly:

"Elizabeth Bathory
Draining her girls in the night so no one will hear
No one comes near
Look at her bathing, splashing her toes
In the night when there's nobody there
What does she care?

All the bloodless bodies
Where do they all come from?
All the bloodless bodies
Where do they all belong?"

As they passed the streetlights came on and died above them, each with a slight discernible *pop*.

CHAPTER THREE

"**S**top!"

"At a shut-down church?" Harvey said, as he stamped on the brake.

"It isn't. Check."

Harvey did, and then did an almost comical double-take. "Shit," he swore. "Never would have caught it."

"I was always a bit stronger than Adrienne. She's a bit better at subtlety. Wards, don't-see-me's, frozen alternatives, that sort of thing."

Adrian Brézé opened the door almost before the car had pulled up against a stuccoed adobe wall across from the building—illegal parking on a narrow one-way street originally laid out by burros carrying loads down to the Plaza market. He could feel Harvey's tiger alertness, the solid weight of the coach gun in his hand, and a like keenness woke in him.

Part of it was instinct: *No other hunter on my ground! Kill!*

Part of it was an old, old hate, like the background music of his life swelling to a pounding chorus.

He walked forward, looking upward at Ellen's second-story apartment. It was only half-past seven, but the night was nearly moonless. The darkness didn't bother him. His breed saw much better in it than humans even with the body's eyes. Beside him Harvey drifted forward and leaned inconspicuously against a car, his hand inside the skirt of his leather coat.

"What is it?" he asked. His head went back and forth. "I can see the building now—two-story stucco, vigas, corner balcony, flat roof. But I'm getting . . . I'm not sure. *Something* more."

"It's—shit! Freeze! Don't move!"

Adrian struggled for words to describe the construct he saw as glinting planes of light, shifting in and out of existence. Possibilities interlinked, ready to fall out of *might* into the *is*.

"It's like a house of cards as high as a skyscraper. A probability cascade. Touch any part of it and the rest falls down before you can switch the causal paths out."

"House of cards? That doesn't sound so bad."

"The cards are giant Gillette razor blades. They'd tangle any mind they hit in feedback loops—cut and rewire all the connections randomly."

"Oh. *That* sounds pretty fucking bad."

He didn't mention the *taste* of it, the wrenching horrible pleasure. The vivid delirious meatiness of pain-soaked blood, the exultant carnal musk of mind-and-body rape, the desolation of death seen coming while bound and helpless. The *power* of it.

If she's killed Ellen, I'll . . . Then the humor struck him: *I'll kill her just the same as I would anyway.*

"Shit!" he said aloud, as his awareness expanded.

The flicker of ordinary human consciousness, disturbed without knowing why.

"The Lopezes are in; the family on the ground floor. Get them out, Harv; nobody's going to stay alive underneath this stuff when it comes down. Powerless or not, it'll slice their minds into sushi. Man, woman, three kids. Get them out *now*. I don't know how long I can hold this. It's like juggling knives with my eyes closed. She had hours to build it, and I'm out of practice."

"Can't you back out? Is Ellen in there?"

He shook his head, and beads of sweat flew into the chilly night, the smell rank in his nostrils. White puffs showed his breath.

"She was, Adrienne used her to source it, but I can't tell if she's still there. And we've already triggered it. I'm holding the whole thing up. It was unstable anyway. Shit, this could fry brains a hundred yards away when it goes. Worse than that. There could be energy release right out here in physical-reality land! Nobody could have done this ten years ago, the world wouldn't have allowed it."

He took stance, feet and arms spread, and began to move his fingers. Luckily the lights were out and there wasn't any through traffic on this street as he shouted:

"*Shz-tzee! Ak-tzee! Tzin-Mo'gh—*"

The blood's borrowed strength poured out of him, but the ancient tongue built his rage, made it fimbul-cold, a living presence in his skull like a fanged smile of bone. Lights crawled across his vision, patterns that repeated inside themselves, spinning away into the heart of a universe of ice and ash and winds like swords.

Beside him Harvey muttered:

"Oh, how I love it when you talk Mhabrogast to me, darling . . . This is gonna hurt inside a silver suit. Here, ol' buddy?"

"That's it, that's the fracture line of the square we're in. *Hurry!*"

The older man holstered his pistol, stripped off his gloves and held the thumbs and forefingers of both hands together above his head. Then he whipped them downward and punched clenched fists forward, as if drawing a line down the joining of two panels and smashing them apart, speaking:

"*I am the Opener of Doors. I am the Watcher at the Crossroads. A-ia-tzin!*" Then, hissed: "*Fuck* me that hurts."

And he was running towards the door, drawing the coach gun again. Yells, crashing; figures flying past in terror. Push *here*. Command *there*. Convince his hindbrain that *this* could happen, then make the universe know it could—

Harvey was pulling at him; he realized he'd fallen to his knees without knowing.

"Get me out," he wheezed.

"Oh, yeah. Pretty soon the local heat are going to be looking for a crazy old Anglo in black leather who chases people out of the house waving a big badass gun."

He was half-conscious of his arm pulled across strong shoulders, and the smell of tobacco and Old Spice; even the burn of silver-pain beneath his armpit was faint. Harvey pitched him into the backseat, where he lay in a shaking fetal ball. The Toyota jeep roared and skidded away, tossing him back and forth. Onto Paseo de Peralta, onto Cerillos Road, into the narrow entrance to the Whole Foods parking lot, then behind the store. Shoppers with their recyclable-paper bags of ultra-expensive organic shiitake mushrooms and handmade bratwurst and garlic-cured artisanal olives stopped to stare; one jumped out of the way with a yell.

Adrian scrabbled at the Styrofoam cooler on the floor behind the passenger seat and pulled out another plastic blood-bag. The cold sticky contents poured down his throat. It was even worse than the last time; he had barely swallowed the last of it before he shoved open the door and vomited it onto the pavement in a rush of red and the yellow liquid remnants of his afternoon breakfast. Another, more slowly; this time he managed to keep it down, like a stomachful of hydrochloric acid. But the strength seeped into him, making the shaking stop and taking the fog away from his senses.

"Oh, hell. Shield, Harvey. Shield for all you're worth. I think I persuaded it to fall in on itself but there's going to be a backwash."

His own arms went around his head, in a gesture as instinctive as it was futile. An impact like an impalpable *thud* struck him, as if padded clubs were beating from head to toe, and a wash of heat that wasn't really there.

"Oh, the bitch. She primed the whole place like a match, too," he said. "But there wasn't anyone alive in the building."

He couldn't see it from here; there wasn't any smoke yet, either. But there would be. He could feel the energy release, like a blowtorch pointed at the sky.

Harvey grunted, hunched over the wheel. "Yeah. Mr. Organic Carbon Molecule, meet Ms. Free Oxygen; on the word of command, screw like bunnies!" Then: "Incoming. From somewhere close."

Reality faded. *Ellen!* he thought.

In her best white evening-dress, with a silvery fringed alpaca shawl over her shoulders. Standing in some no-where, with Adrienne behind her, arms around her, head resting on shoulder. The brown-gold eyes glinted at him beside her fixed blue gaze.

"I driiiink youurrr *miiiiilk shake*," the hot-velvet voice of his sister crooned.

Her lips peeled back from her teeth, and her head darted aside for Ellen's throat.

"You can't—"

That was a security guard, and reality was back. Adrian came upright, wiped his mouth on the sleeve of his denim jacket and reached into a pocket. The man tensed, then relaxed a little as his hand came out and fanned four crisp fifty-dollar notes.

They vanished, as neatly as the Power could have managed it.

"It might be a good idea for your friend to take you home, sir," the man said. "I'll clean this mess up, but you may have had a little too much. Maybe you should see a doctor too. There's blood in it."

"Or maybe I haven't had enough," Adrian said as he sank back and closed the door.

The next container of cold blood went down a little less harshly; he only had to struggle against nausea for a half-dozen breaths, and was never in serious danger of losing the battle. Harvey clenched the wheel as if it was a life-buoy on the deck of the Titanic as he navigated the awkward entrance, waited for his moment and drove across the divider to head south past the Deaf School.

"Where are we going?" Adrian asked after a gray pause.

"Albuquerque. It's the closest place with a real airport. One *we* can use. I just figured something out."

"Tell. I've decided I don't know shit about anything, me."

"You tell me something. Do you fly standard commercial flights when you have to travel?"

Adrian blinked. His mind was functioning again; he was in command of his body. He just *wished* he was unconscious.

"Not if I can avoid it. Shadowspawn—"

"—don't like crowding, yeah," Harvey said. "So what do you do, now that the Brotherhood isn't making you account for all the receipts?"

"I usually charter a small executive jet if one's available. If not, I buy first-class and get sozzled. I drive whenever possible. Trains, in Europe."

The streetlights flickered over Harvey's rugged features as they crossed Rodeo; I-25 was just past there.

"Now, does Adrienne Princess of Darkness Brézé need to buy tickets and take off her shoes and walk through the scanner like the rest of us common sweaty human-cattle peons?"

Something went *click* behind Adrian's eyes. "She'll have her own plane. She travels more than I do, of course, and she's got a lot more money. It's meaningless to her, she can spend like a government. Name of a black dog, of course she'll have her own jet! Which could fly out of Santa Fe Airport—the runway's long enough for medium-sized ones. It would be waiting for her all day, ready to leave at a moment's notice."

"Yeah. She *wanted* us to catch her on the Sunport surveillance cameras and assume she'd come in that way."

"This is all some sort of long-term game," Adrian said.

"We could just refuse to play," Harvey said.

"Ellen," Adrian replied, as if that was a comprehensive answer.

Which it is, he thought.

"She's alive. We know that now. And Adrienne doesn't kill her lucies all that often. At least not right away."

"Yeah. Thanks to me, Ellen's been kidnapped, tortured, raped, bled, and that and worse is going to go right on happening to her until I bust her loose. And if I stop trying, Adrienne will have no reason *not* to kill her."

"You didn't do any of that, Adrian. She did."

"I put Ellen at risk. Anyone close to me is at risk."

"She the only girl you've been involved with since you told the Council and the Brotherhood you were off active duty and they could both go fuck each other?"

Harvey's voice was sharp. Reluctantly, Adrian answered: "Well . . . no."

"And nothing happened to any of *them*, right?"

"Apart from them deciding I was an asshole even if I was rich, and dumping me? No."

"You *are* an asshole, ol' buddy," Harvey said, and Adrian felt his mouth quirk. "But then, every woman I was ever involved with dumped me, too, so I suppose you learned it at my knee. At least you didn't marry three of them."

The older man went on: "Adrienne decided to come after you for her own reasons in her own time. Ellen just got in the way. And at least she has someone *trying* to rescue her. What do you think Adrienne has been doing for kicks and food all these years you've been sitting brooding on a mountaintop? Playing video games and eating tofu?"

"I . . . try not to think about that."

"I'm sure that's a *big* help to the victims."

Adrian flushed, started to speak, then barked harsh laughter. "Getting me angry to get me back on my feet, eh?"

A shrug. "Worked, didn't it?"

"*Mais oui, mon vieux.*"

More gently, Harvey said: "Look, I'm sorry it's your girl. But it's always someone's girl, or guy, or child or mother or brother."

"She's not my girl. I wish she was, but it's nobody's fault except mine she stomped out last night. Ellen has . . . issues. I thought we could . . . be together. And I really like her. But I didn't think it through well enough, and I never told her the truth. I *couldn't*."

"Then let's get our asses in gear. We rescue the girl, we kill the evil witch. *And* we find out what the hell she's playing at."

He turned onto the freeway, the hum of the tires growing as he pushed the Land Cruiser up to the speed limit and change. It was dense dark out here, as Santa Fe faded behind them; the traffic was light even for a weekday evening. The red lights of a Rail Runner passenger train came down the tracks that ran between the strips of highway, swelling and then flashing past.

"You got a cigarette?" Harvey asked.

"Sure," Adrian said, lit two, and drew on one himself as he handed the other over. "You know, Harv, you should stop smoking. I can't get cancer or emphysema or heart disease. Or get addicted. You can."

"Oh, hell, I can probably cure any of that—my Wreakings are good enough for little shit. Or if I can't, I'd just get you to do it."

"Now I'm your enabler?"

"This has just now occurred to you?"

After that, silence fell until Adrian flicked his butt out the window.

"She was waiting for the cascade to fall," he said, his voice coldly rational. "Somewhere fairly close, close enough that she could monitor it. She felt me trigger it, went off to her Gulfstream or whatever it is, and up, up and away. Taking Ellen with her. *Nyah, nyah, can't catch me.* She actually used to say that when we were six and playing hide-and-seek. It made me crazy."

Harvey nodded. "That's the advantage she's had so far, being a couple of steps ahead. Let's not let that happen again, shall we? We're living in a world run by monsters. You don't give them anything if you can help it. We're far enough behind to start with."

"I wish I knew what she'd been doing while we charged into her trap, though. I don't think she was lying on a rooftop, somehow. Not her style."

"Yeah. What was *she* doing at five thirty, when we were setting out to charge her electrified windmill?"

CHAPTER FOUR

"*Átahsaia!*"

The old Pueblo woman who'd been offering the tray of silver knickknacks stared at Adrienne and backed away, slowly. There was naked terror in her eyes, pouched in the wrinkled brown face. The dying sunlight brought the folds out in stark relief, like desert canyons, as it cast the pair's shadows over her.

Adrienne spoke in something that wasn't English or Spanish; Ellen thought it was an Indian language, and she could see the street-vendor understood it. She turned and ran in a lumbering shuffle with her long bulky skirts swaying, shouting:

"*Átahsaia!*"

"I'd have to be *really* hungry," Adrienne said dryly. "Though in the end blood is blood."

Ellen blinked. "What's *Átahsaia?*" she said.

There was no point in not asking, not when even her mind's privacy wasn't her own. It was less disturbing than having unasked questions answered.

Adrienne chuckled. "A cannibal demon. *Everyone* has legends about us."

"Are all the legends true?"

"Only the bad ones. The others . . . wishful thinking on the part of you humans, I'm afraid." A grin, and: "I *love* explaining things to you."

"Why?"

"To feel the way your mind leaps when you realize just how *bad* things are, and then the squirming as you run through the implications and they sink through layers of your consciousness. Stupid people are *boring* that way. Anyone can feel agony when you violate their bodies, but only the intelligent can know true mental torment."

They walked through the tunnel-like entrance and into the court-yard; Ellen felt her stomach growl at the smells, despite the taste of acid at the back of her throat. The body went on functioning, even when the world dropped out from beneath your feet.

La Casa Sena was only a little way up the street from the Palace of the Governors. It had started out as the town place of a wealthy *hacendado* more than a quarter of a millennium ago, the blank outer walls a sign of times when a rich man's house on the remote New Mexican frontier had to be a fortress and a workshop and a barracks as well as a dwelling. Inside two tall stories of adobe made a courtyard around a flagged garden. The planters were bare with winter and the stone bowl of the fountain was dry, but huge cottonwoods laced with lights towered above the roof level.

The maître d'hotel greeted them at the door, beside a little glassed-in cover that showed the deep original household well.

"Ms. Brézé and guest, for five thirty," Adrienne said. "I requested a corner table."

He didn't know her, but he could read her platinum and tanzanite necklace and her clothes—a soft draped black dress by Kokosalaki, with a high waist and a pleated front, the sort of thing that only that sort of slender androgynous figure could bring off. And Adrian was a regular customer, who'd brought Ellen here more than once.

"Your table is ready, Ms. Brézé. And how do you do, Ms. Tarnowski? It's good to see you again. Will Mr. Brézé be joining you ladies this evening?"

"I don't think so, not here," Adrienne said. "We're expecting him to drop in at a little housewarming party I've arranged in a few hours, though."

Within was handcrafted Taos-style furniture and museum-quality local landscapes on the pale walls. Aromatic split piñon crackled in an arched white fireplace. Waiters' heels clacked softly on the tile floors, and there was a murmur of conversation and the gentle bell tones of well-wielded cutlery.

This can't be happening, Ellen thought. *I've come here before. People know* me *here. What if I screamed—*

Adrienne smiled at her. "I *like* it when you scream, *chérie,*" she said. "But carrying you out when you had a fit, and telling everyone about the way you'd skipped your medication . . . tiresome. It would mean missing dinner."

The smile grew broader. "Then I would have to *punish* you. Would you like that?"

"No. Please, no."

"I didn't think so."

The waiter returned with a basket of warm bread and rolls and garlic-herb whipped butter as she took up the menu.

"The paprika-crusted sea scallops first, I think; ancho chile truffle butter sounds amusing. You could have the pan-seared Hudson Valley foie gras, *ma douce*. Then . . . the Colorado lamb shank for me, and the sika venison and wild-boar sausage for you. Followed by the lavender crème brûlée, and the six-layer dobos torte."

The waiter's eyebrows rose. "An excellent combination for you and your friend, madam. And your lamb?"

"Oh, rare, *certainement*. It's not food unless it screams in despair when you bite it."

The waiter chuckled dutifully. "Has madam had time to examine our wine list? We're proud of it."

"It's quite impressive," Adrienne said graciously. "I think a glass of the Rombauer Carneros with the scallops for me. Mildly chilled. One of the 1975 Château d'Yquem to accompany the foie gras for my companion. Then a Burgundy with the entrees; a bottle of the 2005 Richebourg, and open that now, please. And we'll both have a glass of the Cru d'Arche-Pugneau with the desserts. Coffee then, of course, but I'm afraid we'll have to be absolute barbarians and leave at around seven thirty—previous engagement—so do bring me the check early, if you would?"

"I . . . don't feel hungry," Ellen said.

The man ignored her and left with a little skip in his step; a fifteen-percent tip on that order would be more than his salary for a month.

"My stomach is clenched tight and I'm woozy. I'd throw up if I tried to eat. Please."

"I know you are a bit stressed, *ma petite*," Adrienne said, making a graceful gesture. "It's been a difficult twenty-four hours for you. I admit, I can be demanding—perhaps even a little needy, at times. Give me your hand. Yes, I think I can—"

Ellen made herself stretch her hand out across the white tablecloth, palm down. Adrienne took it in hers, fingers interlocking with fingers; she smiled into Ellen's eyes, and lowered her lips to the knuckles. The soft touch seemed to warm her hand, then spread up the arm—up the nerves of the arm, like some heated oil, or like a sauna and spa massage at Ten Thousand Waves up in the mountains. Ellen felt muscles relax she hadn't known existed, and her back slumped against the high rear of the chair, head rolling helplessly.

Gold and blue crept in around the edges of sight as waves of warmth reached her solar plexus and radiated out to the ends of her limbs and back, building on themselves. Her toes curled and her eyes rolled up as tension peaked and released.

"Oh, *God*," she breathed, surprised into a long, soft involuntary moan. "Oh, no, please, *God!*"

She didn't know how much time had passed when she came back fully to herself. La Casa Sena's staff were elaborately not noticing anything whether they had or not, and it wasn't the sort of place where customers would stare too openly. But half a dozen were looking in her direction, if only out of the corners of their eyes. One man moved his hands in a discreet double thumbs-up gesture as she caught his eye.

And Giselle Demarcio was staring at her from two tables over, eyes wide with disbelief, mouth open, a forkful of adobe-baked trout poised forgotten halfway from plate to lips.

Giselle. Manager of Hans & Demarcio Galleries. My friendly boss. The biggest motormouth gossip in town just watched me cream my pants in public. Santa Fe's a small town. Three hundred galleries or not, the art scene's even smaller. Everyone will know inside twenty-four hours.

The deep flush she could already feel turned fiery crimson with embarrassment and spread from breasts to earlobes, and she was achingly conscious of how it would show with her skin, and this off-the-shoulder dress displayed a lot of it.

Oh, God! This is a white douppioni silk sheath! It shows everything!

She squirmed in the seat, and then stopped when she realized that would make it worse.

When I stand up . . . and everyone will be watching to check!

"You're humiliating me!" she hissed.

She stared at the linen of the tablecloth with one hand still locked in the other's grasp.

"Ellen, Ellen, you complain when I make you feel pain; now you complain at pleasure. Some people are never satisfied. I fear I may become exhausted trying to live up to your expectations."

Adrienne turned her hand and kissed the palm. There was a soft wet contact of lips and tongue; then a small quick pain at the base of the thumb, and a steady suction. It seemed to cool away the last of the languorous warmth, but made it impossible to do anything but sit, passive and relaxed. Then she lifted her face away and let go her grip.

Ellen jammed her napkin into the palm of her cut hand and clenched both in her lap, glaring to one side where the wall held no faces. She suppressed the impulse to wipe the light film of sweat off her face or adjust the bosom of her dress against the hypersensitive skin.

"Some say mental torment is bland compared to physical pain and the fear of it. Nonsense. It is *subtle*. Ecstasy spiced with humiliation and shame . . . it makes your blood taste like warm banana fritters with thick vanilla whipped cream and just a *touch* of sharp ginger. And now you are hungry, eh? Really you were hungry to begin with, but I distracted your mind long enough to stop blocking it."

In fact she was ravenous, more so than she could remember being in all her life, enough that she had to make herself not gobble the entire contents of the bread basket. The appetizers arrived, and she gave another small involuntary sound—much quieter—at the rich complex taste of the seared foie gras, with its toasted pistachios and saffron oil. The forty-year-old d'Yquem was a shock; sweet, but with an underlying acidity and tastes of vanilla, mango, pineapples, honeyed peaches and grilled almonds. The feeling that the inside of her body was quivering with cold died away slowly. In a way that made things worse; the more grounded she felt, the less dreamlike the predicament became and the more real the fear. But . . .

If I'm going to die horribly or be tortured by a monster, I might as well enjoy dinner and get my blood sugar level back up first. I can't do anything but collapse into a jelly if I'm in shock. The physical affects the mental as well as the other way 'round.

"A most sensible way of looking at things. I knew Adrian must have good taste. After all, he is my twin."

The entrees arrived, and the Burgundy. The waiter made a small production of pouring the sample glass. Adrienne swirled it, sniffed, held the glass tilted so that the candle flame shone through it, then tasted in a breathy sip.

"Perfect. Nine years, and perfect. Ah, the check."

She dropped her debit card on the tray and the waiter left again. Ellen swallowed a mouthful of the boar sausage and sampled the wine with defiant slowness, then stopped and looked down for a second as the ghosts of cherries and lilac and spices flooded her mouth.

"You're nothing like Adrian," she said quietly, and bit into a piece of bread.

The smooth shoulders shrugged. "Adrian would agree with you, or at least hope you were right. But I suspect from that *interesting* array of paraphernalia at your apartment—"

"That's just a game! It's the one who's tied up that's in charge."

A chuckle. "Not when it's *my* game. Ah, Adrian, though . . . did he never go . . . a little far? Did things never become . . . strange? The poor boy is a mass of inhibitions, but he has the same genes, the same needs, the same abilities, as I do."

I think I'll change the subject.

"How do you do . . . what you do?"

Adrienne reached into her handbag and pulled out a coin. "Flip this. Keep your hand over it each time until I call the toss, then reveal it."

She did. The other spoke every time the coin came down and was covered by her other palm:

"Heads. Tails. Tails. Heads. Tails."

Ellen stared down at the coin. "Adrian . . . said he made investments by flipping a coin. I was angry because he wouldn't talk seriously with me about his work. I thought he was joking, flipping me off, pushing me away."

"Not in the least. He was avoiding lying by telling you a truth you wouldn't believe. Now, again."

A slight frown of concentration, and Ellen's eyes went wider as she flipped and revealed.

"Heads. Heads. Heads. Heads. Heads."

Adrian's sister took the coin back. "Each time, there is a chance of one or the other. Below the muscles of your fingers, below the weight of the coin, below even the decisions you make about how hard to move your thumb . . . down far enough . . . there is a . . . churning. And—"

She flipped the coin into the air herself and moved her hands aside. It struck the candleholder, a butter dish, teetered . . . and came to a stop upright on its edge. Ellen's eyes grew wide. The coin teetered again, and fell.

"—there was a *slight* chance of that happening. The stuff of your mind"— she tapped her temples with her forefingers— "operates on that level, as well. Some scientists have begun to suspect it, though we discredit them."

"And . . . you're not supernatural?"

Adrienne shrugged, in a palms-up way Ellen thought made it as certain as her accent that she hadn't been raised entirely in the United States. She filled her wineglass and Ellen's again, sipped, ate a piece of the reddish-pink lamb and some of the whipped potato, went on:

"Let me tell you a story. Perhaps it is literally true, perhaps only poetically. A long time ago, when humans first spread out from Africa—which was far longer ago than the archaeologists think—a small band of hunters was trapped in the mountains of High Asia, a few families, perhaps twenty or thirty in all. Each year the glaciers rose around their plateau, and the food was less, and the cold was more. It was most likely that they would merely eat each other and die. But one was born who was *lucky* . . ."

Ellen shivered as the other finished: "And then the world became warm and the ice melted, and we were freed and set loose, and for a hundred thousand years we ruled the earth with your breed as our playthings and our prey."

"Legends," Ellen whispered.

Adrienne nodded, resting her elbows on the table and her chin on her knuckles, smiling happily.

"Yes. In those days we believed them ourselves. We were the cruel gods who demanded the blood of men, and carried off their children and tormented their nights. We were Lamashtu and Sekhmet and Smoking Mirror; we were the evil sorcerers and the ogres and the goblins, the lamia and vetalas, incubi and succubae, impundulu and nagual, vampire and werewolf and leopard men. We were why your kind still fears the dark. We call ourselves the Shadowspawn, and for the last century we have ruled the world once more in secret."

"Then you're doing a pretty damn poor job of running it!" Ellen blurted, then clamped her lips shut.

Adrienne laughed. "*Chérie*, has *anything* I've said or done given you the impression that we care about the greatest good of the greatest number? And as for *running* the world—I said we rule it."

She uncurled her fingers for a moment, and held her hands as if framing her face like a picture with the thumbs beneath the chin.

"Do I *look* like a bureaucrat? To run the world would be to spend all our time at meetings, or reading reports, or standing in ridiculous costumes in front of faux-Egyptian temples bellowing platitudes to crowds of groveling worshippers, like a bad science-fiction film. And while you beg and plead and grovel charmingly, my sweet, it's much more enjoyable on a personal one-to-one level. No, no, we rule by ruling the men who run the world. Run it *for* us."

She turned both hands palm-up to her left, in a gesture like a visual *behold*.

"They do all the work."

The same gesture to the right.

"We have all the fun. It's the natural order."

Silence fell as the waiter returned with their desserts.

"You're going to kill me, aren't you?" Ellen said when he'd gone. "That's why you're telling me all this. You don't care what I know, because nobody will hear."

Another laugh. "Oh, I may kill you someday, slowly and beautifully and cruelly. Or not, if you continue to amuse. But if you were to escape, *per impossible*, who would you tell?"

"I'd tell everybody! These days you can't keep things secret."

"Would you start a Web site? *www.MutantVampiresDrinkOurBlood. com*? Why, seventy years ago a writer here in New Mexico stumbled on some of the truth, and wrote a book around it . . . and we let *him* live to an implausibly old age. Though we made sure the publisher wouldn't buy a sequel."

"Adrian would believe me," Ellen said.

"Yes, and you two could sit and tell each other about it. But I have no intention of losing you, *chérie*, not when our relationship is just blooming."

"Why do you do that?" Ellen said.

"Do what?"

"Talk as if we were lovers. Talk as if you loved me. Talk about our *relationship*."

"Ah, but we *do* have a relationship. Granted, it's a predator-prey relationship, but those are very important ecologically."

She took a spoonful of the dessert, ate it with slow relish, then tapped the spoon on the edge of the dish.

"And I do love you. It's a very much more complex form of the way that I love this crème brûlée. But nonetheless sincere. And the more often I taste of you, the more I love. You might call it a devouring passion. Have you never wondered why human beings sometimes feel that way? It's because you all have a trace—sometimes more than a trace, like poor Jeffrey Dahmer—of our heredity. As if deer were part wolf, or antelope part tiger."

She reached into her handbag and took out a cigarette case, tapped a pale ivory-colored cylinder into a holder and bent over to light it from the candle. An off-white tendril rose, scented with rum and something else added to the tobacco. Even then, Ellen was shocked enough to blurt:

"You can't smoke here!"

Heads were turning at nearby tables, but not towards them. A man sniffed and coughed, then shrugged and went back to his soufflé. Ellen had the sudden feeling that she was invisible, that if she stood and shouted and threw dishes nothing would happen.

"Delicious one, I can do anything I want. Anywhere, at any time, to or with anyone. I could rip out the chef's throat if I wanted to . . . though that would be a criminal waste. You'd better get used to the concept."

She looked at her watch, then tucked seven hundred-dollar bills under a wineglass for the tip.

"Time to go. Adrian should be charging in to your rescue about now. Let me see . . . yes, good shielding, but there's that don't-notice-this feeling."

"Adrian *really* loves me," Ellen said stubbornly as they rose; she draped the shawl casually around her hips.

"Which is why you were running away from him in tears when we met?" Adrienne laughed. "*Chérie*, remember that he has my instincts. He just won't admit it."

"What did you do to my apartment?"

"I set a trap. The equivalent of wiring a grenade to the door." She shrugged. "He won't be killed, I think, not if he deserves to be my brother. It's not my plan that he die. Not yet, possibly never. Now, *allons-y!*"

A limousine was waiting outside. Beside the door was a young Asian man, dressed in dark windbreaker, black T-shirt and baggy pants and trainers. There was a button microphone in his ear with the slender thread of the pickup alongside his jaw, and one hand rested inside the coat. Ellen hesitated as he opened the door; the interior loomed dark, as if this was some threshold across which she could never return. A hand pushed firmly at her back, and the man said something in Chinese. Adrienne replied in the same language, her tone sharp.

Then her head came up just as she put one foot inside the door; her eyes pointed eastward past the Cathedral, towards the apartment.

"Oh. The clever boy has brought a friend with him. Yes, we'd better get going. After all, helping Adrian is going to take us quite a while."

"Helping him?"

"Helping him with his identity confusions. You and I are going to help him . . . get down with his bad self."

Softly: "I want my brother back. My brother, my lover, my other self."

CHAPTER FIVE

"**S**till nothing definite?" Harvey Ledbetter said.

"No," Adrian said.

He worked his shoulders; all that tension there would get him would be a headache.

Cold. I must be cold. Do not *think of what Ellen is suffering. My* feelings *will not rescue her, only my strengths, my abilities, my wits. Think only of chances, strategies.*

They rode the escalator nearly alone; Albuquerque's airport was a hub, but not a big one, and air travel hadn't picked up fully again anyway with the economy still limping. There were more people arriving than catching departing flights at nine in the evening, as well.

"No," he went on. "I can't just guess. Not with someone like Adrienne involved."

"Yeah, that screws the probabilities well and good. Just *west*, eh?"

"Just west."

"Hell of a lot of territory in that direction. You want to do the honors at Security, or shall I?" Harvey said, as they walked past the shuttered bookstores and by-generous-definition restaurants.

9:45 San Francisco blinked at them from the Departures screen. *On time.*

"Oh, I'll do it," Adrian said. "I'm bored, anyway."

Harvey put his hand on the younger man's shoulder. "She's counting on you getting frazzled," he said gently.

"Yes. So I won't. I shall not be comfortable or easy, either."

Not as easy as you, my friend, he thought; he could feel the other's cool hunter's patience.

You do not know Ellen. It is not that you do not care, but this is one more encounter in a long war. And you have gotten that which you wished; you have forced me back into this doomed fight.

He didn't resent that—not much. If you could read the truth of men's emotions without effort, you learned to make allowances that those who could take comfort from illusion and ignorance did not. Or else you had no friends.

But Adrienne *must also have desired this. And that is very much a concern.*

They heaved their carry-on luggage onto the conveyor belt as they came to the head of the airport security line, amid the smell and feel of tension and boredom and throttled anger. Harvey walked jauntily into the glass enclosure.

Adrian put the knuckles of his fists together and let the simple electronic nervous system of the machines vibrate in his consciousness. That was hardly a Wreaking at all, no need for glyphs or the diamond-shard syllables of Mhabrogast that cut your mind bloody from the inside. He didn't have to touch anything but electrons in semiconductors, and when your brain held a decryption center intended to break the unique codes inside a human skull, computers were child's play.

The metallic taste put his teeth on edge for a moment, but the scanner showed nothing except the simple form of a man, and harmless underwear and magazines in their carry-ons. The same for him . . .

They collected their gear, stepped into their shoes and walked out through the slowly revolving door into the main concourse; behind him someone's mind muttered:

Kill them all, kill them all—

With a vivid image of a nuclear fireball cracking above a city, the blast-wave throwing aside buildings like confetti and turning bodies to shadows against walls . . .

"Whoa!" Harvey said. "Someone *really* doesn't like goin' through the mill!"

The Sunport had a great bronze statue where the concourse met the two wings of gates; a shaman twice man-height running full tilt, with an eagle headdress and a live eagle or an eagle spirit just at the edge of his outstretched fingers. Two decades of travelers had known it as *Chief Trips and Falls* or *Shaman Destroys Endangered Species.* Adrian smiled grimly at it; there was less charm to legends when you knew their sources. Or to religions, come to that.

"Do you know why I really hate drinking human blood?" Adrian said.

He forced himself not to snarl and turn his mind into a lethal razor as a man bumped into him, walking with his head in a copy of the *New York Times.*

Election Will Be Close; Democrats Confident, read the headline. Knowing who was really in charge also took the interest out of politics, for the most part.

"Moral qualms?" Harvey asked.

"No. It is no crime to abstract a little from the Red Cross; people donate it to help others, and they are helping *me*, and I give them a lot of money. What I hate is the way it makes everyone smell more *appetizing*. I *really* should not be around people."

They turned into one of the washrooms on the B concourse, went into adjacent stalls for privacy and opened their carry-ons across the toilet seats. Adrian checked the magazine, snapped it back into his Glock and holstered it. The knife he slipped into loops on the other side of his jacket; wearing it across the small of the back wasn't comfortable in an aircraft seat, even a first-class one.

The hypodermics with their solution of silver and radioactive waste went cautiously into steel-and-lead-lined tubes sewn into a pocket. A load of that would kill him just as permanently and irrevocably as the wickedest member of the Council of Shadows. The chalks and markers were, ironically, the most dangerous part of his equipment and the ones he *could* let the authorities see.

Or perhaps it is my mind that is dangerous. Yes, without doubt, for the glyphs only focus it. Perhaps the Mhabrogast too, though there I am less certain.

"Ol' buddy," Harvey said meditatively—there was a *chunk* sound as he checked and closed his massive coach gun. "How many people do you figure could mind-fuck the scanner the way you did?"

"Oh, anyone the Council would recognize as Shadowspawn," he said absently. "Half the sworn members of the Brotherhood; you could, it would just be harder, eh? Plenty of independents who think they are magicians or witches or psychics or whatever."

Harvey chuckled as they exited the washroom; Adrian wrinkled his nose as the smells of urine and disinfectant fell away. A hypersensitive sense of smell was another of the disadvantages of his heritage. Not as bad as the cravings, but it added its mite of discomfort.

Of course, dogs and wolves and leopards are more sensitive still, but they seem to mind it less. I wonder why?

"Makes you confident about how Homeland Security's got your ass, don't it?" Harvey went on.

Adrian laughed as well. "Harvey, what do you think would happen to a hijacker who tried to take over an aircraft with one of *us* onboard?"

"It happened. I looked it up last year, had the same thought when we were pulling our team out of Bucharest after we turned Gheorghe Brâncuși's hideaway into a tanning salon. It was in 1972, flight out of Beirut. A Shadowspawn enforcer working for Ibrahim al-Larnaki. That was before he took over Abdul the Damned's Council seat."

"What happened?"

"They hushed up the bodies, the usual. Tell you the truth, I think they got what they deserved. And it isn't often I think people deserve what a bored Shadowspawn mook does when he's turned loose with time to be inventive."

Adrian gave a sour snort. "Have you ever tallied the arguments against . . . what's the current term? Intelligent Design?"

"Can't say as I've bothered since I got over a Baptist upbringing. And I was about fifteen when that happened—decided that anything that said I shouldn't get into Julie-May McBell's pants behind the bleachers after the football game was *bound* to be wrong about everything else, too. Lost my faith with her legs wrapped around me and a bare tit in my hand. But tell me."

"Here's the Power, OK? With enough of it, you can work wonders."

"Yeah. How's that show it wasn't intelligently designed?"

"Because—by sheer accident, by a fucking evolutionary *kludge*—the genes which let you use the Power are tightly linked to traits which make you into a solitary megalomaniac serial-killing monster who has to drink human blood and finds the taste of pain addictive. If that isn't proof of the randomness of evolution, what is?"

Harvey chuckled. "But it could be evidence for *Malevolent* Design on the part of the Big Fellah, right? Monsters with the powers of gods?"

Adrian opened his mouth, then closed it. After a moment he said: "And most of the time I think *I'm* a cynic and a pessimist!"

They came to the desk at B5. Adrian put on his charming smile; he also let his accent thicken until it was as strong as his sister's. For some reason most people in this country found a bit of Parisian soothing and impressive from a handsome young man, unless you met a chauvinist at a time of international tension.

"Mademoiselle, you have two vacant first-class seats to San Francisco, is it not? For standby passengers Adrian Brézé and Harvey Ledbetter."

The harried woman had dark circles under her eyes; he could pick up a little of her weary resentment at the cascade of demands that were always more than she could meet, a life spent trying to do three people's work. She glanced down at the computer:

"I don't think—why, I do! Here's your boarding passes. We're boarding first class and Gold Pass customers right now."

"And we aren't the droids you're looking for anyway," Harvey muttered as they went into the boarding tunnel. "So move along, now."

"*Shut* up, Harv. It's easier—"

"—if nobody notices anything's screwy, yeah."

As they settled into their seats he went on: "Damn, I wish I could always travel this easy. Brotherhood makes us fly coach these days, would you believe it? And no jumping the queue."

Adrian looked out the window at the moonlit slopes of the Sandias, still with a tiny dusting of snow on their gullied peaks. They wheeled as the engines of the Boeing whined and the plane began to roll, the night-lights of the airport a galaxy of colors.

"It's cheating," he said. "I can't afford to give in to temptations. I know what's at the bottom of the slippery slope. Yes, a vodka sour, miss, *s'il vous plaît*."

"Buddy, you are too good for this wicked world."

"No. Ellen is, and now she's in a world a lot worse."

Decision firmed. "Watch my back, Harv."

He let the seat back and arranged himself in as close to the hands-crossed-on-shoulders trance position as he could inconspicuously.

"You sure about that?"

"Judgment call. But we need information if we're not going to waste time. If they're landing in this continent, they'll be where they're going by now. I'll try and grab-link as soon as she's asleep; I can tell *that* easily enough."

A Word, and his mind drifted down through layers of darkness.

"I driiiink youurrr *miiiiilkshake*," Adrienne's voice crooned in her ear.

Ellen gave an involuntary gasp of terror as the teeth touched her throat. Then Adrienne whirled her away.

"No, not yet. Not this time."

Instead she turned and leapt, like a black-haired cat. The young Chinese man who'd played guard in the limousine went down with a startled scream; Adrienne's face was locked into the angle of throat and shoulder. Ellen swallowed and turned her eyes away at the liquid sounds and the scrabbling. She lurched as the big Airbus CJ sped into its takeoff run. When she made herself look again the metallic coppery-iron-salt scent was strong. Adrienne raised her head, blood wet on her chin and her eyes glittering with joy.

God, this is hell. It's absolute hell! Ellen thought.

Adrienne laughed, her teeth red and one hand on the young man's throat.

"Yes, it is. Nor are you out of it," she said as she rose. "Theresa, take care of David. I'm going to freshen up."

"Well, give me a hand, lucy," the briskly efficient middle-aged Latina said.

Ellen did. The Asian man—*David*, she reminded herself—was half-conscious, a limp weight as they lifted him into one of the recliners. His slack grin made her a little queasy, but he came back to himself as the older woman taped a bandage to his neck, went into the kitchenette and then came back and handed him a mug of what smelled like chicken broth.

"Tsk," she said. "The maintenance staff will complain about the upholstery, again. *Gracias*, lucy. Would you like a drink? The bar is available to us."

"You're welcome," Ellen said uneasily. "Yes, a Bloody Mary." That produced a chuckle, and she flushed a little. "But . . . my name is Ellen, not Lucy."

She sank into a chair, uneasily conscious of how grubby her white silk dress was becoming. That was absurd under the circumstances—there was a spray of blood droplets across the hem now too—but the crisp business suit Theresa wore had that effect. So did the ambience of the jet; there was a compartment forward that was probably a bedroom, a central lounge-dining-office area, and the galley and a shower-bathroom at the rear. It was all pale and elegant, curved lines and blond wood and slightly nubby fabrics. The noise of the engines was very faint, and if it hadn't been for the windows and curved ceiling she wouldn't have thought it was an aircraft at all.

Theresa reminded Ellen of the attendants who hovered around the very highest echelon of clients at the gallery. The ones who were sent back later to deliver checks with a lot of zeroes in them. She handed Ellen the drink and sank onto a sofa, sipping her own; it looked like something with tequila.

David's laugh was a little weak still. He felt gingerly at his throat. She noticed a cuff-bracelet on his hand, and a small gold bangle, obsidian and jet, a rayed sun black-on-black with a jagged-looking trident spearing up through it.

He must have lost about a pint. No more than you give at the donor's clinic. Even counting—her eyes skipped over his soaked T-shirt, stuck to a sculpted chest—*the spillage. Christ, it was awful to watch, though. Or hear. I thought she was going to rip him right open. And she might. Or do it to* me, *anytime. I* need *this drink.*

"Lucy is really a job description," David said. "You're *a* lucy. It's not even gender-specific, in English."

"*Una lucy,*" Theresa amplified. "*O un lucy.*"

"*We're* renfields," he finished.

"You?" Theresa said, with a half-scornful smile. She put out a hand palm-down, and waggled it back and forth. "*Masumenos.* Now *I* am a renfield for the Brézé *familia*, like my parents and grandparents before me. You were a lucy to start with, and half one even now."

"As if you've never been bled," David snorted.

"Not since I was a girl, as initiation. And I did not *like* it as you do, *putito*. I endured it. A good manager who can handle IT systems as well as I is much harder to find than someone who can only scream and bleed. Or twitch and moan."

"Lucy? Renfield?" Ellen asked, bewildered.

"An old joke," the woman in the business suit said. "From the time of my grandfather. A joke so old it has become merely the way we speak among ourselves. We renfields are those who serve the Shadow-spawn, knowing what they are. A lucy is . . . you are . . . food and amusement for them."

Well, thank *you!* Ellen thought. *Bitch!*

"Though one may become the other."

Ellen took a sip of her drink. The vodka beneath the tomato juice added to the wine from dinner to make her feel . . .

Dutchly brave? But I have to learn whatever I can. My life depends on it. I've got to stay alive until Adrian comes for me. I can't die like this. I can't!

"How is it, being a renfield?" she asked, trying for cool nonchalance. "As a job. I can see it might be an improvement on what I'm pulling now."

The two laughed again, but with a little more respect.

"It's a little like working for the Mafia," David said. "The money's very good, but you can't quit."

"And a little like selling your soul to the Devil," Theresa amplified. "Half and half, perhaps. There is no God, and no Devil . . . but there are devils, and we serve them."

"The health package is *really* good," David said; he had a neutral Californian accent.

"Full coverage?"

Theresa smiled; there was something about it that made Ellen feel a little uneasy.

"Mostly, you just do not become sick. They lay their hands upon you, as saints were said to do. My grandparents lived past a hundred years."

Both the others snickered; Ellen had an uneasy sense that they were thinking of *her* life expectancy.

"So you get a long life. Unless they kill you first," she said, testing.

That brought shrugs. "Lucy, they can kill anyone anytime," David said. "Where do you think missing persons go? Or those faces on milk cartons? Besides, in any job, sometimes the boss goes for your throat."

Theresa nodded. "We have only one Shadowspawn to fear, one who has a use for *us*. The cattle would fear them all . . . if they knew. Perhaps someday they will; and we their faithful servants will be masters over the herd. *We* know the truth."

Us and we not including me, Ellen thought. *I don't think empathy is high on the list of renfield qualities.*

"They're very territorial about poaching on their preserves," David amplified. "And you don't have to worry about taxes, police, any of that. As long as you're off the reservation, don't piss off the boss or do the sort of big showy shit that's difficult to make vanish, it's pretty well anything goes."

"Sounds like a good gig," Ellen said.

If you're completely fucking crazy, she added to herself. *And have the morals of a rabid weasel.*

"There are some things you should know," Theresa said.

David looked at her; she shrugged. "I *am* household manager," she said. To Ellen:

"There is no privacy from them, not even in your thoughts. And no safety or protection from them anywhere. Once they have tasted of your blood you are linked, linked forever. They can find you if you flee to the ends of the earth and hide in the deepest cave. And whatever they do to you, even a very painful death, embrace it rather than disobey."

David smirked and glanced at the older woman. "There's one other downside to being a renfield," he said. "Your colleagues are going to be the sort of people who are cool with joining the Mafia, or selling their souls to the Devil."

He levered himself up. "Going to go hit the bunk. We'll be home in an hour and a half. Thanks for the chicken soup. Man, I'm looking forward to my own bed!"

Adrienne came out of the bathroom a minute after he'd wobbled to the rear. Her hair was damp, slicked back in a ponytail, and she wore a long loose colorful West African m'boubou robe with wide sleeves, printed in what Ellen thought of as a dashiki pattern.

She and Adrian even walk *a lot alike, allowing for the difference in the hips,* Ellen thought.

That flowing dancer's grace was one of the things that had attracted her to him in the first place.

Oh, God, Adrian, come get me! And I hate waiting for someone to rescue me, but what else can I do?

Though the walk had an unpleasantly catlike quality to it, now that she thought of it. A sense of creeping menace came with Adrian's sister, a fear that she hadn't noticed until it returned.

"Five minutes to the Seversk call, Ms. Brézé," Theresa said. "Do you want me to cancel it?"

"No, no, it's important. Hmmm. There's an idea. He makes a great noise about his progressive attitudes but *is* fond of high Shadowspawn attitude . . . A pity David isn't photogenic right now."

She looked at Ellen. "Take off your clothes."

"What?" Ellen said. Then an involuntary yelp of: "*Ouch!*" as her neck twinged.

"That wasn't a request, *cherie*. This is business. The underwear too. My, that dress is quite ruined, isn't it?"

She tousled Ellen's pale-blond hair, studied the results and nodded.

"Theresa, your pendant for a little."

The manager compressed her lips, but reached behind her head. The slim gold chain held a disk with the same black sun and golden trident that she'd noticed on David's wrist. Adrienne dropped it over Ellen's head, and gave it a twitch so that the sigil was visible just above her breasts.

"Excellent," she said. "Now, I will be talking with an associate named Dmitri Usov. He's an able man but has some quirks. Ah, well, don't we all, eh? Don't speak unless spoken to; if he does speak to you, answer him quickly. Theresa, bring coffee and brandy. Ellen, stand by my chair within the pickup angle and serve them if I move my hand, *so*."

The chair was a deep lounger. Adrienne lay back in it and touched a clearpad control surface in one arm. A sixty-inch screen swung down from the ceiling with a very faint whir of servos, and lit. After a moment it cleared with the pellucidly sharp outlines that meant a high-bandwidth dedicated satellite link.

Ellen blinked. The room that showed in it looked like a set from a Bakst ballet, with samovars and Persian rugs and colorful drapes and icons, clashing horribly with a tumble of electronic equipment. A man in an open embroidered caftan and loose drawstring pantaloons sat on a chair that wasn't quite thronelike—it looked too comfortable—but came close. Two naked teenagers stood on either side; the boy holding a tray with small glasses, a bowl of caviar and strips of toast, the girl the mouthpiece of a water-pipe. They looked Asian, with the extremely high cheekbones, ruddy skin and flat faces found from Mongolia northward.

The man was quite different, sharp-featured, with long pale hair and gray eyes and a thin pointed nose, his torso lean but the muscles sharply defined.

What Vladimir Putin wishes he looked like, Ellen thought. *What he'd look like if he were in his thirties and not ugly.*

She flushed as his eyes slid over her. She'd thought she knew what it was to have a man look at her like a piece of meat.

But I didn't. That's a flip-her-over-and-fuck-her glance, all right, but it's also a literal *piece-of-meat look. Or a bottle-of-good-hooch look. Oh, Jesus this is scary. I wish I could wake up!*

"*Dobry den', Dmitri Pavlovitch,*" Adrienne said. "*Kak vashi dela?*"

"I'm in fucking Siberia in February, Adrienne Juliyevna," he said in good English, only about as accented as hers. "It's *cold*, and that is how I am, and to make matters worse I am in fucking Seversk, which is not even the arsehole of Siberia. It is a chancre upon the lower intestine of Siberia. And I am stuck here until the Council relents. Where are you?"

"On my jet, bound for California." She smiled. "Just think how much better it would be if you were in a castle without central heating or plumbing, and I was traveling by coach or rowed by galley slaves, talking to you by *telepathy.*"

He laughed. "The galley slaves would have their points."

"Not as a means of *transportation.*"

"Certainly not here! If you spit, it freezes before it hits the ground. Though the long nights have been convenient. I have gotten in some excellent hunting."

"What game?"

"Bears by day. Chechens or Tartars by night, mostly. And the odd wandering tourist. Nobody misses them, and they look so surprised. One had *but the guidebook said tigers are extinct here* as her last words, I swear to God."

He smiled. "But we are impolite. First we should honor our ancient heritage with the traditional signs."

He made a gesture with his left hand. "Hail to the Dread Empire of Shadows and the Secret Reign that is to come!"

Adrienne raised her right hand, divided the first and second fingers from the fourth and fifth to form a V, and solemnly intoned:

"Live long and prosper!"

Ellen bit back a startled snort. Then they both stuck their index fingers in their ears, waggled the little fingers and chanted:

"Uga-Chuga . . . Uga-Chuga . . . Bow! Wow! Wow!"

With both fists in the air: "Goooooo TEAM!"

Both dissolved in laughter. "Ah, Adrienne, it does me good to speak with you again, after dealing with the Gheorghe Brâncuşi matter for so long. If you knew how many times I had to actually go through those pseudo-medieval rituals, as if I was some legend-besotted Victorian secret-society occultist like our ancestors . . ."

"You haven't had to deal with the Demon Daimyo of the West Coast as long as I have, Dmitri. Any real progress?"

"Yes," he said. "Progress that can be laid before the Council. Let us toast success!"

He made another gesture, one that seemed natural; forefinger to thumb, like the sign for *OK*, and a finger tapped to the neck. Then he reached for the tray, dipping a strip of the dark toast into the caviar, and taking one of the small glasses.

Ellen almost missed Adrienne's signal. She turned and took the service from Theresa and bent to put it on the sideboard and pour; it had a dark rich aroma, different from anything she'd smelled before. Her flush grew deeper as her full breasts swayed with the gesture; the whole thing made her feel horribly like an extra glimpsed in some obtrusive pop-up ad for an Internet porn site.

"*Za vashe zdorovye!*"

He downed the whole glass, Russian-style.

"*À votre santé,*" she answered and sipped the cognac, following it with black coffee.

"The plutonium was definitely from here," the man in the screen went on. "The cattle who sold it to the Brotherhood agents *thought* they were selling it to the Iranians; I suspect a small, subtle Wreaking on their memories. They have all been dealt with, but the successors . . . I do not know if they will be any better."

Adrienne hissed a little between her teeth. "We really have to do more about this, Dmitri. We are . . . vulnerable."

"Tell me. In my opinion we should never have closed down the Communists, at least their security around closed sites was competent and we only had to control a few key men to control all. That there are so *many* to deal with now is why I've been trapped here, like some exile in the days of Stalin or the Czars."

His face darkened a little. "As if *I* were responsible for Gheorghe's final death! Have you seen my report on his security? A *farce*! Tzigani with knives and shotguns and bandanas around their heads. All that they needed was violins and balalaikas. Maybe their grandfathers were at least formidable savages, but these were merely drunken louts putting on a show, as if for tourists! You expected to see the movie cameras and fog made from dry ice at any moment!"

"Yes, one must move with the times," she said.

There was a short significant pause; they met each other's eyes and then looked away.

I missed something there, Ellen thought.

"I use Gurkhas, as you know," Adrienne said into the brief silence. "They stay bought, too."

"And how was your visit to Santa Fe?" Dmitri went on, taking the mouthpiece of the hookah and drawing a deep bubbling lungful. "You spoke hopefully of it last week."

"Rather productive." Another short pause. "In more ways than one."

"Ah, *ochen' horosho*," he said. Then he looked at Ellen.

"Either you are developing a sense of style, Adrienne, or this is some sort of subtle mockery of mine."

"I? Mock? Impossible, Dmitri. Oh, well, possibly a little of both. I acquired her in Santa Fe, yes. Previously my brother's. Perhaps that explains my desire to show off a little, although he got surprisingly little use out of her. Guilty, I suppose. Such a grubby human emotion, guilt."

"Not just human. *Petit bourgeois*, which is worse," Dmitri said. Then to Ellen: "You are some sort of Slav, girl?"

"I . . . Polish, German, some Scots-Irish, a little Cherokee, sir," Ellen replied.

"And she has the most intriguingly complex psyche, too," Adrienne said. "Childhood trauma, I think. Odd pleasure-pain links."

He replied in Russian, and probably to *her*. Ellen searched her memory and managed to produce what she thought was a polite disclaimer of ability to speak the language, learned when they had some clients from St. Petersburg:

"*Ya poka ne govoryu po russki, Gospodin.*"

"I said, *You have nice tits, too, to go with the psyche,*" he replied with a smile.

What the hell am I supposed to say to that? she wondered, feeling her throat lock on the words. *Fuck off, you posturing moron? Oh, Christ! I can't even* think *it! Or* bite me, *maybe?*

Adrienne sighed. "Dmitri, your lucies have tits. Or even boobs. Mine have *breasts*. Or at least the females do."

"What happened to the Chinese boy with the delectable arse, then?"

"Still delectable, useful in several ways, and currently resting after—"

Adrienne turned her head and snapped aside just short of Ellen's thigh, a biting gesture with an audible *click* of white sharp teeth.

Dmitri snorted. "What a collector you are! Don't you ever just *kill* them, Adrienne? It's like endless foreplay with no fucking!"

Ellen swallowed. She thought the boy holding the tray did too, with an almost imperceptible quiver in his hands.

Adrienne sighed again. "Dmitri, Dmitri, what a . . . gourmand you are. I suppose you even like béchamel sauce."

"What's wrong with it?"

"That it makes everything taste the same, Escoffier's original sin? There's nothing wrong with agony and death, but you miss out on so much if you hurry, experiencing the direct mental overtones as well as the actual blood. Emotional degradation, despair, self-loathing, transference . . ."

He snorted. "Girlie stuff."

"Dmitri, I *am* a girl! When I'm corporeal, at least, and most of the time night-walking too."

"Quantity can have a quality all its own, even for drinking emotions. In mass, they can be overwhelmingly potent. Ah, if you had only been at Srebrenica when the massacre began—"

"Dmitri, I was a child. Besides, my old, do you realize *how many times* you've told your Srebrenica story?"

"Oh." He winced. "Tell me I'm not as bad as von Horst with the *Hindenberg*."

"Nearly as bad as McFadden with the *Titanic*! And he's transitioned successfully to postcorporeal so he'll *never* shut up. You'd think with a potentially infinite span ahead of him he'd focus on the future sometimes."

They laughed again. Adrienne touched the controls.

"I'll do what I can with Tōkairin Hajime," Adrienne said. "He has not any dog in this fight, so he may be reasonable. Michiko listens to me, and she has his ear. She's of our generation. You've earned release, Dmitri. There's definitely going to be a meeting in Tiflis next year, the full Council and all candidate-qualified purebloods. They have to elect a successor to Gheorghe, after all."

"I shall be forever in your debt. And the more so if I can get to Tiflis and a decent climate. We will have to remind Putin of who he really works for, so there are no disturbances."

"Good. There's talk that they may select a corporeal this time, which would be the first since . . . when? 1932, I think."

"Ah. A younger voice on the Council. That would be . . . *progressive*."

"Yes, it would. Possibilities, eh?"

The screen died and hummed upward. Adrienne smiled like a lynx. "That went smoothly, very smoothly. Theresa, you've earned a visit to Jean-Charles."

Ellen cleared her throat.

"Yes, yes, *chérie*," Adrienne said. "Get dressed, and let Theresa have her pendant back. You did very well, putting Dmitri in a good mood. Yes, *dangled in front of him like a piece of steak* is one way to put it, and no doubt you'll feel better with . . . what's that thought there? *Without my ass bare to the breeze?* We'll be landing soon, anyway."

She smiled and linked her hands behind her head.

"Life is *good*."

CHAPTER SIX

Where am I?

Ellen Tarnowski looked around. She was sitting in . . .

It's Adrian's living-room!

The great windows showing an endless tumbled stretch of moonlit high desert and mountain, the lights dim, a fire of piñon logs crackling on the fieldstone hearth and scenting the air. Even the faint smell of tobacco she'd found so irritating was comforting enough to make her almost sob with gratitude.

And Adrian, standing gravely by the mantelpiece, taut and elegant as a cat.

"Oh, thank God!" she burst out. "Adrian, I had the most horrible—"

Full wakefulness crashed back. "It wasn't a dream, was it?"

He shook his head, the silky hair sliding around his lobeless ears.

"I'm afraid not," he said softly, his face stark with misery. "I'm sorry, Ellie. I am so very sorry."

"Then—"

She looked down; she was in a long denim skirt and Indian blouse outfit she remembered. She pinched herself, hard. It hurt, but her surroundings stayed just the same. She had never had a dream like this, not complete with every detail of all five senses.

"Where am I?" she said slowly.

"Your . . . mind is here."

"Where's *here*, Adrian?"

He hesitated. "This is my memory palace. We're inside . . . ummm, my mind. I'm on a flight to San Francisco, trying to find you."

Ellen put a hand to her forehead and clenched it until the fingers dug painfully into the skin.

"And you never thought to tell me any of this before?" she said, keeping her voice from rising dangerously. "We were sleeping together for *six months* and it just never seemed the right fucking time? No wonder I *knew* you were lying to me!"

He crossed and knelt before her, taking her hands. "Ellie, I *wanted* to tell you. But this is dangerous, dangerous stuff, and I was trying to keep you as safe as I could."

"Keeping me ignorant is not *protective*! From now on, you will *tell me things* or I will not . . . not speak to you at all!"

"I feel guilty as hell that I let us get involved at all, but it had been years, I was supposed to be left alone— Ellie, we don't have time for me to tell you two hundred years of history. Multi-millennia, some of it. I need you to help me, and I promise I'll make it as right as I can. Whatever it takes."

She took a long deep breath and forced a degree of calm on herself. Her fingers closed around his with a strength bred from years of tennis.

"My mind is here? Where's the rest of me?"

"Where . . . you were before you went to sleep."

"*I'm still in bed with your crazy vampire sister?*" she half-screamed. "Get me out, get me out, get me out, Oh, God, *the things she* did *to me*—"

Air gasped into her lungs and she forced control on herself and choked down sobs.

"My mind is here? Literally?"

He nodded. "I've got your genetic template already loaded. I'm . . . running you on my hardware. Wetware. Your body is in trance state, like mine—but it's, ummm, empty."

She stared at him. "You drank my *blood*? Without telling me?"

He winced and looked aside. "No. But, ah, it's really anything with DNA in it, you see, which pretty much all body fluids have. So it doesn't have to be blood, strictly speaking, for a link."

"Oh." Then a thought. "But what she said was true? You *wanted* to drink my blood? To really hurt me?"

"I didn't, did I?" he said. "I love you, Ellen. It's just . . . hard for me to show that the way normal people can. But I didn't hurt you."

The lonely pride in it moved her suddenly; the hot anger she'd felt less than two days ago felt as distant as her childhood.

"You're not like her. I said that and she laughed, but I think it made her angry."

"I try not to be like that. I try very hard. Now immediately, darling, you have to tell me where she took you. We might get cut off at any moment."

"I'm . . . not sure. California—"

He gave a small hiss of relief and nodded. She continued:

"South of the Bay, I think. North of LA for sure, and near the coast. Someone mentioned Passo something. We landed, there was a car, but I couldn't see out the windows much. A big place in the country, I think, and everyone was really tired, even Adrienne, we all just went to bed and sacked out. I'm . . . in her room."

"Paso Robles? It might be. The Central Coast. That's very good, that helps a lot. I can put a . . . block in to conceal your memory of this. You'll still be able to remember it, but not unless you've got reason to. Be cautious about that, be *very* careful. She's extremely good at subtle Wreakings . . . mind-stuff."

"Oh, there aren't any *words* for how careful I'll be!"

Then another thought. "Wait a minute. What happens if I just *stay* here? She can't force me back, can she?"

"No. Only I can send you back. If you stay you'd be like this as long as I lived."

Ellen freed her hands and placed them on her knees.

"But if I stayed here I'd be safe . . . well, as safe as you . . . and I could live forever? God, Adrian, that is *so* tempting. She told me I had *all sorts of interesting new sensations and experiences* to look forward to! I'm so *scared* all the time."

He nodded. "Yes. And that'll be just as bad as you can imagine. More than you can imagine. But there's a chance of getting you away from her, and there are drawbacks to staying here."

The room began to fade. Sunlight appeared overhead, grew bright, reflected off marble columns around a pool. Prussian-blue mountains rose in the distance, against a cloudless sky. Scents of thyme and arbutus drifted on warm dry air under the rustling shadows cast by the leaves of live-oaks arching overhead. Cicadas buzzed as many-colored birds flew among great alabaster pots, and flamboyant bougainvillea spilled down their sides in purple and gold.

"This is Maxfield Parrish!" she exclaimed, distracted into delight. "But real! It's so beautiful . . . This is *heaven!*"

The clear cruel laughter of a young girl came from the bushes. Then the water in the pool rippled. Something passed beneath it in a smooth curve. She could see a glimpse of . . . tentacles? She stumbled back from the edge of the water with a sudden sick dread.

"This is my mind, Ellen, and it's not anything like Heaven. It's a Shadowspawn mind, and I'm no more completely in control of it than you are of yours."

Ellen looked at him and spoke slowly: "Could . . . *she* do this to me too? Swallow me?"

Adrian winced and nodded. "We call it . . . Carrying. Any strong Shadowspawn can."

She fought not to scream as he nodded again. Bitterly:

"There's no God, no Heaven, we don't have souls, but we can still *go to Hell forever?*"

"That's . . . probably where the idea of Hell came from in the first place."

Her hands went over her face. "This just gets worse and worse. All right, Adrian. I'll go back. But you get me out!"

A deep breath, and she stood and faced him. "She had a videoconference with a man named Dmitri on the flight from Santa Fe. He scared me nearly as much as she did, even on a flat-screen and eight thousand miles away."

"Dmitri Pavlovitch Usov?"

"Yes. He was in Seversk, in Siberia. There was something about plutonium smuggling, and a man, a very old Shadowspawn, who was assassinated with it."

"Gheorghe Brâncuşi?"

"Yes. There was something going on I couldn't tell, some sort of political thing, I think, an intrigue, a conspiracy. And they mentioned a Council that was going to meet in Tiflis, in Georgia, to elect new members next year. They were saying things without saying them, by indirection. And—"

"No time!" Adrian said; she could see fear on his face. "You've got to go back *now*; she's stirring out of REM sleep. You stay alive, you hear me, Ellie? You stay alive. Do not die! No matter what happens, you stay alive."

He held up a hand before her face, and clenched it into a fist as he spat a *word* that spun into her ears like buzz-saws. The universe shattered and dissolved.

"This town used to be a lot more charming before it realized how charming it was," Harvey said.

They'd spent the night in a hotel Adrian favored when he had to come here, a 1920s late–Beaux Arts one on Nob Hill, brick and marble with an attached spa. Adrian paused under the awning; there was a little square of park uphill, and a big church. The sky was bright with a few fluffy clouds, and the temperature just a little brisk. It could have been June as easily as February, in San Francisco. They turned and headed downslope, towards the Mission District.

"I'm not an urban person. Still, I hate it less than most," Adrian replied.

The streets were busy. More homeless than there had been a few years before, more empty buildings and shops, a little less traffic, but the crowds were still dense and lively on the sidewalks. Adrian detested cities, as a general rule; the sheer crowding grated on his nerves, the smells were bad, and the necessity for pulling in his senses made him feel muffled and thick and half-blind. This was . . . less bad than most.

He'd even been able to enjoy breakfast: buttermilk pancakes and local berries. Mostly he lost appetite for anything but blood quickly in places this dense, which was another reason to avoid them. Then he had spent the rest of the morning standing on the observation deck of Coit Tower on Telegraph Hill watching the Bay and the gulls over Alcatraz, and pulling the smells of salt water into his lungs.

Nothing like as bad as Cairo. Or Calcutta, where he'd once been trapped for an entire memorable month.

Harvey looked aside at him. "Got a jolt there right through my shields."

Adrian smiled. "I remembered the Black Hole, Operation Kali. Convinced me I had to get out or go mad."

Harvey grinned. "That made *me* feel like going over to the Dark Side of the Force too, ol' buddy. Of course, the Council wouldn't have me, these days. Not close enough to pureblood."

Adrian nodded. "I still think it might be faster to just go down to Paso Robles and look around ourselves."

Harvey snorted. "Yeah, *right*. Charge into Adrienne's security and generations of protections with Wreakings soaked into the bedrock . . . it's not as if we could just look things up on Google Earth, you know."

Adrian sighed in acknowledgment. *I am just venting*, he thought.

Nothing, not even human memory, was as easy to nudge with a little Wreaking as digital systems. Even hard copy tended to be burned in fires, or eaten by rats, or mildew . . . or anything else where *luck* mattered.

Harvey went on: "When your parents took you for your *visits* as a kid they didn't go there, did they?"

Adrian smiled grimly. "No, to Europe."

"You've turned to confiding since Calcutta. Getting you to mention this stuff at all was always like extracting teeth with a loop of spaghetti."

"I've been trying not to suppress the memories anymore. They are part of me. Yes, we went to the castle in the Auvergne, to . . . get us in touch with our roots, they'd say today. We thought they were our aunt and uncle, of course, come to give us a holiday. Christ, what a pile that place was! Is, I suppose."

"Yeah, the European branch of the Brézés are a bit conservative."

"Everything but hanging head-down to sleep," Adrian said. "And the place was infested with bats, at that. The attics and the caves, at least."

Then, softly: "We loved it, of course."

"Bet it was in the summer," Harvey observed, dodging a pushcart vendor.

"Of course; every summer, longer as we grew older. Green hills, dusty lanes, mountain forests, ponies for us to ride . . . our *aunt* and *uncle* who denied us nothing, and hinted that we were as an exiled prince and princess. Oh, is there a child on Earth who won't listen to *that?* The delicious sense of being *different*, different and better. Great canopied beds, fireplaces ten feet high, Egyptian gods on the walls of crypts below—"

"Egyptian?" Harvey said incredulously. "You never mentioned *that* before, either."

"Yes, Egyptian, painted in the 1830s, when it was the headquarters of the Order of the Black Dawn, before they discovered Darwin and Mendel. When they thought they were sorcerers and *loup-garou*."

"Yeah, but they *were*. Nobody allowed in who couldn't actually Wreak with the Power. *And* they married each other's sisters. Unscientific, but it worked, sorta-kinda."

Adrian nodded; that had been what kept traces of the ancient, horrible truth alive, there and elsewhere.

His voice went soft: "Then as we grew older, the ceremonies, the first Words in Mhabrogast . . . little sips of blood from the prisoners, mostly wretched *beurs*, like letting a child have a tiny glass of wine with his meal to make him feel grown-up. Staring into pools of ink, and . . . other things. At last one night we saw *les vieux* arise. My great-grandparents, after a gap of fourteen thousand years, the first to survive death. I can remember them *en miá chambra*, beside our beds, like pillars of mist with bright golden eyes, and then people smiling down at us—"

"Whoa, ol' buddy. You realize you're not only talking in French, which is OK, you're talking *Auvernhat* patois thick enough to chisel into building blocks for one of those fucking châteaux?"

Adrian shook himself and smiled. "Sorry," he said, shifting back into General American English. "They put Wreakings on us, of course, to keep us from revealing the truth when we were at 'home.' Some of them still linger down there, twined around the root of my mind. It all seems like a dream, now."

"Nightmare. OK, we're here."

The restaurant was so discreet that it didn't even have a sign; just a big Victorian gingerbread, like so many others that had survived the earthquake and the fire. And generations of vandalism in the dangerous period between being *new and fashionable* and *old and venerable*, when a building was just *out of date and shabby*. The maître d' was just as polished, fitting into the darkly rich interior like a piece of the mahogany furniture or one of the old Persian rugs.

"Ms. Polson is waiting for you and your friend, Mr. Brézé. This way."

Sheila Polson was scowling at the menu as they were ushered into their private nook. She glanced up sharply as Adrian extended his senses; no electronic ears tickled at his consciousness. Just because you *had* the Power didn't mean you had to *use* it rather than some technological equivalent.

Adrian inclined his head slightly. He hadn't met the chief of the Brotherhood's California section before; he'd mostly operated in Europe and Asia when he and Harvey were a team, and the organization was tightly compartmentalized.

She was a medium woman—medium height, medium build, medium unmemorable navy business suit, dark-brown skin and wiry hair cropped short. Only the eyes struck in the mind, and that was because of something in them; otherwise she might have been a paralegal or middling bureaucrat. Though most of those would not have the weapons he sensed, a spring-loaded gun with silver darts in the attaché case leaning against her chair and an inlaid blade in a scabbard sewn into her jacket. And her shoes were made for fast movement, not style.

Her looks said mid-thirties. From what he felt, she could have been that, or possibly a decade or more older. *He* looked to be in his mid-twenties, after all, and she smelled of the Power too. Not nearly as much as he, but considerably more than Harvey. Her mind was tightly warded under a wash of patterned no-thought, so tightly that he couldn't even feel the dislike he was certain was there.

"Hello, Ms. Polson," Adrian said. "A pleasure to meet you."

She looked at his hand as if it were a cobra, or decayed, or both, and then shook.

"This place is a waste of money," she said as they sat. "There isn't a *lunch* entrée under thirty dollars!"

"It's Adrian's money, Sheila," Harvey pointed out. "And since he gives a couple of million of it a year to us, you really can't complain about how he spends the rest of it."

The rangy, graying man glanced at the menu. "No BBQ or hamburgers? Damn. Had my mouth set for a double bacon cheeseburger. Guess I'll have to settle for the *Lapin á la Moutarde Et Au Romarin.*"

Adrian hid a smile; Harvey's French was much less accented than his Texan-flavored English. He could have passed for someone from Tours on the telephone, in fact, as opposed to Adrian. Any Frenchman listening to *him* would have heard some village in Puy-de-Dôme under the overlay of Paris and Sorbonne. With a very old-fashioned tinge at that.

Of course, I spent much time in my childhood with Auvergnats born in the nineteenth century. Granted, they were dead, but they were quite talkative.

"*Magret De Canard Au Porto,*" Adrian said; he was partial to duck breast anyway, and the port sauce, celery root and apple puree sounded interesting.

"I'll have the sliced lamb on mixed greens," Polson said with malice aforethought.

Adrian gave the order to the waiter, and added: "A glass of the Ronceray for me, thank you. Anyone else? No?"

She waited in tight silence until privacy returned. Then:

"You resigned from the Brotherhood, Brézé," she said. "Nobody resigns from the Brotherhood. Why should we help you?"

"Sheila," Harvey put in. "Remember those millions? As in millions of *bucks*? As in, weapons, transportation, living stipends, bribes, special equipment, safe houses, research? Hell, the organization runs on silver and it ain't cheap."

"Stolen money," she said. "Blood money."

Adrian hid his annoyance with a raised brow he knew was intensely annoying in itself.

Fanatic, he thought. *Then again, who else would wage a failing struggle all their lives long?*

Aloud he went on: "No. Directing money to investments that *will* increase in value harms nobody. And before I resigned from the Brotherhood—which, despite your statement, I *did* successfully do—"

Polson's frown said all any of them needed to know: *Because you had no way to punish me except at a cost you weren't prepared to pay.*

"I carried out many missions. But most of all, you should help me because I propose to kill a powerful Shadowspawn who ranks high beneath the Council of Shadows. Specifically, my sister, Adrienne Brézé."

"Ah, there we get to it," she said. "You've left each other alone ever since the last time you locked horns. Why should she come for you? We *know* the Council didn't send her."

Their meal came. Adrian thanked the man, threw his card onto the tray and added a fifty-dollar bill; these were hard times, and a lot of restaurants had taken to raking back a share of tips. Then he took a sip of his wine; the cabernet-merlot-petite Verdot combination had just enough acidity to go with the fatty richness of the duck.

"Why is abstract at this point. She . . . there are personal reasons. In any case, she abducted a young lady I'm very fond of. We know she's taken her somewhere in California, probably the central coast. I need information; all the Brotherhood files on the Brézé properties there, their defenses, layout, everything."

"Specialized weapons, too," Harvey put in.

Adrian nodded. "And since this was a personal vendetta on Adrienne's part, aiding me won't bring the Council down on you any more than usual."

"We should help you get your lucy back?" Polson asked.

The air went still. Harvey's hand made a slight gesture towards his coat before his conscious mind controlled it, prompted by decades of experience with the bubbling edge of violence. Adrian carefully finished chewing and swallowing, laid down his knife and fork, and leaned forward. His gold-flecked eyes met Sheila Polson's, and locked. After a long moment she looked aside, a slight sheen of sweat on her forehead.

"Ms. Polson, I will say this only once. Ellen Tarnowski was my friend—yes, we were lovers. She was not my *lucy*. I don't force blood from living humans, and I don't compel their minds except at urgent need. My sister does. I resigned from your war but I didn't resign from the personal obligations of a human being. I'd be a pretty poor specimen of a man if I didn't do what I could for her. Living with myself is . . . hard enough as it is."

She looked away for an instant, nodded as if to herself, then turned back to him:

"I apologize, Mr. Brézé." At his surprise, she smiled very slightly. "I actually *am* sorry. You . . . must know how disturbing a pureblood is to someone who can sense the Power."

"He don't bother me none," Harvey said, returning to his rabbit.

"You're a loose cannon, Ledbetter, and you bent every rule to breaking point haring off to New Mexico that way."

"I'm also the best field team leader in the Brotherhood, so you're not going to do anything but scold me."

She shrugged and went on to Adrian: "Please describe your encounter in Santa Fe, if you would."

Adrian did; Harvey nodded approval. "He can still do a damn nice after-action report," he added.

"That Wreaking on the apartment building . . . that is . . . not good news," Polson said.

"You could say that," Adrian replied grimly. "If I hadn't turned it in on itself, when the cascade fell it might have taken out everything within blocks. Driven dozens catatonic for the rest of their lives, at least."

"It gets harder and harder to fight . . ." Polson half-whispered to herself. Then: "You were using stored blood?"

Adrian nodded, and spoke with careful precision:

"I drink blood only when I must for major Wreakings with the Power. *As do you, do you not?* What is your rating on the Alberman Scale?"

She forced her eyes back to his. "Yes. Red Cross supply. I'm . . . thirty-eight percent."

"Then you will have some idea of how absolutely horrible an experience drinking cold, dead blood is. It is much worse for me. *Dog-piss* would be more fun."

Polson nodded, stopping her fork halfway to her mouth. Then she visibly put the memory out of her mind and ate.

"We're preoccupied right now," she said. "Believe me, I sympathize with the girl. I've done field work. But right now, the whole world is about to come down on our heads. You've heard about the Council meeting that's been called for next year in Tiflis?"

"No, I had not," he said. "Well, not until last night."

"You heard that Gheorghe Brâncuşi was executed? Formally the meeting's to elect his successor."

Executed, Adrian thought as he nodded. *Or assassinated, depending on your viewpoint.*

"Harvey told me yesterday," he said.

"Christ, Brézé, don't you follow *anything*?"

"It hasn't been on CNN, nor on the Internet," he said dryly. "The Brotherhood has me on their shit-list, and pretty well all the Council's Shadowspawn would kill me if they could and deceive me just for the pleasure of it if they couldn't. Ms. Polson, what part of *retired* don't you understand?"

"Then you wouldn't have heard that they're going to implement Plan Trimback?"

He looked at her, drank the last of his wine, and said: "No."

Harvey tore a piece off the baguette and buttered it.

"Usually they couldn't organize an orgy in a Bangkok whorehouse and they put everything off and off and off because they're planning on living forever 'n' figure they've got time," he said, biting into the bread with a crackle. "This time it's different."

Polson nodded. "We're trying to figure out a counter-strategy—"

"Bullshit," Adrian said crisply.

She glared at him; Harvey grinned and continued methodically demolishing the loaf and mopping his plate.

"I quit because the Brotherhood isn't a threat to the Shadowspawn," Adrian said. "It's a *nuisance*. You kill a few lower-level types—"

"We got Brâncuşi," she said.

"That was *me*, actually, and Adrian's right," Harvey said. "Two members of the Council in thirty years. And that's . . . what . . . less than half of the number of Council heads who've died in faction-fights or family coups. We're never going to be able to *kill* our way to victory, Sheila. There are just too damned many of them now. And they've got the Power."

"You want to give up too, Ledbetter?" she rasped.

"No. I think we should admit that the Power is here to stay. Sure, if you gave me a magic button I'd push till my thumb got sore. But even the Power can't undo the past."

Harvey went on:

"So we need to *use* the Power. Y'know, *you* could have gotten into the Order of the Black Dawn if you'd been around back then. Hell, I might have made it. And we're not evil . . . well, not most of the time."

"The *Order* were evil," Sheila said with flat certainty.

"Yeah, but that's 'cause they were demon-worshipping shits who figured out they could *become* demons. They'd have been just as evil if all they'd had was knives and bad attitudes."

He pointed his fork at Adrian. "Guys like Adrian are our hope. The Power isn't evil either; it's just a . . . technology."

Polson took a long breath. "That's a policy question. We're here to talk about this one instance. OK . . . I'll see what I can do. We do have a lot of information about the Brézé family. We'll get it to you as fast as we can; some of it will have to be dug out of hiding places. But I'm not going to clear everything off our plate just for this."

"We won," Harvey said, when she had gone.

Adrian methodically finished the last of his duck. He would be needing his energy, and ordinary food had its part in that too.

"And Ellen is . . . wherever she is," he said.

He snarled, then controlled the sound. A glimpse at his face in the beveled glass mirror stopped it more effectively. The sharp teeth showed between the drawn-back lines of his lips, and his eyes might have been glowing from a Pleistocene night by the reflected light of a frightened tribe's campfires.

"Christ, Harvey, I don't want to do this."

"You're going at it awful hard for a reluctant man," Harvey said.

His blunt fingers made pills from the last of the bread. Adrian gripped the edge of the table until rims of white stood out in his fingernails, welcoming the pain of it.

"Do you know why I've spent these years *sitting on a mountaintop*, Harvey? Running, meditating, swimming, talking to people at safe remove through a keyboard. Playing tennis when I felt daring? Because that life . . . life on an even keel . . . is one I can control. I don't like what this . . . walking armed towards a fight, thinking in terms of threats and counter-threats and strategy—does to me."

"It ain't all that much fun, I grant you."

Adrian shook his head violently. "No. It is entirely *too much* fun, at some levels. I know myself. I was *made* for this."

"You don't like you nearly as much as I do, ol' buddy," Harvey said quietly, looking away. "Think you might reconsider? You'd be a happier man."

Adrian felt himself smile; the expression in the mirror was worse than the snarl had been.

"Consider my sister, my friend. *She* has an excellent sense of self-esteem, feels comfortable in her skin and enjoys her life."

Softly: "And she has Ellen. For a whole day now. What has been happening, there, in that creature's nest?"

CHAPTER SEVEN

Something chirped in her ear. Ellen woke, yawned, stretched, and frowned. The place smelled different from her own bedroom, and not like Adrian's either, with its faint undertones of expensive tobacco and leather-bound books and juniper. Not bad—fresh linen, flowers, coffee, a spicy scent like eucalyptus—but *different*. She whimpered as memories crashed in on her. Then she realized she was alone in the big rumpled bed, and relaxed. The chirping came again; she turned her head and saw a BlackBerry resting on the pillow next to her.

This is yours, the note on the screen said. *Schedule loaded. First, go get checkup at clinic: 10:00 a.m. Dr. Duggan fully briefed. Don't be late or I will spank you.*

The time display read 9:00. "Am I going to . . ." she started to mutter to herself. Then: "Of course I'm going to go for this checkup. She's not kidding about that spanking. I don't think she means just a pat, either."

She tore through showering and pulling on the cotton dress and sandals provided, clipped the instrument to her belt and grabbed a fluffy kiwi pastry and a slice of fruit-bread from the breakfast trolley. She scarcely noticed the quiet sumptuousness of the great room and the fixtures, except the painting hung to the left of the bed, Adrienne's side. That caught her eye, enough to make her bend close for an expert's quick appraisal.

What a splendid reproduction! she thought, the professional taking over from the personal for a moment; she'd seen the original during her student years at NYU, on a field trip to France. *I don't think I've ever seen a better one.*

A small plaque below had a poem inlaid in gold on some dark tropical wood:

"And when I turned, no face I saw
For the shadow was my own
Death Angel's shadow."

That was certainly appropriate. The painting was by Schwabe, *La Mort et le Fossoyeur*, with the Death Angel shown as a slender dark-haired woman poised over the old gravedigger in the snowy cemetery, her wings making a beautiful curve like a scythe-blade against the willow-twigs and tilted headstones. Ellen had always liked it, as far as she liked any Symbolist work, and the reproduction was striking; it caught the cruel impersonal compassion on Azrael's face beautifully. Then she looked more closely, reaching out to touch and then taking back her hand.

"Wait a minute," she whispered. "Gouache, watercolor and pencil, that's right. And it's *old*, not just artificially aged. Look at the structure of the micro-cracks. And the frame is about a century old too! It isn't a reproduction. My God, the Louvre would never willingly part with this, not for any amount of money!"

Inside her head she could hear: *Oh, quite unwillingly,* chérie. That didn't need any spooky telepathy.

For an instant she sat on the bed, winded and gasping. After shock came a wave of anger; to have something like this hanging in your *bedroom,* exposed to all the possible accidents . . .

The BlackBerry beeped at her, a half-hour warning. She fumbled at it until it came up with a map of the route to the clinic, and ran—that was another thing she could do well, even in sandals—out into the hallway, down a service stair, out a rear entrance, down a long pathway, out through a boundary wall and gate into what looked like a smallish town or large village tucked under the hill where the *casa grande* sat. It wasn't even far enough to raise much of a sweat, not in the cool spring-like weather of a fine February day in the California lowlands.

The clinic wasn't quite what Ellen would have expected; well-equipped, cheery, an efficient-looking receptionist, a waiting room with the usual magazines and a TV . . . Even the smell was nicer than usual, with flower-and-damp-earth scents wafting through an open window to cut the standard ozone and disinfectant. She had just enough time to stop breathing deeply before:

"Dr. Duggan will see you next, Ms. Tarnowski."

A renfield doctor willing to sell his soul to the Devil, she thought, as David Cheung passed her on his way out, with a smirk and a nod and a fresh dressing on his neck. *Or maybe . . . he's more like a* vet?

The doctor turned out to be a her, a pleasantly plain middle-aged woman with a slight Scottish burr and a pile of faded ginger hair pulled back severely. She smiled ironically at Ellen's relief as she ushered her into the examination room. That looked conventional too, if upscale, except for the two replica skeletons in opposite corners. One of the skeletons looked a little odd in ways she couldn't name.

There were even family photos over the desk, a Chinese man and three striking hapa children, two girls and a boy, at various ages up to the mid-teens.

Connections, she thought. *Everyone's story has connections that spin out until they've got the whole world in the web. How did . . . they . . . buy or knuckle her? Why's she working at Hacienda Literally Sucks?*

"Dr. Fiona Duggan," she said, and shook hands, a brisk no-non-sense gesture.

From her expression she guessed her new patient's thoughts.

"Everyone at this clinic is a doctor, Ms. Tarnowski, and a good one. But even if we were no professionals . . . lass, you're the safest person for miles around. Think it through."

Oh. Don't mess with the tiger's bone.

"Bet there's a low crime rate here," she said slowly. "*Unauthorized* crimes at least."

"Ye'd win that wager."

A thought struck her. "Except murder-suicides?"

A grim smile. "Here, murder or any other serious crime *is* a form of suicide. A slow, painful form."

"Oh."

"If it will make you feel better, I was recruited as a second-year medical student in Edinburgh with—I'll say it myself—brilliant marks. And incurable pancreatic cancer; a classic rapid-onset adenocarcinoma. They offered to make the cancer cells have fatal accidents."

"You accepted."

"And so would you, *I'd* wager."

"Why do they need a *doctor*, then?"

She smiled. "The Power is powerful, but it needs knowledge to apply. Imagine them trying to correct your humors . . . only, we don't have humors. We have cells. And there are accidents and traumas and plenty of things too small for their attention. Let's get started."

The only difference between this and the last exam she'd had in Santa Fe was the state-of-the-art equipment; instant blood analysis with only a tiny pinprick sample, just for starters, and the new thinbar scanners that could do things only massive hospital units had been able to manage a few years before. She dressed and sat on the edge of the examining table as the doctor finished tapping at her keyboard.

"Well, Ms. Tarnowski, as no doubt your previous doctor has told you, you're in excellent health. I wish all my patients showed your degree of care with diet and exercise. You might be interested to know that you're also an eighteen-point-nine on the Alberman Scale."

"Alberman?"

"The test for nocturnus genes—the ones linked to the Power, of which there are between seventy-five and one hundred, mostly recessives. Average is around twelve percent."

"Ah . . . thanks, I guess."

"Aye. You should be thankful. There are behavioral complications with a twenty-to-forty result that often have unfortunate consequences."

"Unfortunate?"

"Gilles de Rais. Stalin, Hitler, King Leopold of the Congo Free State . . . Or Joan of Arc."

"Joan of Arc was unfortunate?"

"Think of how she ended."

"Oh."

"Now, it's your special health circumstances we'll move on to next."

Special health circumstances! she thought. *I suppose everyone needs euphemisms.*

"You've been subject to three feeding attacks so far, correct? Typical attack bites on the inner right elbow, the inner left knee, and the smaller one on the left hand."

"Right. None of them seem . . . infected, or anything. Just slightly discolored."

"Nor will they be. *Homo sapiens nocturnus*—"

"Wha'?" Ellen said.

She snorted and pointed at one of the skeletons. "Them. The Shadowspawn. Which is a ridiculously melodramatic name . . . Their bites heal cleanly. It's halfway between predation and parasitism, ecologically, and I've done some fascinating research . . . Well, another time. There's also a coagulant which acts when the wound is exposed to air, and a psychotropic element. A drug."

"I . . . couldn't move while she was, um, feeding. I didn't feel numb or anything, just didn't want to move."

"Yes, standard initial reaction. That effect's strong, but wears off quickly when the mouth is removed. There's an addictive euphoric, too, I'm afraid, wi' a cumulative effect after multiple exposures."

She froze. "*How* addictive?"

"A bit worse than nicotine."

Ellen relaxed, and heard her breath whoosh out. "That's not so bad."

"Mmm, Ms. Tarnowski, nicotine is more addictive than heroin, clinically speaking. The effect on the victim is similar to MDMA, but without the side effects."

At Ellen's blank look, she went on: "Ecstasy is the street name. Intense feelings of intimacy, and sharply diminished fear and anxiety. If you could synthesize it the market would be huge."

"Oh, Christ," she said, hugging her shoulders. "How often . . ."

"That's unpredictable. You'll no' be her only source of blood, of course; that *would* be . . . unfortunate. For them the blood itself is an addictive drug, particularly if it's primed by strong emotion. I've not been able to experiment on that side of things as much as I'd like."

"The marks aren't . . ." Ellen said, and made a stabbing gesture with two fingers at the inside of her elbow. "It's more like a little line with a bit of a curve."

There was a ghoulish fascination to the talk; and it *might* be useful. Something that tickled at the back of her mind said so. Duggan nodded enthusiastically and went to one of the skeletons. She pushed back the upper part of the skull until there was a bony gape and pointed.

"This is a replica. It's the maxillary central incisors, d'you see? Advanced so they're a bit proud and slightly inclined inward. Larger canines would be silly in a human-shaped mouth if you want a clean cut along a vein. These have microserration, so when they're presented at just the right angle they slice like steak knives; the lips and tongue arrange the flesh so that the feeding bite is verra precise . . ."

She wrenched herself away from the details and went back to the screen. "Now, there was a sexual assault with at least one of the feeding attacks, correct? From your reaction to the pelvic exam."

Ellen flushed. "Ah . . . yes."

And that utterly weird thing in the restaurant, she thought. *It's absurd to be concerned about something like embarrassment* now *but I'm still cringing at the thought of that.*

"Only some very minor stretching or bruising, so we don't have to worry about that."

"*We* don't have to sit on it! *I* do!"

S. M. STIRLING

"Sorry for the physician's 'royal we.' Any difficulty in walking or urination?"

"No. Just a bit of a sting when I pee."

"I assume the penetration was manual?"

She thought about that for a moment. "Umm, yes. That's what caused the chafing feeling, at least. I don't remember it all."

Thank God, she added to herself.

"Normal with a traumatic memory."

She handed over a small container with a tube and applicator inside.

"Here's a topical cream. You're fortunate the attack had that pattern."

"I *am?*" she said, trying to control the rising tone of her voice.

"Yes," she said dryly. "The likelihood of a *fatal* feeding attack is much lower that way. There's a mutual exchange of blood when they mate among themselves; in small quantities, but always, as far as I know. I'm no' sure if it's cultural or instinctual."

"Oh."

"Try to cooperate as much as you can the next time it happens; that'll reduce the chance of lesions."

"Just lie back, I suppose," she said dully.

"No. The other thing that makes a fatal attack more likely is passivity or depression on the part of the victim. For lucies, as the slang here has it—"

"Where does that *come* from?"

"Ah, you've no' read Stoker? You should—if only for a laugh. And the film, the one with Anthony Hopkins chewing the carpet, is even funnier."

"I . . . don't like horror films. They upset me."

"Well, you're *in* one now. Lucies. Some of them moved on to other positions here. Some have just . . . stayed. And some have died in what I think is probably inconceivable agony."

"*Slowly and cruelly and beautifully,*" she quoted with a shudder.

"Aye. And that's no' even the worst thing that can happen. So . . . well, a doctor can speak frankly. Make the experience of feeding on you as satisfying for our *Doña Demonio* as possible, because your life *does* depend on it."

"Thanks for the advice," Ellen said; she could hear the mixture of sincerity and sarcasm in her own voice.

That was probably unwise, but she couldn't be strategizing *all* the time.

Or I'll go stark raving mad. This is the sort of advice a horse doctor would give to other horses; don't fight the saddle and signals or it's the bit and spurs and whip for you, and the knacker's yard if you won't perform at all. I think a lot of these renfields must be crazy. And I bet that they do *have a suicide problem.*

The physician smiled. "I'm not easily offended. A doctor can't afford to be. I'll help you as much as I can, Ms. Tarnowski, but that isn't much. I made my choice long ago, and I have a family to think of, as well."

A screen-pen pointed at the skeleton. "That's the world's dominant subspecies. Not us. Even just in the body they've advantages, and there's no fighting the Power at all, whatever the terrorists say."

"Terrorists?"

"A few madmen." She scowled. "Killers who'll murder wholesale, men and women and children. The *nocturnus* at least have their instincts to blame."

That's interesting. The Resistance? And they think you're a collaborator, Doctor? How could *you fight the Power? With excitement: Could Adrian be in it?*

Duggan shook her head. "If you have severe nightmares or problems sleeping, see me, and I may be able to get permission for a mild sedative. We've some good ones."

The receptionist stuck her head in. "Your next appointment, Doctor. Ms. Mandelbaum and her daughter; the earache."

"Right, that's you, then, Ms. Tarnowski. Here's your exercise schedule and a prescription for a dietary supplement. Lots of fluids, mind!"

Ellen looked down at her new BlackBerry. *Lunch, 12:30. You're not on the menu. This time!* and a happy-face symbol with a little blood drooling out of one corner of the semicircle mouth.

"Oh, that's just *side*-splitting," she muttered to herself. Then: "Get a grip on your thoughts."

Which was about like telling yourself *not* to think of an elephant.

The main house was up the hill again, through California-gorgeous gardens only a little subdued for winter, with everything from palm trees to rose pergolas and velvety green lawns and ha-has, brick retaining walls and espaliered lemon trees. It was built in classic Spanish Revival like the town, if in a grander fashion; from the looks at the height of the style's popularity in the earlier part of the twentieth century, like something out of Santa Barbara's Montecito district. There were Andalusian towers and red Roman-tile roofs and earth-toned stucco on walls covered in sheets of purple-and-crimson bougainvillea, with colored tile Moorish-style insets over the arched entranceways, and plenty of wrought iron. Inside . . .

The architecture's first-class if a bit retro, but my, there's some interesting stuff here! If you can get over the number that should *be somewhere else. At least they're being taken care of.*

An eclectic selection: old masters, impressionists and post-impressionists, some late-nineteenth-century academics like Leighton, of the type that had become so popular again, Hoppers and Wyeths. One sculpture she longed to examine, just on the suspicion that it actually *was* Rodin's *Andromeda*. All with no particular organization, as if someone or several successive someones who could fulfill every whim had simply put up anything that took their fancy wherever they chose, like an omnipotent version of William Randolph Hearst.

Which is pretty much what happened, I suspect. Except that everything is good of its kind, if muddled.

The map function guided her efficiently, and she ended up in a large airy room set up as a lounge-study-office, with bookshelves and big mahogany tables and a comprehensive electronics suite; one wall was glass doors between Romanesque arches, open to the mild afternoon warmth and to the sight of a big bowl-shaped fountain plashing in the court outside. Adrienne was sitting—

With a little girl on her lap. Oh, ick, please God not . . . No, wait a minute, that child's the spitting image of her. Has to be a close relative. Couldn't be hers, *could she? And the boy's as close as a fraternal twin can get. As close as Adrian and Adrienne.*

A Great Dane sat beside the boy; the child had his arm around the beast's shoulders, and it was nearly as tall as he. It sat looking up at the Shadowspawn woman adoringly and beating its tail on the floor; then it stood, swiveled its barrel head up and came over towards Ellen with tongue hanging and claws clicking on the diamond-pattern buff tiles of the floor. Ellen slowed step by step, then froze.

This is silly, she thought. *It's just a* dog. She's *the dangerous animal in the room!*

The fear didn't go away. "What's the matter?" Adrienne asked. "That's a delightful flash of apprehension there, but why?"

"Large dogs . . . make me nervous. I was badly bitten once. Sorry. I can't help it."

The Shadowspawn snapped her fingers and pointed, and the dog left after giving her a curious sniff. She relaxed . . .

And now I can remember I have something to be really *frightened of.*

Suddenly she looked after the dog. *Shouldn't it be barking, or going crazy?*

"No, dogs aren't frightened of us, *chérie*," Adrienne said dryly. "That's *Terminators* you're thinking of, which don't exist."

Oh, Jesus, but I wish it was robots!

Adrienne grinned; Ellen *could* see the slight difference in the incisors.

Adrian was always very careful not *to bite or scrape me, now that I think back. Even when things got a little rough, or once more than a little rough. Everyone said "they say they're sorry but they really aren't" . . . but I think he was. A special case.*

"I'm sure he *was* sorry. What exactly was it he did . . . Oh, goodness, but that's an arresting image! You might have smothered! Not to mention spraining your neck. You and I must try something analogous sometime."

She felt her face go crimson. Then she saw what the little girl was doing; she had her hands on the table, cupped as if sheltering a candleflame. Within was a tiny yellow feather, like a shaped golden dustmote . . . and it was bobbing in midair, slowly turning. For a moment she simply stared in wonder. Then her mind lurched:

If you could do that with a feather, you could do it inside *someone, couldn't you?*

The feather fell, and the girl's face scrunched up.

"The air didn't wanna do it! It *slipped*. You should teach me some more special Words and I wouldn't slip. Please, *Maman?* I don't ever say them aloud unless you're there or the cousins or someone."

"Nyah, I did it beehhhh-tttter!" her probably-brother said.

"No, you didn't, Weasel Two," Adrienne said decisively. "And I will most certainly not teach either of you more Mhabrogast yet. It's dangerous if you can't pronounce it properly."

He looked heartbreakingly like a younger Adrian, in shorts and T-shirt and sneakers, his black hair cut in a bowl shape like his sister's. Her mouth began to droop towards a sob, until Adrienne hugged her and kissed the top of her head.

"That's splendid work with the feather. Most children can't do that for another year or two. What else have you been doing? Besides your lessons, *I hope.*"

"Feeding the snake," the boy said. "Gerbils, mostly. Two. But now it just sleeps."

"Well, it won't want any more for a while. Ellen, these are my demon spawn; Weasel One—Leila—and Weasel Two, Leon. One and Two for order of arrival. Children, this is Ellen. She'll be living with us now. Don't you tease her, or you'll be sorry. Now run along."

The girl slipped off her lap. She lifted a strikingly beautiful tow-haired china doll in a frilly dress from the floor beside her mother's chair. The child looked at it consideringly for a moment, and then up at the stranger.

"Hello, Ellen. This is my new dolly. She has hair and eyes like yours. See, blue, they close and open if you rock her like this."

"Ah . . ." Ellen thought, looking down into the innocent face.

And how do you address the Lady Demon's demon spawn?

"Hello, Miss Leila. What's her name?"

"Lucy," the girl said firmly. A broad smile. "'Cause she's *my* lucy."

That was when she saw the miniature bandage around the doll's neck. The children walked away, then suddenly ran, giggling, out into the courtyard.

"Bit of an experiment, so to say," Adrienne said. "Often we foster our children out until after puberty. But I'm actually rather fond of my two little weasels . . . in moderation. Mind you, puberty's the test."

Then Adrienne shrugged and continued: "Come." An inclination of the head. "We'll have lunch over here in the nook. There's a bit of a problem we should discuss."

Adrienne rose; she was wearing jodhpurs with leather inserts on the inside of the thighs, polished riding boots and a *real* polo shirt, with a riding crop in her hands. The golden-brown eyes stared into hers; she remembered with a slight shock that she was an inch taller than the Brézé woman. You always forgot that, somehow, just as she'd been surprised again at Adrian not being tall every time they met again. A thought sprang unbidden and unstoppable into Ellen's mind . . .

"Bettie Page comics?" Adrienne said. "I'm not nearly that pneumatic, and I don't do high heels. I'm actually wearing this because I'm going riding later today. Hmmm. Visualize . . . Yes, I see your point, though. I wonder if one could do that in real life?"

A noiseless servant in a high-collared white jacket brought two fluffy ham-and-scallion omelets with glazed crusts into the nook, along with a salad of fresh greens, walnuts, and slices of small tangy orange and glasses of a pale yellow wine.

"Ah . . . you said we have a problem?"

"Yes. Your former employer, Giselle Demarcio. She's been making inquiries, trying to trace you—which means, trying to trace *me*. That really will not do."

Anxiety turned into real fear with a sudden cold jolt, and the light omelet assumed the texture of mud.

"Please don't hurt her! She's just—I'm a friend as well as an employee. My place burned down. She's probably worried sick about me."

A hand reached out and cupped her jaw. Something *tickled* behind her eyes, and she started to pull back.

"Don't squirm if you're concerned for your friend," Adrienne said—not threatening but abstracted. "This is delicate. I'm probing for memories. It's not like playing back a computer file. They're unwritten and rewritten every time they're called up; it needs concentration. Don't resist. That's right . . ."

She murmured something under her breath; Ellen felt the words as sound, but they didn't resolve themselves into anything she could recall an instant later. She forced her body to relax and tried to think about nothing. The tickling grew, as if tendrils were growing into the structure of her brain, rooting, opening, *merging* with the folds and pathways. *Things* moved in the corners of her vision; little flecks of light swam across her vision, the way they did when you closed your eyes, or opened them in a perfectly dark room. Her head felt *full*, a squirming sensation of penetration.

Then she began to *remember*, impossibly vivid jerky chains of images, as much like briefly reliving as ordinary memory. Herself paddling in the waves on the Jersey shore, the cold salt shock on chubby toddler feet and the taste of salt on her lips and the scuttling alienness of a sand-crab. Her father crying at the kitchen table the night her mother died, and the scent of cheap whiskey and the taste of fear. The first kiss with Paul and the book of art prints falling off the sofa between them, the first day at the gallery, the way Adrian had smiled as he extended his hand over the net and the feel of his palm and fingers—they blurred together, faded, whirled.

It stopped with a grinding shock as Adrienne released her jaw and broke eye-contact; there was a moment of pain, like whiplash of the mind, then it faded.

"Yes, I see. Still, Dmitri is fond of a saying: when a person causes you a problem, remember, no person, no problem. I don't want my little visit to attract any attention."

"Look, if I tell her I'm OK . . ." A hooded glance. She went on desperately: "Please. I'm begging you, please. I'll do anything, just don't *hurt* her. She's always been good to me. *Please.*"

"I *do* enjoy it when you beg, *chérie*," Adrienne said, with a lazy smile. "And as I said, it's really no longer so essential to keep perfect secrecy . . ."

She picked up a control bar and thumbed it; a medium-sized screen flipped up from the center of the table.

"I love these things," Adrienne said absently. "It lets you interact without having to *smell* everyone. We Shadowspawn have become friendly *tout court* compared to the way things were. Scoot over so you'll be in the pickup zone."

Another smile, at a thought that flitted through Ellen's mind:

"No, you don't have to strip this time. It would be socially inappropriate. The number?"

"Uh . . . the videoconference code—"

The query went through; then *accepted* came up on the screen. The image was a little grainy and jerky at first; Giselle had never thought it worthwhile to spend much money on her office system. Then it sharpened to bell-tone clarity. Ellen had never been much interested in hardware, but you couldn't be in the arts these days—particularly the selling side—without knowing something about what the systems could *do*. That meant real capacity, particularly since there was no CGI-style surface gloss to the improvement.

"Uh . . . hi, Giselle. I'm here at Adrian's sister's place, I thought you might be worrying—"

"Ellen!" Giselle's sharp hook-nosed, middle-aged face lit up. "You're OK! Thank God!"

Her voice had a slight East Coast big-city edge, overlain with Wellesley. She went on breathlessly:

"Your *apartment* burned down, there was talk about *arson* and a mysterious man with a *gun* chased the Lopezes out—"

Ellen let out a breath she hadn't realized she was holding.

"—nobody knew where you *were*, nobody's at Adrian's but his *housekeeper*. What's going *on*?"

"Uh . . . I'm OK, Gis. Really. No harm done."

Apart from the blood-drinking and the torture and rape and the speculation about how pleasurable it would be to kill me in an artistic fashion and feel my life flicker out. I must be a lot more in control of myself than I thought I was. I'm not screaming or babbling.

"*Where* are you? Do you need a place to stay? Ummm, if you're actually OK, you realize this is a working day? We've got the Cliffords—"

"Ms. Demarcio," Adrienne cut in, her voice like a purr felt through velvet.

Giselle stared at her with what Ellen recognized as nervous courage, like a bird ruffling its feathers and rearing back at a cat. Owning a quirky, successful gallery in art-happy Santa Fe didn't make you rich and powerful. It did mean you met the genuine article often enough to recognize them.

"Yes, Ms. Brézé?"

"Ellen is a bit upset, what with the fire, and some personal things. So she's decided to come out here to my place and, ah, help catalogue my family's collection. She needs a change of scene and pace for a while."

A sharp glance at the two of them; she saw her boss' eyes narrow. Giselle had always been good at reading body language. Ellen made herself relax from her stiff brace, sway a little towards Adrienne. She smiled and nodded as the Shadowspawn put a hand on her shoulder, winding a lock of pale-yellow hair around one finger.

"That's right, Gis. You know things were a bit, ah, rocky for me the past couple of weeks anyway."

The bright black eyes darted back and forth again.

"Ellen, you need to settle the insurance, the police want to talk to you, you lost all your *stuff.* You should get your ass back to Santa Fe from wherever-it-is. All I could find out was that you got on some *plane* at the airport and went away!"

"No, no, that's all being handled. Really, I'm sorry as all hell to leave you in the lurch like this. You've been really good to me. But I need to get away. To . . . clear things up. And the collection here . . . unbelievable! I'm happy."

A snort. "Ellen Tarnowski, I told you that Adrian was creepy. Told you that these old-money Euro types are bad news for ordinary people who're just jumping on a trampoline while they're flying. Intersecting trajectories aren't a meeting of true minds. I told you months ago that he was treating you like a mushroom and dumping him would be a good idea. Switching to fucking your brains out with his *twin sister* is not! And no, I'm not going to deny the evidence of my own eyes at the restaurant. If that wasn't real, you should be in *Hollywood*, girl, not Santa Fe!"

Ellen gave a panic-stricken glance aside. Adrienne was smiling again.

"Ms. Demarcio, your concern for Ellen is touching. But there are family dynamics at play here you don't understand. Nor is it really any of your business with whom she is, as you so elegantly put it, fucking her brains out."

"Pardon my French."

"*Ce n'est rien*," Adrienne said. "You found my brother Adrian, how is it, *creepy*?"

Giselle nodded. "I don't care who knows it, either."

"No, you're right. Adrian *is* creepy, from your point of view. He is also, as you put it, old money. So am I. That apparently does not bother Ellen, eh? And my forbearance for well-intentioned interference in my private life is not infinite."

"No, Gis, I'm, umm, really having a great time," Ellen said brightly. "Out of this world."

"Here's the number on her new BlackBerry," Adrienne said helpfully, and tapped on her control bar. "Do feel free to call, but not too often."

Baffled, the older woman looked at Ellen. "OK, you're a big grown-up type person, Ellen. Just remember that you've got somewhere to go. I'll hold your job for you—indefinite unpaid leave, OK?"

Ellen felt tears prickle at her eyes. "I . . . I really . . . Thanks, Gis. You're a good one."

CHAPTER EIGHT

"I'm still worried," Adrian said.

"Hey, ol' buddy, it's the mook *this* is aimed at who's got something to worry about," Harvey said.

He spread the parts on the heavy plastic groundsheet he'd laid over the bed with methodical neatness. The west-facing window still had a line of eye-hurting brightness at its top, and the room was flooded with the last light of day. When he was finished he rubbed his hands with satisfaction.

"Once Sheila says yes, she ain't coy. This is the latest and best. Beautiful!"

Adrian nodded, more as a placeholder than agreement. Harvey had a lifelong fascination with firearms; one of the things he most resented about the Power was the way it could make failures happen in complex machinery. Adrian found guns satisfying tools if they worked and could use them well—Harvey had taught him with endless patience—

but they didn't give him a hobbyist's pleasure, the way really good cars did, or gliders, or kitchen gear. If he *had* to fight with anything but the Power or his hands and feet, a knife was more . . .

Aesthetic. Satisfying, he thought. Then: *Name of a black dog, am I going conservative in my fifties?*

The room was smaller than in a modern hotel in this price range, but not uncomfortable; the ceilings were very high, of antique pressed steel, and the wallpaper was hand-printed, a bamboo-spray pattern. The natural linen and floral smell was an intriguing contrast to the fruity gun-oil and sharp metallic steel and tooth-hurting silver of the weapon Harvey was checking, although it took a little effort to prevent his nerves from jangling.

Harvey went on: "See, the problem with my good friend the Monster Truck gun, incidentally that's a *fine* label—"

Harvey nodded to the cut-down shotgun monstrosity, lying alone on one corner of the groundsheet as if sulking and jealous of the new lover.

"—is that it's very effective for a close-range takedown of a Shadowspawn, in body or out, but it sorta makes surprise difficult. And it's real difficult to hit a Shadowspawn who's decided to go elsewhere and fight another day. And when they come out of the wall right behind you—bad news. Y'know, that design feature is just so fucking *unfair* it makes you want to cry."

"Life, my old, is unfair."

"Plus some contract *soldati* cuts loose with a thirty-round mag of 5.56 from a hundred yards and I am well and truly fucked up. And *I* mere human ape scum that I am, don't get to rise again. Have I mentioned life is unfair?"

His big scarred hands moved on the pieces of the rifle, with a swift hard authority. There were *snick-click-chunk* sounds as things fitted together.

"Now this has a whole bunch of selling points. For one thing, it's *just as good* at killing ordinary people as the original, which is a Brit sniper rifle, the L96A1 in .338 Lapua magnum. Only this has a carbon-fiber stock with an ultrapure silver-thread mix. A little silver in the steel of the barrel and action, and surface glyphs and Mhabrogast protectives in International Phonetic Alphabet. Preactivated protectives, of course."

"God!" Adrian blurted, shocked out of polite interest into alarm. "I hope they were *careful!*"

"Ultra, ol' buddy. Not to mention it cost a lot of the conscience money you've been wafting the Brotherhood's way. Jacketed lead-silver alloy bullets—high AG—with active waste filler, pre-fraged so they disperse as long as the target's tangible at all. I had two good shooters backing me up with these when we fixed Gheorghe's wagon. Caught a couple of his people while we were clearing out."

"Shadowspawn or renfields?" Adrian asked sharply.

"We didn't stop to run an Alberman," Harvey said dryly. "Things were a mite hectic. But these rounds do about three thousand feet-per-second. That's under two seconds to impact at max effective range."

Adrian's brows stayed up. "Not much time to *do* anything, if you're not expecting it," he said slowly. "You'd have . . . a small fraction of a second to realize what the silver was, and react. By then—"

"*Give* the man a big cigar."

"I'm impressed."

Then he yawned and looked out the window. "Would you like to get something to eat? I'm not very hungry, but if I have to take blood tonight I want something for it to hit on the way down."

"I was thinkin' of room service," Harvey said.

"Well enough—"

"No, room service with another friend who's coming over. You're not invited."

A little hurt, Adrian nodded. They hadn't seen each other in years . . . Harvey grinned.

"The friend in question is not a brother-in-arms like you, ol' buddy," he said. "But she's a natural redhead and certifiably female, which in this town you can't count on from first impressions. I figure if I'm going to be dead in a week, or if your sister is going to make my eyeballs pop, or my balls, or set my entire skin on fire or use my spinal cord to play a violin concerto or any other of the things she *has* been known to do when feelin' bitchy . . . there's things I want to do one more time first. And not with you. Sorry."

"No offense, my old," Adrian laughed. "I'll go for a walk."

"Next door's fine. Might be safer."

Adrian snorted. "Not with only a wall in between us. I can't afford to close my senses down *completely*. And good friends though we are, Harv, there are certain things I don't care to share with you either. Even only telepathically."

Harvey grinned. "You could go exercise your sinister vampiric charm on some high school girl with perky tits longing for a pale and interesting demon lover."

Adrian frowned in solemn thought, then shook his head. "No, she would expect me to reject anything but kissing and cuddling, no matter how much she wanted more and how tortured I was with desire. Also there would be much conversation about our feelings."

"Talk about *in*human. God, the thought's enough to make a man swear off women. Ones that young, at least."

"Besides, that's the incubus part of the legend, not the vampire. I shall walk the night, commune with my soul, and think wistfully of what might have been."

"The things some men do when they could be fucking. See ya. Watch out for muggers."

Adrian shrugged. "The worse for them, in my current mood."

"Yeah, that's what I meant. We want to keep you calm till we can get you and Ellen back to your mountaintop."

Will Ellen want to share my mountain? Adrian thought two hours later. *Perhaps . . . now she knows the secrets I could not tell her. That would make a difference. Perhaps her kind and mine can share a life, if we know, if we work to . . . make accommodations with each other honestly.*

Then: *But after Adrienne, will she want to come within a thousand miles of anyone who looks like me? Who is like me? All I can do is set her free, and convince her the rest is up to her.*

Tendrils of fog lay along the street; a heavy dew beaded on the surface of his gray anorak. It carried a raw chill, and he could sense the restless power of the ocean on three sides of the city, and smell the salt above the city stinks. There was an aloneness to the brightly-lit night greater than running beneath the stars in his own mountains.

This was Geary Street; he could see the five-story tower of the Peace Pagoda ahead.

Why not? he thought, and turned into the Japanese-style baths. *Heat, and a cold plunge. Then I'll get some noodles.*

It was men's night, and for a wonder there wasn't a line. A few minutes later he was relaxing in the heat of the dry sauna, feeling the sweat break out over his body in a single impalpable rush. He imagined it taking the poisons of the blood out of his body, the savage necessities of the Power.

A shock of very slightly colder air, under the scent of cedar. Two men came in, both young and both Asian—with a little more body hair than most, so they were probably Japanese, and with bands of colorful tattoo over their torsos. Adrian sighed and prepared to block the trickle of consciousness that came through his shields . . .

They had towels over their arms. Both twitched them aside at the same instant, revealing the shielded gloves and the glinting edges of the knives. *Tantos*, twelve inches of slightly curved steel glinting with the silver inlay as the men drew them and flicked aside the sheaths.

"Michiko sends greetings," one of them said in Japanese.

Ellen, he thought in one fractional instant, as his body prepared for combat. *She needs me.*

Then he gathered himself to leap.

Ellen rested her face in her hands and elbows on the table for minutes after Giselle's face left the screen, trying not to think. When she looked up again she was alone except for the sound of the Shadowspawn children romping in the courtyard, and an occasional deep *whurf!* from the dog. The BlackBerry beeped again, from beside a set of house keys:

The rest of the day is your own. Bear in mind . . .

Then it began to play a song—no, it was Adrienne singing, her voice full and sweet:

"Look around and all you see
Are sympathetic eyes,
Stroll around the grounds
Until you feel at home."

"I'm in the thrall of Countess Comic-ula," she murmured. That made her feel better, somehow.

Then: *Your new place is Number 5 Lucy Lane. All should be ready for you by four o'clock. Take a tour around town first.*

"And apparently we're not going to be sharing a room. I am so totally OK with that. It's messy taking your cookies to bed with you anyway."

This time she took her time walking to the front door. The house felt *old*, by American standards at least. Not in the least run-down, it was immaculately maintained and there were discreet signs of periodic refits, but like a building that had been inhabited for generations by the same family. There were touches you hardly ever saw in recent designs, even historicist ones; genuine groined vaulting in ashlar masonry, for starters.

It smelled that way too, of old stone, wax-rubbed paneling, hints of lemon and clean ancient rugs. In structure it was a set of linked E-shapes, and designed to take advantage of the varying levels to look a little less massive than it was; she suspected it was the sort of place where you could discover new rooms for years. Staff went by her now and then, usually with polite nods. She went down a curling formal staircase and out under a portico of columns and arches. The size of the stone-pines and palms and live-oaks, citrus trees and olives outside and the thick bases of some of the espaliered vines confirmed her guess.

The outer gateway in the solid circumference wall had an archway of wrought iron above it, making words: *Rancho Sangre Sagrado.*

"I guess the sense of humor is hereditary," she said; it meant *Ranch of the Holy Blood* and had obviously been there a good long while.

Though it could be a perfectly genuine Hispanic place-name, come to think of it, possibly dating right back to Mexican California or even the Mission era when Spain's flag flew here. Her lips quirked. She'd picked up a fair bit of conversational Spanish in her time in Santa Fe, and if you changed it just a little to *Rancho Sangrón* it meant *Ranch of the Asshole.*

There was a strip of parkland, green grass and leafless oaks and solid blocky cypresses fifty or sixty feet high sheltering the wall from easy outside view, and then the town proper, a little place of a couple of thousand people along half a dozen streets, lined with cherry trees now blossoming in a froth of pink and rose. The only really odd thing about it was the near-uniformity of style, and the fact that there were no boarded-up shops and not many for-sale signs. A civic center had a municipal pool and library and tennis courts; notices on the boards before the steps included those for a farmer's market, the meeting of the local chapter of the SPCA—

I wonder if we get included? she wondered, then saw the fine print: *Sponsored by Brézé Enterprises.*

—and every other little bit of civic self-organization you'd expect, from the Lions and Elks through aromatherapy clubs. A biggish high school showed southward, a golf course, and after that a tangle of minor industrial stuff, fruit-packing plants and wineries, repair shops and a dairy that had a big *All fresh! All organic! All local!* sign, one of the few advertisements she could see.

To the east of town were rolling fields fading into the middle distance with the occasional farmhouse or crossroads hamlet sheltered in its trees. Vineyards marched in geometric rows and silvery-green olives flickered; there were low bare-branched brushy orchards of trees she couldn't name, and flaming apple and almond and apricot in white and pink, interspersed with intensely green fields of grain. The higher pastures to the west, above the mansion, were green too with the winter rains; tongues of forest ran down the low points, growing denser on the high hills or modest mountains that separated this area from the sea.

The people were dead-on small-town California-normal; about half Anglo, more than a third Hispanic, the rest bits and pieces of everything with an accent on Asian and lots of mixing. They bustled in and out of shoe stores and bakeries—the buttery odor of fresh pastry made her mouth water—and stationers and the post office and electronics shops. Mothers wheeled babies, toddlers clutched hands, kids ran, elderly men sat sunning themselves and reading papers or watching the world go by. Teenagers Rollerbladed the brick sidewalks with immersive buttons in their ears, bopping to sounds only they could hear, or stood in groups at the corners.

No, there's one thing odd. You'd expect at least one big Catholic church in a rural town this size, and a couple of others.

She wasn't religious herself, but the thought made something clench a little inside. There was one building that *looked* like a church in the elaborately carved Churrigueresque style, but it had *Sangre Community Theater* on the front, with a banner announcing a Shakespeare revival.

And a little like selling your soul to the Devil, she remembered Theresa saying.

And that her parents and grandparents before her had made the same bargain. This was effectively a settlement of hereditary not-quite-Satanists.

I wonder when they tell their kids? What was that Theresa said about . . . initiation?

Suddenly she didn't want to sightsee anymore, for all the charm that would have had a New Urbanist drooling.

"Excuse me," she said to a middle-aged man sitting on a bench outside a café, eating ice cream from a cardboard cup with two teenagers similarly occupied. "I'm looking for Lucy Lane?"

He smiled at her, and she gritted her teeth. The kids were smiling too, and one nudged his slightly younger companion; it was more than the usual teenaged-male leer.

Oh, yeah, they know. They know.

"Just another block north up Brézé Avenue; left on Armand. It turns into Lucy after the intersection with Auvergnat."

"Thank you," she said between clenched teeth.

Lucy Lane was a cul-de-sac curling around the hill the mansion rode, backing against the perimeter wall. The sidewalk was the same herringbone-pattern brick, and the houses were overshadowed by old plantings that included orange trees in fair-sized front gardens and little walled inner yards. She passed one man sitting on a bench with a set of weights nearby. He was black, tall and impressively built without being bulky, which she could see because he was stripped to exercise shorts, and he had a shaved head and narrow hook-nosed face.

"Hi!" she said brightly.

He looked at her impassively, then lay down on the bench again and began a series of vertical lifts.

Well, that wasn't too successful.

Number Five had a newish Volt in the open garage, with the hood up and the charger cord extended and plugged into a pole-mounted outlet by the garage door.

"You Ms. Tarnowski?" a young Latino said around the open hood when she halted uncertainly.

He was about twenty, in jeans and cowboy boots and a white T-shirt that showed his taut-bodied build, an inch or so under six feet. He let the hood fall with a *clunk* and wiped his hands on a rag; when she shook she felt workingman's calluses.

"Don't mind Jamal," he said, nodding towards the black man two houses up. "He doesn't talk much. I'm Jose Villegas. I'm in Number Three. Just checking your car. Welcome to Lucy Lane!"

"I get a *car*?" she blurted.

He grinned, white teeth in a light brown face. "Sure, Ms. Tar-nowski—"

"Ellen," she said automatically.

"All the fixings, Ellen," he said in perfect California English of a small-town, blue-collar variety. "Me, I'm a mechanic when I'm not . . . you know. So I was checking it for you. Looks good. You need anything done, though, just bop over. Come on in."

The house had the feel of a place that had been cared for but vacant until recently; it was about two thousand square feet, with a living-room that gave on a rear court through sliding-glass doors and re-strained furniture of the type that American Home Furnishings tried to imitate. A slender blond man a little below her height was finishing the connections on a wallscreen TV. He had a handsome triangular face and pale green eyes, and dusted off his hands before offering one.

"Hi!" he said. "Peter Boase, in Number Two. TV and display here, PC in the study, omnidirectional Bose speakers here, there and in the bedroom. All networked to the content library. You've got a high-capacity fiber-optic Internet connection. Hey, it's the President's plan, right?"

"Peter's an egghead," Jose said. "Forgets his own name sometimes. But he sure can make anything electronic dance and sing."

The slender man shrugged. "PhD, physics, so I should be all thumbs and baffled by putting a CD in a player. But you need to be able to

handle equipment the way grants are . . . were . . . these days. Come
on in. Monica will—"

"Coming through!" a woman's voice said.

She came through the front door with a baking tray in gloved
hands. Ellen judged her to be the oldest person present, thirty or a hair
either way, dressed in slacks and shirt and a checked bib apron. She had
pleasantly pretty features that reminded Ellen vaguely of someone, and
curling dark-brown hair held back by a barrette. She was very slightly
shorter than Ellen's five-six, and very slightly heavier; they might have
been sisters as far as face and figure went, coloring aside.

"Hi! Monica Darton, in Number One," she said. "Come on through
to the kitchen. That's where a house starts to turn into a home!"

"Monica's our den mother," Peter said. "She's been here longest,
eight years."

Peter, Jose, Monica, Ellen thought; she had a good memory for
names, and you needed one dealing with the public at the gallery. *And
Jamal is the black guy. With me that makes five, so that's all five houses on
Bloodbank Row . . . pardon me, Lucy Lane.*

The kitchen was south-facing, with a glassed-in breakfast nook, and
a small dining room separated from it by a pierced screen. Monica
set the tray down on a counter. Then she took off the oven mitts and
shook hands in turn.

"Do you want us all to clear out?" she said. "While you settle in
peacefully?"

"Ah . . . no, no," Ellen replied hastily.

*So I could sit and look at the wall and try not to scream? Call Giselle
and lie to her? Wonder where Adrian is? End up lying facedown on the
floor drooling with an empty fifth of vodka in my hand? Seriously consider
slitting my wrists? So . . .*

"Please, stay for a while."

"Good. I'll make some coffee to christen your machine . . . unless you prefer decaf?"

"No, premium grade is fine."

". . . and these are the *best* homemade brownies in town! All local ingredients. Except for the chocolate and vanilla and sugar, of course, but the nuts and flour are, we have the most wonderful farmer's market. I've stocked your pantry and fridge with a few basics and staples, bread, butter . . ."

She bustled them into seats and set out plates and cups and cut the brownies into squares, then brought the pot over from the filter machine. Ellen felt her nose twitch; there was some *seriously* good coffee in there, and if she couldn't have a stiff drink, she could use a cup. Monica went on:

"And I put a lasagna and a salad in the fridge too, in case you just want to throw something in the oven for dinner instead of cooking or going out. There's laundry stuff and basic linens and so on, and a few clothes, jeans and sweats and underwear in the bedroom, and toiletries. You can get the rest of what you need anytime, of course, but we wanted to, you know, help."

Ellen looked at her beaming smile and dazedly bit into one of the brownies. They *were* good.

It's June Cleaver and the Welcome Wagon of Nosferatu Manor, she thought.

"Ah . . ." *If resistance is futile, so's tact.* "You're all . . ."

"Lucies?" Jose said cheerfully. "Yeah."

I'm not surprised. You've all got something about the eyes, this haunted look. I think I probably do too, now.

"*Lucy* is an exclusionary stereotype. I prefer to think of us as *helpers,*" Monica said, a slight trace of primness in her tone for a moment.

Yeah, helper as in Hamburger Helper, Ellen thought.

"It's not as much of a hard-and-fast distinction as the renfields like to think, either," Peter said.

Ellen went on: "This place was empty? Who was here before?"

A ringing silence fell. Everyone looked away for an instant, except Peter, who coughed and explained:

"Mmmm, there's sort of a Lucy Code; you don't ask questions like that, about people who are . . . gone. Though in fact Dave used to live here, before he got promoted."

"He's up at the Company Security barracks now, teaching unarmed combat to the rent-a-cops," Jose said. "And the *Doña* takes him along as muscle sometimes. Good riddance."

A laugh. "Though Peter kicked his ass!"

She looked at the slight blond man with surprise. He smiled slightly and shrugged.

"Only because he was surprised I knew anything at all. I could never have taken him if he hadn't gotten overconfident. He's a professional."

"That's how he ended up here. Came to a tournament up in Paso Robles, and the *Doña* was there. Decided *Hey, I want some of that* and what she wants she gets. No accounting for tastes, I guess," Jose said.

"David could be difficult," Monica conceded.

Her smile broadened and she leaned forward to pat the newcomer's hand.

"I'm so glad there's another girl here now! Some people in town are very nice, but some are a bit standoffish with people who, you know, live on this street. I'm sure we'll be such great friends, Ellen!"

Yeah, Ellen thought. *We can exchange recipes and do each other's hair and compare fucking bite marks, maybe.* "Can I borrow a cup of sugar? Or a pint of blood? I'm out."

"So," Peter said. "What do you think of our little town?"

Impulse made her honest: "It's like Stephen King, illustrated by Norman Rockwell with ads from *Town & Country* magazine."

Peter coughed, apparently choking on a crumb of brownie. Jose pounded him helpfully on the back, looking puzzled but good-naturedly so. He rose and went to the fridge and pulled out a bottle of beer as an alternative to the coffee; it was some local microbrew with an Art Nouveau label that incorporated part of a Mucha poster.

"OK?" he said, raising it and glancing at her.

"Sure," Ellen said, and he popped the cap and drank with a satisfied *ahh!*

"Norman Rockwell is right!" Monica nodded, apparently utterly without irony. "I love it here. It's a wonderful place to raise kids."

Ellen blinked. "You . . . have children?" she said neutrally.

"Two. Joshua, he's ten, and his sister, Sophia, is nine. They're the cutest kids! Adrienne . . . the *Doña*, we usually call her . . . thinks so too and they adore her. I'm dying for you to meet them."

Peter evidently heard the quiver in Ellen's question and understood the sudden tension of her hand on the thick porcelain of the cup. He leaned close and whispered:

"*They* don't feed on children. The blood doesn't taste right. Sour. Green."

Ellen let out a little grunt of relief; it was a welcome alternative to starting a scream she wasn't sure she could stop and trying to kill the other woman with the mug.

Monica went on without pausing; Ellen judged she was the sort of person who found it easier to talk than listen, anyway, in a pleasant-enough fashion:

"I knew that it was the best place right away. Well, after a little while, I was a bit scared at first. It's so quiet and pretty here, and there's no crime, and the streets are safe for children and the schools are just *wonderful*. All charter, you know, with free preschool, and the best facilities in the state, no cutbacks. And there's the health plan, too."

The very best straw and turnout pasture, and the stable is so comfortable, and silver horseshoes, and kindly Dr. Duggan for vet . . .

"That's . . . ah . . . why you moved here?" Ellen said aloud.

The lucies—*the other lucies, let's be honest*, she thought—laughed.

"I ran out of gas!" Monica crowed. "Well, Tom left us after he lost his job and couldn't find work, he wasn't a bad man but he was *weak*, this was down in Simi Valley where we lived, and we lost the house, and Mother wanted to try and move in with her sister in San Jose but we just ran out of gas outside town. And this lady in a Land Rover pulled over, it was about sundown, and asked if we needed help. That was Adrienne. I thought it was so kind of her to put us up."

"Until she dropped by your room that night for a snack, maybe a little hubba-hubba too," Jose said with a grin.

"I thought it was all dreams at first. Nightmares. Everything was so strange. And it *was* kind, I still say. Just . . . there were other reasons, as well." Coyly: "She says my blood smelled attractive."

Ellen sat slowly upright. "Wait a minute!" she said. "You've been here eight years?" Monica nodded.

Then how old is she? How old is Adrian, *for God's sake?*

She took another bite of the brownie.

Maybe these would be better with hash, she thought. *Oh, Christ . . .*

"Me, I was born here, went to school here, graduated Sangre High here," Jose said. "Theresa, you met her, she travels with the *Doña*? She's my mother's cousin, but she went away to Cal Poly for a while—she's got most of the brains in the family and I got all the charm. We've been here since before the Brézés came—"

"1862," Monica filled in helpfully. "That was Don Justin. He was from France. I've been doing a little local historical pamphlet for the library. I work there as a volunteer."

"—yeah, we were *vaqueros* and all that good sh . . . stuff, before they bought the *Rancho*. Hell, the *Indio* part of us has been here *forever*. My uncle was a lucy here for a while on the lane; I figure with any luck it'll be a couple of years for me; then I get a pat on the fanny and told to go get a girl and make some babies to work for the next generation. Meantime I work on the cars and stuff uphill, when I'm not, um, busy."

He grinned. "Hey, you know, some of the girls, they sort of think it's cool for a guy to be a lucy for the *Doña*. Think you pick up stuff."

His smile died for a moment and he took another swig of the beer.

"And no money worries making your stomach twist up so you shake every month. And then there's the travel," Monica went on. "I've been to, oh, London and Shanghai and Paris and Rome and Cairo and *everywhere*. On that wonderful plane."

Taken along for snackies, Ellen thought. *For those midnight cravings when room service is over and you can't go out.*

"I did my graduate degree at MIT. I was at the National Lab in Los Alamos when I started getting some anomalous results," Peter said.

He grinned ruefully. "And I wouldn't stop trying to get people interested, no matter how heavy the hints were. They sent Adrienne in to kill me with a nice little perfectly genuine heart attack or stroke or getting hit by a truck, since she was in the neighborhood on personal business—they're informal about things like that, I'm told. But she decided to give me another option instead. You *bet* I said yes! Actually, I've done some more work here, for her. She can get me all the computer time I need and I'm mostly a theoretician."

"Do you have any outside interests, Ellen?" Monica asked brightly. "I got married right out of high school, myself. More coffee?"

"Thanks. I, um, BA in Art History from NYU. Worked in a gallery in Santa Fe. I was . . . involved with Adrian. Adrienne's brother. She . . . took me away."

Another ringing silence. Monica coughed into her fist and pushed the plate of brownies over.

"I'm sure you'll have plenty to do. There are just *infinite* amounts of art up the hill. And they send some down to the high school and the civic center, now and then, too. Exhibitions."

Bet they don't tell them it's all genuine, Ellen thought. *Or . . . it's a renfield town. Maybe they know that too.*

"I'm sure you'll be happy here," Monica said. She sighed. "Jamal— he's from LA—isn't fitting in well. I've *tried* to be friendly and help him, honest, but . . ."

"Don't think he'll last long," Jose said bluntly. "Man, you can see it in his eyes! And he screams a lot."

"Don't we all!" Monica said lightly; then her smile became almost a simper for an instant. "Why, sometimes, I'm hoarse for *days,* when things get, you know, a little wild with Adrienne."

"No, he screams when he's alone sometimes too. Give you odds, the *Doña's* going to . . . remove him from here, know what I mean?"

"Well, maybe it's just a phase he's going through. I remember my first few weeks here, I *cried* a lot, before I realized how lucky I was. Just sobbed and sobbed and oozed like a puddle. I was, like, *so* silly!"

Getting really creeped out now, Ellen thought. *She's got odd body lan-*

guage. Look at the way she fidgets and pats her hair. Like a smoker who can't . . . oh. The bite's addictive. Addictive as nicotine, and Adrienne's been away. I'm feeling nervous myself. Is that just because I've got really good reason to be nervous, or . . .

"Hey, there's pain in life." Jose shrugged. "A man's got to deal, unless he's a . . ." He glanced at Monica and amended what he'd probably been going to say into a form less blunt. "A sissy."

"Besides," Monica said. "It's not always that bad. Sometimes . . . it's just nice and fun or fun-scary, doing what she wants, and then you cuddle and the feeding . . . it's almost like nursing. You can feel how you're helping this *need*."

Ellen sipped at her coffee again, remembering Adrienne's face on the plane, laughing with blood on her teeth and chin. Hearing her say: *I may kill you someday, slowly and cruelly and beautifully.*

"And she says that then, those times, my blood tastes like warm milk and cookies before you go to bed."

Creeping out getting closer to total now.

Jose looked out the window as he finished his beer. Peter spoke gently, but his tone was dry:

"It's not a tame tiger, you know, Monica, even if it purrs sometimes. Usually, there's plenty of screaming involved."

"Oh, Peter, you're such a complainer! *That's* not always all bad either. It can be sort of . . . exciting, once you're used to it. And when it's, well, very wild and you feel so . . . sometimes then she touches me, you know, *there*, and does that extra-special thing with her mind only she can do. And that feels *so* good!"

Oh, icky-poo yuk, total creeped-outness achieved. A thought: *that thing in the restaurant was with her kissing my knuckles. I wonder if it were . . . could Adrian do . . . Stop that, Ellen!*

Monica's BlackBerry chimed. The tune had words:

"See my eyes so gold
I could stare for a thousand years—"

She opened it and said: "Yes? Oh, Doña Adrienne! Yes, of course."

For a moment she closed her eyes and whispered: "*Thank God!*"

Then: "Shall I make dinner?" A giggle. "Just me? At seven? I'll see you then!"

A brilliant smile at all of them. "Speak of the devil!"

She keyed another number. "Mom? Oh, hi, Mom, I need you to pick up Josh and Sophie from the Judo and dance classes and take them overnight. Yes, I've got company coming. I don't know if I'll be up to bringing them home tomorrow, no. It depends on, you know, how wild things get. Call me in the afternoon. OK? Love you too, Mom! Bye!"

She left with a smile and a wave. Jose washed out his beer bottle and left it upside down in the drainer.

"Well, I'm going to go visit my folks," he said. "It was really nice meeting you, Ellen. You have any trouble with the car, the plumbing, just let me know. The guys from up the hill are on call, but I'm on hand! We usually have a potluck BBQ on Sunday. It's my turn next."

He left; Peter sat in companionable silence for a moment. Ellen drank the last of the coffee, looked down and realized she'd also eaten the last of the brownies without even noticing, which wasn't like her.

"That was David Bowie," she said eventually. "On the ringtone. But aren't the words to that song *See my eyes so* green? I've heard it a couple of times. Giselle . . . my boss at the gallery . . . likes him."

"The *Doña* had him cut a special version for her," Peter said.

Silence fell for another few moments. At last:

"Monica . . ." she said. "Monica's completely insane, isn't she?"

Peter shrugged. "I prefer to think of it as *excessively well adjusted.* She really is as nice as she seems; the Susie Homemaker thing isn't put on, either. And her four-cheese lasagna is to die for."

He grinned. "Though sometimes I feel I should become a vegetarian. It would be appropriate, somehow . . ."

Then he did an alarmingly realistic "*moooooooo!*"

Ellen laughed, despite the crawling sensation between her shoulder blades.

"It does give you more sympathy for their position, doesn't it? God, I feel bloated. I don't generally eat as a displacement activity, but this has been a *rough* couple of days. Forty-eight hours ago, my only problem was figuring out how to tell my boyfriend it was over with us and worrying about how he'd react. Is there any place you can run, around here? I usually do three miles a day minimum."

"There are some great trails in the hills, if you don't mind steep."

"Hey, I'm from New Mexico too!"

"Meet you in half an hour, then?"

CHAPTER NINE

The two killers snarled as they spread out in the big sauna and advanced, lips pulled back to show the wide white gape of their teeth. The air was rank with the scent of their aggression. Adrian answered with a snarl of his own, one that turned into a full-throated racking scream. The wordless challenge-cry of the king predator:

Mine! Mine the land, the herds, the blood, the mates! Mine!

It checked them for the merest fraction of a second. He could feel their intent narrow again, focused like the edge of their knives; they were Shadowspawn, and powerful. Not as powerful as he, but there were two of them and the silver-inlaid, glyph-warded knives were deadly, annulling luck, canceling the Power's ability to heal the wounds they made. Adrian knew a single instant of irony; that was the same sort of weapon he'd learned to use when he was the Brotherhood's fosterling. The two sides of the ancient struggle were more closely linked than either would admit.

Then his intent was as pure as theirs. One came in, lunging leopard-fast up the stairlike seats, sweat gleaming across the bright patterns printed into his skin. The knife ripped upward towards belly and genitals. Adrian swayed his hips aside, fluid and sure, and lashed out with the ball of his foot as he pivoted on the other. The man rode it, flinging up one arm to take the impact and tumbling down the wood-sheathed tile of the benches, coming to his feet and shaking his head at the base.

His companion was already attacking, the knife flashing in a blurring X-figure of slashes before him. Some remote part of his mind spoke in Harvey's voice; memory held a tinge of sunlight filtering through the boards of a barn somewhere in the Texas hill country too, and the sweaty feel of a practice-hilt in his hand.

If it's a knife-fight, accept that you're going to get cut and cut bad. Just make sure the other mook's worse-off.

Adrian lunged into the other's attack. That broke his rhythm for the merest second; he'd been counting on the unarmed man retreating. Silver-veined steel slashed down his deflecting forearm and into his thigh, like a razor of sun-hot fire.

Pain! Painpainpainpain—

Blood-scent, his own, rank and terrible; the knife-arm slipped free of his grip and whipped back for the stab up under the short-ribs. For an instant they were locked chest-to-chest, and Adrian's other hand flashed up and clamped on the back of the knife-man's head with fingers like iron rods.

"*Sh'tzeeeez ak-ot!*" he spat, while their faces were close as lovers'.

Mhabrogast *commanded* the mind; the Power flowed out of him. The man's galvanic reaction sent him to the floor in a twitching, writhing, heel-drumming fit, and hurled Adrian back. A thin keening sound came out of him, endlessly. Adrian snatched up the knife where it had fallen; more pain lanced up his right arm, without the shielding glove. The other blade-man halted his rush and poised in a wary guard.

Then he smiled thinly. Adrian's leg buckled under him. The blood was flowing too fast, and he couldn't spare the focus to clamp the vessels from within. On one knee he kept the blade pointed out, swaying as gray gathered around the edges of his vision. Cold seemed to be blowing around him, despite the dry heat of the sauna—

"Hey, asshole!" a gravelly voice said cheerfully.

The tattooed Shadowspawn turned in a blur of speed. The massive *bummpf!* of Harvey's coach gun seemed to flow into the motion, and the knife-man jerked backward as the soft slug struck his face just above the nose and smashed open his skull with a dull wet cracking sound. Pinkish-white-gray tissue and blood spattered on the tiles and mats. Harvey took another step forward and brought the other barrel to bear on the head of the convulsing figure on the floor.

Bummpf!

"Good Shadowspawn," he said with satisfaction, breaking open the weapon's mechanism and slipping in two more shells. "Good 'n' *dead.* Dead-dead, too, not just body-dead."

Adrian let the savage focus slip away from his mind. Harvey caught him as he buckled; even the burn of silver in the leather jacket was distant. He felt himself laid down, and the towels turned into tourniquets.

"Let's let the Council cover things up, ol' buddy," he heard, as if from another room or another year. "Got to get you to a doc."

Hands clamped on his wounded arm and thigh. The pain was there, but didn't matter.

"And let's see if I can Wreak a little, here, partner, before we move you."

"Ellen," Adrian whispered.

Then he screamed, as Power flowed into the open wounds.

The welcome wagon hadn't tried to unpack her personal possessions. Ellen's bags rested on the king-sized bed. It was made up with fresh sheets, and the walk-in closets and the drawers of a tall rubbed-oak armoire held the sort of thing Monica had mentioned, clothing that could be bought off the shelf on short notice. The room had a half-empty feel anyway, no knickknacks or pictures on the walls. The window opened onto the small interior yard between the house and the *casa grande*'s perimeter wall; it let in a sweet scent of cut grass.

She'd packed the bags to a quick command of *Take what you can't replace with money*, and evidently her subconscious had been functioning. All she remembered from the time was a blur of terror, but they were full of a jumble of things like Mr. Wabbit—loved into shapelessness when she was small—and her family photographs and other mementoes. She hesitated; taking any of them out would be like admitting she was living here. Then she defiantly put Mr. Wabbit on the shelf over the head of the bed.

"There. Keep an eye on things, you wascally wabbit!"

She dressed in sweats with a sports bra beneath and a headband and a pair of very good running high-tops, and started stretching outside the house. The Lane was very quiet; Jamal had finished his routine with the weights and was sitting on the bench. He stared expressionlessly at her, made no response to her wave and then went inside.

Peter showed up; his gear was well-worn. The bruises and sore spots made her wince a little and go slowly at the limbering-up motions; he waited patiently.

"Ummm . . . Jamal *really* isn't friendly, is he?"

Peter sighed. "I've had exactly one sentence from him since he arrived last September. From LA, I think."

"What was that?"

"*I'm nobody's bitch, you faggot, so fuck off.*"

"Ouch!"

"Yes." A hesitation. "I usually sort of resent that; I'm not gay, I'm just *small*, for Christ's sake! But . . . it's hard to feel hostile to someone in his position. And I have this horrible feeling that he replaced me at the bottom of the list."

"The list?"

"The one she'd kill if she felt in the mood for that. The one she would miss least afterwards. Don't mention that to the others, by the way. I just violated the Lucy Code."

Ellen winced. "Double ouch. Let's run, shall we?"

He nodded, relief on his face: "How tough do you want it?"

"Not too-too, in new shoes—though these feel like suede gloves for the feet. And I'm still feeling a bit rocky in spots."

"I usually run in the mornings, when I can. Care to join me?" He held up a hand. "I'm not hitting on you. Not that you're not attractive, but . . . that sort of thing is not really practical for any of us here."

"Why do men always *apologize* for not hitting on you all the time including the grossly inappropriate ones?" Ellen asked, with a wry quirk to one corner of her mouth. "It's like *sorry for not interrupting you incessantly* or *I regret that I can't breathe onion in your face.*"

"Because we wish women *would* hit on us all the time," he answered promptly. "I realize the reverse isn't true."

They set out slowly, warming up as they left the end of the cul-de-sac. There was a brick bicycle path at first; that faded out as they worked their way onto a dirt path that snaked beside a seasonal brook under eucalyptus and native oaks. She kept quiet for half an hour, simply feeling the push of legs and flex of muscle, enjoying the body doing what it was supposed to do. It cleared her head as well.

"Did you . . . have anyone in Los Alamos?" she asked after a while, pacing the words to her breath.

"Not seriously, lately. And I'm very glad things were that way."

She nodded. He went on: "You were really involved with Adrienne's brother? And he didn't . . ."

"No. Things got sticky, but he never . . . well, obviously he never drank my blood! I didn't know about *any* of this stuff; that was a big part of why we were splitting up. He wouldn't *tell* me things. I knew he was keeping a lot of secrets. He's a good guy, basically. I can see now looking back how hard he had to fight not to . . . do things. I may have unintentionally been tempting him."

Peter nodded. "Left up here, past that clump of bamboo. You know, they can play games with your memories, if they can get close to you for a while. Break your brain-codes. You *sure* he didn't do that?"

That made her miss a stride; then she laughed harshly. "That's like trying to prove that the world wasn't created six minutes ago!"

"Yeah, classic non-falsifiable hypothesis. Sorry!"

"No, I can't be sure. I'm morally certain, though. Thanks for giving me *another* creepy thought to keep me awake!"

"*De nada.* Do you hate him for getting you into this?"

"No," she said.

Odd. I wasn't certain that I didn't until just now.

Aloud: "No, what Adrienne's done is Adrienne's fault, and they hadn't had any contact for years. She's got some twisted love-hate-desire thing going on with him, at least on her part; he hates her and he's afraid of her. All he wanted was to be left alone and live something as close to a normal life as he could. I was part of that, I think. And she . . . wants . . . me because he did. I get this really creepy feeling that to her . . . messing . . . with me is like fucking *him*."

"I don't know if I could be that objective. And, yes, the *Doña* tends to give you that creepy feeling, doesn't she?"

Soon they were moving up a pair of ruts through dense pasture and onto a ridge. The conversation went in spurts; the usual origin-story you exchanged with a new friend. Her small-town Pennsylvania coal-country roots, the struggle to get to New York and work her way through NYU, the way paintings had taken her to another world. His professional-class Minnesota background, physics a door into the nature of things. The way they'd been fifty miles apart for years and never even dreamed the other existed.

"This rock is a good place to turn. It's all chaparral for a bit after this—limestone slope. Good steep ground but not this late and not unless you're up to it."

"Woof!" Ellen said, leaning over to get her breath under control.

Her lungs seemed dry and inflexible for a few moments, and her skin heated by a flush like an interior sunlamp. The air was cooling, but that felt good.

"I needed to run off the sugar, but I'm still more wiped than I thought."

Peter nodded. They trotted on a little more; the sun was to the left and a little ahead, making the bare branches ahead black outlines. She stopped again when they rounded a clump of oaks and found themselves facing a small group of white-face cattle, up to their bellies in the deep green grass.

"They're OK," he said as he noticed her freeze.

"They're *big*. I like cows best already disassembled."

When they'd moved off she turned and said: "You got in trouble for something about the Power, didn't you? That's why . . . they . . . wanted you dead. Or someplace like this, fully under control."

Peter nodded. His handsome mobile face turned to the shadows in the east. "How much mathematics do you have?"

"Hey, Art History BA, remember," she said. "I can use TurboTax if I concentrate very, very hard. If it's obscure technical terms in Renaissance Italian painting you want, I'm your gal."

He sat down on a stump. "OK, short form. The Power doesn't come from inside the Shadowspawn brains. It can't. Brains just don't generate that much energy. What they do is *modulate* the Power, tapping it from a deep level. Like a transistor in a radar set. They step it up or down and shape it. But the energy comes from somewhere else. Follow me so far?"

She nodded, and he continued: "What put me on to it was results on probabilistic analysis of—"

"Whoa! Artsy math-aversion reflexes kickin' in! Let's get going, then. You know, what puzzles me is that we . . . our ancestors . . . were ever able to overthrow them."

He rose and they trotted slowly downward. "I suspect it's because there just weren't many in any given spot, back when humans were rare."

"A sort of lions versus zebra thing?"

"Exactly. But now the upper limit's vanished. And their numbers and their genetic purity have been increasing *fast* the last hundred years. It explains a lot. Think of the early legends . . . you know those?"

She smiled at him, mopping at her face with the sleeve of her sweats. "*Art History*, remember? It's obligatory to know the loves of Zeus and that sort of thing."

"You know how crazy the world seems in those myths? How . . . anything-can-happen? Dreamlike and arbitrary?"

Her eyes went wide in alarm. "You mean it *was* like that?"

"Around the Shadowspawn, yes. Probabilities start to blur into each other. The damned *luck*! They're probably the reason we believe in luck in the first place. There's no such thing, really—not as sort of a personal possession, or a muscle that's stronger in some people than in others."

"Except for *them* it actually does work that way."

"Right. And it explains so much else, too."

"Like why the Greeks thought ghosts needed blood? And why so many gods demanded human sacrifices?"

"Yeah, but more fundamental things as well. Why do humans want gods at all? Why do we believe in them without proof?"

"Oh. There *was* proof."

He nodded. "For a hundred thousand years we *had* gods, for ninety-six percent of the existence of the human race. And spirits and ghosts and survival after death—for some."

She shuddered, and he made a hands-in-the-air gesture.

"You know the really ironic thing?" he said. "I think that if we could *understand* the Power, we could use it. I mean, everyone could. We'd need something like a very capable, very specifically tailored quantum computer. But all they're interested in is keeping potential competition down."

She frowned. Running downhill was harder, or trickier, than going up, but her balance adjusted automatically.

"Why don't they do that themselves? Surely they'd be in the best position to investigate the Power."

Peter laughed, half-genuine amusement, half-bitterness. "What animal does Adrienne remind you of? Not *a bitch*, please. Really."

"A cat," she said instantly. "I like cats, but they're not tame. We can have them around because we're stronger and smarter. The big ones we put in zoos or nature parks."

"Smart! We're apes that became more like wolves. Shadowspawn are apes who became like wolves and then decided they'd rather become like cats instead. And what do cats do if you leave them to themselves?"

"Hunt and play at hunting. Torture mice. Eat. Sleep. Groom themselves. Fight other cats for territory and mates. Screw."

"Exactly. I—"

An engine sounded from around the curve of the track ahead, the whining burble-hum of a new electric-drive hybrid. They stopped in surprise as a TARDEC utility vehicle stopped, a low-slung boxy body of angled plates on four oversize wheels, the sort of thing you saw on news reports from dry dusty places where things went *boom* a lot. It didn't bristle with weapons, but there were antennae and the man beside the driver was looking down at some sort of display screen. Another followed it.

The riders looked like soldiers; at least they had body-armor, which Ellen could recognize from the news, and bulbous helmets with sensor visors ready to be flipped down, and each had an ear-mike with a little thread-microphone at one corner of their mouths. They carried odd foreign-looking assault rifles as well.

Eight of them were Asian, but not quite like any she'd seen before. Short barrel-chested bandy-legged men, tough and stocky with the weathered skin of those who'd always been out-of-doors in all weathers; they swung down and spread out, going down on one knee facing outward. They were relaxed and alert, their eyes never stopping; their sense of tensile presence reminded her of good tennis players, even in their heavy boots and gear. Besides the usual military paraphernalia their belts held big inward-curving chopping knives.

They don't seem like a brute squad, she thought. *Just . . . focused.*

The ninth was a white man, older but very fit, with gray threads in his clipped brown mustache, and very cold gray eyes. They met hers through the growing shadows . . .

This one knows, she thought. *He's not one of them, but he knows. Maybe the others don't, maybe they do, but he* really *knows who he's working for. What he's working for.*

"Hello, Dr. Boase," he said; his voice was clipped upper-class British.

"Captain Bates," Peter replied neutrally.

Then he turned his head to her: "I'm Harold Bates, head of site security here for Brézé Enterprises, Ms. Tarnowski. Were you heading in for the evening? It's a biggish bit of wilderness to be out in, on foot and after dark."

His voice was impeccably respectful. Ellen nodded when Peter said cautiously: "Yes, just heading home."

"Cheerio, then."

He switched to a fast-moving language, evidently the one the soldiers spoke, and the two runners stood aside as they climbed back into their vehicles and drove by.

"Who are the soldiers for? It's not as if they need guns to keep us from running away."

"They have enemies," he said, and shook his head when she would have gone on. "Later."

Adrian! Be careful! she thought. Then: *Would men with guns have any chance against . . . well, he must be able to do all that stuff too?*

It was full dark when they were at the head of the trail again where it joined the Lane, and chilly enough that she felt she'd be glad to get indoors; during the day this gentle climate was enough to make you forget it was only the middle of February. There weren't any street-lamps along Lucy Lane, only little lights over the courtyard doors. That left the ambient level low enough that the frosting of stars and crescent moon were helpful. And a trickle came through an open window in Number One.

They were about to walk by when a shriek of raw pain stopped her in her tracks. Peter took her arm and tried to urge her along. Then she heard pleading. Monica's voice, high-pitched and urgent:

"Oh, Addi, *don't.* Don't! Please! Not there—*ow! That hurts. It hurts so bad!*"

Another scream, then a delighted laugh, and a low moan broken with choked-off muffled sobs: "Ow . . . ow . . . oh, owwwww . . . ow . . . ow . . ."

The noise fell behind her. They stopped outside Number Five.

"I guess this wasn't a milk-and-cookies sort of evening," Peter said quietly. Then: "And Monica keeps *forgiving!*"

He was quivering; she could feel that. She touched his arm.

"This is just so totally awful, isn't it?" she said quietly.

He nodded. She took his arm again and it felt rigid. Then he began to shake; she hesitated, then pulled his head down on her shoulder. The sobs were soundless, but the tears soaked through the fabric of the sweat suit. His arms came up to embrace her clumsily. After a moment he straightened and wiped at his eyes with the palms of his hands.

"Thank you," he said, and cleared his throat. "Sorry."

"Sorry for what, Pete? Look, I'm not hitting on you either, but I don't want to spend the evening with a pillow over my head. Come on in and have dinner and we'll talk about something else. Maybe watch a movie. OK?"

He nodded wordless gratitude.

CHAPTER TEN

"**W**here—*Adrian!*"

Ellen was in a hospital room; greenish beige walls, linoleum floor, ceiling tracks for curtains. The air smelled of disinfectant and pain and lousy food. The smell that had been ground into her soul during her father's long dying as the accompaniment to guilt and anger and relief. Adrian was lying in a cheap hospital gown, the sort that fastened down the back with ties. It looked shockingly incongruous on his beautifully balanced, lean-muscled body, which she'd only seen either elegantly dressed or naked.

There were bandages on his arm and another large dressing on his thigh, which was held up in a rest. A tangle of tubes dripped plasma and saline into his veins.

"Adrian!" she said again.

His eyes turned towards her and blinked. "Oh . . . sorry . . . Ellie," he said in a slow, blurred voice. "Let . . . me . . . do something about . . . this."

The world seemed to flux somehow. Before she could decide what was happening they were both standing on a beach. It was wide white sand, with a wind whipping up little gusts around their ankles and waves coming in from the east knee-high, hissing almost to their feet. A brown pelican flapped by over the water, intent on its own concerns, and gulls eyed bits of flotsam.

Adrian was in chinos and a loose shirt of beige natural cotton, barefoot, tanned darker than she remembered him last. Ellen looked down at herself; so was she, and she was in a bikini and straw hat. The air was warm and moist, blowing from the ocean and into the low scrub and occasional palm tree inland with an intense salt cleanliness.

"This is that place we went on the coast in South Texas," she said slowly. "Last spring. Just after we got together."

He shrugged. "I can change it if you like. It was a happy time, for me."

His accent was a little stronger. She'd never inquired about it before; he didn't like to talk about his past.

"For me too. You grew up in France, didn't you?" she said now.

"Partly, some time every year as a child, and my foster-parents were French. California, for the rest, until they . . . died. Then all over the world. Texas, more than any single place."

A hand went over his tousled black hair. "Where are *you* now? That is important."

"I'm . . . asleep in my . . . in a place Adrienne put me. I'm alone in the bed, too."

"Good." He relaxed a little. "We may have enough time, then. This link is stronger than I thought."

She blinked. "I remember now! I remember the last time you brought me to a place like this! I didn't forget, but I didn't think *of* it until now!"

Adrian nodded. "And I really am in a hospital bed," he said. "In San Francisco. Two men with knives tried to kill me. Shadowspawn . . . perhaps indirectly set on me by my sister."

"What happened?" she asked anxiously.

He *looked* healthy, body glowing like a fine slender racehorse, every muscle moving distinctly under the olive skin. But that meant nothing *here*, wherever.

"They died. I lived, due to a friend named Harvey Ledbetter who arrived most opportunely. I was badly wounded, I am afraid, but I will recover. I'm very sorry."

"Sorry?"

"It will delay me."

Ellen smiled at him, and got a shy answering expression. "Thanks, Adrian."

"It's nothing. Let's walk up the beach, and you tell me what has happened with you."

She did; he winced now and then. "You're with some sort of . . . Resistance movement, aren't you? The doctor called you terrorists."

Adrian smiled crookedly. "Not entirely without justification, from a renfield's point of view. The Brotherhood is not squeamish about collateral damage, particularly to servants of the Council of Shadows."

"Then it's all *true*, what she told me?"

"True enough, if you allow for viewpoint."

She stopped and looked searchingly into his eyes. "You . . . aren't like the other Shadowspawn?"

"I was raised to think of myself as human. It isn't easy. That is why

I have been so much alone. And . . . your type of human . . . aren't instinct machines, and neither are we Shadowspawn. Some humans are good and some less so, according to the choices they make. I shouldn't be able to blame everything on my genes either. Shadowspawn *do* blame their genes, but that's an excuse. The fact of the matter is they were raised to evil, and they embrace it."

She put a hand on his shoulder, and he covered it with his. "You should curse my name," he said.

"Adrian, you just fought two men with knives for me and got cut up. You could have been an all-powerful monster. Judging from the way Adrienne acts, it's fun. You *decided* to be a human being. An asshole sometimes, but who isn't? I'm just getting my mind wrapped around this stuff but that part is pretty clear."

They laughed. "And now you know where I am. I'm—"

She paused, frowning. Her mind felt perfectly clear; clearer than it had been for days, unhazed by fear and tension. But she couldn't *say* where she was.

"I don't think I know, exactly," she said slowly. "Somewhere in central California . . ."

"You know," Adrian said grimly. "You've been blocked from saying it. It's a Wreaking on your memory and volition. Small, subtle, but it would be dangerous to break it—with me weakened, certainly. You'd only notice it if you tried to tell someone who *didn't* know."

"But that should be a clue!" she said hopefully.

They walked again, holding hands this time. The cool salt water ran over their bare feet, and the wet sand made for good footing. Curlews bobbed and probed in the shallows with their absurdly thin curved beaks, crying *wheet-wheet-wheet.*

"Not as much of a clue as I'd like," Adrian said. "Ellie, it's *easy* to fox records with the Power. The Brotherhood are looking in *their* records, and those are far more complete."

"You've been fighting with the, the Brotherhood?" she asked, squeezing his hand. "Against the Shadowspawn?"

Now he looked out to sea. "I did. For twenty-five years—"

"Thanks for telling me your real age!"

"I *couldn't*—"

"I'm teasing, dummy!"

"Oh. Thank you for *that*. I . . . retired a few years ago."

"Why?"

"Because it was futile. I was the strongest Wreaker the Brotherhood ever had, but there was only one of me. The others were far weaker; and the Council has all the resources of the earth at its call, the governments and the police and the armies and the security forces. All I could do was kill—some who deserved it, many who did not. It didn't *change* anything."

"Wait a minute," she said. "To use this Power for big stuff, don't you need—"

"Blood. From the Red Cross, and handsomely paid for."

"Oh," she said with relief.

He grimaced. "God, it tastes terrible. And the things it does to my digestion, and the headaches . . . I can't even completely cure those with the Power, because that would require *more* of it. That was another reason to retire. On my mountain, or here, I could . . . grapple with the cravings, the drives. Learn a degree of peace."

"Your sister . . . seems to enjoy the taste."

"She's drinking live hot blood, and primed with strong emotions. It's . . . a powerful drug. Dead blood is an entirely different story."

She squeezed his hand again. "I hope you can get me out soon," she said. "Jesus, it's . . . creepy here. The people all act as if it were *normal*. Even the ones she *hurts*."

"To them it is," Adrian said. "People adapt. If they could not, humanity would not have survived the first rule of the Shadowspawn. But, Ellie . . ."

"Yes?"

"This isn't just a personal thing between me and Adrienne, as I thought at first."

"It's certainly *partly* a personal thing! There's all sorts of overtones in her voice when she mentions you. And she thinks about you a lot. Even her children look like you!"

Adrian froze, so suddenly that his hand tugged her to a halt; he was a slender man, not large and so graceful you forgot the solid density of him.

"She has children?" he said neutrally.

"Twins, a boy and a girl, around six or seven. Oh, God, talk about *creepy*! You didn't know?"

"No, I did not," he said in a voice empty of all emotion, so much so that it was as notable as a shriek. "I had no idea."

Then he shook his head. "It doesn't matter. But there is some great matter at stake here as well, somehow tied up with me and Adrienne. The Council of Shadows is moving, contemplating . . . enormous actions. There are factions and factions within factions; that is natural to Shadowspawn, even more than to humans. Please, listen to all that you can. Adrienne likes to talk, when she thinks it safe."

Ellen nodded. "Does she ever!"

He stopped and took both her hands in his. "And . . . I hate to say this, Ellie, but until you're rescued, that advice from the renfield doctor is good. Stay alive! Whatever it takes."

"I'll do my best. And *you* get better and get to work, *hombre!*"

She leaned forward and kissed him gently. Adrian's arms went around her, and she stiffened. He let them drop and step back.

"Sorry—" she began.

A shake of the head. "It's natural. You're sensing . . . what I am. Sleep well, Ellie, and hope."

He reached out and touched thumb to one side of her forehead and little finger to the other.

"Sleep well, and don't think of this unless you must."

A *word*, and sleep returned. She woke for a moment, grasping at the fleeting stuff of dream, turned over and hugged Mr. Wabbit against her and drifted down into the velvety blackness once more.

"Woof!" Peter said. "You *do* run a lot, right?"

"Told you," Ellen said smugly.

"God, you long-legged people—it isn't fair!"

They came down the bike path at a loping trot, then slowed to a walk.

"So it does solve one problem," Peter said; she'd grown used to the way he skipped mentally among topics.

"What, *another* one?"

She liked Peter, but his mania for explaining and systematizing could probably wear, after a while.

He nodded vigorously and drank the last of the water in his bottle. "All those old legends, and the books and movies . . . none of them could explain why, if there were creatures with such power around, they didn't rule the world."

"The answer being, as soon as they're around, they *do* rule the world. They just don't like publicity."

"Exactly. It's horrifying, but it's . . . intellectually *satisfying* as well. And the dislike of publicity is probably a holdover from the secret societies they started out with—the occultists and ninjas and whatnot."

"Boy, your hobby rides you hard, doesn't it? And there's one good thing about it all."

"What? That's a first."

"We don't have to blame *ourselves* for the way the world's screwed up. It's them, goofing on us."

Ellen mopped at her face with the towel hung around her neck as he laughed, breathing deeply but not panting; after a solid day's rest and two good nights' sleep her body was starting to feel *right* again.

The world feels wrong, but my body is back in tune.

The third run had been best of all so far, and the weather was cooperating—it had rained in the night, but the morning was cool sixties, with scattered clouds over the hills to the west. Sweat mixed with the smells of crushed grass and wet dust.

"See you later," Peter said, as they came out onto Lucy Lane. "I've got some remote time on the Stanford machine. I'm working on—"

"—something I wouldn't understand if you told me twice. Tear 'em up, tiger," she said. "Let us know when you've solved the mysteries of the universe."

Or invented a zap gun to kill Shadowspawn. Only they'd read your mind and know about it beforehand. God, that's depressing!

They walked past Number One, and Monica waved to them from the doorway. Peter went by with a nod and a wave back, but Ellen stopped. Evidently the Sangre schools had a uniform policy—white shirt and blue shorts for boys, shirt and pleated navy skirt for girls— and Monica was seeing her two off. They hurried by with a polite murmur of "Hi, Ms. Tarnowski."

Which makes me feel ancient *beyond words*, she thought, as she returned the greeting.

And . . . I wonder what they know? What do they think about the times Mom has . . . company and they have to stay with Grandma? The boy's eleven and the girl's nine; you do *think about things at that age. What does Monica's mother think, that it's some sort of deeply weird kept-woman arrangement? Could you live here eight years without a clue about what's really going on?*

Monica looked after them fondly as they ran swinging their book satchels and lunch boxes and folded Netbooks, the morning sun bright on their light brown hair.

"How are you?" Ellen asked.

"Oh, I'm fine," she said. "Thanks, though."

"I, ummm—"

Monica laughed. "Oh, you heard me screaming the other night, did you?"

"Sorry. I was walking by that evening. And you were, uh, sort of laid up yesterday. I wondered what happened, especially . . ."

"Since it'll be happening to you too." A smile and a shrug. "Nothing too bad. I mean, the screams were real, but when . . . I just let it rip, let the hurt flow right up the throat, you know? It helps and she likes it."

"What happened, exactly?"

"She came in and said, 'Tabasco sauce in the Bloody Mary tonight, Monica,' and right away I knew I was in for a wild time. Then she just flipped me over on the sofa, yanked off my underwear and—"

She held up a hand with the extended fingers together, moved it sharply upward, clenched them into a fist and pumped it up and down. Then she giggled again, rolled her eyes and blew air over her upper lip.

"Let's just say I'm *glad* she doesn't have bigger hands! You know what I mean."

"Ah . . . yeeee*ah*," Ellen said with a wince. "Fisting."

"That's what she told me it's called; I'd never even *heard* of it before I came here. I don't really like it all that much even when it's, you know, not so *abrupt*."

I found that out in my own apartment and I'm not inclined to giggle about it. God, I hope your variety of crazy isn't catching!

"I think that's harder on the guys," Monica said thoughtfully. "But you know how guys are. They're sort of shy, really. They don't like to talk about things."

Ellen thought, in what was almost a prayer:

God, Adrian, you're coming to get me, aren't you? I swear, I'll never keep a cat again. The mice and birds would haunt me.

And, as prayer sometimes was, it felt . . . very slightly reassuring.

Monica went on: "But then she fed—it's very soothing when she feeds—and then she was, umm, *really* nice to me."

She absently touched the Band-Aid at the base of her throat.

"You play tennis, don't you?" Monica went on.

"Yes?" Ellen said, blinking at the non sequitur.

"There's a ladies' club that meets at the community center courts; I go after I finish up at the library most days. Care to play a few games this afternoon? I'm not very sore anymore, and the *Doña* can reach us there if she wants you for something. She's reasonable about that. You only have to clear it with her if you're out of town for more than a few hours. Besides, she was with Jamal last night."

"Ah . . . why not?" Ellen said.

I do like playing tennis. Why not, indeed? They're probably not good enough to give me much of a game, but you never know.

Just then an ambulance came up the street and stopped in front of Number Three. Two paramedics trotted inside pulling a gurney. Both women froze, then exhaled again as they came out with a living man on it.

Adrienne followed; she was dressed in black motorcycle leathers and boots, and made a beckoning gesture, leaning back against a massive low-slung machine with wide tires, arms crossed on her chest.

Like something alien, Ellen thought; it took a slight mental effort to make herself walk to the driveway. *Like something alien and sleek and deadly. All of which are truer than God. Much truer.*

"He's just dazed, I think," the mistress of Rancho Sangre said absently when they came up, looking after the emergency vehicle. "Possibly a mild concussion. Jamal is"—her voice dropped to a purr "—very *strong*. And very, very grumpy at breakfast sometimes. Of course, I'm not usually a morning person myself."

"Well, he should know better than to *fight* you, Doña Adrienne," Monica said disapprovingly. "Really, some people are just plain *rude*."

Then she cleared her throat and touched the corner of her mouth for an instant.

"Ah, thanks," Adrienne said, and used a thumb to wipe up the red trickle that ran down to her chin.

She licked it off, scrubbed her face with her sleeve and went on:

"No, it's actually entertaining, at least for a while. Now, I'm going up to San Francisco. You're not up to it, are you, Monica?"

"Ah . . . on the motorcycle?"

Adrienne nodded. Monica smiled and patted the air behind herself for an instant.

"It would hurt a lot," she said, almost clinically. "Riding that *long*, I mean."

"You wouldn't be very mobile when we got to town, either, which would be tiresome. We wouldn't want to shock Jean-Charles. Ellen, sluice off, pack yourself some underwear and socks and an extra T-shirt, and your toothbrush. We can do some shopping while I'm there. *Vite!*"

She jumped at the snap and hurried, flushing with annoyance at herself.

Fear burns itself out, she thought. *I can't be afraid of her every moment of the day. Not that I don't want* to, *I just can't, the way I couldn't run for twenty-four hours a day either. But I can be* nervous *a lot longer, the way you can walk farther than you can run. I* do *wonder why we're making this trip. Surely she'd want to stay here behind . . . oh, defenses or something? If I'm bait for Adrian.*

When she returned Adrienne was astride the big red-black-and-yellow touring bike; it had a V-shaped logo on the front with the trident-and-black-sun inside it.

I don't like motorcycles. They're insanely risky.

"What can I say, I'm *lucky*," Adrienne said, and grinned beneath the raised visor of the full-face helmet. "There's a spare padded jacket in the touring bag—that streamlined trunk thing behind the rear seat. You'd be chilly without that, even with me to break the airflow. And a spare helmet. Put 'em on, spread your thighs over the bitch seat of this vibrator on wheels, and let's go!"

Just then Monica hurried up. "Some lunch!" she said, and tucked a plastic-wrapped parcel into one of the fared saddlebags beside the rear wheel. "In case you want to stop at someplace pretty and picnic!"

"Monica, you are a wonder," Adrienne said and stood on the kick-starter. *"En avant."*

The big V-twin engine roared into life, but then the sound faded to an oddly muted drone. The inside of the helmet seemed to *adjust* itself slightly, pressing more tightly against her ears.

"Automatic selective sound-damping," Adrienne said, tapping her ear; the voice came through faultlessly from the mike in the helmet's chin-bar. "Customized experimental military system, filters things like engine noise. I just *love* modern technology!"

Ellen mounted; the touring machine had actual if sketchy seats, enough to cradle the butt and hips at least, and her back was against a padded rest. The Shadowspawn's torso pressed her, and she could just see over her helmet.

"Arms around my waist," Adrienne said. "It's the closest you'll get to a seat belt."

She obeyed hesitantly, feeling the other's back pushing against her breasts and belly through the down jacket's fabric, and the taut muscle beneath the leather as she gripped.

"It's a bit late to be shy, *chérie*," Adrienne observed. "Hang on!"

"Eeek!"

She did, gripping convulsively as the big machine seemed to hang on its spinning, smoking rear wheel for an instant, then came down and caromed out of the little lane like a wet melon seed squeezed between two fingers.

"Whooooop! Whooooop!" Adrienne caroled.

The cycle leaned far over as they cut right, dodging a delivery truck. Speed built to a blur, and the wind tugged at her head. She hugged desperately, hands joining below the other's ribs as they headed south. After a few moments that was for sheer warmth as well as safety. The air caught at her jacket and made it flutter sharply, like an awning in a high breeze, a continuous crackling sound; the vibration sank into her bones, with the deeper note of the machine beneath.

"We're on Highway 46 here," Adrienne said as they turned west. "Pretty country, but it's even nicer when we hit the coast."

The only parts of California Ellen had seen before had been the Bay area and LA. This *was* pretty, in a way different from both the forested East and the austere piñon-and-juniper high desert around Santa Fe.

Here rolling green hills rose out of the occasional patch of flat land, like a rumpled padded quilt on an unmade bed. Tongues of oakwood and trees she couldn't identify rose up the notches in the high ground, with sheep grazing in ridge-top meadows. Vineyards pruned and stumpy for winter made geometry across the lower slopes with the first yellow traces of wild mustard beneath, and blazing orchards of cherry and almond were slashes of color against the green. The smells were fresh and moist and the air grew a little warmer as the sun rose; now and then there was an overwhelming sweetness of blossom or a pungent waft from livestock.

Adrienne drove the near-empty road and through the little hamlets with a hard decisive snap that was somehow never jerky, overtaking whatever came her way with a surge that pressed her back against the passenger and Ellen back against the rest. Uneasily, she remembered that Adrian handled the sports cars he loved in very much the same fearless way, as if he were pushing his own nerve and muscle down the controls into the machine.

She peered over the other's shoulder at the all-glass screen controls; they were doing ten miles above the speed limit, on this winding roadway.

"Customized engine," Adrienne said after a while. "Four-stroke fifty-degree V-Twin with 1731 cc displacement. Single overhead camshafts with four valves per cylinder, self-adjusting cam chains, hydraulic lifters. But they jiggered the compression ratio for me and the frame's special alloy, lighter than the standard. I think I'll give Jose one for his birthday; he loves it."

I don't speak Mechanic, Ellen thought.

Then her mind stuttered slightly. It was *impossible* to censor the way you talked to yourself!

"You sound like some of my elders." Adrienne laughed; there was a hard edge to it, but Ellen didn't think it was directed at her. "A lot of them don't like machinery either. At least machinery that doesn't involve shoveling coal into a boiler."

"The ones who make the middle-management demonic career path hell?" she asked.

"But yes!"

She took one hand off the handlebars to gesture for an instant, and Ellen felt the muscles in her thighs and stomach clench in sudden terror. Was that a wobble in the front wheel?

"Also, their *attitudes*. Few people change much past their twenties. In this my breed and yours are not so different. Perhaps in the Old Stone Age this was of no consequence; one millennium was much like another. But now matters are different, and that, my sweet, is a matter which concerns *you*."

"Why? You'd all want to . . . drink my blood, wouldn't you? Torture me and mess with me?"

"Yes. But *they* rule the world, remember? And not just at dinnertime."

"Oh."

Ellen winced. *That explains a number of things.*

"Imagine again; the ruling elders grew up in the time of the First World War, more or less—a little older than *my* parents. That was when Shadowspawn powerful enough to survive death became more than a very few. *Their* parents were Victorians, born before Bismarck's men shelled Paris."

Ellen gave a sly chuckle. "Sexist assholes?"

"Oh, you have *no* idea. Exactly *two* women on the Council, in this day and age!"

"How many on the Council altogether?"

"Thirteen, naturally! Though that is not the worst of it. They have nineteenth-century habits of *thought*. They do not think of interlinkages and unintended consequences and feedback cycles. This matter of you humans overbreeding and ruining the world, for example."

"You're *environmentalists*?" she said incredulously.

"If you plan to live . . . well, exist . . . for ten thousand years or more, you really do not have much choice, my sweet. But *les vieux*, they also just *hate* the modern world, many of them. It is not the place in which they grew. They do not understand it; they feel *alien* in this century, alien to the buildings and the clothes and the music, the very fabric of life. They want the changes to *stop*. Hence their solution to the problem is . . . far too drastic."

"Drastic?"

"They plan to destroy human civilization. Let only a few hundred million survive, as peasants."

Eeerk! Ellen thought; for a moment she forgot the rushing passage of the roadway.

That's insane, it's got to be insane even by . . . vampire-monster-sadist-werewolf-Saruman-on-steroids standards!

"Precisely. *Quelle connerie!* I *like* the modern world. Well, much of it. Yes, yes, there are too many humans; they must be trimmed back, faster than our pressure on governments to promote birth control can accomplish—"

"That was *you?*"

"Of course. Do you think the Chinese would have given up hope of sons on their own? And our sabotage of the economy—"

"That was you guys too?"

"*Chérie*, you thought it was *by accident* that all over the world so many intelligent people made the same mistakes at the same time? Yes, these measures are inadequate. We must intervene more directly. But I do *not* want only a few peasants to survive. Peasants are *boring!*"

Her voice rose. "I like fast cars, and motorcycles, and my jet! I like towns where the streets are *not* rivers of shit! I like movies and the Web and digital music libraries and BlackBerries and video-on-demand! I like a good selection of lucies, ones who do *not* have lice and who can carry on an intelligent conversation and have interesting, sensitive minds to torment and degrade! I adore the Louvre, and the Getty, and the Hermitage and the Rijksmuseum and good restaurants and fashion shows in Paris or Milan and Château Lafite Rothschild and the London theater!"

The voice rose again. "Idiots! *Izidingidwane! Baka tare!* Fossilized imbeciles! *Cretans! Èrbǎiwǔ!*"

By then they were moving north on Highway 1, the narrow two-lane coastal strip. The torrent of multilingual insults melded into a sheer howl of rage, not deafening only because the headphones damped it. Acceleration rammed the Shadowspawn's dense compact torso back into her, and the engine was loud even through the helmet as the wheel screamed against the earth. Everything blurred around them as the cycle surged forward.

"No!" Ellen screamed herself. "You'll kill us both, *nonononono!*"

They took the curve lying over so far that her left knee nearly brushed the pavement. A minivan loomed up in front of them, and the motorcycle skimmed between it and the rocky cliff-face of the road-way, close enough that she could have reached out and touched either one, if her arms hadn't been locked around the other's waist. A swerve outward and another leaning turn, with asphalt rushing by so close to the right that she could see every crack from deferred maintenance. She couldn't even close her eyes or look away as death loomed up in the form of a rust-eaten Honda Civic with three horrified faces staring through the glass.

A screech, a skid, a rooster-tail of sparks and they were off the road and off the earth. *Thud* and they landed again, the gas suspension on the rear wheel clanging as the piston met the stops, then corkscrew-ing down a rough slope of grass and sand towards the beach and the ocean. Adrienne standing, crouched to throw her weight from side to side to keep the massive touring bike from overturning. Swerving in a sideways break that threw white plumes twice head-height from both wheels as they scrubbed off velocity.

It came to a halt, and silence crashed in as Adrienne killed the engine, kicked down the stand and leaped to the ground. She danced around the cycle screeching exultantly, tearing off her helmet to let her black mane fly in the wind off the blue, blue Pacific, punching her fists in the air.

"*Whooop! Whooop!* I am *supreme!* Now *that* is the way to burn off tensions!"

Ellen half-fell, half-crawled, half-dragged herself off, swaying as her knees threatened to buckle, dropping the helmet at her feet as she gasped in cool salt air. It felt icy on the sweat that drenched her face.

"I nearly peed myself! I nearly peed myself!"

She clutched at her stomach, fighting nausea for a long moment, staggering a few steps away and back.

"Oh, God! Oh, God!"

Adrienne was laughing, eyes blazing and spots of red in her cheeks. Ellen braced her hands on the seat of the motorcycle, straining to control her breathing.

"You could have killed us ten times over!" she said, voice trembling.

"Only five, if you count the ones where I had to use the Power to shift probabilities. The rest? Matchless skill and reflexes like a leopard, *ma douce*. Oh, if only you could see your face! And your mind, it's like an eye that has stared into the sun!"

"Stop *laughing* at me!"

Adrienne did. The smile died away, and the gold-flecked brown eyes locked with hers. She sank down with her back against a rock that jutted up through the sand of the beach and patted her lap.

"Come and lie across my knees like this," she said, her voice husky with a growling undertone. "That was an effort. Now I'm a little hungry again."

Run, Ellen's mind whispered suddenly.

The fear of crashing into rock and metal and feeling her bones crackle like overstressed bamboo suddenly gave way to something older and more primal. A hundred thousand years of instinct spoke:

Run. Hunter, predator, walking death, it smells your blood, runrunrunRUN!

The Shadowspawn laughed. "I'm twice as fast as you and half again as strong," she said, in that deadly velvet tone. "I'd chase you down in ten yards. Or I could just use the Power and make your pants fall and trip you. That would be fun, but not for you, and you wouldn't like the mood I'd be in then. Come *here*, lucy."

Ellen felt a whimper building up in her throat, and suppressed it. A remembered sentence ran through her mind:

Make the experience of feeding on you as satisfying for our lady demon as possible, because your life does *depend on it.*

"Excellent advice."

She forced herself to walk towards the waiting smile and moistened lips and the fixed eyes, each step as slow and heavy as running in a dream. She sank down on the sand. Breath and heartbeat fluttered.

"To my right, facing me, *chérie*. Now lean across. Lay your head on my left shoulder, arm around my waist, the other around my neck."

She did, and knees came up to support her back. The collar pressed against her face with a buttery-soft smell of fine leather and a slight acrid one of sweat and the scent of verbena hair wash. A hand stroked her nape, her throat, and then cupped her jaw, holding it firmly so that her neck arched. The other hand rested on her hip. Lips touched the hollow below the angle of her jaw, soft and wet, and the tongue. A breathy whisper:

"This won't hurt at all."

A hardness, teeth pressing against taut skin. *The feeding bite is verra precise.* Terror built to a peak; she could feel herself quivering as tears threatened to break free.

"Just imagine I'm Adrian . . ."

A *sting*, sharp and slight.

A torrent of emotions fell through her mind, but her consciousness refused to analyze them, and they died away. Suction against the cut, steady and insistent. Coolness spread out from the incision, as if all the fear and tension were leaving her body with the blood. She relaxed with a slight tremulous sigh and felt her mind slow, spinning downward into a bright wash of no-thought. Her eyes fluttered half-shut, filtering the bright sunlight off the white sand and the glitter of water into a blur; there was no drowsiness, only a complete disinterest in moving from where she was.

The gentle liquid sounds of the feeding were distinct; and a soft purring growl, more felt than heard where Adrienne's throat pressed against hers, working with the swallows. The *shsshshshssh* of waves and gull-cries ran beneath it. At last the mouth lifted from her neck. There was another slight sting as the air struck the wound; Adrienne put a finger against it and the sting faded to a very faint itch for an instant and then was gone.

The Shadowspawn's head tilted back. Ellen could see her turn her face upward with eyes closed for an instant, lips parted. They were red with the blood, and beads of it trickled from the corners of her mouth. The tongue came out slowly to lick them up.

"You know," Ellen said in an abstracted murmur into the other's shoulder, "I can tell I'm going to be frightened and grossed out in a little while, but right now I'm not. You look so *happy*."

"Oh, I am."

"Good. It makes me feel sort of nice." She sighed. "I can see how this gets addictive. A floating drifting feeling, like the afterglow. How did I taste?"

Adrienne smiled and kissed her lingeringly; there was a faint flavor of salt and metal to her mouth.

"It's a pity you can't appreciate it. Two distinct layers of fear, and anger, dread, longing, resignation, courage . . . like a very, very good beef bourguignon garnished with sautéed pearl onions and mushrooms. The sort cooked with a really fine Burgundy and a bouquet garni from a farm stall. Fresh egg noodles with it, and the sort of *pain Poilâne* bread you get in the morning at that place on the *rue de Cherche-Midi*, with farm butter. Paired with a reasonable Saint-Émilion; even a Château Ausone, perhaps."

"I'm . . . glad I'm a gourmet meal, at least," Ellen said.

"Honest *cuisine bourgeois*, but very good of its kind."

She felt as if she were flying in a dream, one of the slow ones, down towards normalcy. It was in sight below, but not there yet. There was no hurry. Right now, normalcy had serious drawbacks. They rested quietly for a few minutes, listening to the gulls and the surf. Then Adrienne chuckled, rose, and pulled her up by her hand, dusting sand off them both.

"It's a lot more pleasant for you when you relax into the bite, isn't it?"

"Yeah. I can move now, but I feel . . . like I'm laundry just through the wash. All light. Don't you get a charge out of stalking and pouncing, though?"

Adrienne nodded. "This isn't quite as . . . hot . . . for me, but it's more nuanced, too. Are you hungry?"

"I could eat. Yeah, now that you mention it, I *am* hungry. I only had some milk and fruit before I went for the run."

"Let's see what Monica packed in the way of solid food. Ah, excellent! Two baguettes, butter, tapenade, thin-sliced ham, some Appenzeller style cheese, olives, dried figs, all Casa Sangre organic homemade, and two beers."

She stood looking out over the Pacific. "Pity I have an appointment in San Francisco. It's a pretty spot to linger."

CHAPTER ELEVEN

drian watched.

This is not real, he thought. Then: *No. It has not happened yet, and might not. But it is very real.*

A file of trucks and two Humvees passed down a street in San Francisco—Market, he thought. The soldiers in the utility vehicles were in the uniforms and body-armor and equipment of the US Army, often ill-fitting as if salvaged from others and worn for want of better. The trucks were civilian, dirty and battered-looking, on the edge of failure from bad maintenance. Every building was closed. Not far away a body lay half-out of a broken shop window, two bottles of liquor still resting below it with the contents mostly spilled. Flies buzzed, and the wind blew through the steel-and-glass canyons, but there was only a distant hint of engine noise. Parked cars along the edges rested on the rims of flat tires, but the center was clear except for patches of broken glass.

A poster in red-and-black on one intact plate-glass expanse shouted:

Emergency Quarantine Regulations—Please Read! Its edges were ragged, as if it had been there for some time.

The vehicles' exhaust was faint; stronger still was a sweetish-rank scent he knew well.

The little convoy stopped. An officer dismounted, and then a short slim figure Adrian recognized as his sister. She was in the same uniform and wore a pistol at her hip, but without the standard insignia of rank. Instead a black patch on her shoulder held the image of an upthrust three-tined golden trident, jagged and irregular and barbed. If he'd looked closer he sensed that it would have been held within a rayed sun, black-on-black. It was the glyph that had once been the secret sigil of the Order of the Black Dawn, and for a hundred and twenty years that of the Council of Shadows.

"Two days at least," Adrienne said coolly, looking down at the body. "In this climate, possibly as much as a week. Have the workers load it, Colonel Hawkins, but I think this district is more or less clear."

The officer was a hard-faced black man in his thirties. He had the blank eyes of someone who has seen things he can neither forget nor deal with, and is running on a precarious mental slope to keep his balance. He hesitated, and she went on impatiently:

"It's quite safe, Colonel Hawkins. Look."

She stooped and touched the bloated flesh. Men and women in overalls and dirty white face-masks and heavy plastic gloves jumped down from one of the trucks and took ankles and wrists. They carried the body over to another truck and slung it in with an efficiency that spoke of long practice. It landed with a soft *thud*.

"Then the plague really *is* over, ma'am?" the soldier asked. "Christ, I thought it would go on until nobody was left."

"Quite over, Colonel," she said. "Not one person who's received the new vaccine has developed Dalager's Parasmallpox; and we have more doses on hand than the remaining population of the world. There are still eighty million people in this country alone. Nine-tenths have been vaccinated already, the rest will be by the end of spring, and we can end the quarantine lockdown and begin to rebuild. With the new World Council to allocate resources we can do it everywhere. Rebuild on the new basis."

"Thank God," the man said; his shoulders slumped a little. "I don't know Thing One about this Council, the way communications have been screwed up the last couple of months. We haven't even heard from National Command HQ in weeks, just Regional in Redding. But if the Council's ended the plague, if they can do that . . . well, they've got my vote. Geneva can be capital of the world and good luck to them."

He laughed, a rusty sound. "Though with a World Council running things now, I may be out of a job."

"Don't worry," she said. "The world cannot become *that* peaceful, truly. Not as long as human beings are human beings."

The man snorted and nodded. "Damn *right*. I've seen . . . enough of that lately. People will be crazy for a while yet and then they'll be, well, people."

Adrienne gave a long slow smile. "I'm sure the Council will find a need for your services. There are always . . . recalcitrant elements. Keeping the peace will be your task. Keeping *our* peace. You'll have . . . powerful new backup, too."

The Seeing cut off. He drifted in darkness; shapes rushed by him, like subway trains roaring down through a darkened station. Adrian *pushed*, looking for purpose in a universe of chaos. Then he could see again.

See, he thought. *I am Seeing.*

*   *   *

The same street showed, and on the same day and hour. But here the buildings leaned crazily, scorch marks showing where flames had burst out of windows. One had fallen across the intersection, and lay in a tangle of girders and shattered concrete still held together by the rebar. Cars littered the street, many with their doors and hoods still open, stopped where they had been stricken all at once. A group of men and women waited in the rubble, guns and clubs and knives clutched in their hands; they were skeletally thin, and wore a patchwork of rags and hair and dirt. He could smell them, the scents of madness and bodies sick and starving.

Other men came down the street, dressed in tough nondescript uniforms and carrying assault rifles and grenade launchers. Their leader stopped, raised a hand in a gesture Adrian recognized, spoke a *Word*. The ragamuffins tensed; then one sprang up, screaming and slapping at himself, then gouging his own eyes into bloody holes in his face. Three more simply slumped over, dead before they hit the ground. Another leveled a pump-action shotgun at the newcomers and pulled the trigger.

Crang!

The shells in the magazine gang-fired, and he ran three steps waving the spouting stumps of his arms below a ruined face and then toppled to lie still. The rest broke in panic, scuttling like rats back into the tangle of ruins. The newcomers opened fire, short accurate bursts, the empty shells sparkling in the sunlight as they spun up and the flat elastic *crackcrackcrack* echoing off the dead buildings. The *shoonk . . . boom!* of grenade launchers sounded.

Their leader stopped and removed his helmet. Pale hair showed beneath, pale eyes, a sharp-nosed Slavic face, though his followers were of half a dozen races. His eyes were faded blue, with tiny golden flecks visible only when the light struck at an angle.

"*Kakoy naverh trahaviy!*" he said, with limitless disgust in his tones.

Adrian's observing mind translated automatically:

"*What a fuckup!*"

"We return," he continued in English. "There's obviously nothing worthwhile here."

The pointed nose wrinkled at the corpses, and his upper lip rose to reveal his teeth.

"Not even any clean blood, and I am *hungry*. We go!"

Adrian sat upright—or tried to. The restraints around the wounds in his forearm and thigh stopped him, and the tubes and holders rattled where lines dripped plasma and saline and carefully metered drugs into him. He sank back with a hiss at the sharp stabbing pain and looked around the room by rolling his head from side to side.

"Hospital," he muttered.

The institutional smell, clean and dismal, was unmistakable; the tray of congealing food somewhere near made it even plainer with its scents of overdone green beans and reconstituted mashed potatoes. Green-beige walls, linoleum on the floors, tracks on the ceiling for privacy curtains to be drawn around the beds. This was a smallish room, set up for two patients.

Waking up in hospitals without being sure exactly how he'd gotten there was no new experience. But . . .

Wait. I'm retired. I haven't done this shit for years and years.

Memory crashed in, the killers with the silvered knives in the Japanese bathhouse. Ellen. His sister.

Ellen woke me up. I could feel *it. It's been a while. I was deep in trance, and then the link with Ellen.*

He shivered, and continued to flog his mind back into working order. There was a drained feeling to it, as if he'd been Wreaking at high level without blood, forcing the Power to feed on himself.

Harvey, he thought.

The other man was lying on the next bed with his boots off, limply asleep. Adrian blinked in shock at how *old* he looked, silver stubble showing on his cheeks and the eyes fallen in a little.

When did that happen?

In his mind's eye Harvey Ledbetter was always a vibrant thirty-five, a tireless mass of gristle and bone and lean muscle and sharp penetrating blue eyes. Adrian was alert now, however weak his body. He let his head fall back on the pillow and closed his eyes, because that weakness made them prickle with half-shed tears.

All human beings are mortal, he thought. *Including those you love, Adrian. Prepare yourself for more of this grief, unless you plan on dying soon.*

The other bed creaked. He opened his eyes again; Harvey was sitting up, stamping his feet into the boots and lacing them, rubbing at his face. The grin was back, and the sparkle in the eyes that made you forget the gray and the wrinkles and the way the hands were getting knobby.

"You look like shit, Harv," he said—or croaked.

"Said Mr. Kettle to the honey-bucket. You look like shit that's been through the baby twice. Hold one."

He went out; a few minutes later he returned with a big mug. Then he put a hand behind Adrian's head and put it to his lips. The scent of the blood hit him a second before that, revulsion and longing together. It was almost *warm*. He looked a question.

"Usual source, just a bit fresher. Pretty well straight from the donor. You need it, ol' buddy. We got connections here, but it ain't altogether a Brotherhood establishment. Drink before someone comes by and asks questions."

He drank. For an instant it tasted only of salt and metal, a sign of how drained he really was. Then it was like tofu—stale tofu with an overtone of slightly spoiled milk. There was only the mildest quiver of nausea as it hit his stomach, empty though that felt.

"Ahhh," he sighed. "My God, don't give me this Grand Cru Burgundy too often, Harv."

"It's back to the rotgut as soon as you're out of here. I was gettin' worried. You were in a trance lockdown—I had to jimmy those with a Wreaking—"

He pointed at a bank of monitors, which were now showing his *real* heartbeat and respiration and blood pressure. It would have been hard for the older man; everything came from his own reserves.

No wonder he looked so exhausted!

"—but it didn't seem to be doing you all that much good, not like a real healin' coma. Thought I might have to hold your nose and pour the blood down your gullet my own self."

Adrian made a dismissive gesture. "Ellen woke me. Adrienne was . . . feeding on her."

"You've got a pretty close link with that girl, don't you?" A grin. "Don't work with just *blood*, does it?"

"Dirty-minded *salop*," he replied. Then: "Ellen is becoming acclimated to it, developing the addiction pattern. That was . . . not pleasant to observe. She was very frightened, and then . . . nearly ecstatic."

Harvey sighed. "Look, ol' buddy, you knew that was going to happen. It actually makes things easier for her and less likely to get on the receiving end of an overfeeding frenzy—which in case you hadn't noticed, is *fatal* while blissing-out isn't."

"She has an addictive personality. She knows it and deals with it well. But in this situation she is more vulnerable."

Harvey shrugged. "She can go through detox when we get her back. Concentrate on getting healed up so we can *do* something about it."

Adrian crossed his arms and rested his hands on his shoulders. Breath in, out, in, out . . .

A few seconds later he opened his eyes again and hissed, "Damn those knives! I'm healing only a little faster than . . . ah . . ."

"Us normals," Harvey said cheerfully. "Well, that's what the blades were designed for. Sort of ironic, isn't it? The Shadowspawn using 'em, that is."

They had been witchfinders' tools originally, the predecessors of the Brotherhood as the Order of the Black Dawn and kindred groups were of the Council of Shadows.

Adrian shrugged. "I'm going to give it another try. Flash cards for me, would you?"

Harvey grunted agreement; he pulled out a set of blanks the size of playing cards and spent a moment marking them with the artist's pencils from Adrian's pack.

"OK," he said. "This is the *s-at'lauissi it'k-baiy* sequence."

Adrian sank back again. As the glyphs were held before his eyes he murmured words—Words, rather, one of the earliest patterns children learned when the Power came on them.

I've failed World Lit; now I'm back to using alphabet blocks.

There was a soft heavy resistance, the lingering traces of the knives in his flesh. Let the pattern grow stronger, let the Mhabrogast syllables echo in his mind, louder and louder, until his personhood felt their edges . . .

He was gasping when his eyes opened again, but the pain in arm and leg had grown to a fiery itch. There was no way of avoiding *that*, and he set himself to ignore it.

"More," he croaked.

Harvey lifted his head again. The blood vanished as if his tissues were soaking it up, but his head felt less light. Then water, and he sighed.

"I'll be walking in a day or two. Real recovery . . . not too much longer."

"If we live that long," Harvey said grimly. "Got the make on those two mooks we assisted to shuffle off. Definitely Tōkairin clan muscle, partners who worked together regular. Up-and-comers."

"Why?" he said, mystified.

"Could be general principles. They did edge out the Brézés for top-tiger position on the West Coast back when."

"As if I cared! They know that."

"The two you got were part of a security detail run by Michiko Tōkairin. She manages that for this section of the West Coast. Old Hajime lettin' family feeling overcome prejudice about the weaker sex."

"Tōkairin Michiko," Adrian corrected absently as his thoughts spun. "Surname first."

"Well, excuse me your exalted multiculturalist poobah-ness. She ain't really Japanese. Hell, strictly speaking you could argue whether she's human."

"And she's a sibling-of-blood to Adrienne. And definitely not the weaker anything."

Harvey made a grimace. Among Shadowspawn the sibling-of-blood relationship was a kind of fictive kinship; it also had sexual overtones but mainly referred to shared kills.

Not that that is altogether different from the way actual *siblings among Shadowspawn act*, Adrian thought.

The older man reached under the bed he'd been napping on and hauled out a cardboard take-out box.

"Whatever the reason, if she came after us once, she may again. Put the cops on our trail, or Homeland Security spooks, too. We're not official Brotherhood and we're vulnerable."

"I shall live with it," Adrian said. "What have you got there?"

"Chicken *bánh mi* sandwiches on sourdough with cilantro, chilis and five-spice. And some croissants that actually taste like croissants, which ain't so easy to find this side of the Atlantic."

Adrian accepted one of the sandwiches gratefully; the mere scent of it drove out the smell of limp green beans and reconstituted mashed potatoes and mystery-meatloaf from the trolley out in the corridor. Accelerated healing required *food*.

"And Sheila came through with the report on the Brézé-clan properties," Harvey went on.

He carefully cut the cards he'd marked with the glyphs—ideographic Mhabrogast—into confetti-small pieces and scraped them into a plastic Ziploc, to be burned later.

Then he wrapped his mouth around a huge bite of his sandwich. Indistinctly:

"Whole *lot* of Brézé properties, but there are only three or four likelies in the Central Coast area."

Adrian's lips thinned. "That is the problem. I got a visual impression with that . . . feeding incident, and the distance was less. Adrienne and Ellen were traveling. She's *moving*, Harv. Where?"

"Getting closer, you said?"

"I think so."

"Then maybe . . . we need to talk to the Tōkairin honcho ourselves."

Adrian looked at him in surprise, and he went on: "Michiko likes Adrienne. Hajime don't. I'll put out feelers, but if he accepts, it'll be you he wants to talk to. I'm just an ape, remember?"

"How could I forget, my old? You *are* an ape."

Harvey laughed. "Now you need some more sleep."

"Yes." He sighed. Then: "No. First I must tell you of the Seeings I had, before the feeding woke me."

He did. Harvey whistled. "Sheila was right. They *are* plannin' something a mite drastic."

"Several things. Those were unrealized alternates. They both felt . . . loose, not nearly determinate. And Adrienne and Dmitri were in both. Somehow something *we* do affects those outcomes."

Harvey's mouth twisted. "Neither of 'em's what I'd call desirable."

Adrian shrugged, half-conscious. "Ellen. I must rescue Ellen. The rest . . . it can wait."

Harvey leaned over him and smiled, a tender expression incongruous on the rugged bristly face.

"Right, ol' buddy. You get some shut-eye."

"Ellen," he murmured, and sank into the waiting darkness.

Hungry, Ellen thought, as the motorcycle burbled to a stop amid a small parking lot. *Stiff. Cold.*

She'd been drifting for most of the ride through the endless outskirts and suburbs south of the city. Now they were in San Francisco's core, bright and lively. Ellen shivered again as she glanced at the people and traffic.

It's all a false front, she thought. *Now I know what's real. And oh, God, how I wish I didn't.*

"We'll get you warm and fed, *chérie*," Adrienne said.

The restaurant was on Post Street, near Union Square; Ellen had a confused sense of recently-renovated antique magnificence, arched ceilings with mosaics and Art Nouveau marine-themed lamps. For a moment she felt hideously underdressed in her plain jeans and rumpled T-shirt and wind-tangled blond thatch; then her stomach twisted at the subtle scents.

I look like I'm homeless!

"And I'm in motorcycle leathers," Adrienne pointed out. "This is San Francisco. Nobody would bat an eye if you were in a bustier and pink boxers with your head shaved."

The maître d' came up, smiling. "This way, Ms. Brézé. Ms. Tōkairin just arrived and is in the Sevruga room."

He had the art of being deferential but not oily. The door to which he ushered them had an unusual addition; two Japanese-looking men in expensive suits flanking it, standing with their hands crossed. Within was a small private dining chamber, restrained in white and beige, the walls mostly covered in a wine library—bottles on slightly inclined shelves. There were a couple of nautical-fisherman paintings as well. The round table could have held four comfortably. The young woman sitting there was alone, and—

Wearing a Sailor Moon costume? Ellen thought.

Certainly a manga-version of a Japanese schoolgirl outfit—white sailor blouse, blue skirt and red bow. Her raven hair was up in a complex design held by long golden hairsticks and a comb; Ellen recognized it from an Edo-period print by Koryusai. The face below was classic as well, doll-like and pretty; she was a bit shorter than Adrienne, which put her three inches below Ellen's five foot six.

"Adrienne!" she said happily, rising.

"Michiko!"

She extended a hand and they touched fingertips, a greeting Ellen had never seen before. There was a sense of *something* passing between them, of words spoken too quickly and softly for her to hear.

They also exchanged several sentences aloud in Japanese before Adrienne switched to English:

"Not blond anymore, I see."

The Asian girl smiled and indicated her hairdo. "Grandfather! He wanted something more traditional, I gave him *traditional*."

The two Shadowspawn women laughed and sat. Michiko went on:

"How *do* you get that sweaty authentic look with the leathers? On me, it's always like a twelve-year-old trying to butch up."

"The authenticity is simple. Put them on and then drive a motorcycle for three hundred miles."

"That's going a bit far."

"Ichirō?"

"He's in Japan with the kids, supervising them while they learn to contemplate raked sand and rocks and the other profound Buddha-Shinto-ninja-clan shit. As if human nations and traditions meant anything to *us* anymore!"

"The Wreaking training and the physical side are useful," Adrienne said. "But I sympathize. On the other hand, Tōkairin Hajime's father thought he *was* a human being for most of his life. It's only natural your grandfather still thinks in those terms."

"Your Brézé-clan Old Ones are miracles of flexibility by comparison."

"We were . . . in at the beginning. We've had more time to adjust."

Ellen hovered uncertainly for an instant, then sat as waiters brought a tray of drinks and platters of Kumamoto oysters on beds of shaved ice and rock-salt and seaweed, with thin-sliced buttered brown bread on the side.

"Ah, I can always rely on you, Jason," Michiko said in a friendly tone to the man overseeing them.

To Adrienne: "When I come here, I just put myself in Jason's hands. I'm like putty and he's never gone wrong."

Then to the man once more: "What's with? Not the Staglin Chardonnay this time?"

"I'm recommending this cocktail instead for the oysters. Skyy 90 vodka infused with Antiguan black peppercorn, Manzanilla dry sherry, shaken, served up with cucumber."

"*Definitely* linked to the pleasure principle," she replied, sipping one. "Jason, if only you were straight, or at least flexible, what a lover you'd be!"

"Not even for you, Ms. Tōkairin," the slim handsome man said with a smile of his own. "Enjoy!"

"Ah . . ." Ellen said, when the staff had withdrawn. "I've never actually eaten a raw oyster before."

The slanted eyes considered her. At first Ellen thought they were the normal brown so dark it was almost black, but then she could see tiny golden flecks here and there.

"A new lucy?" she asked, glancing at Adrienne. "You always did favor those Marilyn Monroe types on the distaff side."

Wait a minute, Ellen thought suddenly. *I* do *look a* little *like Monroe.*

She'd studied Warhol's prints closely at NYU and half a dozen people in the class had pointed it out, some far more often than she liked. The resemblance had been even stronger before she took up running and tennis intensively.

And come to think of it, Monica back at the ranch looks a fair bit like Norma Jean Mortenson before she went blond and got discovered. Is that a thing *with the Brézés? Oh, that's a bit of an ick . . . Well, some guys just have a subconscious preference for a* type, *I suppose . . . Adrian may have liked my looks, but he stayed for* me. *I was the one who broke it off.*

"Though I should be charging you corkage!" Michiko continued with assumed umbrage. "You're perfectly free to hunt in San Francisco while you're my guest—we put that in the peace agreement—and it's not as if we didn't have a wide assortment. Bringing your own fresh bitch to bleed is almost a slur on our hospitality!"

Ellen fought to control the spike of resentment. From the smiles, that was absolutely futile, and Adrienne chuckled.

"*Chérie,* you're my lucy. That means you *are* my bitch, in several senses of the word. Here. Take a sip of the cocktail—"

Cool, sweet-pungent, a tiny peppery bite, then white ice-fire down the throat.

"—then put a tiny bit of these marinated scallions on the oyster, a squeeze of lemon, and use the oyster fork to help the whole thing *sliiiide* in. Then take a bite of the brown bread."

Ellen let the morsel and shell-full of liquid drop into her mouth. It *was* good, if a little strange—salty and meaty and fishy at the same time. The earthy texture and half-sweet taste of the brown bread and butter cleared her mouth.

"Like kissing the Pacific Ocean on the lips," Adrienne said.

To Michiko: "But this is the one I took from dear Adrian. And quite unusual in herself. Less pillowy than Monroe, too, judging from the films."

"Oooh, she was *Adrian's*? Mind if I take a look?"

"Be my guest."

This time the gaze took her seriously. Ellen decided she preferred dismissal. The eyes locked on hers, and she found she couldn't look away. The sensation that followed was purely mental, but the exact equivalent of having someone put a fingernail on the base of her spine and run it slowly up to her neck. She shivered involuntarily. Michiko reached out without breaking the eye-lock and took her hand, put her thumb on the web between the little finger and the next and pressed sharply.

"Ouch!" Ellen said; she barely suppressed the impulse to snatch the hand back.

Michiko's teeth came together with a *click*. She began to turn the hand to expose the wrist, her mouth opening again as she bent forward, lips curling back in a way that made her suddenly look far less human. Ellen's breath caught as she shivered, and she looked over at Adrienne with her eyes wide in involuntary appeal.

OK, aren't I supposed to be your *bitch?*

The other Shadowspawn chuckled and rapped her friend's wrist with an oyster fork.

"Ta-ta-ta, Michi, I said *look*, not *taste*. You know how I hate people touching my things."

"Oh," she said with a start, and released Ellen's hand. "Sorry. Still, I see what you mean. There are depths there. I wonder how her blood would taste as her heart skipped and quivered and stopped?"

"Absolutely marvelous, I'm sure. That *is* always a treat. But then she'd be *dead*, and no fun at all. I have plans for this one."

Michiko shrugged as she squeezed lemon on an oyster.

"There's always more, even of the special ones. The planet's over-populated, after all. And Adrian will come after you whether she's alive or dead."

"Be careful, or you'll start to sound like Dmitri."

Michiko made a gesture of theatrical horror, throwing up her hands; one of them held an empty oyster shell.

"Oh, no, not *that*. I don't kill what I can't eat. Well, usually."

"Dmitri is definitely a gourmand. Still, he's earned release. And he has the supreme virtue of being useful."

"Ah," Michiko said, and ate another oyster. "Well, that's about the only good news I've got for you tonight. Grandfather *will* extend Tōkairin patronage so that he can attend the meeting . . . and leave Seversk in time to prepare."

"Seversk, that oozing chancre upon Siberia's lower intestine," Adrienne said with a grin. "Still, it's a good place to reminisce about Srebrenica."

Ellen kept eating through the Shadowspawn laughter. Four oysters were just enough to remind her that it had been a long day since lunch.

And that I lost half a pint of blood, she reminded herself grimly. *This cocktail is going straight to my head.* Then: *So what?*

The longer the time that passed, the less . . .

Peaceful, she thought. *Dreamy, peaceful, pleasant, right-and-proper.*

. . . the memory of Adrienne's ecstatic face, turned to the sky, mouth open with Ellen's blood trickling from the corners.

I can remember thinking at the time that I'd be grossed out later, and

I remember now how good it felt then. And I really don't like the way Michiko keeps glancing at me, as if I were one of these oysters. Eating with people who think of you as food is nerve-racking.

"The bad news is that he's pretty much decided to support option Trimback One," the woman in the elaborate hairdo went on.

Adrienne sighed and took the last oyster. She replied . . . and it was in Japanese, as the head-waiter came in again.

"Champagne-cured Monterey sardines for you, Ms. Tōkairin," he said triumphantly, laying out the appetizer. "With French fingerling potato salad, micro beet greens, and sauce verte."

Another flourish. "And for you, Ms. Brézé, artichoke-stuffed local calamari, with Iacopi Farms white bean puree, mizuna, and preserved Meyer lemon *bagna cauda*."

Another plate was deftly twitched from a server and set in front of Ellen:

"And for the pretty blond lady who looks so hungry, seared hand-line-caught Ahi tuna, accompanied by yellow foot chanterelles, braised salsify, and wild mushroom consommé. Now with *these*, I recommend the Paul Hobbs Russian River Valley Chardonnay."

Ellen took a forkful; the tuna was almost as much like rare steak as fish.

Oh, my, this is good! But why are these Shadowspawn all such foodies? Adrian was too. I had to add an extra mile to my run to keep from inflating like a blimp, and he never gained an ounce.

"Because we have much sharper senses of taste and smell than you do, *ma douce*," Adrienne said. "And very active metabolisms. When we're not in trance, it cranks right up. Our bodies are treating it as a brief hunting season, but we don't have to wait out glacial winters anymore."

"You've got her verbalized thoughts already?" Michiko asked, raising a thin black brow. "It takes me a couple of days at least."

"Our acquaintance has been brief, but intense," Adrienne said. "And even though he didn't feed on her, there was a ground-link between her and Adrian. I could taste it the first time her blood hit my tongue."

"Kinky," Michiko laughed.

"Delightfully so. I'm disappointed to hear about your grandfather. I had hopes he'd be reasonable."

"He wavered, but the al-Lanarkis talked him around. Convinced him we could handle things like the reactors melting down after the EMP."

"Oh, now we're going to rely on our *administrative abilities* to pull things through? Name of a black dog!"

Adrian used that same odd curse, Ellen thought. For a moment her throat squeezed shut; then she took a deep breath and doggedly kept eating.

"Adrienne, you're preaching to the converted here. The Lanarkis don't have to worry so much; it's mostly camels and goats out in their bailiwick anyway."

"And then there would be the burning cities, and the refineries . . . Oh, what's the use? You're right, Michi; I don't have to convince *you*. We'll just have to hope we can convince a quorum at the Council meeting, or at least block hasty action."

"I'm getting ready for Tiflis," Michiko agreed, sipping at her wine. "My, this *does* go well with the cured sardines."

"I hope you'll have all the East Asian data so we can circulate it— and nothing too technical. PowerPoint, with lots of *pictures*. You've got better access there than I do. My cousins will have Europe more or less sewn up—the downside to Trimback One is fairly obvious there, enough so that even a lot of the postcorporeals are *en courant.*"

"My people are working on it," Michiko said. "We'll have it in good time. And I've got just the expert for calculating the spread on the initial exposures."

I suspect that my people *here means something like* my horses, Ellen thought.

"And I'm learning Georgian," she went on. "*Me minda ts'avide tbilisshi.* It's so much better when you can understand them, and I expect to do a little hunting there."

"Who are you learning it from?" Adrienne inquired.

"An adjunct professor down at Stanford named Vakhtang Choloqashvili. Darkly handsome and—"

She giggled and put a hand to her mouth; when she went on it was with a fake-guttural accent:

"In Georgia, are *real men*! Are like wild"—with a crook-fingered grabbing gesture—"*bull* of ze mountains!"

She went on in her normal mid-Californian voice: "He's just beginning to suspect that the nightmares aren't really nightmares. He gave me this *look* the last time I drove down for a tutorial, and his hands were shaking."

"I could teach you a few words," Adrienne said, and they snapped at each other with a sideways flick of the head and a mutual *click* of pearly teeth.

Literally snapped, Ellen thought, and turned her eyes down to her plate.

The gesture had looked absolutely natural, and playfully flirtatious.

God. Oh, God.

"I should be fully fluent by the time things are concluded," Michiko said. "Then I could console his grieving widow. She'd need someone who really *understood* her, all alone in a strange country."

She glanced at Ellen. "Aren't we *awful*?"

They both laughed at her involuntary mental wave of agreement. Platters of Maine lobster claws and Dungeness crabs and Kona Blue sashimi came in and were enthusiastically devoured amid gossip about people and places and politics Ellen had never heard of; what she *did* grasp would have killed her appetite a few days ago if she'd believed it. Now she found she could push it all out of her mind and concentrate on each bite; it *might* be her last meal.

At least if it is, I can console myself that I didn't die with the taste of KFC on my tongue. Adrian managed to turn me into a bit of a foodie too.

It helped that the conversation shifted unpredictably among at least five languages, two of which she didn't even recognize. Jason returned to consult about the desserts; or dictate them, as far as Michiko was concerned:

"Chocolate blackout cream cake, dulce de leche, raspberry sorbet, and sweet and salty peanuts," he said, setting the plate before her. "I'd suggest the Late Harvest Sauvignon Black-Semillon, Rancho de Oro Puro. And coffee? Ethiopian Yirgacheffe, perhaps: a slight cherry fruitiness but also the bitterness to balance the unctuous sweet here."

"This Rogue Creamery cheese from Oregon looks *very* interesting," Adrienne said; she was perusing the menu.

"It is, it is," Jason replied. "Cold smoked over hazelnut shells, sharp and sweet together. To *die* for, ma'am."

"I'll go French for the wine. Loire Valley?"

"Excellent! We have a very nice Vouvray Moelleux . . ."

"I'll have that. You pick for my friend here. She needs corrupting and I suspect you're good at that, Jason."

"We'll soon get rid of that wholesome schoolgirl innocence!" Jason said. "Depravity is the way to go."

He probably thinks I'm some sort of cheap hookup! Ellen thought. *Some student putting out for glamour and a taste of the high life.*

When you were in terror of death it was *absurd* to be concerned about social embarrassment. She found that perfect fear did *not* drive out shame.

They just synergize.

"Then the quince-apple turnovers for you, miss, with brown sugar pecan ice cream, and cinnamon caramel sauce. A white Riesling, I think. The Anderson Valley Navarro Cluster Select."

It appeared, and tasted as good as it sounded. She was distracted enough that something almost escaped her:

"—parasmallpox."

Her ears pricked up at that.

"Well, at least *something* went right," Michiko said, chasing the last crumb of the cake around her plate.

"The Congo field tests were just what we'd hoped."

Michiko clapped her hands together. "Stopping things *just* where we want. My family would be perfectly happy with ten million on the West Coast."

Adrienne nodded. "And the humans would offer their necks to us out of sheer gratitude to the savior gods."

"Mmmm," Michiko said dreamily. "I can see establishing this ceremony, somewhere, where they offer a youth and a maiden to me every year. Like a *kami*, you know? Something beautiful and sad, with music and dancing."

"Exactly. And then we could have all the modern conveniences and *still* be absolutely sure they'd never, ever be dangerous again, or learn anything we don't want them to know. Now *that's* what I call a Dread Empire of Shadow!"

"Wonderful," Michiko breathed.

She bowed her head for an instant. When she raised it again her eyes were moist.

"Adrienne, it's a beautiful vision!"

Oh, God! They're talking about destroying the world!

Michiko sighed. "I just hope we can convince enough of the others. And on a personal note, things turned out fine with Adrian; you got the note?"

"Yes." She frowned. "That was a little close to the mark."

Michiko shrugged. "It's a high-stakes game with a *lot* of powerful Wreakers involved. Nothing lost except two of my least favorite cousins. And all's well—"

"—that ends well."

"I'm going out clubbing now. Want to come along?"

"Not tonight, Michi. I know how *that* ends up. We wake up together with blood-soaked sheets, headaches, and an empty going into rigor mortis between us."

"You didn't have any complaints last time," she said with a wink and a pout.

"He was just a pickup," Adrienne said with a smile.

She looked over, and Ellen felt a slow flush traveling up her throat.

"As I said, I have *plans* for this one."

Michiko laughed as she rose. "I can imagine."

They repeated the fingertip-touching gesture. "Thank you, Michiko. You've been *une vrai amie*. We can do this!"

CHAPTER TWELVE

At four hours past midnight, Adrian Brézé shook off dreams of dread and fear, of savage pleasures taken and bestowed. Of rapturous abandonment of self.

Ellen's asleep now, at last, he knew as he woke. *Yes, that's a minor Wreaking on her, a sedative.*

He could tell that, though not the precise location; simply that she was near, and slept in a mix of exhaustion and Power-driven unconsciousness that turned aside the chances of waking.

Pauvre petite. *Caught in the contentions of demons. Poor girl.*

Then a wry correction to himself:

Unfortunate young woman? It doesn't feel right to say it that way, but she always disliked being called a girl unless she did it herself. I was too much around oldsters as I grew, and too little around ordinary folk. I was born in the sixth decade of the twentieth century, but I'm not really a child of my own time. Or of any year. Or I am part of many? Of the age of chipped flint and the Empire of Shadow whose memory haunted all the ages after? Of the nineteenth century that saw its rebirth, of the twentieth that lived beneath it and thought its evil dreams their own, the twenty-first that may see its final triumph? Adrian Brézé is home no-where and no-when. Forever out of time, out of place.

He let a Mhabrogast phrase run through his head: *Amss-aui-ock!*

That was *being-becoming-now*. The sensation was like thinking in syllables of razor-edged glass. They cut him away from his flesh. A brief flash of pain, and he rose and looked down at his own birth-body lying in the hospital bed, shivering as the slight shock of the separation died away.

Out of body, too, now. And Harv was right. I do *look like shit. It's been a long while since I went night-walking. You don't see yourself in a mirror as you do with a stranger's eye.*

He was thinner than he should be, and looked older, and with lines of pain in his face even asleep. They smoothed out a little as the empty body sank into the coma that would sustain it, heart beating once or twice a minute, breath imperceptibly slow. He flicked his mind at the monitors to keep them reporting all was well, and passed his hands from head to toe of his physical form. The wounds felt full of flickers of light to his senses, a tingling on the hands as the cells lived their accelerated lives.

Healing well, he thought. *Yes, I can leave tomorrow.*

Then he looked down at the body he was wearing. It was the default, his hindbrain's picture of his physical self, partly read from the paired helixes of his heredity and partly through his somatic memory of his life. He tried to see himself as another might. He was naked, of course; what most would have called a slender man a few years short of thirty, a little below medium height, with the muscles of a runner or gymnast or dancer. The scars showed, those graven on the memory of his cells and mind. The four long parallels across the right thigh were still vivid; he'd never been able to shed those.

Adrienne's parting gift in Calcutta. My mind doesn't want to let that go, on some level.

The other marks of blades and bullets were long-faded and nearly gone, just as they were on his birth-self. New red lines on his left forearm and thigh stood out, anticipation of healing, freed of all pain.

"Stop admiring yourself and get going," Harvey said. "I don't like the idea of a meet with Hajime anyway. Yeah, and I know it was *my* idea."

He could see the night-walker's shape, even when Adrian wasn't trying hard to manifest. The rifle he cradled in his arms was a shrilling note of *wrongness* in the darkened hospital room; night-sight goggles were pushed up on his forehead.

"You ought to have me in closer overwatch," Harvey grumbled.

"The old bastard said he'd give me an hour's start if he decided to kill me," Adrian said reasonably. "He has an antique sense of the proprieties. I certainly wouldn't trust Michiko with a safe-conduct like that. But if he or his men detected *you* . . . you've killed too many Shadowspawn, Harvey. There would be no mercy for either of us."

"Not as many as *you've* killed, personal-like."

"They make allowances for me because of my blood."

Harvey sighed. "Well, I'll be listening. I may not project all that well, but I can *hear* at these ranges. If things go south, I'll head east."

Adrian nodded wordlessly. He dressed from the suitcase in dark slacks and a black long-sleeved cotton knit shirt and slipped on moccasin-like shoes; it was possible to *imagine* clothes for the aetheric body, but easier not.

A moment's concentration showed nobody alert outside; a sleepy duty nurse at the station near the stairs, and minds tossing in the restless sleep of the ill in the other rooms. Their dreams grew evil as he walked past, endless ones of flight and fear and pain and fangs lurking in the dark. The nurse shivered and turned up the space heater beneath the desk and rubbed her hands together.

And that fear I cannot help, not without wasting time and energy I cannot spare.

He couldn't help the impulses that made his lips want to curl back from his teeth, either, or make the meaty appetizing scent of their blood less appealing. The lust was even stronger in this form. The dim night-lights were bright as daylight to his eyes, though everything had a slightly silvery sheen. Detail leapt out at him without shadow.

They have reason *to fear. Nightmare walks here.*

Even a great city was quiet at this hour, and not many lived in this district save in hotels. A few stray dogs and cats sensed him; one brindled tabby stared with unwinking green eyes and carefully circled around him. Webs of energy spanned the night, though, flowing in wires, humming through the air. Particles sleeted into the atmosphere above, leaving rippling curtains of fire along the edge of the atmosphere that shielded him.

At last he was in South Park, an oval of trees and grass in a district where the mathematical complexities of computers laid a sparkling shimmer to his eyes when he let them see. A long dark limousine was parked at one end of the park. He walked towards it and bowed his head.

"Master Tōkairin Hajime," he said, in Japanese. "I humbly greet you."

Even to Adrian's senses the Master was barely distinguishable from a living man; his form would be as tangible as he wished. He wore a black and dark-beige hakama kimono, the practical garment warriors had used, with the two swords thrust through the obi-sash. He didn't bother with the complex antique hairdo, though; it was cropped close in a silvery-gray cap. His long lined face was that of a man in his sixties—probably because someone born in Yamagata Prefecture in 1890 simply assumed core-deep that the face of authority had wrinkles.

Only the eyes were visibly different from those of a corporeal; they were unmixed gold. The swords were real, and silver-threaded; the warning pain of the metal that the Power shunned radiated through the lead-lined scabbards. Adrian bowed again, in unspoken respect at the strength of will and Power needed to carry them. Hajime hadn't been as close to purebred as Adrian, not that far back. But anyone who survived the birth-body's death for long tended to gradually grow in their capacity to Wreak. His mind was like a surface of mirrored steel, revealing nothing. It was a little eerie, not to be able to sense intent before speech.

There were two men behind the Master, in dark suits. They were Shadowspawn, but corporeals, young and fit and very alert; he could sense the knives beneath their jackets. The driver was a human, a renfield carefully *not* observing what passed.

"Adrian Brézé," the old man said. "Traitor, why have you come to my territory and killed my people? Why do you think you can do so and live?"

"Master Hajime, I have come to your territory only because—"

I must speak as he expects. In his terms, it is true.

"—because what is mine has been stolen from me. This is not a matter of Council and Brotherhood. I renounced the war long ago, and would have stayed in my own house if left alone. My sister Adrienne came to my territory and took a woman of my household to California. And now somewhere in the vicinity of this city; I can feel it through our link."

And nobody of your generation among Shadowspawn likes Adrienne— that I know of, he thought.

Hajime shrugged his shoulders; the cloth of the kimono's layers rustled.

"What is one human?" His voice went taut with venom. "The earth *swarms* with them. Adrienne has the leave of my granddaughter Michiko to come and go here, and to use the properties we left to the Brézés."

"I resigned from the war, Master. I did not become less than a man. The woman was *mine*, on my ground."

He thought he saw a slight flicker of respect in the blank gold eyes. When Hajime spoke, the voice was still cold:

"And you killed blood of my blood. The peace agreement specified that no Brézé would enter the city without permission. *You* have no such leave. You came, you killed."

"Only to defend my life," Adrian said calmly.

"That is not what my granddaughter says. She says that she sent her cousins to observe you, when you intruded without leave."

"That is not how I perceived it," Adrian said carefully.

Do not, do not, do not *accuse his well-loved granddaughter of lying!*

"I merely defended myself. My birth-body is still lying badly wounded by warded silver-blades."

Silence stretched. "A man will strive to protect his own, even if it is only his own dog," the Master said at last, grudgingly. "I will therefore forgive the intrusion. Provided that you leave immediately, and give up this mercenary Harvey Ledbetter, the ape who dared to kill his betters.

You did badly to bring him into contention between us. He *is* of the Brotherhood, and under sentence of slow death."

Adrian swallowed. "In honor I cannot yield either the woman, or the man who assisted me—"

"What do you know of honor?" Hajime spat. "I am the twenty-fifth head of my clan. We Wrought with the Power long before the Order sent its *missionaries* to Japan. Before Meiji, before the West. Great lords went in fear of us, paid us tribute, sought our aid in their wars."

Little Wreakings. The sort of thing Harvey can manage, Adrian thought behind his shields. *Until the Order of the Black Dawn went looking for its equivalents in every country of earth, to teach them how to reconstitute the genome.*

The old man went on bitterly: "What are the Brézés but the heirs of a secret cult? Yes, you stumbled across valuable knowledge. That did not prevent *us* from taking this territory from your line twenty years ago, and its Council seat. And now you stand here asking the favor of the man who killed your parents—"

"Only their birth-bodies, Master. They live yet, undying, as you do."

And I would like nothing better than giving them the final death!

"—against your own sister! Go. Count yourself lucky I do not demand blood for blood."

"I must have the woman, and I will not yield the man. Give me this, Master, I beg. Then I will leave and cause no more trouble for you and yours."

Hajime looked at him expressionlessly. Events trembled on a precipice of *might-be*.

Remember that you hate Adrienne and her corruption of all tradition. That you fear she plots Brézé revenge for the West Coast coup. Know that

I have no such ambitions. That you dislike her influence on your favorite granddaughter.

He could feel the balances shifting towards him, like the weight of his own body on the parallel bars. Then he whirled, grappling with the *push* of the Power. For a moment he was blinded, the keening, whining snarl of Mhabrogast echoing in the ears of his mind. The moment toppled from his fingers, slipping away from potential to certainty.

"You say *must* to me! *Ebisu! Kokuzoku!*" Hajime spat.

The hand darted to the hilt of the katana and the blade came free in a hurtful dazzle. Adrian threw himself backward, and his body *flowed* as the clothes fell free. When it landed it was on all fours. Hajime's eyes went wide, and his followers froze for an instant with their knives half-drawn. The form that faced them was twice the weight of a lion, a spotted tawny bulk whose fangs curved nine inches from its upper jaw. They gaped in a killing scream as the lower mandible dropped out of the path of the stabbing canines.

Bless reconstitutive DNA technology, he thought, in some corner of his mind that was still human—or hominid.

The rest of it blazed with the fury of the great killer, with the wealth of scent and sight that poured in through senses keener than even his own breed possessed. A racking scream rose into a deep full-throated roar, and the stump tail on the powerful hindquarters quivered. He leapt—and twisted in midair to avoid the long slash of the sword. That brought him down between the two corporeals. A plate-broad paw sent one spinning to crash into a tree five yards away, clutching at his rent stomach and shrieking in pain. The other threw himself flat and slashed. The scent of Shadowspawn blood filled the air, stronger and ranker than human, driving him to frenzy.

Adrian dodged with more than human—more than Shadowspawn—speed. The silver edge of the knife struck hairs from the ruff around the smilodon's neck. They sparkled into nonexistence as they separated from the energy-web of the night-walking body; he could feel the cold shock up and down his spine and into his skull. His strike cracked the arm behind the weapon, but he leapt again a fractional second ahead of Hajime's blade.

The old man was fearless; he was even smiling grimly as he took stance, straddle-legged and katana up in the classic position.

"I will not assume the tiger," he said. "Only the *kami* know how you took the spirit of *that* beast into you. Come!"

Actually I took in its DNA after the Brotherhood used my money to finance a reconstruction, the distant part of his mind that thought in language gibed.

The sabertooth crouched and snarled again, coming forward with one huge paw placed at a time. Faster, faster, a bunching of hindquarters, the leap with forepaws outstretched and jaws open to a hundred and twenty degrees for the killing stab—

He twisted just in time, writhing in midair as the whistle of cloven air warned him. Even so the impact was stunning—the raptor stooped at fifty miles an hour, an eagle whose body was the size of a collie. The tiger-sized claws slammed agonizingly into his ribs instead of puncturing spine and skull. The five-foot bird's great curved beak raked down his side, probing for the soft belly, and wings twice man-height long hammered at his muzzle.

The smilodon rolled, squalling and striking. The eagle leapt free . . . and *flowed*. The black tiger wasn't as large as the sabertooth, but it was a blur in the night. Paws rammed back and forth as the predators reared and shrieked and struck. Adrian jinked desperately as he felt the sword approach again.

There was no possibility of fighting both these enemies at once; the Power flashed the knowledge into his inner selfhood, as he felt their minds striving to lock his paths dark. Only one choice did not end in his final death. Mind and body followed it with desperate precision—

Back. Back. Then *up*. He flowed again, and wings caught at the air.

Harv! he called, with agonized strength. *Get my body moving!*

Adrienne Brézé pulled the borrowed coat around herself and bowed deeply, keeping the smile off her face.

"*Konbanwa, Tōkairin-sama,*" she said politely. "Good evening, Lord Tōkairin."

"Good evening, Miss Brézé. My thanks to you," Tōkairin Hajime said gruffly, switching the conversation into English. "I will not say that you saved my life. You tried to do so, though, and may well have saved the lives of my men, who are of my family. I am under obligation to you."

What he really means is giri, Adrienne thought. *Something rather more serious. Which is exactly what I had in mind. Besides keeping Adrian from spitting himself on that sword.*

The ambulance bearing his wounded men howled away; the police were examining the surroundings in increasing puzzlement. The night-walkers were as imperceptible as shadows to them, as long as they willed it.

"*Dômo arigatô gozaimasu,*" Adrienne said, and bowed again. "I am your granddaughter's guest, and therefore *your* guest. It is also a disgrace to my family that the traitor acts so, in violation of our solemn agreements. On both accounts I was obliged to do whatever I could."

Both the *thank-you* and the gesture were in the *extreme polite* form, the one used mainly by women in Japan when Hajime was a young man. She could see the very slightest relaxation in the stiffness of the Tōkairin clan-head.

"I am obliged," he repeated.

"I will, of course, leave San Francisco immediately, for Brézé possessions or neutral land," Adrienne said. "I am deeply ashamed of how I have brought a Brézé family dispute onto Tōkairin home territory. What must you think of me! I'll begin packing and close down the town house you so kindly allowed us to secure after the . . . readjustment."

"You will do nothing of the sort!" Hajime said. "I will not allow an outlaw to drive out a guest of my family! Besides which, all the West Coast is in a sense Tōkairin territory, even if not under our direct control. Our patronage extends over all Shadowspawn in the area. We represent them on the Council of Shadows."

"Very true, Master Hajime," Adrienne said. "But I would not dream of causing you the slightest inconvenience. I was only visiting here for social reasons. Shopping, and so forth. Women's matters. And to visit with Michiko-san, of course."

He snorted. "And you will stay and amuse yourself as you please for as long as you please. Whether by shopping or hunting . . . What about this woman your outlaw brother claimed you took from him, by the way?"

Adrienne made a graceful gesture. "He never even fed from her, Master. She was running wild when I acquired her, not under his control at all. I do not think he considered her in his possession."

She let her shields drop enough that he could read her for an instant. Intent-to-deceive was the easiest emotion to sense, and she was being honest both in form and spirit. Allowing your own thoughts to be tasted was a great concession among their kind. He nodded as her screen went up again.

"And . . . well, Michiko has kindly invited me to hunt and feed as I will here, but I thought it would be more polite to bring . . ."

She let the remark trail off. Hajime nodded. "Very polite," he said, and now his voice was a little impressed.

Not the idea you had of me at all, is it, you costumed dinosaur? Adrienne thought behind her smiling mask. *I'm so demurely respectful that only the possibility of projectile vomiting endangers my manners.*

"Even excessively polite," he said. "I wouldn't have it rumored that Tōkairin hospitality is grudging. And these swarming American mongrels are so many that killing a few is a service to us, not a burden."

"Michiko was kind enough to say the same, but, of course, from yourself I must accept with thanks."

He nodded. "Go. I insist that you send to me immediately if you have more trouble with this renegade. Here, or elsewhere in our province! The next time we meet him, we will deal with him. The man obviously knows no sense of decency or obligation at all. In which I begin to believe he is very unlike his sister."

"*Dōmo arigatō gozaimasu,*" she said again. "How extremely kind of you."

"*Dou itashimashite,*" he said dismissively.

Her smile was brilliant. "With your protection, Tōkairin-sama, I am sure he will be no trouble at all! And I've already enjoyed my visit very much. Very much indeed. You must allow me to return your hospitality in some small way soon."

He inclined his head. She bowed again—not so deeply as she had the previous two times, which could have been subtle insolence, but enough to show profound respect.

Her body flowed once more as she straightened and let the coat fall, changing forms with a fluency he would find impressive in itself. The

ten-foot wings of the giant eagle bore her upward with massive strokes
that raised a circle of dust and litter for an instant. The slightest hint
of cold fire in the east told her that she should seek the sheltering flesh
soon, but she wheeled above the spire that bore the two setback stories
of the Brézé town house for a few minutes anyway.

Then she swooped in and landed; a canvas chair overturned with a
clatter. A flowing, and she stood in her own form amid the chill silent
darkness. Hearing and smell grew stronger, sight weaker; her mind
raced for an instant as the fierce pinpoint focus of the raptor's specialized intellect dropped away and her sense of *self* expanded into the
larger hominid brain. With it came words:

*I've been having an extremely good time, she thought. With Michiko,
with Adrian, and with you, Master Hajime. And not least with Adrian's
little lucy, while I waited for Adrian to be his usual bumblingly straightforward self. She made herself come out to me right over there only a few
hours ago . . .*

Adrienne was singing softly as she leaned on the marble railing of the
terrace and the stars wheeled around to midnight:

"And we who hold high places
Must be the ones who start
To mold a new reality;
Closer to the heart!"

Ellen climbed out of the heated pool, toweled down and wrapped
the thick robe around herself. Then she filled her wineglass from the
last of the bottle and walked out to join her. The Brézé town house was

the uppermost two stories of the St. Regis Hotel tower, forty floors above the SoMa district near the access ramps to the Bay Bridge. It was the sort of *apartment* that had a two-story waterfall in the lobby and six fireplaces and twenty-two-foot glass walls in the living-room.

She'd rapidly been losing her ability to be impressed by that sort of thing. Except . . .

This is what Adrian could *have had. No, it's just a* sample *of what he could have had. An emperor's life, including the power of life and death, and immortality with it. He could have been a* god *in shadow, and he chose—chooses every day—to give it up.*

More primal concerns crowded the thought out, and even the panorama of San Francisco's hills jeweled with night, dark water defining the edge of the world and the East Bay cities glowing across it. She leaned on the railing beside the Shadowspawn and carefully set her small glass of wine on the marble; it was something called *Tokaji Aszú 1924*, which meant nothing to her, except that it tasted very nice and was rather sweet and hit like a toppling statue.

"You're a little drunk," Adrienne said.

She was naked and evidently perfectly comfortable that way despite the chilly wind that had dried her long black hair. She brushed feather-tufts of it back from her face as she turned her head.

"I'm terrified, is what I am," Ellen said.

It had been surprisingly easy to learn there was no point in *not* talking to someone who could riffle through your mind like a search program through a computer.

Through Ellen dot doc, she thought. *Talk about being an open book!* Aloud she went on:

"So frightened I'd do anything to just make it *stop*. The booze helps a little," she finished and took another small swallow.

"Tsk, tsk, using *that* to drink just for effect . . . So what are you frightened of? Me?"

"Always."

"Sensible girl. Frightened of Michiko?"

"Fucking *right* I am! She wanted to *kill* me, didn't she? That was what she was talking about. She'd be killing me right now if you'd let her. Killing me slowly and I'd know it every second of the way and she'd *drink* it. Oh, Christ."

She gripped the stone until the wave of hot-cold fear finished surging up from her abdomen, then washed across her face and receded.

"Probably," Adrienne said calmly as she sipped from her own glass. "In fact, she's probably picking up someone as much like you as she can find to kill that way right now."

Ellen closed her eyes for an instant, struck with a sudden stab of unbearable pity for someone she'd never see or know. A girl who was just meeting dark gold-flecked eyes and a sharp white smile, whose story would end in a scream before the sun rose.

"I think you gave her an itch she couldn't scratch," Adrienne said. "You have the most *interesting* mind."

"And I'm frightened of the *world* now. It isn't the world I thought I was living in! As if suddenly I'd wandered onto another planet or another dimension or something."

"Like having the lid of the Abyss whipped out from under your feet?"

Ellen nodded. "Finding out about *you* was bad enough. But tonight I really realized there's a whole *world* of . . . of Shadowspawn out there. There always was, just a step or a thought or a chance away."

"You met Adrian on a tennis court. Which led to meeting *me*, of course."

She nodded again. "So one of you might have killed me anytime, like something walking out of a nightmare. One of the nightmares where you scream and scream and it doesn't make any sound, and the *thing* drags you back to the basement to *do* stuff to you and everyone ignores you as if you weren't there . . . and worst of all is that I know I can't ever go back to the way things were on Wednesday. Because they weren't actually that way, I just thought they were."

Adrienne chuckled. "A Greek philosopher once said that knowledge was the treasure nobody could take away from you. That's not even literally true. I can make humans forget things. So can vodka or a ball-peen hammer! But it's stupid even on its face. A wiser one said that no man can step twice into the same river, which translates as: *You can't get a lost illusion back.*"

Ellen nodded, finished the sweet wine, and took a deep shuddering breath.

"What do you want?" she made herself say.

"Everything, forever," Adrienne said. "But you mean right now?"

She gave a sideways glance and rolled a hip into a playful bump against Ellen's.

"Well, it's been a long exciting day, but the night is young, and I'm naturally nocturnal. Let's have some fun, you and I."

"Do you want to . . . hurt me . . . that way?"

"Not tonight."

Her hand stroked Ellen's back slowly, from the neck to the base of the spine and back, over and over.

I mustn't tense up. Remember what Dr. Duggan said.

A flicker of another voice; it slipped out of her mind before she was conscious of it.

I mustn't. My life depends on it.

Instead she made her back arch and tried to push everything but the mere sensation out of her mind.

There's nothing wrong with having your back stroked, if you just think about the thing itself.

Adrienne stepped behind her and began massaging her taut neck and shoulders. Strong fingers worked at the long muscles along her spine.

"Mmm," she said aloud, and thought:

Okay. If I'm not getting hurt, the sex doesn't gross me out by itself. There were a couple of hookups at NYU, remember, Ellen? That was just sort of . . . bland and not worth trying again. If this were a fantasy you were having, it might even be hot. Christ, it is *sort of hot, in a skanky, degrading, horrible Oh-God-please-no-no-no sort of way. You can do this.*

The velvet voice continued in her ear, a murmur: "Sometimes I will give you pain, sometimes pleasure, sometimes utter horror. Sometimes all three. Tonight it's Option Number Two."

Another deep breath. "I'll try, I'll really try. But . . . I don't know if I can."

"We'll see." Adrienne finished the Tokay and smiled, taking her hand and tugging her gently along. "Come, *chérie*, come. Let's play."

An hour later she stared up at Adrienne's face where she leaned on one elbow, their bodies touching from neck to toes. Strands of the other's black hair stuck to her neck and breasts, tickling sweat-slick skin that felt as if it had thinned to taut foil that might burst. She tried three times to speak, gulped air and said:

"Wha—wha—what did you *do* to me?"

"Well, I would have thought *that* was obvious!" Adrienne chuckled.

"Just now your mind was like . . . sunlight flickering through beech leaves at noon. Delightful!"

She rested a thigh across Ellen's; the voice was a lazy purr as she trailed damp fingers across the other's stomach in an infinite series of tiny tight circles. Ellen felt as much anger as boneless relaxation allowed.

"You're doing things to my . . . my brain or something!"

"Not unless you keep your brain *here* . . . Oh, you mean *that special thing*, as Monica puts it? No. Just feedback. I can sense every tickle of sensation, even when you're not aware of it yourself. Especially when"—she moved—"we're close. There's a reason for the *demon lover* legend too, *ma douce.*"

A memory flashed through her: a conversation with Giselle about Adrian when she was hashing out her relationship problems with her boss-slash-best-friend.

Best sex I ever had. Like magic. Like every part of his body was reading mine, just right!

"Just so," Adrienne said. "It runs in the family."

"God, how I hate you."

"I know. But I'm not *bland*, eh?"

"No. That was fantastic. But you're not as good as your brother, either."

Ellen flinched, but the thought had been in her mind anyway. The caressing hand moved suddenly and clamped on her groin, tight enough to be just short of discomfort.

"Let's see if you think so when you know what that *special thing* is like—"

"No! N*nnnnn!*"

For a long instant she thought what she felt was unbearable agony.

Then she made a single convulsive movement and locked in a shuddering arch, collapsed, tried to arch up again. Everything vanished except a wash of gold fire that radiated out from the contact at the center of her, out to the very ends of her being and back. She screamed as unbearable tension and its release combined in the same moment, one that stretched on and on in surging waves.

Reality returned like a tide slowly going out. Their lips met; arms and legs intertwined.

"I still hate you," Ellen whispered into the curve of her neck. "I'll always hate you."

"You have odd ways of showing it. You were already rosy pink, but you just went red, with spots!"

A nuzzling at her neck. "A taste, a little sip for the flavor."

The sting was very slight, and her body relaxed as if she'd been plunged into a warm bath; the panting and quivering died down, which was reassuring.

Since I thought it might be nerve damage.

A tongue lapped up the slow trickle from the little cut, taking the drops as they welled up. Languor spread out from it, calming, a floating drifting feeling. It was less passive this time; all the sensations were distinct, and her hand tangled in the black mane, holding the other's head to her neck.

Oh, God, but this feels good too. Double the afterglow. It is *addictive. Oh, God, if it were Adrian . . .*

"Like . . . cookies and milk?" she said when it ended.

"No. Coconut-chocolate macaroons and eighty-year-old Tokay."

"God, why don't you just do that 'special thing' thing to *yourself,* if you can?"

Adrienne rolled over on top of her and looked down, head cocked to one side. Ellen stroked her back, rubbing hard into the muscle from beneath the shoulder blades to legs and back. The Shadowspawn wriggled and purred against her, breasts and stomach and hips touching, thigh between thighs, utterly unselfconscious in her enjoyment of the moment.

It was disturbingly like petting a cat.

Human-sized . . . naked . . . wet . . . musky . . . horny cat lying on top of you and licking drops of your blood off her lips. Molested by a man-eating tiger. Oh, Christ!

"We *can* do that to ourselves," Adrienne said after a moment, her eyes heavy-lidded. "But we generally don't."

"Why don't you?"

"It's something every Shadowspawn discovers how to do around age thirteen. Then their parents put a Wreaking in their hot little minds to stop them. By the time you're old enough to take the inhibition out, you realize that churning your own brain into puréed oatmeal with an endless feedback loop of orgasms is not a good idea."

"What a way to go!" Ellen said, laughing unwillingly.

God, this is weird and awful and I do hate her passionately. On the other hand it feels great *and spending the night fucking like a ferret in heat is a lot better than booze to make me forget for a while,* she thought.

Her hands and lips were moving.

Bring it on, Princess of Darkness! Maybe I *can make* you *scream!*

"I do like a positive attitude," Adrienne said, and kissed her deeply.

Her mouth tasted of salt blood and of desire. Then she knelt up and put her hands behind Ellen's head.

"Let's start by trying this, then. We have a few hours until I have to spread my wings and fly. Now *concentrate.*"

CHAPTER THIRTEEN

Adrian gave a gasping scream as he felt his body wake. Waken from a nightmare of being caught by the sun in night-walker form, of his self peeling away in flakes and strings of fire . . .

"Ah, you're with us again," Harvey said. "Give it a few minutes and maybe you'll stop wishing you weren't."

He stubbed out his cigarette, flicked it out the window and pulled over. Wet gravel pinged and crunched under the wheels as the car slowed and stopped.

"Sorry this is cold," he went on, sliding into the rear seat.

He put a blood-bag from the cooler to Adrian's mouth. It wasn't *very* old, which made it a little less horrible; he must have stocked up at the hospital. Adrian gasped again, drank, retched, clapped his hands to his mouth.

"Water," he rasped through his fingers. "Then more."

He drank and swallowed the pills the other man shook into his hand. Then he curled around himself, hugging knees to chest. Gradually the shaking and chills and the sick pain behind his eyes and in his temples subsided, along with the missing spots and bits of glitter in his vision. He became conscious of something beside the gray misery inside his skull, took Harvey's arm and used it to help lever himself upright; a sleeping bag he hadn't noticed fell away from his shoulders, and he clutched it back for the warmth. The thin cotton of the hospital gown only emphasized the chill against which the car's asthmatic heater strained.

It was a nondescript Toyota Venza, flaking red and old enough to be unremarkable, smelling of ancient cheap stale tobacco, his own cigarettes which Harvey had presumably plundered and nameless things and children and dogs.

Harvey probably lifted it, he thought.

Some absent corner of his mind noted that they'd have to dump the hot vehicle; he could simply buy something from a used lot. Outside was the gray of a Central Valley wintertime tule fog, thick enough that he couldn't see more than ten yards in any direction. The world was a bubble of cold, dark-gray nothingness, with a few bare-limbed trees along the edge of the field dripping moisture on flat black mud. The air was heavy with it, a chilly, silty smell with an undertone of manure and vegetable rot.

"Name of a black dog, it looks and smells just precisely the way I feel!" he said.

Inside, somewhere in the depths of his mind, there was a dull wonder that he didn't say: *I do not care. Back to Santa Fe, me, and goodbye to you, Harvey!* The physical misery was enough to swamp emotion; the memory of Ellen was distant. It was a commitment of the will that kept the words unsaid.

A Taint in the Blood

To love someone is not to feel loving continuously. That is impossible, for humans or Shadowspawn either. It is to always act that way.

"Bit strenuous?" Harvey asked.

"You might say," he said, letting his head fall back. "What a fuckup. Adrienne was waiting for me again. After," he added bitterly, "spending the previous four hours humping herself blind with Ellen and taking little sips of her blood in the very short inactive intervals."

"Bad?" Harvey said sympathetically.

"I blocked as much as I could. She wasn't hurting her to speak of this time, but . . . The bitch is doing it to jolt me, I know it. She doesn't realize how close a high-link I have with Ellen, but she knows *something* is getting through."

"She *is* doing it to jolt you," Harvey said. "And to score points; that *I drink your milk shake* thing, which she's been doing one way or another since you two learned to walk. She's also probably still got the hots for you, since the Calcutta thing."

Adrian winced. "Yes. That was a bad time."

"Five gets you one *she* doesn't think so."

"And . . . to Shadowspawn that isn't incompatible with a desire to kill me slowly. Quite the contrary."

"Right you are. And she was also doing it because she just likes humping herself blind and ain't too particular about the 'with who' part long as they're good-lookin'. How precisely did she wreck the meet?"

"Preactivated Wreaking," he said. "A bit like that one in Santa Fe, only smaller and more . . . concentrated. The trigger was complex beyond belief. It was keyed to Hajime's state of mind; truly, the very *act* of deciding to listen to me. If he'd been completely hostile on his own account, nothing would have happened . . . you see the difficulty, and the cleverness of it?"

"How was it placed? Keyed to the ground?"

"No, dynamic. Like a floating spiderweb strung between buildings, with a seeker function. Hanging ready to exist, and when it existed there was only one place it could possibly be."

"Someone must have slipped her a sample of him from his mortal remains; you'd need a ground-link for something like that," Harvey observed clinically.

Adrian nodded: "It cascaded the probabilities of his decision negative until only the black paths were left, and he never noticed."

"She's gotten better," Harvey noted, resting his big hands on his knees and staring out the windscreen at nothing. "And she was always good."

Adrian nodded. "Things went downhill from there. He decided I was attacking him, went for his sword—which he really knows how to use—and I had to switch form."

"What to?" Harvey asked.

"The smilodon. I wish I'd had more practice with it. The animal mind swamped me; that never would have happened with my wolf. I can think about as well with that as in man-form, now."

"Would the wolf have been enough muscle for the job?"

"Well . . . no. I took out his backup men, but he's far too good with that sword. I wanted to leave then, but the sabertooth took me over and I was just going for Hajime when *she* hit me."

"As?"

"The biggest damned eagle I've ever seen, and stooping, falling out of the sky. Probably from one of the tall buildings. It must be some real species of bird to be that tangible, but . . ."

Harvey took out his BlackBerry. "Describe? This we gotta know about, soonest."

"Christ, my head . . . the body was the size of a child, perhaps five feet long. Wings twice that, broad and strong, not slender like a falcon's. Long head, strong legs and claws like a tiger, literally. Broad tail. Mostly I noticed the claws and beak."

He indicated his flank, and Harvey reached over to draw aside the hospital gown. The lacerations there didn't break the skin, but they were blue and purple already, bruises that twinged savagely every time he moved, adding to the pain of his half-healed knife wounds.

"Well, I'll be damned," the older man said when the results of his search came up, shaking his head in reluctant admiration.

"You found something?"

"Haast's Eagle."

He showed Adrian the picture; the younger man frowned, squinted, then nodded. Harvey read, swore again.

"New Zealand," he said. "Went extinct about 1400, but there are skeletons and such. Guess you ain't the only one can figure out that DNA reconstruction gets you a broader set of forms for night-walking."

"Most birds are too fragile to be much use in a fight against another walker," Adrian said.

"Right," Harvey said. "But this little critter is pocket dynamite, 'bout the weight of a medium dog. Evolved to hunt those cow-sized flightless birds they used to have. Says here it attacked at fifty em-pee-aitch and hit about as hard as a concrete cinder block dropped on you from six stories up."

"That sounds very, very right, except that concrete blocks aren't *sharp*."

Adrian rubbed his forehead. "The hell of it is that she and I *do* think alike. At least at the problem-solving level . . . If I hadn't sensed the attack at the last fractional second she might have severed my spine and Hajime would have killed me before I could regenerate. When I managed to beat the bird away, she went into tiger form—Amur type, but black. I broke contact and ran; flew myself, as a peregrine."

He glared at Harvey. "And *you* kept me flying at top speed to catch this damned car with my body in it until it was nearly dawn!"

"Better than *them* catching *us*. Somebody high-powered was looking. I'm pretty sure we lost 'em. Three gets you ten cents it's Michiko got the tissue sample or whatever for Adrienne from her granddad that let her set that trap," Harvey said. "You up to solid food?"

"I'm not sure, but I'll try," he replied.

The food was bread, butter, cheese and hard-boiled eggs. The first few mouthfuls were tentative, feeling his way around his abused stomach. Then he was ravenous, and forced himself not to gobble. When his share was finished he was able to force down more of the blood. The itching became worse in his arm and thigh, which was a good sign, and he flexed them cautiously. The bruises would heal much faster. They were only transferred tissue damage anyway, his soma-memory convincing his body that it had been attacked when he returned to the flesh.

"Let's get *somewhere*," he said.

"Son, we're between Stockton and Bakersfield on the west side of the Central Valley. There ain't no where to *be* there in, thereabouts. Specially in these days of ongoing national readjustment."

"I need to rest and heal. There is no alternative to that."

He slumped back against the door, ignoring everything until Harvey drove them into a motel and helped him into their room with an arm over his shoulder. They were the only occupants, and the mattress smelled musty with disuse, but the room was blessedly warm and dry. He lay half-comatose as Harvey stripped off the hospital gown, checked the bandages and covered him in blankets. His mind sank into the shadows.

"Hello, Adrian," Ellen said with a smile. "I'm *almost* getting used to this. Not as much of a mental shock when I . . . appear."

She looked around the motel room. "Ewww."

Adrian gestured from the bed, and the world changed. Now they were sitting; she still found *that* abrupt transition a little startling. There was the same sensation of doors opening in her mind, of memories three-quarters gone snapping back into place. She looked around; this was more complex than the confined landscapes she'd seen before.

Bright sunlight shone on tiled roofs and whitewashed walls descending a steep slope beneath them to a small harbor, and a Christian cathedral in a style half-Moorish . . .

"It's Amalfi!" she said. "I love that town. I've only been once, on a package tour in university. Two days for Florence, would you believe it!"

"It's a favorite of mine too." Adrian nodded, lighting himself a cigarette. "I spent some time convalescing at an *alberghetto* here once."

A striped umbrella shaded their table. Bright blue ocean stretched to the horizon, and mountains rose around the town. The air had a smell of spicy bushes and the sap of the umbrella-pine growing in the center of the little plaza, and of fruit and blossom from the rows of lemon trees to one side on the terraced hillside. Other couples and individuals chatted with lively animation and plenty of gestures, but when she tried she couldn't quite make out words.

Adrian was in white linen shirt and pants and thin leather shoes on bare feet, with sunglasses pushed up on his forehead, tanned nearly brown. Ellen checked herself and found that she was in a cool pale traveling ensemble of silk blouse and cotton skirt, with elegant leather-strapped sandals fastened with wrought-gold buttons. A white woven hat with a trailing band rested on the table, and loose strands of hair sun-bleached almost as pale lay over her shoulders.

Can't say he doesn't have good taste! she thought.

A waiter approached.

"*Un Limoncello, per favore,*" Adrian said in fluent but slightly accented Italian.

"*Subito, signore. Bello gelato, naturalmente . . . Noi lo facciamo con i limoni che crescono qui davanti, è una specialità, qui lo sanno tutti. Lo prende anche la signora?*"

Adrian looked over and raised a brow at her. A little dazed, she nodded. He answered the man:

"*Si, certo. E dei biscotti di pasta di mandorle.*"

The pale yellow liqueur came, and the plate of marzipan-like biscuits made with ground almonds, not as sweet or nutty as the American equivalent but sharper-flavored. She sipped and nibbled.

"I was going to say this is a bit dreamlike, but that's sort of redundant, isn't it?" she said. "Everything even *tastes* real. Realer than real. The people?"

"Not really people. Made from edited memories. Tangible in this state, but not . . . self-actuated."

She nodded. "I'm asleep, I think. The last thing I remember is lying on my face and Adrienne sort of . . . slapping me on the butt and telling me I'd earned some rest."

Adrian looked away, taking a draw on his cigarette; he held it between thumb and the first two fingers, next to his palm.

That's why he never took me seriously when I said he should quit! Ellen realized suddenly. *He wasn't really brushing me off; he can't* get *cancer or anything. That would be* bad luck, *and he doesn't have that! Wait a minute, it just occurred to me, they can* cure cancer *and they never told anyone?*

"Adrian," she said dryly, and he looked back at her. "I like the fact that you're concerned for me. It's sweet and wonderful, actually. But you can spare me the pity."

He flushed. "Sorry," he said. Then he smiled slightly. "I seem to be saying that a lot around you, Ellie."

She nodded. "I'm already an abuse survivor . . . well, no, I'm back to being an abuse *victim*, actually, since I've been kidnapped by an abuser. But I'm not a child anymore, and I know the coping strategies, Adrian. And I know they're strategies, not something wrong with *me*. It's a lot harder with someone who can read your mind, but at least I don't have the sense of betrayal I did before. I'm in no danger of Stockholm syndrome. I know all about that."

"OK," he said. Then he touched one finger to his forehead and flicked it out, a sort of sketchy salute. "I should remember that you're not just the damsel in distress. Sorry . . . touché."

"I need to know how this link thing works."

He took a deep breath. "It's stronger when I want it to be, or when we're physically closer, or when you're feeling . . . any intense emotion or sensation."

Ellen laughed involuntarily; she clapped a hand to her mouth.

"My turn to say sorry. You mean you could . . . could *feel* it when your sister was scaring the daylights out of me on that motorcycle or drinking my blood or when we were in bed?"

"Yes. Not all the time, and secondhand and much more faintly, but yes."

"That sounds sort of . . . perverse."

"It is, even by Shadowspawn standards; it's one reason they're so . . . jealous . . . about their, ah—"

"Lucies. Stop trying to shield my delicate sensibilities, Adrian! I hated that attitude when we were together, but you didn't *listen*. Right now I *am* a lucy. It's not my fault and I don't feel disgraced about it. Angry and frightened, yes. Defiled, no."

"Touché. I throttled back as much as I could. It's . . . a very strong link. Much more so than I expected. More so than she understands, I think—and hope. She almost certainly doesn't know about *this*, that we can communicate. But she knows I'll be getting flashes of emotion and physical sensations."

Ellen shivered. "I hope to God she doesn't decide hurting me more would be the way to get back at you."

"I also . . . Me too. This environment scrambles my linguistic reflexes!"

A thought occurred to her. "How come you all seem to be so multilingual?"

"It's easy for us. The language center in our brains is enlarged and linked to the telepathic faculty."

Ellen shivered, reminded of a voice saying, *I'm learning Georgian*.

"Time to fill you in on what's been going on," she said, putting briskness into her tone. "You know about the motorcycle trip? Well, when we got to San Francisco—"

"Name of a black dog! We were probably less than a mile apart, and her laughing at me all the while! If I'd known where, I could have gone after her."

Ellen winced, and he cursed, first in French and then in a string of other languages.

"Ouch," she said. "Hadn't thought of that. Anyway, Adrienne took me to this restaurant and we met a friend of hers. A woman named Michiko—"

"Tōkairin Michiko?"

Ellen shivered again. "Yes. Talk about *scary*. She wanted to kill me, Adrian—wanted to kill me with your sister. I think she would have liked to do it right then and there."

Adrian nodded, looking down at the table and taking a sip of the yellow drink, chilled in its small ceramic cup.

"Yes. They're blood-siblings. It's . . . sort of a mix of friends, fictive kinship, and lovers. And it involves joint kills. That's a very . . . intense experience."

"They were talking about some plan to, to wipe out half the human race with smallpox, some genetically engineered variety, they called it parasmallpox. And I got this horrible feeling that that was *better* than some other plan they were criticizing!"

"It was," Adrian said grimly. "The other plan involves EMP . . . a way to burn out all the technologies the world depends on. The Council of Shadows calls it Operation Trimback, Option One. I suspect it wouldn't work as smoothly as they think."

Ellen nodded quickly. "Yes! That was what Adrienne's been saying. She doesn't want that—*drastic*, she called it—a plan. She's *angry* with this other plan. Michiko was the same way. I think she . . . looks up to Adrienne. Admires her. But I wasn't catching everything they said."

Ellen frowned, concentrating. "There was something about *field tests*, in the Congo."

An appalling thought occurred to her. "Adrian . . . does that mean they were testing it on *people*?"

"Yes." Gently: "Ellie, Shadowspawn are the ones responsible for virtually everything monstrously bad in the past hundred years. Just before World War One, there was a great scandal in Europe because one Alsatian shopkeeper was put in jail for one weekend for offending a Prussian officer. That was before the Council secured the world."

Ellen shivered. "She said more, about drugs and vaccines, and stockpiling them."

"That fits," Adrian said.

"So after we left the restaurant, we went to what she called the *Brézé town house*."

Adrian's brows rose. "That used to be on Nob Hill, but it was destroyed twenty years ago, when the Tōkairin ousted the Brézés as the foremost Shadowspawn clan on the West Coast . . . long story."

"This was *new*. The building wasn't more than ten or fifteen years old max, a big luxury hotel with . . . sort of super-condos on the upper floors. The town house was a two-story penthouse on the top of the tower, huge, glass walls, pools . . . like something out of a Modernist fantasy of Haroun al-Rashid's bachelor pad."

Adrian cursed again. "The St. Regis Hotel! We were within *walking* distance of each other. And that's where she launched herself when she stooped on me."

Ellen felt her eyes growing wider and wider as he described the meeting and the fight that followed.

"You can . . . you can *actually* turn into animals?" she said. "Literally into fur-feathers-and-fangs actual *animals*?"

"Technically it's . . . well, for all practical purposes, yes. As long as we have . . . *les vieux* say, *taken the spirit of the beast into ourselves*. In fact, it's a DNA sample you need. Nearby. Swallowing it is best and most permanent."

"Then . . . those Norse berserkers . . . Sigurd with the wolf-skin he wore . . ."

"Mostly just psychotics with delusions. But some, yes, they had enough of the inheritance to do it."

This is truly *weird*, she thought. *But hey, Ellen, weird is the new normal for you.*

Then she went on: "OK, she took me back from the restaurant to the town house, we had a swim, a sort of strange philosophical chat which scared me quite a bit, she led me off to bed and we had lots of hot sweaty writhing sex and a little feeding—"

She smiled with a crooked twist of the lips at his carefully controlled expression:

"Adrian, hold the pity again, will you? Yeah, I'd *much* rather she couldn't force me to do things. Being helpless is *not* fun, not in reality. I want it all to stop, and badly. But if she *is* going to make me do things, which right now can't be avoided, forcing me to eat wonderful elaborate meals and then have hour upon hour of multiple orgasms just *so* totally beats 'feeling nauseated piss-your-pants bowel-loosening terror' and 'screaming in agony as sensitive tissues tear.' And . . . the high from the feeding doesn't actually *damage* me, does it?"

"It's addictive."

"I know about that, and I've gone cold turkey on things before when I thought they were getting too much of a hold on me. I was even a smoker for a little while and sweated bullets stopping. That's why I kept getting on your case about the cigarettes; and it made me *crave* one myself in the worst way."

"You never told me that you'd smoked. See, I am not the only one to keep secrets!" he said, trying for lightness and just about achieving it.

Ellen leaned over and prodded him in the ribs. "That'll teach you to ignore a lady's complaints! And I have to watch it with alcohol too. But the . . . drug . . . isn't physically harmful, is it?"

"No. As far as I know, there are no harmful effects apart from the feelings it causes, and the craving. It evolved to make the victim willing to be bled, not to hurt them."

"OK. It might totally screw the head of someone who didn't know what was happening, but I can tell the difference between the way the feeding makes me feel friendly and actually *being* friendly; I know that even when it's happening. The . . . effect itself actually feels pretty good."

His smile was broader, and he made a gesture with both hands and bowed his head slightly.

"You are a stronger person than I thought, Ellen. Many would be totally shattered in your position, but you are keeping your wits about you. Forgive me for underestimating you."

In fact . . . she looked at him speculatively. *You know, buster, if you'd approached it the right way and just* told *me about things instead of trying to* protect *me all the time . . . I might have surprised you. I might yet.*

"Provisional forgiveness given. OK, I go to sleep—I was surprised how easy that was even at the time because I was feeling shivery and jazzed, the way you are when you're tired but can't sleep—"

"Partly a Wreaking."

"OK, she zapped me into enchanted slumber, went out on the terrace again, turned into this big-ass eagle—"

"Her body stayed in the bed; that's one reason she put you under a Wreaking. We're . . . very helpless in that state."

Ellen's eyes narrowed, and she surprised herself with the flood of savage images that filled her mind for an instant.

"Oooooh, *wouldn't* I just like to get *her* helpless. With a hammer and a sharp wooden stake!"

"Ellie, you don't need a wooden—"

Ellen laughed. "It would still *work* if I drove it through her heart, wouldn't it?"

"On a tranced body? Quite well."

"And then I could hit her in the head with the hammer for a while and see how funny Countess Comic-ula thought *that* was!"

Adrian laughed, but looked at her seriously a moment later: "If you get the chance, take it. But don't hesitate, strike to the heart or brain, and then strike again and again. We are . . . very hard to kill, with anything but a silver weapon."

"Silver makes it easy?"

"About as easy as killing an ordinary person. The Power has no grip on it. We don't know why."

"I've never killed anyone. I've never even really *wanted* to kill anyone, just get away from them however I could, but I'll make an exception for you-know-who. So, she was . . . her body was lying there?"

"Yes, like this, in a sort of coma."

He halted for a moment and crossed his forearms, each hand resting on the opposite shoulder, before he went on:

"The aetheric form went out onto the terrace in her default daywalking shape. Then it waited until it sensed the Wreaking turning Hajime against me, transformed and attacked. You have to be careful in animal form. You're . . . still you, but you *are* the beast as well. It can be hard to retain purpose."

"Thanks. And so Adrienne swooped down to rescue Michiko's grandfather. Who she hates and despises. Who *Michiko* sort of hates, I think, or at least resents an awful lot."

"We're not a very social species and I think Tōkairin Hajime hasn't quite realized what it means. His grandchildren are so much closer to pureblood. Seventy-five percent and up. He's about two-thirds, and he was raised by people who were less than half. There's more human in him, and he's trying to run his clan as if it were made up of humans."

"But then why did she *rescue* him?" Ellen puzzled. "I don't think she's the sort who just swoops in to save the day."

Adrian frowned and sipped again at his drink. "That's the question; though maybe what she stopped was him spitting me on that damned silver-plated katana. Was she trying to use me to kill him without any blame attaching to her? But then as you say . . . or was she trying to get *credit* with Hajime? But what for? And she didn't try to pursue me in winged form—that eagle looked fast, and it could have twisted the head off any bird-form I have. There is some elaborate game here, one with multiple strands, multiple objectives."

"Which right now we don't know. How long do I have here?"

"Probably a while. It's natural for us to sleep most of the day and wake in the afternoon." A small smile. "Notice how many mad dictators had work patterns like that? Not a coincidence."

"Then . . . this may sound odd, Adrian, but can we take a walk? I'd like that."

He smiled, the charming expression with a hint of shyness she liked, and they rose and walked down the steep streets hand in hand. He bought them *gelato*; they fed the pigeons in front of the cathedral, and she explained the details of the frescos—his knowledge of art was broad but without system, a jackdaw's accumulation picked up in spare moments. He seemed at first amused and then impressed as she told—showed—him the links between the High Medieval techniques in the thirteenth-century building and the Quattrocento and the Renaissance.

"We should have talked about this more," he said at last.

"Says the man who used to derail any conversation that wasn't commonplace!"

Adrian laughed ruefully and ran a hand over his hair, taking off his sunglasses and hanging them through the neck of his shirt.

"When you begin on a basis of lies . . . even lies of omission . . . the areas you cannot talk about grow and grow, I find."

"We don't have to lie now. It's . . . almost worth it all."

"I'm glad to be honest, but I *don't* think it's worth what you've gone through, Ellie."

"I said *almost.*"

They wandered on by the busy harbor, amid a smell of fishing-boats and yachts, tourists and locals and thin, wandering, wary cats. The sun declined into the Mediterranean, and the terraces of stone and stucco above them took on a green-blue translucence. At last she took a deep breath and asked:

"Adrian, after this is over, if—*when*—I'm back in, ummm, real life, do you want to try again? With the two of us."

"If you do. I would like that very much. But—"

"*Don't* tell me how I'm going to be feeling then, Adrian! *I* don't know that yet!"

He laughed, a wholehearted sound. "Touché once more, Ellie!"

He took her in his arms; he was just an inch taller than her, perfect height for a kiss. It grew lingering.

"Dammit, I don't want to go back!"

"It's time."

"All right. Zap me back, then. And we're going to *win*!"

*　　*　　*

Adrian slept, woke in darkness to stumble to the bathroom, hardly noticing that his leg would bear him once more; drank enormously from bottled water by the side of the bed, slept again and woke clear-headed, the wounds itching less fiercely.

And smiling, he thought for a moment. *And it has been a while since that happened.*

"You're looking a mite more cheerful," Harvey said.

He was sitting at the table, making sandwiches from commercial rolls and convenience-store cold cuts. His coach-gun was on the table by his hand, and Adrian was awake enough to feel the slight drifting chill of a no-see Wreaking, not powerful but enormously subtle.

"It's calories," the Texan said, jerking a thumb towards the pile he'd made. "That's all that can be said for it. Except that the preserva-tives will keep your corpse lookin' pretty without the expense of an embalmer."

"It is to food as the Red Cross supply is to blood," Adrian agreed.

He limped carefully to the table and looked at the platter with dis-gust. But he ate, trying not to think of the taste.

"At least it's morally permissible to eat decent *food*, most of the time. It compensates for the foul blood, a little."

"You're *still* looking cheerful and you just bit into that so-called salami."

"I high-linked with Ellen. She's . . . much better than I expected. And she had some information for me. We have an agent in the en-emy's camp."

He filled the older man in on the relevant details.

"That might be useful. If there were a lot of bodies around this

Congo site, we could maybe isolate the virus strain; their lab, now, that'll be somewhere else. Somewhere with reliable electricity, which the Congo doesn't have."

"Neither does California, compared to the old days."

"It sure does compared to the fucking *Congo*, ol' buddy."

"A point."

"You know," Harvey said after a moment, "I'm startin' to feel a mite guilty about this."

Adrian looked. "How so?"

"Now don't misunderstand me. Ellen's your obligation, and you're mine. OK, that's *giri*, as our buddy Hajime would put it. We go through with this, and Adrienne most certainly needs killing. But the fact of the matter is we've got information on something damn big the Council has planned for the world, and we're not doin' dick about *that*. What good's rescuing Ellen if she dies of . . . whatever it was?"

"Dalager's Parasmallpox," Adrian said. "Although, in fact, I could cure a virus."

On a limited scale, went unspoken.

"And if they're planning that, or some faction of 'em is, from your Seeing it's not too far in the future. That means they're already gettin' it ready. If we knew the rest of 'where'—where the labs and storage shit are—there might be something that we could do about it."

Adrian snorted. "Except that would mean the other option I Saw. I'm fairly sure that my sister is the nexus point between the probabilities, with us important mostly as we affect her."

"Yeah," Harvey said. He leaned back meditatively, staring at the ceiling. "That other un *definitely* sounds to me like an EMP attack. That would account for the stalled cars and such."

"Could that be done to the whole world?" Adrian asked; his mentor had always liked keeping up with weapons technology.

Harvey bit into one of the sandwiches himself. "Oh, sure. Most of the big powers got specialized high-altitude nukes for EMP work; mebbe the Council's behind that. And the Council could set 'em off; squeeze on the leaders, mind-Wreaking, or just send in teams to Power-fuck the control systems, then launch enough to blanket the planet, minus the poles and oceans. Instant Ay-poc-al-ypse without much blast damage or fallout. 'Cept when all the reactors in the world slag down and suchlike. So you see why this has to be stopped."

Adrian's mouth quirked. "Harvey, how often have the Brotherhood been able to stop one of the Council's larger schemes?"

"Well . . ." The older man looked out the window.

It was raining, a dark persistent mist falling out of the sky onto the parking lot and the little strip of dead or half-alive stores and fast-food eateries beyond. His voice was reluctant:

"Not too often."

"Ah, that is how you say *never* in Texan?"

Stung, Harvey frowned in concentration. "We got Baron von Ungern-Sternberg, back in 1919. They were going to make him Dragon Emperor of the East. He was a bad one."

Adrian began ticking off points on his fingers. "But the Brotherhood never even realized the Council was behind the Black Hand and Prinzip. That's World War One. They'd been grooming Hitler for years even then—"

Harvey nodded reluctantly. "Little bastard was a *battalion runner* on the Western Front for four years, most dangerous job in the TOE. And he lived. Now, that's not right or natural. Must have taken some special Wreaking to beat the odds that way."

"And Lenin's stroke, so perfectly timed to put Stalin in power. And the Great Depression. And—"

"OK, OK, you're right. We still got to do some serious thinkin' about these schemes."

"*We* have to rescue Ellen and kill Adrienne, Harvey; that's why I'm here and not in Santa Fe, looking out over the arroyos and moving more supplies into the sub-basement. When Ellen is free and Adrienne dead, you and Sheila and the Brotherhood can concoct whatever futile schemes you wish, and I will take her back to New Mexico and guard her, if she will let me. In the meantime, send Sheila a memo."

The blue eyes grew somehow distant and savage at the same time.

"You know, I'd off your sister in a moment and it'd be a right good deed. But I'd like to get me Hajime, I'd like that very much."

Adrian looked at him. "The only difference is that Adrienne has not yet had the *time* to commit so many crimes."

He sighed. "And now I will keep watch while you sleep."

"I can—"

"Drop dead from exhaustion, Harv? Believe me, I will wake you as soon as possible."

CHAPTER FOURTEEN

"This one is just for clothes, *chérie*," Adrienne said. "Really, I thought you'd be more interested in the last. All the things we bought there were replacements for your own . . . gear."

I got all that stuff on the Internet, *dammit!* Ellen thought, her ears still burning.

Not in a sex store with attendants asking questions about whether I like plugs or clamps! And playing up to you as if you were . . . well, you are *the top and I* am *the bottom, but it was still embarrassing!*

"You should become more comfortable with your identity. Now, clothes."

The establishment was so exclusive that it didn't resemble a store at all; it was more like a wealthy family's house with stockists-cum-models on call, amid a smell of rich fabrics and flowers and upscale consulting rooms. The owner beamed delight at Adrienne; he was a middle-aged man with a gray mustache and a rather blocky build, immaculately dressed in a three-piece suit and shoes that had to have cost more than Ellen had ever made in a month.

"*Ça va*, Jean-Charles?" Adrienne said, as she drew Ellen in through the door by the hand. "I am sorry for the short notice."

Except that she didn't quite say that, Ellen realized suddenly.

She'd used the standard French casual greeting, which meant roughly *How goes it?* Ellen spoke fair basic French and understood and read it much better; that and some Italian were pretty well compulsory in her field if your area of study was Western art.

She pronounced it something like cha va, instead.

"*Tu dit-moi 'Ça va'?*" he replied, drawing himself up and crossing his arms. "*Rien pendant toute une année! Infidèle!*"

Well, that's friendly, in a gal-pal sort of way, Ellen thought. *They must have known each other a* long *time.*

Adrienne made a shrugging gesture, almost apologetic, and continued in the same language:

"Jean-Charles, I never promised you a monogamous relationship. I was in *Paris* three times in the past year. In Paris, one buys clothes, is it not so?"

She's got an accent in her French, I think. Something nasal and quick, faint, I didn't notice it until I heard it together with someone who doesn't. Regional, maybe?

"Ah, it could be so," he said, and opened his arms. "And you are here now."

They exchanged an embrace and kiss on both cheeks. He held Adrienne at arm's length and said:

"My God, it *is* over a year since I saw you and you have not changed *at all*. In the ten years since we first met you have aged perhaps one or two."

"Oh, three or four, certainly."

"While I have gone gray and wrinkled. In a very distinguished way, but still, gray; and you were not a young girl then. How do you do it?"

"I have told you *so* many times. Wicked sorcery and the drinking of human blood, my old. Besides, there is a wrinkle. One. Here, beside my eye, you see?"

He laughed easily. "And I thought you were called Brézé, not Bathory," he said.

He doesn't know, Ellen thought, and relaxed very slightly.

Then he turned to Ellen and raised an eyebrow at her rumpled jeans, clean plain T-shirt and padded jacket; not entirely out of place—Pacific Heights *was* still part of San Francisco—but not exactly fitting in either.

At least my hair's combed and I had a shower and the underwear and bra are fresh, she thought mordantly.

Adrienne was in a severe outfit of dark blue, with a modishly asymmetric skirt that came to a point beside the left knee, and a gold-link belt; it somehow made her look a few years older.

"This is a young friend, Ellen Tarnowski," Adrienne said. "She lost all her possessions in a fire. I need a complete outfitting for her. I have taken her under my wing, as one says."

Elegant, batlike wing, Ellen thought, and saw a sardonic look in the gold-flecked eyes.

God, telepathy adds whole layers of meanings to conversations even when you don't have it yourself.

"You have certainly given us something to work with," he said enthusiastically. Then to her: "A pleasure to make your acquaintance, Ms. Tarnowski."

Another lift of the eyebrow to Adrienne. "Ms. Darton . . . she was here only two months ago . . ."

"Monica and I will always have a deep bond."

"You are a constant and faithful friend, Adrienne."

Or a collector, Ellen thought. Then she remembered Dmitri Usov saying *Don't you ever just kill them?* and the hopeless caged desperation in his lucy's face. And Tōkairin Michiko's avid eyes when she wondered how the last living drops of Ellen's blood would taste, as her heart quivered and died.

Let's hear it for collection! she thought fervently. *At least until I get out of this madhouse-slash-Hell.*

"Never are you out of it," Adrienne whispered in her ear. "Abandon all hope, remember?"

Then she went back to her discussion with the designer. The premises included a laser scanner in a changing room that made a complete three-dimensional model of her body. When she came out it was already on the screen, and the proprietor and Adrienne were consulting over the curiously sexless silver shape.

"*Oui, mais*—" the owner said. "With such a complexion and such a figure—magnificently traditional, a veritable maize-fed American goddess—it would be criminal not to—"

"*Mais non*, Jean-Charles; you make her sound like a prize Jersey at a state fair in Wisconsin. She is also a woman of great intelligence and sensitivity, an artist. Look at that face, those eyes—"

Ellen offered an occasional comment as clothes appeared on the figure or mysteriously wafted out of the depths of the establishment; once or twice they took her seriously, or more often gave her pitying looks and then ignored her. Once the man did a series of quick impersonal measurements with a tape, and several times models came in wearing one item or another. Then a cloud of assistants descended and bore her off to fitting chambers, expanses large as a living-room;

fine chairs and rugs, and only the mirrors and mannequin stands and the sewing station that let down from the wall to show their purpose. Tucks, pins, hems, voices advising:

"This skirt is just right for madam, but it needs to be longer, Madam has such elegant legs, she can carry off the longer length as other women can't . . ."

Another: "This slip goes with this dress and it will be better if we change your bra. The thong will show—let's use the elastex full undergarment instead . . . These pantyhose . . . try these shoes, Miss Tarnowski, no, I think the satin *Eau de Nile* slippers are better for this one . . ."

One of the assistants flipped up her BlackBerry:

"Jack? Shoes. Size seven and half medium, satin *Eau de Nile*, evening and dancing . . . Bring five or six examples . . ."

But they *aren't really treating me like an object,* Ellen thought suddenly, as one of them stepped back glowing with enthusiasm and clapped her hands together.

These are artists at work. They're having fun. *They've been turned loose in a candy store with a gold card. Or they're painters suddenly given the key to the supply closet. That's why they keep asking* me *too.*

"Madam is a true champagne blond, very natural, very beautiful," one said around the pins clenched between her lips. "Your complexion can carry off many difficult colors, even this sunset pink, most women would *kill* to have madam's figure; it makes dressing you a pleasure . . . God, if you only knew what we have to do to make some of the cows who come in here look like human beings. Talk about being masters of disguise—the CIA have nothing on us . . . Someone get Margaret and tell her to bring her emergency kit!"

Margaret guided her to one of the chairs and put a towel around her shoulders and went to work on her hair.

"My God, it's all real," she said, fingers and comb deft. "Look at this color, and the density! You could grow this to your ankles like a silk waterfall if you wanted. But what have you been *doing* with it, madam?"

More clothing, and double doors opened to show a long corridor nearly as wide as a room. Ellen walked down it, with the critical group spacing themselves out to see how the outfits looked at a distance as well. At the end around the ell was an ironing board and cleaning station. Jean-Charles made an occasional entry at discreet moments, spoke an imperial word and left.

"Good," he said at last.

She'd returned to the original room, feeling oddly diminished in her jeans and T.

He made a final note and turned to Adrienne: "That's settled, then. A final fitting? In any case, we should have the complete ensemble ready by . . . oh, the end of the week. You have priority, of course."

"Your work is always right the first time," Adrienne said. "In any case, I have perfectly competent seamstresses at home when it's a matter of tiny adjustments to a hem. It's your creative genius I need. Also, of course, a few things for her right away. I appeal to you, my old friend!"

Jean-Charles turned to her, tapping his hand on his chin. "A fire, you say," he muttered. "*Pauvre petite!*"

Then, decisively: "You are wandering around our windy city in that junk, a girl of my own daughter's age!"

He snapped his fingers. "Martha! The brown and turquoise running suit with a pale blue shell and a tan shell, the ones Richarda models. Also, bring the off–royal blue wool dress, the camel coat . . . Francisco wanted to change the design on that anyway. Grab those nice lined wool slacks . . . in a dark olive and a chocolate, and one of the asymmetrical jackets in that dark ivy and black pattern. We should have two or three silk blouses in tan, lilac and green, oh, and that twinset in nile. That should help! You *cannot* be with nothing but those jeans. Just a few things to tide you over this week."

Ellen found herself flushing. "*Merci, Monsieur,*" she said, trying for her best pronunciation. "*Vous êtes si très gentils.* So very kind."

He really is, she thought, her eyes prickling a little. *I haven't had much of that lately.*

"It is nothing," he said, smiling at her. "I am merely following my trade."

Adrienne smiled herself and pulled a checkbook out of her handbag. Hats, gloves and pantyhose appeared as if by magic, and Ellen tried to pay attention.

I have to wear them, after all.

"Good deeds should not go unrewarded."

She filled in the check. Then she tore it from the book and slid it across the table to the man.

"After Mademoiselle Tarnowski's so-gracious words, I feel like a whore to charge anything," he said. "But one must live."

"You are a *grande horizontale* in the ancient mode, Jean-Charles," she said; they laughed and exchanged another set of cheek-kisses.

"I am a veritable Liane de Pougy, then! I shall write a novel about our liaison!"

They were laughing together as the assistants reappeared with his list, to bear Ellen off one more time.

At least I feel less conspicuous walking beside her, Ellen thought when they came out onto the street.

She'd been chilly before. The fine double-knit merino wool of the running suit and the knit silk shell fit like her own skin, but they were supremely comfortable as well.

And this stuff feels fabulous. Like my clothes are stroking my skin all the time.

Ahead steepness fell away to show the Golden Gate Bridge soaring above water royal blue, and the hills of Marin green with the winter rains. It was sunny but brisk, and she was glad of the suit's jacket. She put her free hand in the right pocket; Adrienne had her left again, swinging it like a happy child as they walked.

Though inconspicuous is an odd way to feel considering I'm wearing six months' salary.

"Or conspicuous in the same way as others," Adrienne observed.

"Why are you doing this?" Ellen asked, genuinely curious.

"Well, we *could* have stayed in and found other ways to pass the time until my meeting. The replacements for all that . . . equipment you lost have arrived by now, I'm sure. There's that nine-thonged braided silk whip with the delightfully explicit dual-purpose handle . . ."

Errrk! Ellen thought, flushing with a complex play of emotions.

"I wasn't *objecting*, Adrienne! Ah, it's weird, but yeah, I *like* the clothes. They're fun. I've always gone funky before because it was what I could afford."

"Well, even wearing a burlap potato sack you *would* look like Aphrodite rising from the waves."

"Ah . . . thanks."

"No, truly. You should develop a more positive self-image. And, of course, you are supremely bite-able, which is a matter of the psyche and mind as much as the body, though physical beauty helps. Have you noticed how much Michiko wanted to drink your blood, even though she was sated? I think nearly every Shadowspawn you meet will. Adrian certainly would have too. How it would have tortured him, the scent, the pulse beating so close to his lips! You are like a sweet, fragrant golden peach one longs to taste."

"Ah . . . thanks, I suppose."

I think. Sort of. That's sort of eerie and creepy and . . . thinking of Adrian . . . sad. If I'd known . . . I mean, if I'd known and hadn't run screaming for the hills . . . Poor Adrian! I was teasing him all the time and I didn't know it. He must have willpower like titanium steel.

"I like having beautiful things," the Shadowspawn went on, giving her hand a squeeze. "You deserve the proper settings. Also there are some . . . social engagements coming up, if things go well. I want to show you off to best advantage—for yourself, and as a sort of subtle statement about Adrian. He has quite a reputation as . . . a person of formidable, dangerous talents, you know."

"He does?"

"Oh, certainly. He has killed more Shadowspawn than any living . . . well, more than any corporeal."

Good for you, Adrian! she thought. *You're the* only *Shadowspawn I've met I don't* want dead!

Adrienne laughed. "I won't miss most of the ones he got. He very nearly killed *me* at least once, and vice versa . . . not unusual for brothers and sisters of our breed. As is passionate love. Love, hate, they are closely linked."

I wish he had *killed you,* Ellen thought.

It was automatic, but she winced. Adrienne laughed again, and freed her hand for a moment to administer a slap to the fundament that made her yelp and jump.

"Keep that up and I'll think you don't appreciate me," she said.

"I *hate* you. And not in any ambiguous way, either!"

"Of course. It adds a delicious spice to things. But to return to Adrian . . . whom you seem to be falling in love with again, perhaps by way of contrast to me . . . That I have his lucy strengthens *my* reputation."

"Sort of like . . . running off with his flag, or stealing his car, or something?"

"Exactly. And so I wish to display you to best advantage, and because it amuses me. But keep in mind that I'm not a tame tiger, Ellen. Peter was quite right about that."

Yesyesyesyes, she thought, nodding.

"I promised you many new and interesting sensations and experiences. This is one of them. There are going to be others that you'll find much more stressful. I suggest you learn to live for the moment."

She's jerking me around.

"Of course I am. I am a sadist! But not a guzzling brute like Dmitri; he's the type who gave werewolves a bad name. I'm going to devour you utterly, Ellen, in several senses of the word, but slowly, artistically, a sip at a time. You may or may not survive the process, but it's going to be interesting for us both."

"Oh, *Jesus*."

"He's a myth, alas. Now the Tempter . . . *that* was real."

The thought was appalling, but . . .

Perhaps I'm getting jaded. Losing my capacity for horrified surprise at the fact that the world has turned into a theme park for demons.

They walked down to Fillmore and turned towards the Bay, blue and white below; then into a café with an inner courtyard, a cheerfully bustling place, patrons sitting at marble-topped tables amid a mouthwatering smell of pastries baking.

"Adrienne!" a woman's voice called.

Ellen recognized Michiko; there was a slender preoccupied-looking black man with her. Beside them were a pale-faced spiky-haired girl in black trailing clothes wearing a pillbox hat with a net half-veil, and a Native American man in shirt and vest, pants and boots. He had the broad brown beak-nosed face of one of the Southwestern tribes, with a lean trim body; his hair hung down his back in a single braid beneath a headband, and there was a gold hoop in one ear.

"*Hon Da*, Adrienne," he said, rising in a motion like a cougar coming to its feet on a rock.

"*Hon Da*, Dale," she replied.

They exchanged the finger-touching gesture she'd noted before; this time there was a trace of . . .

Cool and wary, Ellen thought. *They're sort of . . . respectful of each other. And he's giving me the eye too. So's Michiko, in a pouty sort of way.*

Suddenly the drape and cling of the running suit made her feel even more vulnerable than she knew she was.

I wish I was wearing a burka, only they could still see my mind. Why do all these monsters find me so attractive, *for God's sake? Or is* appetizing *the right word?*

"She was Adrian's, eh?" he said. "Nice. He must be slipping. I heard he'd gone soft."

"Eccentric, perhaps," Adrienne said.

She repeated the gesture with Michiko. The three—the Shadow-spawn, she realized—took one end of the table.

He's got those gold flecks in the eyes. Not enough to see easily, but they're there when bright light strikes.

They began talking earnestly; unfortunately, they did it in some language she'd never heard, though she suspected it was the dark man's.

That left her . . . *Below the salt*, she thought wryly.

A plate of tarts and sweet fruit breads and cinnamon rolls and tiny puff pastries was placed between them.

With the other lowly food-and-amusement types.

"Hi," she said to them. "I'm Ellen Tarnowski. I'm Adrienne's . . . lucy."

The spiky-haired girl grinned. "I heard about you. I'm Kai, Dale's blood-bitch."

She nodded towards the man with the braid. "And he and Michiko were talking about you a bit. Pleased to meetcha."

She had a rapid-fire voice and a quick smile, and irregular-pretty features. A little younger than Ellen, with a tough, wary look around her dark eyes. They traveled up and down the blond woman's form.

"Michiko said you were hot. I sorta agree, in that classy blond way . . . That's natural, right? You show a canary with your pants down?"

"Yes," Ellen said, startled into honesty.

Then she glared. *Shall I inquire about* your *pubic hair?*

Kai smiled again, unabashed. "I'm mousy brown so I go for this ink-black look—it's a Wreaking, not Clairol. Michiko said Adrienne wouldn't throw you into the pot. Got kinda shirty about it."

The black man shuddered. "She . . . killed a girl last night. One that looked like you. I had to watch. Oh, Jesus, all the blood, the sounds she made, and she bit her and bit her and then she'd stop and the girl would wake up and scream and beg me to help—"

He collected himself. "I'm Wayne Jackson. I'm . . . with Michiko. I am . . . was . . . an epidemiologist at Stanford."

He knotted his hands together. Kai looked at him with a slight sneer.

"Wuss. You better get your act together or *you're* not going to last long, not with *her*. Show some positive 'tude, dude!"

Then she lit a cigarette. Ellen blinked; in San Francisco that was worse than beating kittens to death in a public place, but nobody seemed to notice.

Kai looked around proudly: "That's me, not Dale or the others. I'm a twenty-six."

At her look: "I've got twenty-six percent of the Shadowspawn genes—there's this test they have."

"The Alberman?"

"Yeah, that's it."

Unexpectedly, Wayne spoke: "Someone . . . like me did it for them back at the end of the last century. Twenty-six is high, for the general population."

Kai nodded. "It happens sometimes just by accident, or a Shadow-dude has some bitch and forgets to hex the sperm. I can do some Wreaking now that I'm trained, just little shit like my hair, but it's lots of fun. Dale says it's why I'm alive after my *happy childhood* and wasn't some strung-out OD'd junkie or something. It makes you lucky, sorta, kinda."

"It sounds . . . useful."

Adrienne's children could spin little feathers. What could this malicious grown-up child do?

"Oh, shit, yeah," Kai said, around a mouthful of kiwi tart. "That's why Dale didn't off me when we met. He could feel it when he got his mind into me."

She giggled. "Along with his teeth and dick. He lets me help with a kill sometimes, get guys or chicks thinking it's a hookup and lead 'em in. He usually doesn't like to string it out the way most Shadowspawn do. Or I get to watch, which is totally hot, or do other stuff. You done any of that yet?"

A Judas-goat lucy, Ellen thought. *Eww. Whole new vistas of ewwness.*

"No," she said, her mouth a little dry. "I'm . . . new to this."

"It's cool, I think. I was always into the pain stuff, I was *so* this death metal fangirl, but I never got to *do* a lot of it until this. I've been Dale's for four years now."

Wayne seemed to have gotten some self-possession back. He ate a little sugar-dusted *something* and sipped at his coffee.

"Michiko asked me some hypothetical questions at a public lecture. They were off-the-wall, but I answered. Then she decided she needed my services full-time."

"Yeah, services," Kai said, and licked her lips.

He sighed. "Well, professors don't get hit on by gorgeous young rich women very often and taken out and . . . And then there were teeth in my throat, and the world . . . went crazy."

He looked down into his coffee cup. Kai snorted again and ate another chocolate-and-cream pastry.

"How did you . . . meet Dale?" Ellen asked her.

"Picked me up at a concert in Tucson. He *totally* started feeding right while he was boning me that first time and I still thought he was just this awesome Indian dude, and it was like, totally great. You had the feeding and sex at the same time thing yet?"

"Ah . . . no," Ellen said. *A bit late to be shy, as Adrienne said.* "Close together, though."

"That's good too, but with the timing just exactly right, *wow!* I'm the only regular lucy he's got right now. We travel a lot—that's cool too. He does things for the Council. Killings mostly, you know, people who find out stuff they shouldn't or get out of line, sometimes even a Shadowspawn. They call him the Shadowblade. Is that awesome or what?"

"Aren't you worried that—"

Kai shrugged and washed a mouthful down with her coffee.

"Nah. Dale says he's going to Carry me when he finally offs me— you know that soul-eating thing they can do?"

Ellen's mind went blank for an instant.

Did I hear that? There's so much . . . I am never going to get used to this. I don't want to get used to any of this. Help!

Kai nodded. "He's already done the temp version a bunch of times so he can do the extreme stuff to me without killing me. Well, killing my body; he's killed *me* in there about . . . oh, thirty-six times. All sorts of ways, and it feels just like the real thing. The first time I didn't know what was happening and thought it *was* the real thing. Shit, talk about a crazy ride!"

Wayne blinked at her. "What's that like?" he blurted. "Dying, I mean."

"Kinda interesting. Like, there's this complete rush. Especially when you learn to ride the pain and fear. I figure it won't be much different when he does me for real. Pretty weird in there, yeah, but I'm not your vanilla sort of girl and I get to live forever. Or as long as *he* does. And when he lets me I can see and feel what he's doing, which is just *bitchin'*. And when you think about this destroy-the-world gig they're gonna do, it all gives me a lot better chances than most people."

"You want to live forever . . . in there?" Ellen said.

That being my own particular nightmare right now. Even with Adrian it would be terrifying. In the mind of a monster forever . . . and you couldn't die, or even go mad . . .

"Why not? Lots of company. Meantime it's all fun. Especially the feeding part; there just *isn't* any shit you can buy that gives you a high like that. I haven't wanted a hit of anything else since Tucson except cigarettes and I've cut way back on those. And the sex is just fucking *extreme*. How'd you end up with Adrienne? Those Brézés are seriously big mojo with the Shadowspawn."

"I . . . was her brother Adrian's girlfriend. She . . . took me away from him."

"No!" Kai said. "Kinky! I heard about her brother, too. Those two got this feud thing going. He's like, a boogeyman to a lot of the Shadowspawn. Even Dale gives him respect."

She subsided, looking up the table at *her* Shadowspawn; the conversation had shifted into English, more or less.

"*Ga no iwai,*" Michiko was saying thoughtfully.

"Prayer for Long Life," Adrienne said. "I like it. It's been ten years since his last?"

"Exactly ten come May, and fifty since his Second Birth. I think it would be a . . . *good gesture* . . . to invite him to Rancho Sangre for the celebration."

"Which is where we'd need *your* unique talents . . . Dale Shadowblade," Adrienne said. "I have to admit, you do no-see better than I do . . . and that's something I rarely say."

The Indian looked into the distance. "OK. You make a lot of sense, Adrienne. Option One would be fun for a while, but that devastated wasteland thing, no."

He grinned. "My father would have loved it; he was deeply into that old-time Swallowing Monster and Bear-man on Nabîanye mountain stuff, wanted the world to be like the old stories. Michiko's right too, though. We've got to get free of all that human leftover shit, tribes, countries. It's just not relevant to us."

Michiko nodded; she had a sleek modern look to her today, hair parted in the center, sunglasses, a sleeveless white silk blouse, dark trousers tucked into high-heeled boots and a coat hanging off the back of her chair, like an up-and-coming lawyer on her day off.

"Wayne," she said, and snapped her fingers. "Come here and talk to us."

He did, fumbling up a laptop from a case at his feet and taking the spot between Adrienne and his Shadowspawn as they moved their chairs aside for him.

"Tell us about those spread patterns you were working on," Michiko went on, playfully running her fingers over the back of his neck. "With the aerosol release of the initial pathogen."

To Adrienne: "Wayne's got me talking like an intellectual when I'm with him. You know, he even *screams* with an impressive vocabulary?"

Wayne stammered for a moment, closed his eyes, then opened them. Adrienne spoke, her voice warm:

"Michi, we all have our individual needs, but we—collectively speaking—need him coherent right now."

Well, there's a first. The Yonsei Horror actually looks abashed! Ellen thought. *Take one spoiled rich girl sorority bitch and add* murdering sociopathic sadist*, and put it all in one awful package with superpowers. And she's not even as scary as the Apache Devil there. God!*

The scientist took a deep breath, let it out, and began to speak in a voice that was almost calm:

"With a fourteen-day contagious latency period, what you'd need would be aerosol release at a limited number of major transport hubs . . . I've got graph projections here."

"Pictures are good," Adrienne said. "A lot of our relatives are *not* intellectuals. Not given to complex verbalizations, shall we say."

"As in, some of 'em are stone stupid," Dale said, and laughed. "One thing the Power doesn't guarantee is that you'll be *smart*. We don't average dumber than humans, but when there are only a few thousand you sure *notice* the dumb ones more."

Adrienne had been studying the graphs. "You're assuming a very high average number of contacts."

"They'd be the most highly mobile individuals, too," Wayne said. "Ideal vectors."

"What cities?" Adrienne asked. "The fewer the better. Complex plans have a tendency to go wrong, even with the Power."

"This list."

"Twenty-seven?"

"If you want to be absolutely certain."

"Thank you. You've made a definite contribution to our plans."

Ellen could see his face twitch. The Shadowspawn all laughed, a wicked snickering.

"Then we're agreed?" Adrienne said. The others nodded, and she raised her coffee cup.

"To Option Two! And the Dread Empire of Shadow, with decent plumbing and high-speed Internet!"

"Oh, thank God!" Ellen said.

She was in the great high-ceilinged glass-walled living-room of the mountaintop house again. Standing near enough to the fireplace to feel the warmth on her skin, dressed in a long soft robe of dark cloth.

"Ellie!"

The embrace and kiss were wordless for a long time.

"Where are you?" Adrian said into her ear.

"In bed, alone. She told me to go to sleep quite early. I think—"

She could feel his lips move in her hair, and there was sound, but it slipped out of her consciousness.

"Yes, you're under that *sleep-now*."

"I thought so."

Ellen dropped her head into the hollow of his shoulder, her breath almost a shudder of sheer *relief*; it wasn't until the deadly tension was gone that she realized how tightly it had drawn skin and muscle and tendon. He felt it, and began to knead her shoulders.

"Bad?" he said.

She raised her head with a sigh. The living-room was lit only by the low crackle of a piñon and juniper fire, scenting the air and casting a pool of ruddy flickers around the hearth. The full moon washed the crags outside with silver and darkness, its light falling on the sofas and settees and bookcases.

Ellen sank down cross-legged on the sheepskins that were heaped before the fire; Adrian joined her, and they leaned against each other in companionable silence.

This is like how it was when things were good with us, she thought. *Only better. How to Save Your Relationship: Get Abducted by His Monster Relatives.*

After minutes he asked again: "Where are you?"

"Still in San Francisco," she said.

"Adrienne?"

"Mostly she's been . . . *shopping* today. Shopping with me, of all things. Clothes and accessories and lingerie and perfume and jewelry and getting my hair done. Even books and some pictures, all bundled up and sent back to the ranch, to the place she put me in on Lucy Lane. It's . . . weird; she *knows* I hate her, and she even *likes* that, she doesn't expect to change it. It's all like I was a room she was decorating, or a *doll* or something."

Adrian sighed into her hair. "She had quite a few dolls, as a little girl. She'd dress them and talk with them and have parties . . . sometimes I'd help her. She liked my hobbies too, the piano, watercolors. We were both passionate about horses, and swimming."

"But sometimes a doll would disappear?" Ellen said.

She hugged him closer; the solid lean muscularity was infinitely comforting, and the familiar clean but slightly acrid smell of his body. Even the fact that it was like his sister's didn't make it less so. It wasn't *exactly* the same; deeper and heavier somehow. It must be the scent of Shadowspawn, subtly different from her kind.

"She'd say *Francine was* bad, or *Isabelle wouldn't do what she was told.*"

"Eerrrk!"

He nodded. "And that would be the last of that one. Once she cried because a doll was gone, and our mother—we thought she was our aunt—said, *Let that be a lesson to you. They don't grow back.*"

"It's hard to imagine you as kids. Either of you."

"Oh, we were," he said softly. "It gives you a . . . different perspective. There was always a rivalry, but sometimes . . . yes, there was love. Love as puppies or kittens love, straightforward, there like sunlight or rain. It is easier for love to curdle into hate than become indifference. Both link you tightly. We have become utterly different, but we both started out on the same road. What else?"

"And we had lunch with Michiko and . . . this other Shadowspawn. An Indian—he looked like an Indian, maybe a Hopi, maybe Apache or Navaho—named Dale."

She could feel him stiffen for an instant. "Dale Shadowblade?" he said.

"That's what they called him. You know him?"

"Know of him. We've only . . . briefly been in proximity. Otherwise one of us would be dead, the true death."

"He's bad?"

"An enforcer who works for the Council as a whole, freelance. Mostly he's famous for being unseeable."

Ellen nodded. "That must be what Adrienne meant when she said *your special talents* to him. She's planning this get-together—"

"Now what could that be?" he asked when she'd finished. "An assassination? But she *saved* Hajime yesterday. Or could she really want a reconciliation, hoping to persuade him to change his stance on Operation Trimback?"

He shook his head and then looked down at her where she rested one cheek on his shoulder.

"You have kept your head about you, my darling Ellie. This is the break we need."

"You're sure?" Ellen said; she fought to keep her hands from turning into claws and digging painfully.

"There will be many, many Shadowspawn there, crowded together. And their guards. Frictions, jockeying for position, cross-purposes. Not a one-on-one duel between defender and attacker. Everything will be . . . *confused*."

"It will? Adrienne . . . is smart."

"We don't do organization well, not on a large scale. Yes! This *will* be the opportunity we need! And I *will* get you out of there!"

The kiss turned heated. After a moment, she took his hand and slid it onto her breast.

"You are sure?" he said, looking down into her eyes.

The hand moved, sliding up over the curve, touching the stiffened nipple through the cloth of her robe. She gasped slightly at the jolt of sensation, and the way her skin seemed to glow all over. The golden flecks in his irises glittered like mica seen in the depths of a cave, catching the firelight.

The Power, she thought. *That's what they're a sign of. This is the man the Shadowspawn themselves fear.*

"Adrian, when a woman does that, she's generally *sure!*" Softly: "I want to do this because *I* want to, with someone I really like. Someone I love."

The hand turned insistent, and his mouth came down on hers. She scrabbled at the buttons on his shirt . . .

Minutes later she linked her fingers behind his neck.

"Adrian?" she said breathlessly.

"Yes?"

"I haven't suddenly become made of porcelain. I like to feel how strong you are. Come *on!*"

He snarled then; she felt a brief surge of fear, and then it turned to a savage excitement. Her long legs wrapped around him as he drove forward, lifting her in an arch off the sheepskins until only her neck and shoulders touched . . .

"So," she said much later.

He lay against her; one hard arm was across her stomach, and his breath tickled on her collarbone, like butterflies in the golden glow. There was still a little tension in him; she could feel it in the muscles of his back as she stroked it, like hard living rubber under the sweat-slick skin.

OK, she thought, with a catch in her breath and a flutter beneath the breastbone. *Here goes.*

She slid down a little more and slipped an arm behind his head; he stirred and murmured drowsily. Then she arched her neck up and began to pull him down towards the base of her throat.

He growled, a low rippling sound in his chest. Her heart beat faster as his hand gripped her shoulder, hard almost to the point of pain. The lips touched the taut skin—

"No!" It was half a shout as he came fully awake. "What are you doing?"

She caught his face in her hands to keep him from scrabbling too far away.

"Well, *that's* an invitation too, lover," she said firmly.

He reared back. "You don't know what you're talking about!"

"Yes, I *do*. I'm talking about helping you with what you need. I'm your lover, right? That's what lovers do. And, buster, I expect to enjoy it too. That's part of the package as well."

"You want me to drink your *blood*?"

"Yeah. Exactly. I want you to drink my blood. Not more than I can spare, of course!"

He quivered. "I've spent my life fighting not to—"

"You've been fighting not to *take* blood. That's wrong. That's like rape. Now that I know about it, the way you fought it makes me love you more."

He panted, then seemed to come to self-control. "Then how can you ask me to give up the fight?"

"I'm not. I would *never* try to sabotage what you've done."

She took a deep breath herself. "I'm . . . a little scared here, myself, Adrian. But . . . I'm *asking* you to drink some of my blood. It'll make me feel very good too. That's like making love, as far as I can see."

"You're . . . addicted—"

"Not right now. I got a fix night before this as far as the goddamned drug in Shadowspawn spit goes. This is about you and me."

Softly. "Come on, Adrian. This is your mind. I'm not physically here. We're safe, right? I've thought about this."

"I don't want to hurt you! If I drink here, it'll *feel* exactly the same as reality for both of us . . . until we wake up, at least. How could I stop myself when we're back together in the real world?"

"That's just it. If it's just the same, you can *test* whether you can stop. And . . . even if you can't, here, this time, I . . . won't be angry with you. We'll just know that it's not an option. But I think you can."

"Nothing can stop me, if I start," he said desolately.

"Yes. *You* can stop you. So *I* can stop you. I'd say, *No, can't spare any right now* and you'd stop and go back to the horrible stuff from the blood bank."

His gaze turned from its inward lock, and a smile warmed them without quite reaching his lips.

"You trust me that much?" he said quietly.

"I trust you that way with other things. You're a lot stronger than I am physically, and I always knew that, so I trusted you every time I got into bed with you, or even was alone with you. Trusted you not to hurt me; trusted you not to make me do anything I really didn't want to. I couldn't physically stop you; I had to rely on your being a . . . good person. How's this different?"

"I . . . the need is very strong," he said softly. "And I'm not a good person. I just try to act like one."

"Adrian, that's what a good person *is*; someone who controls what they *do*. You're what you do, not what you think about doing. And even your crazy sister can stop feeding on me when she decides to, and she doesn't care about me at all, not really. I trust you with my *life*."

"You would have to," he said somberly. "I . . . don't . . . Who could be worthy of that?"

"Adrian, you've got the Power. If we're going to live together, the only way I can do it is knowing you won't use it on me against my will. But you can't stop being what you are."

"Ellie, more than anything, I don't want to hurt you."

"I know. I really believe that now. That's *why* we should try this. But not if you say no. It's got to be both of us."

He turned on his stomach and put his face in his hands; she could feel his back shake with muffled sobs as she stroked it.

"It's all right, Adrian. Whatever you decide, it's all right."

She cuddled against him. Gradually the tremors ceased. He wiped his eyes with the back of his hand as he turned over to face her, unselfconsciously.

I haven't often seen a man who can do that, she thought.

He regarded her levelly, the gold flecks in his irises glinting a little. "You are sure?"

"Yes. Well, I'm feeling fluttery and breathing quickly and my heart's racing, but yeah, I've *decided* I want to try it. *Bite* me, for God's sake. That's an *order*."

She brought their faces together. "I need to do *this* with someone I love, too."

One arm went under her shoulders. She let her head fall back against his biceps and arched her neck again. Then she put her arms around his shoulders, hand behind head.

"Do it."

The mouth touched her throat, and she felt the familiar motion of the lips and tongue arranging the angle.

The feeding bite is verra precise.

For a single instant a stab of cold terror went through her, like ice water in her chest and stomach, and something inside her screamed:

What . . . are . . . you . . . doing! *Nonononono!*

Then the teeth, hard against the skin, and a faint growl, rumbling, deeper than Adrienne's. The sting of the cut, as the incisors moved in their exact lateral slice. Instantly the fear vanished. Warmth surged through her, deeper as she made no resistance. The blood flowed strongly under the hard insistent suction of the feeding, but she could move a little, though lights swam in front of her eyes. Her free hand stroked his throat, feeling the swallows. Peace was utter and complete, a fulfillment that needed nothing more.

"Oh, yes," she murmured. "Yes. Take it. Take what you need." She waited for a time that stretched. Then:

"That's enough, lover," she whispered.

Nothing changed, except that his grip on her shoulder tightened. She tugged at his head and pushed at his jaw—feebly, the lightest touch against the ruthless predator's strength she felt. Her mind forced her lips to move:

"That's enough. Adrian, stop. *Stop!*"

One more long moment . . . and his mouth broke away from her neck with a small wet sound, and he rolled over onto his back, shuddering. The cut itched fiercely for a moment, then almost vanished; she was just barely aware of it.

Ellen gave an exultant wiggle. "Oh, *my*," she murmured, and raised herself on one elbow to look down at him.

His eyes were closed; there was a slight smile on his lips, where beads of her blood glistened darker than rubies in the firelight.

"Your mind was like . . . moonlight making a path on water," he said.

"You say the nicest things," she chuckled, and leaned down to kiss him.

The blood tasted of salt and metal, like the sea but with a hint of organic muskiness.

"I wish I could *taste* that the way you do," she said, with her hands on his shoulders.

"I think . . . here . . . you can. Let me try."

His hand buried itself in her tangled gold hair and held their foreheads together. There was a tickling behind her eyes . . .

"*Oh!*" she said.

Like golden light poured down the throat until the tongue tingled with it, like the taste of song, like the thing that wine tried and tried and failed to be, like an infant's memory of mother's milk, and caramel and spices and the first sip of darkly rich hot chocolate on a winter's day.

"Oh, *God*, no wonder you want it!" she blurted.

His eyes opened. "Now you know."

"Now *we* know."

CHAPTER FIFTEEN

"So, any contact?"

"Yes," Adrian said.

He finished dressing and leaned against the musty-sour smelling wall of the motel room and hissed as he cautiously stretched the healing leg. The Power could speed the process, but he still needed to make sure there weren't adhesions if he was going to recover full use. The pain was deep but not shrill; he monitored it carefully.

Pain is just a sensation. Let it go by without paying too much attention. It's paying attention to pain that hurts.

"OK, that was informative," Harvey said dryly.

Adrian grinned. "I had a nice long chat with Ellen."

And fortunately woke up first, so I could attend to the . . . evidence.

"She's . . . nothing worse has happened to her. Except that Adrienne forced her to spend a day *shopping* together. Adrienne was buying her clothes and seeing to her hairdo."

Harvey's worn face scrunched. "Hell, *that's* a new one, and I thought I was something of an expert on Shadowspawn brutality. 'Course, it would only be hell for *me* to be forced to spend a day looking at clothes 'n' shoes and shit. Lots of females like that stuff."

"How perceptive. You were divorced three times, Harv. I wonder why? At least I *like* shopping, within reason."

"They all left you too!"

"Yes, but that was because I wasn't human, not because I was but did it badly like you, my old. To a woman, forced shopping is probably a subtle but horrible form of psychosexual dominance behavior."

"I think I liked you better depressive," Harvey said dryly. "Why so cheerful?"

"Amid the dresses and pantyhose, Adrienne had lunch with Michiko . . . and Dale Shadowblade."

"Oooohhh, *shit*." The humor died out of Harvey's eyes. "That is one mean motherfucker, even in the crowd he runs with. This is *good* news?"

"Hell, yes, Harv. Because of what they all discussed. Ellen could not get all the details; much of the conversation was in languages she did not know. But Adrienne is using the credit she got with Hajime to get him to have his . . . not precisely a birthday party. A celebration called Prayer for Long Life. "

Harvey snorted and finished pulling on his leather jacket.

"Interestin', on account of he's been dead since I was about ten, and I'm no spring prairie chicken."

"They've adapted it to take Second Birth into account. And Adrienne is trying to convince him to have it at her estate."

Harvey's blue eyes went blank with calculation. "Oh-*ho*. Slip you in amid the inevitable screw-ups? Me as backup? Get Ellen out?"

"And kill Adrienne." Adrian nodded grimly. "No point without that. We may have to run. Hajime could come after us in New Mexico easily enough. But it *is* an opportunity."

"I can see that would make a man happy. Maybe *too* happy. I'll plug into the Shadowspawn rumor mill. Too easy to get details, and it's a trap. Hard, but they're there, probably genuine."

Adrian's grin grew wider. "And Ellen wants to come back to me," he said. "Now that we can be . . . honest with each other. I never really thought that would be possible."

Harvey whistled softly between his teeth. "I was *hopin'* things would turn out OK for you two. But I wasn't holding my breath, exactly."

"Neither was I. But Ellen was . . . quite convincing."

"Got mentally laid, did you? That *does* tend to cheer a man up."

Adrian made a rude gesture, as much as he could with one knee clasped to his chest.

"I have never been loved . . . loved for *myself*—you understand? At most, only for the mask I wore, and that for a little while. This is . . . marvelous."

The older man hesitated. "You realize, you're her lifeline right now? I'm not saying she's not honest, but . . ."

". . . but her feelings might change once she is no longer in Adrienne's power. Yes, that is possible, but I don't think it's likely. And that, my friend, makes me feel very good indeed. Even more anxious for Ellen, but . . . good."

He finished the exercises and walked over to his bed. His nose wrinkled slightly; the sheets hadn't been used before they arrived, but they'd been musty. Now they smelled stale with his pain-sweat and faint traces from the bandaged wounds. He still sat. This whole place smelled bad.

"And I was thinking also of larger matters."

"Uh-*oh*. Sex and philosophy. That's a dangerous duo."

"*Salop*. No, I meant what you said to Sheila the other day. The Power is here to stay. And while it's good that Ellie trusts me, humans cannot live on our individual forbearance. We must learn how to . . . to untangle that kludge evolution handed us. The blood and pain and death, they are *accidents*. With the Power itself, and enough knowledge, we could make it the common inheritance of humanity."

"Well, yeah. Except that almost all the people with a lot of the Power are your unesteemed sister's sort. Can you see her working as a receptionist?"

"We could be . . . doctors. Therapists. Even police."

"Christ, Adrian, you gonna start singin' *kumbaya* next?"

"Harvey, we have switched roles in a week." Adrian laughed. "But seriously, a lot of it is the way we are *raised*. You raised *me* from my early teens, and I didn't turn out so very bad, eh?"

"Yeah. Now I'm playing pessimist. OK, first order of business, let's sort out the files on the Brézé properties and figure which one is going to be the site of this monster jamboree. Ellen said it was an all-day trip on a motorcycle?"

Adrian nodded. *"Denn die Todten reiten schnell."*

"She's not dead, but she does drive damn quick," Harvey said, completing the bilingual pun. "Speed demons, both of you. Still, it was all on two-lanes . . . OK, here's the possibilities . . ."

This stuff does make riding a motorcycle more comfortable, Ellen thought.

She was in a suit of tight leathers, canary-yellow with red trim, as they rumbled through the streets of Rancho Sangre at sunset. The wheels of the machine ground fallen cherry-blossoms under their treads. Cooking smells drifted from homes and restaurants; it was dinnertime, in the early-February gloaming.

I'm also less scared, she thought. *For one thing, Adrienne didn't drive like a complete maniac on the way back. And she hasn't fed on me today.*

"You didn't need to be terrified and I wasn't frustrated and angry at the world," Adrienne said. "And while your blood is unfailingly delicious, I snacked elsewhere in San Francisco. Pretty drive on the inland roads too, isn't it?"

"Yes, and I had more time to pay attention."

"It comes to me that you are feeling less totally isolated and hopeless and psychologically crushed than I would have expected at this stage in our relationship," the Shadowspawn said thoughtfully. "But I can't quite tell *why*. It's a pity. I am so looking forward to your abandoned misery and the transference and identification with the aggressor and so forth."

"I . . . ah, sorry . . . Look, I could *try* to feel more crushed . . ."

"Oh, that's very sweet of you, but there's no problem. The full pleasures of your abject emotional degradation can wait. We're not in a hurry. Anticipation has its own spice, and I'm a little busy right now anyway."

Eurrrrk!

The motorcycle swerved inward in front of the police station, a blank wall of stucco with a gate of wrought iron; a round machicolated tower showed at one corner. Less than a minute after she kicked down the stand and took off her helmet to shake her hair free the police chief was standing at not-quite-attention on the sidewalk. He was a man in early middle age; Hispanic, Ellen thought, lean and grizzled. Beside him was the Englishman she had met before leading the patrol of

Asian soldiers—Gurkhas, they were called. He gave her a small polite inclination of the head before standing at parade rest.

"There's a problem, Captain Bates?" Adrienne asked.

"It's Jamal, I'm afraid, ma'am," the ex-soldier said. "Shortly after you left, he . . . went missing. He took hiking clothes and food and headed up into the high country. Southwest, I think."

"Tsk," Adrienne said. "That won't do at *all*."

Her head swiveled, the tousled black hair swirling about her shoulders; a frown of concentration grew between her brows.

Once they have tasted of your blood you are linked, linked forever, Ellen thought to herself.

"Yes," Adrienne said, opening her eyes again. The gold flecks seemed to glitter. "Southwest. Not far, either. Working his way south through the hills on foot."

"Suicide by cop, pretty much," Mendoza said. "I *told* you we didn't have to worry, Bates. I grew up here."

The Englishman smiled, a thin, eager expression. "My men could use the practice tracking."

Adrienne chuckled. "Oh, Captain Bates, this is Rancho Sangre of twenty-first-century California, not Tara in antebellum Georgia. We don't chase people with bloodhounds and drag them back in chains. Besides, it wouldn't be safe. Safe for your men."

Looking over her shoulder, Ellen could see the corner of her grin. She turned her face, but not before she saw both men blanch a little.

"Safe, ma'am?" Bates asked carefully.

"There are large, predatory beasts in that area at night. Or there will be. Mankillers. Very dangerous."

Despite herself, Ellen shivered and laid her head between the other's shoulders.

Adrienne sighed and made a gesture with one hand, palm up and fingers cupping. "It's a pity. Jamal . . . Jamal was so deliciously *meaty*. Like jerk pork. It was nice to have that on hand."

I'm more like dessert, Ellen thought. *Oh, Jesus. The poor man.*

"You wouldn't say *poor man* if you knew more about Jamal, *chérie*," Adrienne cast over her shoulder.

The police chief cleared his throat. "The . . . preparations for your parents' arrival are at the *casa grande*, *Doña*. From San Simeon, this time. There will be no repercussions requiring your attention."

"Oh, excellent, Chief Mendoza. I can always rely on you."

"There was a child, I am afraid. A baby girl, perhaps four months. Jose's mother is taking care of her."

Wait a minute . . . a baby?

"Good. We wouldn't want the poor mite to be traumatized. Speaking of which, it's fortunate you're both here. We're going to be having a bit of a gathering, a *do*, in May. About thirty to thirty-five guests, though I won't know for sure until they RSVP. Plus their personal renfields, lucies in some cases, and other attendants. I'll be contacting Paco for supplies and Theresa will be managing the household side, but you'll need to put the usual preparations in hand for storing the refreshments. Please consult and organize. I don't want any complications."

Bates looked . . .

Professionally interested, Ellen thought. *Mendoza, the policeman, he's gone a little gray. Refreshments for a Shadowspawn house party . . . storing the refreshments . . . oh, Christ!*

"Immediately, *Doña*," Mendoza said.

"Ma'am," Bates added. "That'll be . . . about eighty?"

"That should do," Adrienne said. "It's a party, one shouldn't stint."

"And the wastage we can expect?"

"Around fifty percent, but it's impossible to be precise; we can always use a few extra workers afterwards. I'll try to arrange the shipments starting in mid-March. Do tell Dr. Duggan."

She nodded to both, put her helmet back on and peeled off into the traffic.

I'm not going to ask. I'm not going to ask, Ellen thought, gripping her tightly. *I'm not even going to* think *about asking.*

"You'll be much happier that way," Adrienne agreed.

She pulled into Lucy Lane. "Ah, the weekly barbecue!"

A spicy, smoky smell came from Number Three, the babble of a crowd, and the sound of a guitar.

"Perhaps I'll drop by for a snack myself later," Adrienne said, reaching back and giving her a slapping pat. "Off you go, *ma douce.*"

"Hi!" Ellen said, putting her head in the open door of One Lucy Lane.

I'd like to have someone I know a little with me when I brave that crowd at Jose's. New kid . . . new lucy . . . on the block and all that.

"I'm here!" Monica replied. "Kitchen! Come on in!"

Ellen followed the scents of baking and cooking to the steamy warmth. Monica was in her frilled bib-apron again, with her jacket slung on the back of a chair.

"Good to see you again," Ellen said to her smile.

Which is actually true. I think she really is *friendly. And she must be a basically strong person or she'd be a lot crazier than she is. Eight years with Adrienne! I'm feeling pretty crazed after that many days.*

"Sorry I couldn't be here to help with the setup, but I've brought a good appetite," she said aloud. "We only stopped for a taco at lunch."

"That's what makes a barbecue a success—appetite! I'm just getting my contributions ready. The kids are already over there and things should really start in about half an hour."

Monica stopped her bustle for a moment to eye the nile twinset and earth-toned skirt Ellen had changed into; the FedEx parcels had been waiting for her at Number Five.

"*You* had a shopping weekend," Monica said brightly. "And a successful one."

Her kitchen and dining nook had a lived-in look; scrawled crayon pictures by her children tacked up to a corkboard on a cabinet, dog-eared recipe books, a slightly obsolete terminal fastened to the door of the refrigerator that had a couple of spots on the touch-screen, bowls soaking in the sinks. It smelled wonderfully of fresh bread and home-made mayonnaise and pimentos, and Ellen's stomach twisted.

The mid-floor island had a series of dishes standing ready—green salads and potato salad in bowls covered in plastic wrap, a basket of crusty homemade baguettes with a dish towel over them, and plates of cookies glistening with half-melted chocolate chips and studded with walnuts.

"Isn't Jean-Charles wonderful? I go up just for him a couple times a year, and more often so I'll have an excuse to wear some of the things! Rancho Sangre is lovely but it's not a real dress-up town. Peter and I go to the opera there, and sometimes Adrienne goes with us."

"You like opera?" Ellen said.

Monica nodded. "I know I'm not a college graduate like you—" she began, sounding a little defensive.

Ellen made a *wave to a halt* gesture. "Monica, I'm the first person— well, the first woman—in my family *ever* to go to university. If I hadn't been desperate to get out of Allentown for personal reasons *I* probably wouldn't have gone. I'm a small-towner and all my family were coal miners and steelworkers for a hundred years. And housewives and secretaries and the odd elementary teacher or whatnot."

Monica relaxed slightly. "Same here, SoCal version. I have some friends there in San Francisco, though it's, well, difficult. But Jean-Charles makes you feel like you're his little sister and he's giving you advice."

"Yes, actually, he *was* very nice," Ellen said honestly. "I really enjoyed . . . part of that. We had a dinner with one of Adrienne's Shadowspawn friends, and a lunch with her and another one and some . . . other lucies. That wasn't as much fun. Though the food was great and I tried to concentrate on that."

I'll leave out the politics, and the threat of universal destruction, and Kai. Shit, I wish I *could forget that little bitch! Not as scary as the Shadowspawn but even* more *revolting.*

"Oh, you poor darling!" Monica stopped to give her a brief hug. "The other Shadowspawn, they're *awful*. I absolutely *hate* the way they look at me. It makes me feel . . . all cold and alone and shivery inside. Though the *Doña* would never let any of them hurt us."

"Uh . . . yeah," Ellen said.

Only she *gets to hurt us. You can see how she and Adrian started in the same place. But the difference!*

She frowned for an instant. *It's odd . . . I haven't heard a thing about Adrian in days, but I feel like I know him better than I did before we broke up . . . as if the breakup didn't happen, somehow. Things will be different, once I'm out of this. And I can't just wait. I've got to keep looking for something I can do.*

The other woman looked in the oven, shook her head, and murmured: "Not quite ready." Then she went on:

"So tell me all of what you did. Did you stop for a picnic on the way up?"

"Uh . . . yeah. Thanks for the stuff you packed for us. Adrienne did this berserk driving thing, frightened the bejesus out of me, and—"

"Fed on you while the blood was juicy and tingly," Monica said succinctly. A reminiscent smile:

"I think I know the spot. She's done that to me, and before I realized that it was safe no matter *how* fast we were going I was *terrified*. Now it just *scares* me. Then I actually . . . well, she made me take off all my clothes and wash in the ocean before she drank the blood, and the water's *cold* there. I was head-to-toe stark naked goose bumps right there on the beach while she fed. Thank God it was summer and even more that nobody came along!"

"I was going to ask you about the feeding thing, a bit," Ellen said. "I've noticed that at first it just made me want to stay still—"

"But now you don't feel so paralyzed, and it gets better and better?" A smile. "Starting to really like it, aren't you?"

"Well . . . yes. I might as well, if it's going to happen regularly anyway. I'm still scared spitless beforehand."

"Oh, *that* doesn't change. It's more of a nice-scary for me now, but she still looks so . . . so *predatory* when she's about to feed on you, doesn't she?"

Ellen nodded. *Oh, yeah. Because she actually* is *being predatory and you know she's actually, really no-kidding going to bite you and* drink your fucking blood. Aloud:

"But while she's drinking and for a while afterward it's pretty nice."

"That lovely drifting feeling when you feel like you love the whole world and everything's so right? And the way the blood makes her face shine with happiness, that looks so beautiful too?"

"Mmmm, yes. What's it like if she *doesn't* bite you for a while?"

"Terrible," Monica said matter-of-factly.

She poured them each a glass of white Zinfandel and sat at the kitchen table across from her.

"First, after four days or so, you just get . . . itchy and nervous and you can't concentrate and it's all you can think about. Then, after about a week, your skin feels like it's going to crawl off of you and slither into a corner and cry. Then, after two weeks—that's the longest it's been for me—it still does, but you don't care, because you feel like your best friend just died and it's all your fault. Dr. Duggan says it gets better after that—she's helped some lucies who got retired—but I'm not interested in finding out."

"*Ouch,*" Ellen said. *Sounds like quitting smoking, only worse.* "Well, I asked."

"That you did. I want her to go on biting me as long as possible. So what else happened?"

"We went to the town house."

"God, isn't it *gorgeous*? That heated infinity pool on the edge of the terrace, where it makes you think you can swim out over the city?"

"Yeah. And, um, we made out. I mean actually made out, not the . . . painful and really absolutely frightening stuff. A little feeding with that. I didn't know if I could relax enough to actually get going, but I did."

This time the smile was sly: "Like having a tiger in the sheets with you when she gets in that mood, isn't she?"

"Ummm, yes. That's just exactly what I thought."

For good and bad. You can't forget the claws and fangs are there, even when it's purring.

"And oh, don't the little nips of feeding add to it? You just wish it could all go on forever."

"Except that your brain would explode and run out your ears or your heart would rip loose or something."

"Mmm-*hmmm*," Monica said, then continued thoughtfully: "That part was hard for me at first. I was, you know, very shy and prudish and only twenty-one, and I was very religious then. For a while I thought I must be, you know, a bad person."

"That must have been hard."

A shrug. "Sometimes life *is* hard. We both know that. And I'm not a bad person, I think. I just . . . came to terms with things. I'd never been with anyone but my husband. And now I've never been with anyone but him and Adrienne."

Ellen hesitated. *Well, let's be helpful and honest at the same time*, she thought, and went on:

"It wasn't my first time with a woman, more like the third, but it was the first time it was more than, 'Oh, this is interesting but not something I'd like to make a habit of.' So I think it's that Shadowspawn mojo at work."

The more so because Adrian is also dynamite in the sack, even more so than his sister, but that would *be oversharing. God,* even better in bed than his sister. *That's an odd thing to be able to say. Or even think.*

Monica nodded. "Well, it was never very exciting for me with Tom. I wondered what all the fuss was about. It was always over so quickly, and I wondered if other women were having a better time."

A sigh. "Now that I look back on it all, I'm sort of regretful I didn't try more to find out what I wanted. I envy you being able to go to college and have all sorts of experiences. I thought he was sort of, you know, *small* too . . ."

She made gestures with her hands. Ellen looked and said clinically:

"No, that looks about average to me. Unless he's *deformed*, size doesn't really matter. A lot of men don't have a clue and then, yes, it's sort of dull from our point of view."

"Oh, I know all about *that*."

Ellen blinked at her. *Didn't she just say she'd only—*

Monica chuckled, with the sly note back. "You know about the night-walking?"

"About how they can get out of their bodies and turn into wolves and tigers and birds?"

She laughed. "Silly, if they can turn into *birds* and things, it's even easier for them to turn into *other people*. She likes to . . . come to us lucies . . . night-walking, sometimes. Not very often—she says she wants to enjoy her birth-body while she's still got it—but every once in a while."

"Oh," Ellen said. Then . . .

Think of the implications, as Dr. Duggan said. Eerrrrk!

That must have shown on her face. Monica went on gently: "She can be anyone she's bitten. The first time she turned into *me* right in the middle of things I nearly jumped out of my skin, let me tell you!"

"Ah . . . that would be extremely strange."

"At first. After a while, it was sort of flattering. I knew I was pretty and had a good figure even after the kids, but that convinced me I was, you know, actually really hot stuff. And I felt so *naughty*. You can tell it's her—the personality's *her*, no doubt about it—but it's really *you*, too. Or she could be you with me, or me with you."

"Ah . . . yeah, I suppose it would be, umm, interesting."

Errrrk!

"And, of course, she can be a guy, night-walking."

"She can? And—"

"Everything works, right. Anyone she's bitten; Jose, Jamal, Peter, lots of others." A giggle. "Except that it's a guy who can read your mind, and knows exactly what it feels like from the other side as well."

"That sounds . . ."

Oh, Jesus, Ellen thought, as her heart skipped in alarm. *Keep calm, Ellen. It's . . . well, yes, it is weird, but weird is now your normal, and you can deal with the icky part.*

". . . like it might be fun now and then."

Monica nodded. "It's always fun when she wants it to be, whatever shape she's in. And when she wants us scared or hurt . . . well, then we just have to go with that."

Yes, we do. But I got away from being hurt. And now I'm right back in it, only worse. And you're in a position where you need to think it's all right. I won't think that. I just won't.

There was a silence for a moment, and then Monica rose, looked in the stove again, turned it off and then faced around with her hands on her hips.

"I'm not stupid, you know," she said.

Ellen blinked. "I never said—Monica, I never *thought* you were—"

"I'm not crazy either. I know she hurts me, really hurts me, and that's going to happen sometimes. Whenever she feels like it. I just . . . I've decided to accept that. She cares for me in her way, but she *needs* to hurt. The Shadowspawn aren't *like* us; they're like cats and we're mice. I was *born* a mouse, I just didn't know there were such things as cats. OK, I'm a mouse, and I'm lucky my cat wants to play with me and not finish me off."

"Do cats enjoy hurting mice?"

"Yes, they do," she said flatly. "Adrienne told me. She can read their minds . . . well, their feelings."

"Oh."

Damn. I always hoped they didn't.

"So I can take that, it's not all the time. I'm not going to let it spoil my whole life. My life was *over* when I came here. I was going to end up homeless . . . I *was* homeless. I just didn't know where to go or what to do or how to take care of my babies. Mom's sister couldn't have put us up, not for more than a few days. Things . . . things worse than anything that's happened to me here could, would, have happened. And bad things are going to happen to the whole *world*. There are good parts to this, lots of good parts, and my children and I are safe. So there!"

"I'm not judging you, Monica. You're doing what you have to do to survive, and this is my second time 'round. At least this time it isn't someone I should have been able to trust absolutely."

"Oh," Monica said, then: "*Oh.*"

She put a hand on Ellen's shoulder. "I'm so sorry." A hesitation: "Does Adrienne know? Because . . . well, you know how it is about trying not to think of something . . ."

Ellen shrugged. "I'm pretty sure she does. She did that memory-searching thing on me the day after I got here, and I had flashes of things right back to when I was about four. It . . . started a long time after that."

Monica put her fingers by her own temples and wiggled them. "Doesn't that reading your memories thing make you *itch* inside your head?"

"Yes, it does . . . Monica, you've been very good to me. I think you were right that first day: we *are* going to be friends. Let's get this stuff out and have a good time at the barbecue, shall we?"

*   *   *

Adrienne looked up and tossed aside her copy of *Architectural Digest* as the door opened. A nude Shadowspawn woman walked through onto the terrace, her face and forearms and breasts dotted with blood. Beside her sprawled and slithered a ten-foot Komodo dragon, three hundred pounds of reptilian predator with red-running serrated teeth.

"*Bonsoir, Maman, Papa,*" she said, embracing the woman and kissing her on both cheeks.

There was a faint tang of blood from the drops there—cooling, but still savory, like a slightly overripe banana.

"*Bonsoir, Adrienne . . .*" the woman said.

Then she looked down at the reptile, her tone becoming exasperated:

"Oh, for the love of *God*, Jules, I know it's your favorite new toy, but really! It *smells!*"

It did, of carrion and death. The great predatory lizard reared; there was a blurring, and it was a man on one knee with a hand touching the ground. He rose and returned Adrienne's embrace gracefully; then the pair both stood while servants cleaned them with hot, scented damp towels and dropped loose robes like Adrienne's over their heads. They and she had a family resemblance; the pair were a little below medium height, dark-haired and olive-skinned, with a look of vital, well-preserved early middle age.

Their eyes were hot gold, like pools of molten metal with darker flecks crawling through them in slow motion.

"Our baggage and servants should be here momentarily, Adrienne," Julianne Brézé said. "But it is great fun to fly in to the tower on one's own wings. And the refreshments were lovely! I was always partial to blonds."

"So am I," Adrienne said. "I have an absolutely wonderful new one you must meet. She has the most interesting mind."

"We heard," her father said. "Stealing Adrian's lucy! Not that the boy doesn't deserve it, with some of the things he's done. He always was a strange one."

"He'll come 'round eventually," Julianne said. "He's our boy at heart."

She smiled, blood crimson on her teeth before she licked them clean.

"Those two were absolutely delicious . . . They were really very thoughtful of you, *ma fille douce*. And it was so *sweet*; the man kept trying to *protect* her, and she kept calling his name. Marvelous!"

"Chivalry is not dead," Jules said. "Not Californians, from the accents?"

"No, my renfields picked them up for you . . . tourists at San Simeon, in fact. I've had them combing the possibilities, with the party in mind."

"Ah." Jules sighed. "The Enchanted Hill was such a pleasant place in its prime. A shame to think of it being overrun with gawkers."

"There were some fabulous parties there when we were a newlywed couple," Julianne agreed, and then laughed softly: "Particularly the parts that our host didn't allow into the papers."

Jules nodded. "What a pity William didn't transition successfully. Still, he was genetically marginal—a tragedy more common in his generation."

An attendant set out wine, bread, olive oil, a selection of cheeses and dried fruits and nuts. It would have been chilly for humans, but the Shadowspawn reclined comfortably around the table, nibbling and sipping, enjoying the jeweled arch of the heavens and the new moon. Wood burned in iron cages at the corners of the terrace, reflecting on the water of the pool below.

"So, what is this of *Hajime* invited to the estate?" Jules said. "Speaking of the *party*."

"Oh, Jules," Julianne said. "You're not still angry with the man for killing us?"

"It was grossly offensive," Adrienne's father replied.

Adrienne smiled. "And you've been very good about living in a reclusive way down in La Jolla since then," she said. "With me as public head of this branch of the family, the Tōkairins felt . . . easy and unthreatened. But now . . . now I think it's once more time for the Brézés to spread their wings here in California, a little."

The molten eyes turned to Adrienne. "Oh, my darling girl, whatever could you mean?" her mother said. "We were simply taking our time adjusting to the postcorporeal state."

White teeth gleamed in the night, and all three laughed. A servant's hand shook a little as she poured more of the wine. A few red drops spilled on Adrienne's wrist; she considered them and then slowly licked them up.

"We should talk. And then, if you have a taste for midnight flight, perhaps we could do some hunting together. There's a little loose end you could really get your teeth into."

"Let me give you a hand!" Peter said.

He took the big ceramic bowl of potato salad out of Ellen's arms and put it on one of the picnic tables. Others jumped to take the rest of the precariously-piled loads from the two women. People were milling around the walled rear yard, and into the house through the sliding-glass doors. Japanese lanterns bobbed overhead, casting shifting light.

More than half of the attendees were apparently the Villegas clan, but a substantial number of Monica's tennis and library-volunteer friends were there too, and their spouses and children. Fiona Duggan was attending, with a Chinese man a little younger than she. Most families seemed to have brought a dish, including enough cakes and trifles and empanadas to make her feel guilty just looking. The sheltered walled garden was comfortable if you had a jacket, but there was a constant traffic of laden plates into the house and empty ones coming out. Children ranged from teenagers—the male ones giving her wistful looks—to a small fair-haired baby being dandled and admired.

Oh. That's where the . . . little girl from San Simeon went.

She was too young to cry much, though she looked around dubiously.

She'll forget. She's really too young to know her mother's gone. And growing up a renfield . . . well, better that than some things.

The big brick barbecue pit smoked over the oakwood coals at the edge of a flagstone patio, with Jose presiding—or attempting to, as his father and uncles crowded around offering advice with bottles of beer in their hands. A long spike over one end held a yard of *carne al pastor*, thin-sliced pork loin dripping with little sputters and spurts of flame. Smells pungent and meaty and spicy drifted on the air.

Jose flourished a knife as long as his forearm and sliced off an edge from top to bottom onto a plate of tortillas. More of the flat wheatbreads warmed on a *comal*, a flatiron, supervised by Jose's rather stout mother and a doe-eyed, strikingly pretty girl who was probably his sister from the way they teased each other. Chicken thighs and breasts and drumsticks sizzled, and some hamburgers and bratwurst, and steaks that smelled as if they'd been marinated in lime and garlic and pepper . . .

"The brats I brought, they're one of Minnesota's national dishes,"

Peter said. "These things always turn into an amoeba party when Jose's putting it on."

"Amoeba party?"

"Multiplication by division. He has a lot of relatives," Peter said. "Beer or wine? The Rhône de Robles is good, but . . ."

"Beer, thanks. More cooling!"

He fetched her one, a light pale ale from the Rancho Sangre brewery.

"Maria's—Jose's mother's—adobo chicken mole is just great," he went on. "And Frank Milson, he's the husband of one of Monica's tennis buddies, makes this amazing cowboy beans and bacon thing."

She loaded her plate with everything he'd recommended, and a red chili tamale with shredded pork and an ear of roast corn, and circulated. That was prolonged by Monica dragging her off for a complete rundown on her hours at Jean-Charles' establishment to an admiring and envious group. Evidently an outfit from him was a rare and coveted reward in female renfield circles, much less a complete wardrobe.

Then she returned to sit beside Peter and the doctor at the end of one of the outdoor tables, a folding model that was a little unstable on the clipped grass.

"Hello, Dr.—"

"I've been in America a generation now, Ellen. Fiona will do," she said.

Then she grinned. "I've not brought any haggis, honest. Though it would have to be certified *organic* haggis here. You'll find few towns this size with healthier populations."

"I've noticed," Ellen said. "Why . . . oh, of course . . . Fiona."

She nodded, with an odd smile.

It's a show ranch, she thought. *But a* people *show ranch. We're the palomino horses and certified Angus cattle. Or . . . well, considering all those jokes they tell about sheep and shepherds, maybe we're the cute bouncy waggle-tailed big-eyed fleecy flock of pedigree ewes and rams.*

She concentrated on eating for a while; everything *was* good, and she'd gotten used to spicy in Santa Fe, where even the chocolates could have red chili.

From here a big pepper tree shut out most of the stars . . . and the lights of the *casa grande* over the wall and on its hill. There was a pleasant burble of voices, mostly talking in English but liberally flavored with Spanish words, sentences, inflections and occasional conversations. Ellen ate and let the ambience flow into her. It was more relaxed than she would have expected, and for a long moment she closed her eyes and imagined she was anywhere else.

What Peter was saying brought her back to reality: ". . . and I think I've got a handle on a really rigorous mathematical description of why the Power can't affect some materials—"

"I wouldn't, if I were you," Fiona said softly.

Peter blinked at her. "Why not? That's what I'm *supposed* to do."

"Indeed you are," Adrienne said, and reached around Ellen for a forkful of the potato salad on her plate.

Eeeeek!

Ellen fought not to spill her food for an instant. The talk didn't die at the *Doña*'s presence, though it did drop several octaves. Ellen noticed a number of older people glance nervously at their teenage or young-adult children. Some of those were giving Adrienne the sort of glances usually reserved for the *extremely cool*; others looked a little apprehensive themselves. The Shadowspawn was wearing a loose caftanlike robe; it looked comfortable but not the sort of wear for stealth.

How did she sneak up on me like that? Did she—

"No Wreaking needed. I just move very quietly when I want to, and you humans have the most terrible hearing," Adrienne said to her.

I wonder how far away she can read thoughts?

"That's for me to know and you to worry about, *chérie*."

And now I'll never be sure if she's standing behind me!

"No, you won't. Ah, that was a very nice shiver up the spine you had just then; it gave me this almost irresistible impulse to pounce on you. You're such a *flirt*, Ellen!"

"Not intentional," Ellen said tightly.

"As if that mattered, you teasing minx!" Adrienne snapped teeth at her playfully, then went on to Peter:

"Though the good doctor has a point too. It's occurred to me from time to time that my enthusiasm for things modern may be misleading me. That understanding the Power could have disadvantages. After all, we don't really need to understand it to *use* it, and if other people understood it better than we did . . . that could be unfortunate."

"Ummm . . ." Peter frowned. "Well, *you* could use it better if you could understand it."

"Yes, but . . . you're thinking about your work right now, aren't you?"

"Of course."

"And it might as well be in Swahili. I can read your thoughts but they're meaningless to me, even the bits of what's apparently English interspersed, and . . . is that some sort of graphic notation? Worse, because I could learn Swahili in a couple of weeks without particular effort. I couldn't follow the mathematics and theory in your head without *years* of very hard work. It's odd. I can decipher computer code easily enough."

"I think that's a different order of representation," Peter said judiciously. "It's not just knowing a language, it's knowing a lot of facts *in* the language and understanding their relationships. Knowing English doesn't make you an expert on Shakespeare. You *could* do physics, with enough time and work, I think. You pick up concepts well."

"But the number of Shadowspawn who could is quite limited, while we can all *use* the Power. It's the difference between being able to walk and being able to learn ballet."

"Why . . . oh, yes, limited talent pool," Peter said. "Bell curves."

"You get the most fascinating spike of intellectual pleasure when you realize something, Peter. It's part of what makes you interesting. Like one of those minimalist-cuisine dishes, with a little dab of ahi and a single artfully arranged French bean and a thin calligraphic drizzle of some sharp-tasting sauce. Ascetic, but a pleasure nonetheless."

Ellen looked between them, puzzled. *She's not the only one listening to a strange language.*

Adrienne turned to her for a second: "It doesn't matter if only one human in ten thousand has a natural talent for physics. That's still millions in total. For *us* one in ten thousand means one or two individuals in the entire race."

"Oh," Ellen said. She smiled. "Guess that shows why I'm *cuisine bourgeois* and not minimalist."

"You're very good of your kind, my sweet. Just as Monica and Jose are two varieties of honest American comfort food, like this potato salad or the *carne al pastor*."

Peter nodded enthusiastically, sticking to the original thread: "And science requires a *community* of trained minds. Which is why I've been so slow here."

Ellen winced; even on short acquaintance she'd noticed how he would follow a line of argument anywhere, once he had his teeth in it. And looking at Adrienne's smile . . .

That's an unfortunate metaphor.

The Shadowspawn nodded. "The last time we did anything like that was back in the nineteenth century, when Brézé adepts researched how to bring back Mhabrogast from the fragments we had."

"How?" Duggan said, obviously taking mental notes.

"Using reconstructive philology boosted by the Power . . . If you cut the possible answers down to a reasonable number, then the Power can tell which is most likely right, which gives you more information for the next deduction. That was scholarship, not real science, though."

"Do you want me to stop the work?" Peter said anxiously.

"No," Adrienne said slowly. "Not for now. It's all in your head, after all."

Then she smiled. "We can talk later, but I had some other topics in mind. Ellen has given me some *interesting* ideas on how we could pass the time agreeably. Drop by the *casa* in an hour or so and don't plan anything but rest tomorrow. Dr. Duggan, a word with you. There's a bit of an extra load for your clinic coming up, I'm afraid."

The two moved off into a corner of the yard; Adrienne ate a tortilla wrapped around some of the pork loin as they spoke with their heads close together.

"Interesting ideas?" Peter said, looking at Ellen with his eyebrows raised.

What . . . Oh, God!

"Ah . . . Peter, it's not my fault—it's *really* not my fault. I'm sorry!"

"*What* isn't your fault, Ellen?"

She took a deep breath, closed her eyes and then opened them again despite the heat she felt in her cheeks.

"Ah . . . OK, there's no way to say this without being embarrassed, at least not for me. I'm . . . well, I sort of like some kink stuff, some of the time. Fairly often. Nothing extreme! Not edgeplay."

"Like?" he said curiously, and took a swig of his beer. "Really, it's all right, Ellen. I'm not easily shocked either."

"Ah . . . I'm a bottom. Ropes and chains. I like being tied up. Tied up and beaten with whips. *Symbolic* whips! Well, partly symbolic, they sting, but . . . It's a *game*, Peter. All consensual, safe-words, that sort of thing. When Adrienne found my . . . my gear in my apartment, she thought it was hilarious. She ordered a duplicate set in San Francisco. God, we went in this shop and . . . *I* got all mine on the Internet before. I thought she was just going to use it on *me*, Peter. As a joke."

"Oh," he said quietly. "Well, whatever happens, it's not your fault, Ellen."

His mouth quirked. "Compared to direct Power jolts in your pain centers or sensitive parts, it's probably not bad. See you later."

CHAPTER SIXTEEN

"**O**h, Jesus wept, now what?" Harvey asked, panting as they toiled up the last, almost vertical stretch of the dune. "You auditionin' for a remake of *Rocky* now, boy?"

"I've gotten soft," Adrian said.

He pushed himself to the top and stopped, feeling the burn in his thighs, and the way the cool wind off the Pacific flushed the wet warmth of his soaked T-shirt to instant chill. He paused for a moment, testing his leg for any twinges from the healed wound. There was nothing but the clean strain of hard effort. Then he pulled the practice blades out of his rucksack.

"Not so much in body, as in mind. I have to be a warrior again if I'm to free Ellen and kill my sister."

"I haven't gotten *soft*. I've just gotten goddamned *old*, Adrian! Hold up!"

Seabirds wheeled overhead, or skittered long-legged through the low waves below. The air smelled wet, salt, cold, and faintly of the wrack along the high-tide line.

Harvey joined him, bending over and resting his hands on his knees for a moment to suck in more air.

"Y'know, boy," he said, taking the wooden blade. "If this were a movie instead of real life, we could have a great *montage* right now. It'd be more economical."

"Montage of what?"

"You know, little short clips of us doin' all these sweaty manly warrior things, and then they skip to the part where we're all toughened up for the fighting. Saves the waste of good killing and bikini time in an action movie."

Unwillingly, Adrian grinned at him. "Instead we have to *do* all the sweaty, manly warrior things."

"You do. Ol' buddy, you're going in close. I'm going to be hanging back with my fancy sniper rifle. Nothin' wrong with my trigger-finger yet, as opposed to my reflexes, my knees and my wind. I leave that personal-style stuff with knives to you youngsters."

Adrian snorted. "I'm fifty myself."

"Yeah, you're fifty years old chronologically and physiologically maybe twenty-eight. You-um purebred Shadowspawn prince. Me-um lowly human ape scum. I've seen quite a bit more than fifty years and I feel every physio-fuckin'-logical one of 'em."

"You have a guarantee you won't be face-to-face with Dale Shadowblade?"

Harvey straightened and looked out over the blue-gray Pacific waters and the endless ripples of white foam that stretched eastward.

"No, but I can guarantee you I'll be dead if I do. Couldn't have handled him by my own self on my best day, even in a silver suit. Less I took him by complete surprise."

"I'd like to know what he's doing now," Adrian said grimly.

"Well, I bet it ain't running up a sand dune."

"And we need to know. We need a great deal more detailed information."

"Anything from Ellen?"

"I haven't dared risk a high-link with her lately, not for more than a few moments. The multiple feedings and . . . closeness . . . mean that Adrienne is deeper and deeper into her mind. I have to be cautious."

He smiled, and Harvey looked at him dubiously.

"But there's another way, and it'll be easier than running up and down dunes. I did manage to tell Ellen about that. She agreed."

Softly: "I would never set a compulsion on her, unless she agreed."

Then Adrian's smile grew into a grin. "And now, my old . . . old . . . *old* friend . . ."

He crouched and held the knife in the ready position. Harvey groaned and took his in a thumb-on-hilt dagger grip, his other hand stiffened into a blade across his chest. They began to circle.

"Age and treachery beat youth and strength," Harvey grumbled.

Adrian lunged, his feet sending up spurts of sand. Harvey countered with a backhand slash to the face; he dodged and dove to the side with a shoulder roll that brought him back upright out of reach.

"But I have both age's treachery *and* youth's strength," Adrian taunted genially.

Harvey said: "Just makes you want to—"

Harvey launched himself forward, pivoting on his hands and kicking out. One boot thudded painfully into Adrian's thigh, and he fought not to topple. The edge sliced upward in a curve that whipped the edge across his abdomen.

"—*cry*, don't it?"

"I'm going for a drive before I go home," Ellen said.

"God, how can you have any energy left?" one of Monica's tennis-club friends said. "After beating us all into the ground on the court."

They sat around a table not far from Rancho Sangre's civic center pool. The early-May sunshine was warm, this Sunday afternoon, another perfect golden Californian day. All had tall frosty glasses of fresh lemonade or iced tea or soda before them—or in one or two cases, something stronger. The place was more like a private spa than the usual bare-bones public facilities towns had; there was a pleasant clubhouse with a café, a bright well-equipped gym and a big circular swimming pool with a fountain in the center, besides tennis courts and much else. The yelling children splashing in the water made a pleasant burring background to conversation, and the smell of chlorine mingled with cut grass and lilac blooming along a wall.

"Ellen's improving our games," Monica said proudly. "She beat me to flinders back in February, but now it's May and she just had me running like a mad thing!"

The other women ranged from their twenties through late middle-age, and initially hadn't seemed much different from any other clutch of small-town, middle-class Californians. One was head of the town library; another principal of the high school; there was a pediatrician, a dentist and the town clerk, and several teachers. The housewives had an architect, a surveyor, the winery and dairy factory managers and others of like ilk for husbands. Dr. Duggan was there, along with her older daughter and several of the others' offspring, one of whom was attending Cal Poly and had given Ellen a serious game.

Let's see . . . most of them have these little black-sun-and-trident pendants or bracelets somewhere visible; maybe some keep theirs tucked away, like I do. And apart from that everything's normal . . . until suddenly it isn't.

"Monica," one of the matrons said. "Do you know if the *Doña* is going to have an initiation ceremony soon?"

Like that, Ellen thought. The simple physical well-being of hard exercise and a hot shower faded. *Then it* isn't *normal, like that.*

"Yeah," a honey-blond teenager named Sherry added.

She was the coed's younger sister and about sixteen, very pretty in a wholesome way, but the type a student from India she'd known at NYU had said was called a *tung admi* where he came from, a tight lady. In American terms she had no more than ten years before a lifetime battle with the waistline started. Sherry went on with a note of complaint:

"Like, I'm *months* overdue, we've taken all the classes and practiced and watched the videos and everything. I want my pendant before we take the SATs!"

Like that. It's the normal adolescent lust to grow up, I can remember that pretty vividly, but . . .

The freckle-faced youngster looked at Monica. "I . . . ah, Ms. Darton, is getting bitten as cool as some people say? A really big rush?"

"Not the first time, dear," Monica said, to her visible disappointment.

"I *told* you, Sherry," the college girl said. "But you'd rather listen to junior year geeks who *don't* know what they're talking about."

Sherry looked mutinous, and Monica went on gently:

"It doesn't hurt, only a little sting, but you're just . . . very calm, the first few feedings. After that, yes, it starts to feel extremely nice, but that'll only happen if you become a lucy, and that's not likely."

Calm, as in, you can't move while you watch them drink your blood, Ellen thought. *Of course, before the feeding you feel* scared, *or in the case of my first time* agonizing pain and bewilderment and terror *and then afterwards you feel horrified. Or maybe not, if you grew up with the idea.*

"What's involved in this initiation?" she asked aloud. "I've only been here a couple of months, and I'm a lucy and a new one at that, so . . ."

The college girl answered: "Oh, there's this ceremony, with your family and friends. Everyone sort of dresses up—"

"Black robes with hoods," her mother said. "That's traditional. It's held up at the *casa grande*. There's a big room just for initiations. Like a chapel. In a way."

"— and there's chanting and kneeling and stuff like that, and you pledge yourself to the Brézés and the Shadowspawn."

"*Our blood and souls are thine, thou who will live and rule when we are long dust,*" her mother said in a reminiscent tone, obviously quoting from memory. "*Take, drink. With our blood and lives and bodies we worship thee.*"

"Then the candidate goes up—"

"*Naked!*" the younger girl said breathlessly, her eyes glittering.

"—well, yeah," her older sister said, with affected worldliness. "You wear this white robe, and then you stand up and let it slip off and go up in front of everyone. Which is *so* totally *hideous* if you're overweight and you've got a big wobbly butt or something like poor Madison did on my night. I thought she was going to *die* of embarrassment right there, or cry, or hurl. Or if you're a guy and *little* like Bob Tyler. So watch out, Sherry."

"I am *not* fat! I've got a twenty-five waist!" Sherry said hotly.

"Didn't say you were. But think about that next time you see a milk shake. At least you can *do* something about it, which is more than poor Bob could."

Turning back to Ellen: "And you lie on this stone altar thing—it's got padding—and you put your arms around the *Doña* while she bites your neck and feeds on you while everyone watches. She's naked too, and God, what a *body*. Like Monica said, Sherry, it just makes you feel . . . calm. Not much blood, a sip from each, and then you get your pendant and a *black* robe and everyone gives you a hug and a kiss on both cheeks and you sing."

Her mother crooned a verse:

"Spawn of Shadows
Rule our nighted hearts—"

The elder daughter nodded. "Then there's a big party. It's a bit like a sorority or fraternity pledge."

Sorority Sisters from . . . Heeeellll, Ellen thought, keeping an interested smile on her face. *Oh, Christ!*

"Or like a first communion, in other places," someone else said helpfully. "Or a bar mitzvah."

An older woman tinkled the ice in her drink; she was a well-preserved sixty-something, neat in her tennis whites and billed cap, with blue-white hair and a fresh pink face and eyes like an ancient snake.

"Tame, tame, tame. Now, in *my* day, when Don Jules and Doña Julianne were heads of the family here, if you were pretty you were likely to get *deflowered* as well as bled, right there on the altar in front of everyone. Don Jules had my brother, Henry, on our initiation night, and then me right after. *My* mother fainted dead away watching. But Mother wasn't born here, of course."

"Oh, *wow!*" Sherry said, her face wavering between fascination and dread. "That would be so totally *extreme.*"

"Yes," the older woman said softly, swirling her drink again and looking into the distance.

Then, in a normal tone: "*That* changed my perspective on things, let me tell you. Of course, most girls were virgins at sixteen, in my day. Are you, Sherry?"

The girl's mother glowered at her as Sherry blushed crimson. Monica put in:

"Doña Adrienne doesn't do that very often. Though," she added thoughtfully, "her parents *are* visiting, so maybe they'll give you an initiation to remember, Sherry."

"Well, I'm off," Ellen said brightly, looking at her watch.

"Would you like to catch a movie later?" Monica said. "I'm taking Josh and Sophie to the new Disney, the *Snow White* remake. We *finally* got 3-D here."

"I've, ah, got a heavy date tonight," Ellen said. "Up at the *casa.* I'm supposed to meet the *Doña's* parents, and then, ah, you know. I was hoping I could drop by your place to make sure the dress is exactly right. She said *look nice.*"

And she said don't plan on anything energetic tomorrow, *too. Which means she's got something . . . whimsical planned. Oh, Jesus.*

"Oh, of course," Monica said. "Have fun on your drive! See you about seven, then."

Everyone else waved or called goodbyes. Ellen went out through the stucco and wrought-iron entrance to the civic center, got into her Volt and let her head drop onto the steering wheel while she struggled to keep her breath even. The knowledge that she couldn't just wake up and be back in a sane world was a cold, thick lump in her stomach. She craved a cigarette and a couple of stiff vodka-and-orange-juice mixes.

I'm craving being bitten, too, she thought. *It's been everyone else but me for the last six days and I need it. My skin's itching and I'm starting to resent the others. I want it and I'm scared of the other stuff she's going to do to me and I still want it.*

"I've got to get *out* of this place!" she said to herself, resisting the urge to beat her forehead rhythmically on the padded surface of the wheel. "Got to, got to, *got to!*"

The temptation to just point the car in any direction but west and accelerate was overwhelming. She fought it down and began taking deep breaths: in until the chest creaked, hold for the count of three, slowly exhale, repeat. It had seemed silly when she'd first started it after her therapist talked her into yoga classes years ago, but it *did* help. When she was sure her hands wouldn't shake anymore, she turned the key. The quiet hum of the electric motor sounded as she pulled out into the street; a glance at the gauge showed nine-tenths charge, enough to get all the way to Paso Robles and most of the way back before the gasoline engine kicked in.

Warm air poured in as she drove; the outskirts of town passed quickly, with its *Rancho Sangre Sagrado elevation 666 pop. 3964* sign. Then a stretch of countryside mostly in vines and orchards and olive groves with the odd horse-ranch, rising towards hills westward where the grass was turning gold between tongues of forest, more open to the east. And then the outskirts of Paso Robles itself, with a scatter of outlet stores and fast food . . .

It looks so normal *I could cry,* she thought. *I even love the sight of some boarded-up stores.*

She parked in a side street near the town center; she was wearing a pants-and-blouse ensemble with a worked-leather belt and a sun hat, casual-chic. The man at the podium-desk of the Craftsman restaurant greeted her with a smile.

"Mr. Ledbetter will be waiting," she said.

Why did I say that? Who is Ledbetter? *What am I doing here—*

Adrian rose from the table as she entered the starkly elegant room. For a moment time and memory dropped away; then they came crashing back into her mind, like a surf-wave that crumbles a sand-castle on the beach. Tears started from her eyes, but she blinked them away in her eagerness to *see*.

He was smiling at her, but there was something grave in the expression as well. Only a little taller than her, but with a hard, slender masculinity; after not seeing him for three months she was struck again by his *presence*, the way he dominated any room he was in. His face was tanned dark, so that the golden flecks in his eyes stood out more vividly, and there were sun-highlights in his raven hair.

He looked more stark than he had in Santa Fe, but with some of the distance gone from his expression, less of the remoteness that had frustrated her. She started towards him and extended her hands; they were trembling slightly.

Adrian caught them in his, and kissed each one gently.

"*Ma belle* Ellie," he said softly. "It has been so very long."

They flowed together.

Harvey cleared his throat

Damn, Adrian thought.

He broke the kiss, pulling himself away from the touch and taste and the lovely tormenting scent that was like a memory of peach and lilac and apple blossom.

"Ellen, my old friend Harvey Ledbetter. Sort of a mentor in my youth, an unofficial elder brother always, brother-in-arms for many years, and my comrade in this business."

Ellen extended a hand. Adrian found himself surprised at how much he wanted these two to like each other. The Texan smiled as he shook, an expression that transformed his homely lined face.

"Pleased to meet you, Ms. Tarnowski. Glad to see what Adrian thought was worth fighting for. Can't say as I disagree, offhand."

She laughed. "I won't say any friend of Adrian's a friend of mine," she said. "But any *really good* friend of Adrian who risks his life for Adrian and for me is a friend of mine."

Harvey shrugged. "Adrian and I have saved each other's butts so often we lost count years ago," he said.

"Harv, could you give us ten minutes?"

The older man hesitated, then said: "Sure."

"Do we have time?" Ellen said.

They sat, each holding the other's hands across the table. Hers were warm and slender and strong in his, still with the thumb-callus a tennis player developed on the right hand.

"We will make time," Adrian said decisively. Then: "How much I wish we were just . . . enjoying a dinner together."

"Me too. Oh, *yeah*."

He cleared his throat. "I'm nervous . . . I know this is short notice, Ellie. But we are at war, and that says *hurry*."

He freed one hand to reach into the pocket of his jacket, and brought out a small velvet case. She looked at him, and he nodded. She took it and snapped it open; within was a plain band of platinum and gold, with a small flawless diamond. His heart tensed with fear as she sat motionless for most of a minute. Then she looked up, with tears jewelling her eyelashes.

"Will *yes* do? Even if I can't keep the ring right now?"

He felt his grin grow. "It is an abominable cliché, but you have made me a very happy man."

Harvey arrived back from his walk around the block at the same time as the wine; Roederer Brut L'Ermitage, *Tête de Cuvée*. Not technically champagne—it came from Mendocino—but more than close enough, and *good* champagne at that. The sommelier popped the cork and poured the tall flutes; Ellen extended hers towards him, and he to her. They sipped; tastes like baked apples and buttery crust, apricot and delicate vanilla bean flowed across his tongue with the tickle of the bubbles.

Then all three of them clicked their glasses together. "To better luck than I ever had," Harvey said. "Three divorces," he added to Ellen.

Adrian cocked an eyebrow at him. "Yes, but you were always drunk when *you* proposed, Harv. Marry inebriated, repent at leisure."

"I see you *are* good friends," she said. "Men don't insult each other that way unless they are."

Adrian spread his hands. "And now to dinner and business," he said. "Barbarism, but there you are. I want to proceed to the wedding and the honeymoon as soon as humanly . . . in a way . . . possible."

Ellen's face went grim. "Me too. Christ, that place . . . it really gets to me. Especially when I can't remember *this*."

She frowned. "Though Adrienne says sometimes . . . not that she can tell anything specific . . . but that I don't seem as *crushed* as I should be."

Harvey sucked air through his teeth, and Adrian nodded.

"You don't consciously remember, but your emotional *attitudes* do. She thinks we have only a base-link, and would be hoping that your torment would slide over to me. We could not keep up this pretense forever."

"Honey," Ellen said, "I *so* do not want to think of the terms *forever* and *Adrienne* in the same sentence! The more so as it's literally possible."

Just then the appetizers arrived. "I ordered for you," Adrian said to them both. "I hope you don't mind."

"Adrian, you always picked something interesting," Ellen said. She grinned: "Now I know it's because you have *superhuman* taste."

He shrugged; you had to be careful about that too, if you could taste things others couldn't. The waiter set his burden before them; little plates of braised Berkshire pork belly with caramelized apples and celery root, herb-roasted meatballs with buttermilk potato puree and green peppercorns, and crisp calamari . . .

"Now, tell us of everything you have observed," Adrian said, nibbling on one of the meatballs. "*Everything*. However insignificant."

She did; she didn't have a trained agent's skills, but she was observant and intelligent, and so new to the world of the ancient conflict that she saw details others might have missed. Adrian felt himself hiss a little when he heard his own mother and father had arrived; his mouth twisted a little at the news of the mysterious baby.

"The parents are dead," he said. "If my mother and father flew in, they would be ravenous for blood when they assumed human form again. Transformation drains the Power. And it is a . . . courtesy to provide a kill for a guest, among Shadowspawn."

"Ew," Ellen said; she stopped chewing for a moment, then resumed doggedly. "I haven't met them yet. I'm supposed to go up to the *casa grande* for that tonight."

"Be very careful."

"Hey, I'm careful *all the time!*" Then she stopped and looked at both of them. "You aren't taking notes?"

"That would be bad tradecraft," Harvey said, popping one of the calamari into his mouth. "Especially for this. You can remember detail if you know how. Mnemonic training's traditional in the Brotherhood, too."

"What *is* the Brotherhood?" Ellen asked.

"You've heard of witchfinders?" Harvey said.

"Didn't . . . they sort of torture innocent old women and that sort of thing?"

Harvey's mouth crooked. "Enemy propaganda . . . no, a lot of them really did do *that sort of thing*. But some of them were after the *real* evil magicians."

Adrian nodded. "Like my unesteemed ancestors. The Brézés were leaders of the Order of the Black Dawn for centuries."

Ellen nodded sharply. "That thing everyone in Rancho Sangre wears—" She pulled out her pendant.

"That is their symbol. Was theirs, and is now the sigil of the Council of Shadows. The Order were . . . Satanists originally, or for a very long time. Black magicians, *loup-garou*. They could use the Power. A little, weakly—"

"About like I can," Harvey said cheerfully.

Adrian nodded. "And as the Order set out to find its counterparts, so the Brotherhood did, until both were worldwide. Unfortunately the Order was much, much stronger by then."

"We don't have time for general background," Harvey warned.

Adrian dipped his head. "Now, Ellie, here is what I will be doing, as much as you need to know. I will be attending the . . . Prayer for

Long Life. Invitations were sent widely. One to a recently deceased Shadowspawn."

"Wilbur Peterson." Harvey took up the tale.

He produced a file from the attaché case. "This is a case where written records are necessary."

He slid a photograph across the table. It showed a man in his thirties, dressed in an archaic white-tail jacket and black bow tie, smiling with a cocktail glass in his hand. There was a vague resemblance to Adrian, and the hand on the stem had three fingers of equal length, but his hair was lighter.

"He died . . . body-death . . . in 1960," Harvey said. "By then he'd already sorta retired up to a little country place he had in Sonoma. Got more and more reclusive, then got rid of most of his renfields, then stopped talkin' to other Shadowspawn except to warn 'em off. 'Bout two months ago, he sat up all night with a case of bubbly, and toasted the sun."

Ellen looked a question at Adrian, and he answered: "Unlike the sign of the cross, silver works, and the aetheric form is just as vulnerable to sunlight as the legends say."

"Tanning lamps?" she said hopefully.

"Not powerful enough and they don't have the full range of particles. Annoying, merely. Direct sunlight for more than a few seconds is always deadly."

"Why did this man . . . this Shadowspawn . . . stay up and die, then? When he could live forever?"

Adrian shrugged. "Why do men commit suicide? Probably he had grown tired of his un-life. The weight of grief and loss becomes too much."

"Adrienne said that's why so many of the really old ones *hate* the modern world and want to destroy it completely," Ellen said.

Adrian smiled grimly. "She is not as different as she thinks, Ellie. She wants to stop it *now*."

"So you'll pretend to be this guy?"

"And set up your rescue; the Brotherhood are helping us. My own birth-body will be nearby, with Harvey guarding it. A night-walker whose body still lives cannot be told from a postcorporeal."

For an instant Ellen rested her forehead on her fingertips, and her elbows on the table.

"I wish . . . we could just *go*."

Adrian shook his head. "She would be able to haunt your dreams, and to know where you were, even if we buried ourselves in a silver-lined cave."

He saw her stiffen, and then scrabble in her purse. "Here."

It was an ordinary flash memory card of the type Office Depot and a hundred others sold, a cheap twenty-four gigabyte model.

"There's another lucy, a man named Peter Boase, we're friends," she said quickly. "He was a physicist at Los Alamos. This Council of Shadows sent Adrienne to kill him."

Harvey raised one eyebrow. "Adrienne's a bit high powered for that sort of routine duty. They must have taken him serious. So why ain't he dead, instead of providin' the lady with refreshments and frisky recreation?"

"Adrienne has him working for *her*. I remember, a while ago, he was talking about *why* the Power can't grasp silver. I didn't understand a word of it, and neither did Adrienne."

Adrian took the chip. "Now that is very interesting," he said.

"He was, ah, occupied up at the *casa grande* again yesterday, and sort of stayed in bed today, so I dropped in and copied everything."

Adrian hissed. "Dangerous, so dangerous. The very desire to conceal something stands out like a flag to the Power!"

"I'm very much aware she can read my mind, Adrian. It's like being naked in public *all the time*."

He flushed and made a gesture of apology. Harvey glanced at the younger man. "Not just a pretty face," he said slowly. "To think that clear with a Wreakin' messing up your head . . . not easy."

"Harvey, take this," Adrian said, tapping the chip with one finger. "The Brotherhood must examine it."

"How does it feel?" Harvey asked. "Got any baggage weighing its paths?"

Adrian gripped it in one hand. The other made three precise motions over it, and he murmured under his breath:

"*Or-ok-sszee, m'naiii-t—*"

After a moment he opened his eyes again. "Now, that is extremely strange," he said.

"Not important?"

"*Nothing*," he said. "Neither important nor unimportant. It is as if there are no potentials *at all* attached to this. As if its world-line vanishes rather than spraying out into a fan of possibilities."

"Hmmm. That *is* odd," Harvey said.

Then Adrian turned back to Ellen. "I am so proud of you!" he said. "Your mind is supple. It bends, but like good steel it does not break and springs back when the pressure is removed."

She shrugged. "I'm proud of myself, right now!"

The main courses arrived. Harvey looked at the food and grinned.

"Black truffle agnolotti, chanterelles, Loch Duart salmon, brown butter béarnaise . . . that's your idea of a working dinner?"

To Ellen: "You probably know what a food snob this boy is."

"*Oh*, yes," she said, and rolled her eyes. "I remember once it was late and I suggested we stop at Blake's Lottaburger, and he just *looked* at me. Like I had some skin disease or something. Then he insisted on driving an extra *twelve miles* to Bobcat Bites."

Adrian laughed. "I have been eating worse than that, often enough lately," he said defensively. "You shouldn't take anything this *salop* says seriously. He is the one who taught me to cook—and well, too."

The desserts came out, and for a moment they could relax and be happy. Then he reached into his jacket and held up a piece of paper. Her eyes fell on the glyph and fixed, unwinking. Then her fork went back to her whiskey-raisin carrot cake.

"Oh, God, Adrian, I wish you were here," she murmured softly, as they rose and left.

"Name of a black *dog*!" Adrian swore. "I have to leave her like that . . . I cannot even pay for the whole dinner!"

"Now *that's* petty. And if you're feelin' helpless . . . well, it's a lot worse for her, ol' buddy."

CHAPTER SEVENTEEN

"How do I look?" Ellen said.

Monica made a turning motion. "Wonderful, actually. I wish I had your figure."

"You do," Ellen said, turning around slowly.

The shoes were low-heeled, but it was a while since she'd worn anything but sneakers and sandals and flats. The coral below-the-knee dress had a princess seam bodice and flared skirt, under an open-fronted turquoise jacket with a neckline gathered into the band. She went on:

"Pretty much exactly my figure. You could wear this with only a little alteration."

"No, I *used* to have it. You're . . . thirty-five, twenty-four, thirty-five?"

"Just about."

"Add an inch or so all 'round for me. And I'm a little shorter than you. Maybe I should start running every morning too."

"An inch isn't a real difference, and you're certainly welcome to join Peter and me!"

"I think you both look pretty," Joshua said.

Ellen smiled at him; at ten-going-on-eleven he was just after the age when boys find women totally uninteresting as such, but well before actual reflexive lust snaps in, and he looked at her with an almost detached critique. His sister, Sophie, was simply entranced by the dress, taking in the details over and over again. They were both in their pajamas—rabbits on hers, some sort of tentacled thing on his—which fit in with the well-kept but very slightly worn look the living-room had, the inevitable result of two active children in an ordinary-sized house for years.

"You're going to meet the *Doña*'s parents," Sophie said. "I wish *I* could meet them. They're probably really cool."

They're mass murderers, Ellen thought. *I've been perfectly glad to put this off for a while. But no point in scaring a kid.*

The door opened, and Adrienne walked in, dramatic in a classic black dress with platinum and sapphires on throat and wrists. Both the children stood politely; she smiled at them, nodded to Monica, then raised a brow at Ellen.

"My, Jean-Charles did not labor in vain! Impressive! Well, nearly time to go. I thought we'd stroll up. My parents are eager to meet you, now that they're well settled in with their things."

Suddenly Joshua spoke. "Ma'am?"

"Yes, Josh?"

"Do . . . you drink my mom's blood? Is that what her being your lucy means?"

Monica started and flushed. "*Joshua!*"

Adrienne chuckled and made a soothing gesture. "You can't avoid rumors in a renfield town, Monica, and they're getting to the age when little people hear things. Better they hear from us than in the school-yard at recess."

She turned to Joshua, bending a little so that their faces were level.

"Yes, that's part of what being my lucy means. I'm a Shadow-spawn . . . you've heard that name?"

"Like . . . like vampires? With superpowers?"

"Vampires are just a story. Very silly stories. Shadowspawn are for real. We aren't catching, like a cold or the flu; we're born that way. Superpowers . . . well, we can do many things your type of people can't."

She sat on the sofa and folded a piece of paper there into an ori-gami bird, holding it out on her palm when she finished. Then she hummed . . . and the wings of the bird began to vibrate to the same rhythm. She slowly lowered the hand, and the bird stayed suspended, hovering. Then it moved, circling and swooping around the children. Sophie gave an exclamation of awed delight as it paused before her face, and Joshua's mouth fell open slightly as it circled his head before it flew back to the table, stopped and hovered, then settled gently down.

"It's called the Power, Josh, and it's . . . magic, really. That's why we Shadowspawn rule the whole world, as I do here in Rancho Sangre. And to use the Power, we need to drink blood."

He swallowed, and visibly gathered himself, his face flushed with determination.

"Does . . . does it hurt her when you drink the blood?"

"No," Adrienne said easily. "I only take a little at a time from her, and that doesn't hurt. It's fun for both of us."

He was silent, but visibly unconvinced. She sighed and patted the sofa cushion to her right.

"Monica, I think they're old enough. Come here."

Monica hesitated, then sat beside her and cleared her throat.

"Come here, Josh, Sophie," she said, with a creditable effort at calm. "Stand right here where you can see things."

They did; Sophie clutched at her brother's hand, her face a little pale, blinking rapidly.

"Now watch closely, and you'll see it's not anything bad," Adrienne said.

Ellen flushed herself, with embarrassment. *I'd feel even more weird if I turned around or went out*, she thought, and tried to will herself invisible. *And, God, I want the bite myself right now. Want it! Want it!*

The children gasped as lips peeled back from Adrienne's teeth in a way human equipment couldn't quite do. Monica sighed, slid her arms around the Shadowspawn and leaned across her lap, turning her head and arching her neck with her eyes closed. Sophie gave a little cry and then put a hand to her mouth as Adrienne's head moved in the precise predatory grace of the feeding bite. Monica sighed again, a longer sound, and stroked the back of the Shadowspawn's neck, her face soft with pleasure.

The children relaxed as their mother straightened up a few seconds later and smiled.

"See?" she said, her voice slightly dreamy. "Just this little nick."

She pulled a Kleenex from the box by the couch and touched it to her neck; the small incision had already clotted when she took it away and went on:

"And it feels nice while she drinks from me, really. It's . . . natural. Like the way flowers make nectar for hummingbirds. It's what we human people are for."

Sophie looked calmer and nodded. Joshua hesitated again, then said:

"Ma'am? Sometimes when we come back from Gran's, Mom . . . looks like she hurts."

A little Tabasco sauce in the Bloody Mary tonight, Monica, Ellen thought grimly.

"Ah," Adrienne said. She paused, looking up a little in thought, then went on to him:

"That's because we play together in other ways, too, and sometimes we have so much fun we play a bit rough. You play soccer, don't you?"

"Yes, *Doña*," he said.

"Well, sometimes that gets rough, eh? Someone gets their knee skinned or a bruise. Sometimes they even cry. But it's all fun, *hein*?"

A dubious nod.

"It's a bit like that. You're really not old enough to understand about those things yet. Now, you and your sister come here. Stand with your heads together. That's right . . ."

Her hands came up and cupped their heads, thumb at the corner of the eye and little finger behind their skulls. Her voice dropped to a murmur as she brought her face close to theirs.

"It's time for little children to be sleepy. You're sleepy, aren't you?"

"Yes . . ." they both said slowly, in eerie unison.

"And you're happy that I answered your questions, aren't you? Now if anyone says silly things, you'll just laugh because you know the real truth."

"Yes . . ."

"And you'll be glad that your mom is someone very special for me and gives me what I need, won't you?"

"Yes . . ."

"So why don't you let her tuck you into bed and kiss you good night?"

Monica rose and took their hands; they were yawning and stumbling as she led them away. Over her shoulder she mouthed: *Thank you.*

All the Lucy Lane yards had rear gates that led to the *casa*'s gardens.

"That . . . actually was rather nice of you," Ellen said as they went through Monica's and walked up the stairs. "All things considered."

"I like watching human children gambol, like lambs and puppies. I suppose it's an instinct to preserve the stock of our prey."

"Oh," Ellen said. "It was still actually sort of nice . . . for someone as evil as you are."

"Ellen, you have absolutely no *conception* of how evil I am. Though I am having a wonderful time gradually showing you."

"I'd bet Monica thinks it was nice."

"She did," Adrienne chuckled. "And believe me, I've already thought of several rather *rough* ways for her to show her appreciation."

"How was the blood?"

"Surprisingly good with so little priming. Almost bubbly. Refreshing, like a sip of sparkling cider."

The truck backed into the warehouse. Adrian helped Harvey heave the big sheet-metal doors closed, the edges sharp under his gloved hands. When it was done the overhead lights came on, two long-endurance fluorescents making a puddle of visibility in the mostly empty space. The vehicle was an anonymous Chinese-made model of no great size, but low on its shocks; he wrinkled his nose at the exhaust stink in the confined space, and at the older smells of oil soaked into the concrete floor and nameless cargoes.

Harvey shot the bolts that held the exterior door closed. A man and a woman jumped out of the truck's cab, dressed in nondescript dark clothing, boots and knit caps, both youngish and moving well. They nodded to him as they came around to open the padlocked rear door of the truck, then turned to face him.

"Anjali Guha," the woman said. "This is Jack Farmer."

Guha was slender and fine-boned and dark, and spoke faultless English with the slightest trace of a singsong accent; Farmer was of medium height but broad in the shoulders, blue-eyed and with close-cropped sandy hair and a snub nose. They both shook hands; the brief contact confirmed what he'd suspected, that they were high enough on the Alberman scale to Wreak consciously.

Somewhere between Harvey and Sheila Polson, he judged.

They could feel his Power, as well, and bristled slightly at it. There was an ironic twist to his smile.

The Brotherhood has become an asylum for those with enough Shadowspawn genes to Wreak, but not enough to be accepted by the Council, he thought.

Both were armed; he could feel the warded knives, the man's point-up under his left armpit, the woman's on her back with the hilt just below her collar.

"This is what we could cull from Wilbur Peterson's stuff," Guha said. "And what we could duplicate that would have been there if the *banchut* hadn't gone hermit."

"Gone batshit," Farmer said, and smiled. "A batshit *banchut.*"

"Right. Krishna, but you've never seen such a ruin. Cobwebs, dust, stalactites of plaster under the leaks in the roof, stacks of ancient magazines and newspapers, reels and reels of old film movies worn out from being played over and over . . . old, dried moldy bodies, too, thrown down the stairs into the basement. And the *smell.* Like a ghoul's lair."

"Just a couple of old renfields, enough to guard him by daylight," Farmer said. "They were still wandering around stunned after he stayed up to kiss sun, when we moved in."

"They're dead, I suppose?"

"Yeah," Farmer said; his voice held a gloating overtone. "And we got a *full* debriefing from the bastards first."

Guha gave him a glance. "Farmer, don't be more of a *banchut* yourself than you can help, OK? It has to be done. You don't have to enjoy it so much."

"They're *traitors*," Farmer hissed with sudden vehemence, the sound like a snake in the darkened empty room.

"You can both play a renfield?" Adrian asked.

He shot a glance at Harvey. The older man was leaning one haunch against the open back of the truck, his arms crossed. He gave an ironic shrug and smile, as if to say: *They're what's available.*

"We've done it before," the senior Brotherhood operative said; *she* shot a look at her partner. "We're still alive."

"For days at a time, in a gathering this size?" Adrian persisted.

"No," she said reluctantly. "Never with more than three Shadow-spawn, and never for more than a few hours. There *aren't* Shadow-spawn gatherings this size very often."

"This will be considerably more difficult than a brief impersonation. Stick close to me; close as glue. Say nothing that you don't have to—"

"We're not working for you, Brézé—" Farmer began.

Adrian crossed his wrists in a sudden snapping motion, the backs of his fists outward. Thumb and forefinger came out, thumbs touched . . .

"Sseii-*tok*!" he snarled.

Focus gripped him. Possibilities shifted, like planes of greased crystal sliding over each other. A sensation ran up his spine, and something went *snap* behind his eyes.

Farmer had begun to recoil into battle-stance. One heel hit an oil-spot, at precisely the angle needed to make the rough gripping surface of the boot turn frictionless. He went over backward with a muffled yell, turning to a yelp as his shoulder struck the ridged steel of the truck's folded loading ramp. His hand flashed towards the hilt of his hidden knife, but Adrian had flowed forward, and the edge of his foot rested on the man's throat.

They both knew that required only a flex to crush his larynx and leave him choking and drowning in his own blood.

"Listen to me, imbecile. Will you be sensible?"

A nod, and he eased up on Farmer's throat, ready to smash down in a stamp-kick if he went for the knife.

"I'm in this operation on my own terms, not under Brotherhood discipline. You're under *my* command in this. Your life may be worthless, but mine is not, and my fiancée is infinitely more important than either of us. Every one of the guests in this circus of demons could crush you like a *cockroach* at the least suspicion of what you really are. Understood?"

The man glared, then nodded.

"Show me you mean it."

Another glare, but he let his shields slip enough for Adrian to sense agreement—qualified, grudging, but real. He stepped back and extended a hand.

"We're on the same side, Farmer," he said.

The other man took it, and Adrian pulled him to his feet. Guha snorted.

"Let's get this over with. If we're going to play renfields . . ."

They went around the other side of the truck. Harvey sighed, went with them, and returned with two small disposable hypodermics full of dark venous blood.

"Here you go," he said, rolling his eyes. "Preservin' the proprieties."

"Tell me which one is Farmer's, so I will know why my stomach's upset," Adrian replied dryly . . . but quietly.

He shot them both into his mouth with a thumb on the plunger and swallowed; the taste was mildly pleasant, about like a drink of cold soda-water on a hot day. It was fresh, at least; and he could display a convincing base-link to both of them if someone prodded at them with the Power. A Shadowspawn had to be able to protect his renfields.

Guha was rubbing at the sleeve of her jacket as she came back, and talking to her partner:

"And he's *already* given us intel that may mean the survival of the Brotherhood, Jack," she said.

Harvey spoke: "Something *that* important?"

"We can develop hardened refuges against EMP," she said, apparently missing the slight tinge of irony. "And . . . well, I don't know officially, but we've got teams going to the Congo and we're gearing up some bio-labs."

Adrian nodded. Keeping the Brotherhood from disappearing in the wreck was a more realistic plan than trying to stop Operation Trimback altogether . . .

But I find myself less enamored of realism, these days. If I was truly realistic I'd be back in Santa Fe, drinking myself into a stupor. Or doing what Peterson did.

"Let's get this stuff out. I have to familiarize myself with it."

The trunks were just that; old-style, brass-bound leather and wood. Most of the clothes and gear within had a deep musty smell of age, beneath the mothballs.

"The newer ones will have to do," he said. "Discard the rest. We must persuade them that he was never so far gone as to neglect everything."

Adrian sorted until the remaining garments were presentable to a Shadowspawn nose; all deeply out of fashion, but that wasn't unknown among older postcorporeals. And there were a few private possessions—a golden locket with a picture of a woman in the short hair and cloche hat of the 1920s, a massive wind-up wristwatch, a collection of letters and a few books.

"*Jalna*, by Mazo de la Roche," Adrian said, reading the title on the spine.

It was leather-bound, worn but almost desperately well cared for, and it had the author's signature on the flyleaf and a publication date of 1927.

"He had that one with him when he sat up for sunrise," Guha said. "Must have meant something to him at one time."

"Or just a link to life. I had better read it, and the letters," Adrian said thoughtfully. "There is a chance he knew my parents, and they will be at the Rancho. Still, Shadowspawn are no better than others at remembering small details for sixty or seventy years."

"These are the weapons," Farmer said; no Shadowspawn would travel unarmed.

A revolver, the grips black bone; he could feel silver on the interior pawls that moved the cylinder and the spring that drove the hammer.

"Webley Mk. VI," Harvey said with interest.

He took the weapon, broke it open and examined it, smiling a little in satisfaction that it was functional.

"It's a .455 caliber, top-hinged, 1915 model. This antique hand-cannon's got stoppin' power to spare but it's a wrist-breaker; you'd better practice a bit."

Adrian nodded. He was very strong—even for a pureblood Shadowspawn—but he wasn't particularly massive. Harvey was forty pounds heavier, and mass counted in absorbing recoil. The bullets were silver as well, rougher than modern rounds but probably effective. There were two warded and silver-edged knives, not much different from those made today if you liked straight double-edged daggers; he weighed one in his hand, satisfied. A Council trident-and-sun was set into the pommel of each.

"Good. We have about a week before the official opening of the . . . Prayer of Long Life, enough for me to reinforce the Wreakings to disguise your minds."

Harvey grinned. "You two are goin' to be hearing a lot of Mhabrogast."

The two Brotherhood operatives winced. So did Adrian; he would have to *think* in it, not merely recite phrases. That did odd things to your mind. It had only two tenses, the *fixed* and the *potential*, just to start with; it was a language for solipsistic monsters.

"I will be one of the first guests to arrive, in bird-form. You will be my faithful renfields, and—"

He sketched out the preliminary plan he'd developed. By the end of it they were all sitting on trunks and crates, eating shrimp po' boys from a place Harvey had discovered here in Paso Robles and drinking Duvel beer that had started out in Belgium before it ended up in plastic glasses in California.

"That's a lot more risky for you than for us," Farmer said, when he'd finished.

"I need you for the first two days. After that, all you could do would be to die. I suppose you have your suicide imperatives primed?" They both nodded. "I don't have that option, either."

He stood and got the markers and chalks out of his knapsack. "This is a splendid place to work with. We'll need a rope to scribe some circles . . ."

Several hours later Farmer walked away with his hands clutched to his head. Adrian blinked as he watched the Brotherhood's operative carefully avoiding obstacles that weren't there, and forced his mind not to see what they *might* be. His nose twitched; Anjali Guha had a wad of tissues pressed to hers, to stop the blood. Neither of them was used to Wreaking at this level; neither was he, anymore.

"That will do for a start," he said, and they both groaned. "We can continue tomorrow night. No more than four or five more sessions."

He thought Farmer sounded less resentful. *Now you have some idea of what you'll be dealing with*, Adrian thought. *We speak of minds that can rip the fabric of reality as if it were tissue. And who have the dispositions of malicious children, the type who pull the legs off one side of a spider to see it walk in circles.*

"Now let's get some sleep," Harvey said, wielding a mop to erase the glyphs drawn in a looping tracery outside the circle. "Early day tomorrow."

The walk to the motel they were using was short, but even with an adept's training sleep came slowly. Rancho Sangre was not somewhere he'd ever been physically, but his parents had lived there for decades, and Adrienne since their body-death. It was graven in the history of his life; and now Ellen's world-line was woven with it.

What is happening there now, Ellie? I'm coming to you, as fast as I can.

*   *   *

"I am pleased to meet you, sir, madam," Ellen said formally to Adrienne's parents.

Should I curtsy or something? she thought. *In this Jean-Charles creation I'm wearing at least it wouldn't look ridiculous. But I never learned how anyway. Polite will have to do. And . . . they're Adrian's parents too. God, in a skanky sort of way this* is *like being taken home to meet the folks.*

"No, you're not glad at all," Jules Brézé said. "But it was polite of you to say so. By all means, call me Jules. This *is* America, after all. My parents were the ones who came from France."

He advanced and took her hand. The contact had a slight shock to it, psychically cold and somehow *wet*, though the hand felt absurdly normal for a man who'd died before she was born; there was even a faint smell of wine and mint on his breath, beneath an expensive cologne.

His eyes were the thing that made what he was unmistakable, like pools of living gold. His wife came up beside him and reached out to touch Ellen's hand as well. Both flared their nostrils slightly to take her scent; it was an oddly animalistic gesture. She could remember Adrian doing it when he forgot himself, but then she hadn't had the context.

"Oh, I see what you mean, darling," Julianne said over her shoulder to Adrienne. "One longs to *consume* her. Her mind is like a rose carved out of finely marbled meat until the petals are translucent, scented with fruit and flowers and blood."

Errrk, Ellen thought. *That's an . . . arresting metaphor. All my life I thought my only talents were for tennis and art history, and now I find out I'm A-1 Shadowspawn fodder too.*

"Even more entrancing than the others," Jules said to his daughter. "My dear, you have without a doubt inherited the family's discerning tastes."

The elder Brézés were in slightly old-fashioned evening wear: a beautifully tailored suit and a long off-one-shoulder gown and slightly bouffant hairdo, like something she'd seen on the TV as a little girl back before the turn of the century. If she'd met them at a launch party at the gallery, she'd have put them down as extremely well-conditioned late thirties or early forties, with a sleek timeless look that appeared effortless and cost heavily; Adrienne's mother was a bit fuller-figured than her daughter, and her hair not quite so dark.

They had the same slight Continental accent as their children, but there was also an indefinable difference in the way they treated their vowels and used contractions, a tinge of slow clipped harshness. The English language itself was in the process of changing out from under them.

"I'm glad I'm . . . interesting . . . Jules," Ellen said.

"My dear, you are positively *appetizing*," Jules said, bowing over the hand and releasing it.

Errrrk, Ellen thought again.

Adrienne laughed. She was standing by the carved-stone fireplace; the spring evening was cool enough that the low crackle of flames on the split oak there seemed justified. She had a snifter of brandy in her hand, and a cigarette in her ivory holder. Mark and Renata were the elder Brézés' lucies, a golden-haired younger man and a slim dark woman of about thirty, and they were reclining on the sofa, chatting easily to each other about some cultural event in Los Angeles.

"So, what do you think of the Rancho Sangre art collection?" Julianne said. "Adrienne has added to it, but we and our parents did a good deal."

"Ah . . . it's very impressive. But eclectic and hardly organized at all," Ellen said, both of which were true.

Jules shrugged. "It was a case of *I know what I like* with us, I'm afraid. Adrienne is more enthusiastic. I'm sure you'll work immense improvements."

"I've gotten a preliminary redistribution roughed out and approved by Adrienne, and we're going to start moving some items soon. Before the, ah, party."

Both the elder Brézés smoked—slim dark cigars for him, and Turkish cigarettes in an ivory holder like Adrienne's for her. The way she held it . . .

By God, that's the way they used to do it in old movies! Ellen thought. *Not an imitation, it's completely unselfconscious, and apparently they really* did *wave it that way. Really old movies, silents, back when it was a daring novelty for women to smoke in public. And the way the two of them talk . . .* When *were they born?*

"More than a century ago," Adrienne said.

There was that sense that *something* passed between her and her parents. They both laughed, Julianne more ruefully than her spouse.

"Yes, implausibly long ago!" she said. "The habits you acquire in youth stick like glue, I find."

No wonder Adrian smokes! In a way, he's the same generation as my grandparents.

"That's another reason we used to use foster parents a good deal," Adrienne said. "To keep children from getting *too* out of period. Even so, when I was excited over something early in our acquaintance Jean-Charles gave me an odd look and said my French was splendid but sometimes he wondered if I'd learned it from Napoleon the Third."

Jules nodded. "We're still working out how to deal with such things," he said. "It is all too easy to become . . . lost in memories and in dreams."

"Do you have any elder brothers and sisters?" Ellen asked her Shadowspawn, intrigued for a moment.

"Two. Jacques and Jeanne. They went to Chile with their mates as . . . missionaries, you might say, seventy years ago," Julianne answered for her daughter. "They're still there. Even still corporeal! Though they'll transition soon, I'm sure."

Ellen shivered a little. *Missionaries.*

Julianne held out her snifter. The blond young man rose and filled it from the decanter of Martell X.O., and brought Ellen one as well.

"What do *you* think of the Getty's repatriation policy?" he asked her.

"Mark!" Julianne said, gently reproving.

"We've heard these family stories so *often*, Julianne!" he said defensively.

Ellen sipped. She'd never liked brandy before she met Adrian; if you were going to drink something concentrated and harsh, vodka went down easier. He'd enjoyed showing her the difference between liquor-store brandy and actual cognac . . .

She closed her eyes for an instant and shoved the thought of his face smiling at her away, concentrating on the taste instead. This was as good as the type he favored, but different, heavier and smokier; a hint of dry fruit, and of almond and vanilla. It went down smoothly, but with a bite that warned it had to be taken seriously.

I've got to remember not to drink to relax tension or suppress fear, she thought. *It's too tempting. It's always been too tempting for me but now especially it's too tempting. It's bad enough the way Adrienne feeding on me blisses me out. I'm getting too psychologically dependent on that, too, not just physically; it's the only time I'm not afraid.*

"Ah . . . I'm generally in favor of returning works that weren't legiti-mately acquired, but I think they've got to draw the line somewhere," Ellen said. "You can't send *everything* back where it came from, just because the descendants don't approve of many-times-great-granddad's bargains!"

I'm actually enjoying this, she thought, as that conversation went on.

Mark Jensen knew what he was talking about; he wasn't a profes-sional, she thought, but he obviously cared deeply. Renata was mostly concerned with contemporary folk-art, but had something to say. The Brézés had seen artistic fashion change and change and change again.

After a while Leila and Leon were brought in to visit with their grandparents; evidently midnight was a perfectly normal time for Shadowspawn children to start thinking about bed. Adrienne smiled benignly.

"I'll let you enjoy yourselves," she said, and took Ellen's hand. "Come, *chérie*. The evening is young, and our own personal carnival of the perverse is about to start."

CHAPTER EIGHTEEN

top, Adrian thought/projected.

Harvey did, and sank down with a slow smooth motion, soundless despite the twigs and last year's leaves.

So much for too old for this shit, Adrian thought.

He was as quiet himself. The night buzzed and crickled with insects; it was a little rank with the scents of new spring growth. Ahead and miles downslope to the northeast the lights of Rancho Sangre were a glow through the darkness of early evening.

The patrol he'd detected came into sight in a little clearing a hundred yards below, all going to one knee at the edge of the open space. The grass there was tall, still a little green with May; it was starred with rose and owl's clover, columbine, lily of the valley and forget-me-nots, purple and yellow bush lupine and drifts of golden California poppies. The breeze blew from them to him, carrying the harsh scents of male sweat and gun-oil from the Gurkha mercenaries amid the sweet lingering fragrance of the flowers. Their rifles had argent rounds, the silver alloy a slight gritty-tingling sensation in the night.

I'm glad I *am not too proud to wear body-armor!* Adrian thought.

Two more were Tōkairin retainers in close-fitting black, including masks across their lower faces, with swords slung over their backs. The trickling menace of inlaid, glyph-wrought blades hummed past the sheaths. The black-clad men's eyes needed no technology to see through the light spring night; they had the distinctive sharper, ranker body-scents of Shadowspawn.

He could feel their attention fanning out. Automatically his mind *pushed.* Slightly, subtly, switching pathways to the ones where they missed/ignored/didn't notice any evidence that something was amiss, which was the highest probability anyway.

With them was a huge gray wolf. It *blurred* for an instant, sparkling with energies to Shadowspawn sight, then became a naked man on one knee, dark and lean and scarred, his beak-nosed brown face still raised to sample the air.

I'm impressed, Adrian thought. *I couldn't tell he was night-walking except by deduction. And the way the soldiers are afraid of him. I can smell* that. *The other two are in-the-body.*

"Jirō, Kenta?" Dale Shadowblade asked softly, in the quiet conversational tones that carried least. "You catch anything?"

The narrow gold-flecked dark eyes of Hajime's clansmen scanned carefully. One hesitated for an instant, his hand going towards the sword-hilt that jutted over his left shoulder, then shook his head.

"No. Though there are so many Wreakings soaked into the earth and rocks here I jump at my own shadow! Like *kami*, only real."

"Yeah, the Brézés have been busy. Let's get the circuit complete. I gotta get back to town to meet Michiko and . . . a friend."

Another silent blur, and the wolf turned its long muzzle. Adrian let his own eyelids drift down as the yellow gaze seemed to meet his. Then it turned and bounded away. The men followed, scarcely less silent or less swift. After a long moment there was a quiet *whoosh* of breath from behind him.

"Now, that was just a mite nerve-racking," Harvey said quietly.

"You could say so. Or that my luck is very strong," Adrian grinned, with an expression halfway between relief and sheer exhilaration.

Danger too can be addictive. I had forgotten . . .

They waited another half-hour. Patience was a hunter's virtue . . . or a sniper's, if there was a difference. Then they began their step-at-a-time progress. Adrian paused with his foot in the air.

"Wait," he said. "Wreaking."

Old, old and strong. Keyed into the volcanic rock, like the structure of its atoms, but at a far finer level.

Trace the linkages. If-this-then . . .

"Step on that and you break your leg," he murmured. "And trap it in that crack, so that any attempt to free yourself causes more damage. If you are sentient at all. *Unless* it recognizes the Brézé blood."

"DNA."

"Whatever. Let me convince it . . ."

He drew a small sharp knife and nicked one finger with the tip. The scent filled his nose, but it would fade quickly; he *willed* the tiny wound to dry. A drop fell, and soaked into the porous stones beneath. He felt a response, and a glyph showed for a moment where the blood had struck.

"*Ai-siiii.*"

Congruence/recognition/fitness. With it came a ghost of the mind that had set the trap, many years ago, a snicker of gloating anticipation of pain and the long dying of someone crippled and helpless.

"My grandfather's idea of a joke," Adrian said, letting out a shaky breath.

"This is like walkin' through a garden of carnivorous plants," Harvey grumbled slightly.

He was in the same splotched dark charcoal-gray outdoors clothes—better than black at night. A heavy case on his back carried the knocked-down rifle and more than half their gear, but there was only a light coat of moisture on the older man's face.

"Tired of the sweaty manly stuff yet, old friend?" Adrian asked under his breath.

"Before we began," Harvey said, as they moved slowly on, stopping every few yards.

He had a small electronic device in his hand, and a thin wire leading to an earpiece. A grunt from him froze them both.

"OK, got a blip. Your sister ain't relyin' on hex-marks only."

"How *progressive* of her," Adrian observed dryly.

"There. Lemme . . . cracking the code . . . Sheila comes through again . . ."

Harvey indicated a live-oak, its roots writhing into the fractured stone of the hillside like a slow-motion strangling.

"Visual and audio pickup. Now foxed, you can relax. Sorta. A little."

Beyond the rock grew steeper. A rattlesnake stirred at his passing; its dim reptile brain obeyed the prompting of instinct and probability, threading away deeper into its hole. Then a deep cleft appeared.

"Bingo. Here's that observation post. Good ol' Brotherhood, thinking ahead."

"To opportunities that never occur," Adrian said dryly. "Let's get set up."

"And have ourselves an MRE," Harvey said, as they ducked into the sheltering cave. "Yum!"

His face was darkened with camouflage paint, but his grin was white at Adrian's expression.

"We made it."

"For now," Adrian said sourly. "There are three days yet until the . . . festivities. My sister may order another sweep."

"Or come 'round herself."

Adrian sighed as he set down his heavy pack. "I doubt it. She has much to occupy her, besides her usual . . . diversions."

"My parents were quite taken with you," Adrienne told her.

Then she pivoted and struck.

Crack.

"*Uh!*" Ellen gasped.

Crack.

The nine tight-braided thongs of the silk whip hissed through the air and slapped against her lower back. It melded into the aching glow that stretched from her shoulders to her thighs after the slow, deliberate lashing. The pain was much more than a sting, considerably less than agony. That lurked, though, if the damage didn't stop. Already her sweat stung like fire in one place where the skin had been broken a little.

And I can't make it stop.

Some corner of her mind thought that, as she slumped against the padded cuffs that held her arms spread above her head. Vision blurred with tears and sweat; the smell of her own was heavy in her nostrils, and the subtly ranker scent of Adrienne's, under the flowers and clean linen of the *casa grande*'s main bedroom. The chain-rack was suspended a few yards from the foot of the great bed, running up through a pulley on a rafter.

There's no safe word here.

"That's because I'm not a tame tiger, Ellen," Adrienne's voice laughed in her ear. "I don't jump through hoops when the whip cracks. You do. That's the way *this* circus works."

A hand traveled down her back, cool and delicate, fingers lingering at the base of the spine.

"Have you ever thought of a tattoo here, *chérie*? A phoenix, perhaps, or a monarch butterfly, or some Celtic knotwork to emphasize these little dimples and the curve . . ."

"A *tramp stamp?*" she said incredulously, shocked half out of her daze.

"Well, you *are* such a pain-slut, Ellen. Yes, I definitely think it would work. We'll do it tomorrow."

The hand clenched hard on one buttock. Ellen arched again with a strangled grunt.

"Hurts good, doesn't it?" the taunting voice said.

"Yes."

Which is true. God, how I hate you! That's true too. What are you doing—

"*Unhh! No!*"

"Delightfully dual-purpose."

"*No, please!*"

"No, what?" she laughed. "Is that: No, stop! Or: No! Don't stop!"

Ellen let everything but the flood of sensation drop out of her mind. When it receded she forced her legs to lift her again. Adrienne stood before her, and looped the whip around her neck to draw her close. The gold-flecked eyes stared into hers after the kiss, and her skin twitched at the sensation of her mind being riffled through like a collection of pages. The silk slid free and was tossed aside.

"Shall I feed?"

"Yes," Ellen said, bending her head back to bare her neck. "Oh, *please*, yes."

Lips and tongue touched her throat, caressed the vein. Then:

"As the sadist—which I am—said to the masochist—which you are—*no*. Not yet."

"Oh, God, how I *hate* you," she whimpered

The thought resounded in her head with the iron ring of certainty, beneath the burning *need*.

Adrienne walked over to a table—eighteenth-century French, stone on cast-bronze legs—and wiped her hands on a hot damp towel scented with lemon and tossed it into a hamper. Then she poured herself a glass of a pale yellow wine and turned, leaning with a bare buttock braced against the smooth stone, eyes sparkling and taut nude body sheening with sweat. Her gaze fixed for a second, and the tumblers inside the cuffs opened with a *click* as the dance of stress and molecules aligned precisely. Ellen fell to the linen cloth that covered the carpet and tried to make her limbs work under her own command again.

"I'm going to feed later, so don't worry. Crawl on over. Start with the toes," Adrienne said, extending a foot.

Perfectly nice toes, Ellen thought, as she did. *Nothing wrong with kissing clean pretty toes, in the abstract. Nice high-arched feet. Nice ankles, for that matter. Very trim calves. Muscles like a ballerina. Thighs, OK, skin like satin, a little salty with sweat . . .*

"You're stronger than you seem, Ellen," Adrienne said thoughtfully, some time later, stroking her hair, her voice slowing as her breath did. "You're enjoying parts of this a great deal, aren't you?"

You know I am. Though I'd much rather it was Adrian and it was my idea. Sort of odd to be talking mentally with your nose pressed into someone's navel and your arms around their ass, but what the hell.

"It's not that you don't really hurt," Adrienne said. "You do, but the reactions to it go off in all sorts of intriguing tangents inside your head. I wouldn't have thought that a masochist would be so much fun for a real sadist, but it's actually quite a delightful romp in a wholesome Girl Scout sort of way."

Well, it isn't as if it was consensual, Ellen pointed out. *I'd bolt in a minute if I had a chance and have nightmares about you for years. You must be enjoying my fear and sense of boundary violation and the emotional contortions I have to go through to keep from getting really incoherently angry at being treated like a toy. I'm not enjoying any of those one little bit. I just . . . suspend them.*

"Yes, that's all extremely nice. And the deeply buried feelings that you deserve to be treated like this, which you continually deny; that's exquisite. Like a hint of red chili in a creamy sauce. We can build on that together as our relationship deepens."

Ellen gritted her teeth as the other laughed with delighted cruelty at the uncontrollable surge of anger/guilt/pain.

Though there's actually a sort of erotic frisson from being completely honest with someone I hate so much, too, she thought. *It's a bit like talking dirty but more so. And knowing you're reading my mind and sensations is like being naked twice. Naked inside, not just skin. I'm starting to see what you meant about devouring me and it's scarier than anything else.*

"And there are the images you keep having of driving a stake through my heart. I've seen that one quite often and it's very entertaining. How *did* Adrian like this sort of thing? The ritual, so to speak."

He was . . . conflicted. Afraid to let himself go. I understand that better now.

Adrienne laughed again and sipped. "Long-denied desires *are* hard to contain, which is one reason I don't deny them in the first place. Stand up."

She put the glass to the other's lips; it was sweet and cold and had a fugitive taste of flowers in Ellen's mouth, clearing the salt and musk. Then a quick flick poured the last of the wine in a cold stream along Ellen's collarbones. Adrienne began to lick up the droplets; Ellen shivered at the slight gentle contacts, running a hand up the back of the other's neck.

"Mmmm," she sighed, hugged the Shadowspawn's head against her breasts and thought:

That's nice, but oh, God, stop dicking around and bite *me, will you! It's been a week! But not* there! *Please!*

"In due time. Your blood would be too sweet right now; a savory—some garlic butter, so to say—will make it taste better. Perhaps it's time to move on to a little horror? Ah, now that sent some real fear through the system!"

She stood back and gestured to the huge bed. Ellen got into it and lay back, the cool cotton grateful against the heated glow of her skin. Adrienne lay down too, arranged her head on the pillow and then crossed her arms on her breast so that each hand rested on the opposite shoulder. Her eyes closed and she let out a long breath.

That's the horror? Ellen thought, holding back a flood of relief. *We go to sleep? I need the feeding, but maybe I could sleep first . . .*

"Over *heeeeere!*" Adrienne's voice called.

"Shit!"

Ellen leapt convulsively and scrabbled backward against the carved African ebony of the headboard. Adrienne was back by the table, arms folded and grinning. *And* she was lying beside Ellen . . .

Oh, shit. She's hardly breathing. That's not sleep. It's trance. She's night-walking. That's her aeth-something over there.

"My aetheric body. Exactly, *ma douce*. And that little shriek and the way your heart went pit-a-pat and the emergency clench of those superb buttocks was worth the effort in itself."

She looked at her tranced physical self, and made a little punching gesture upward with both fists along with a *mmmmph* of wordless satisfaction:

"I am *such* a *hottie*! You're a lucky lucy, Ellen, truly."

Ellen swallowed and swallowed again, edging backward until as much as possible of her was crammed against the wood.

"Of course, I admit that sometimes I can be a complete *bitch*, too . . ."

This time Ellen followed the instant of transformation; a wavering glittering flow more sensed than seen through the eyes, like a prickle . . . and a bitch-wolf was sitting and watching her, yellow eyes gleaming, gray-black fur, tail curled around its front paws. She shrieked again and wrapped her arms around her shins, trying to cram herself into an invisible ball, but she couldn't make her own eyes shut as the wolf came to its feet.

It's huge, it's huge, she thought.

Big and elegant, dark fading to brownish-cream on the belly, eyes golden. The teeth were very white as it snarled, the sound low and guttural. It stalked forward, insolently slow, head down and ears laid back, the fur bristling. Then another step, faster, faster, crouching, the long smooth leap—

Ellen did shut her eyes then, screaming wild and high as she waited for the fangs to close in her flesh. There was a *thump* as weight struck the bed . . . and then nothing. Terror made Ellen will her mind to stop operating at all, but terror also made her force her eyes open.

Adrienne was lying on her side, head up on one hand, like an impossible double vision with her slumbering physical form beyond. She winked.

"Now admit it. *That* was scary. Woof-woof-woofity-woof!"

"You vicious *shit*! I *hate* dogs. They *scare* me, since I was a little girl!"

"Technically that was a hundred-and-forty-pound Canadian timber wolf, not a dog." Adrienne laughed. "Consider it a literalized metaphor. Didn't they cover that in your English Lit courses?"

Then she sat up and stretched, looking down at her own body and stroking the slumbering form's cheek. "I learned how to do this when I was about thirteen—young to be night-walking. Think of the auto-erotic possibilities."

Ellen forced her breath to slow. Was that the faintest rank dog-scent still in the air?

Could scent molecules come off a body that's made out of random energies? Oh, shit!

"Ah . . ." she said, collecting herself.

Get into the conversation or she'll think of something else to make your mind leap and quiver.

"Not real practical for a girl, I'd think."

Oh, eww! she thought, at images that sprang unbidden. *Auto-necrophilia?*

"Oh, there are ways. But, of course, if you can turn into a wolf or a tiger, human beings are easy, provided you've got the template. That's probably how the legend about turning into a vampire or a werewolf if you were bitten by one started, but it's really the other way 'round. For example . . ."

Ellen blinked. Then she was looking at a woman taller than Adrienne, blond, full-figured . . .

That's me!

"In the pseudoflesh," Adrienne/Ellen said, wiggling closer and giving her a lingering kiss. The lips were fuller and softer, the taste of the mouth subtly different.

"Have you never wanted to make love with yourself? I can assure you that you're very good in bed. Ah, Monica warned you, I see. Still, there's some interesting fear and horror there."

Oh, God, now I've got to fuck my own ghost?

"It's more like making it with me wearing a you suit, but let's give it a try, eh?"

She took one of Ellen's hands and placed it on a breast; the firm-soft fullness was eerily familiar/not . . .

Half an hour later Ellen whimpered: "Well, don't *stop* . . ."

Then she opened her eyes and screamed again. Adrian was kneeling between her legs . . . Adrian to the last detail, except for the wicked slyness of the smile, her/his hands busy again.

"I could be *this* form when I was thirteen too. Just think of the possibilities. Autonecrophilia indeed!"

"Oh, *God!*"

"Let's play a game, *chérie*. You pretend I'm Adrian, and I'll pretend I'm you pretending I'm Adrian. I *warned* you this was going to be a carnival of the perverse."

It's not going to hurt. I know what's really happening. Get a grip, Ellen, she thought, repeating it like a mantra. *Get a grip. Don't lose it. Get a grip. Pretend it* is *Adrian. You'd be going berserk with joy if it was. Get a grip.*

"That's exactly what I had in mind," she/he said, grabbing Ellen's ankles and levering them back and up.

Weight pushed her down, shoving the sensitive bruised skin of her back and shoulders against the cloth until a flash of fire ran across them. Adrienne looked down at him/herself for an instant, poised above Ellen.

"This is easier because it's a Shadowspawn body and one so similar to mine except for the XY thing, but there are the most *intriguing* differences. On the downside, the sensations are all so much more localized; the rest of your body might as well not exist. On the up, there's this tremendous *focus*. As if everything in all the world was reduced to the need to . . . *thrust*."

"Uhhn!"

"Like that. Now move with me . . . and *grip* . . ."

Later, a panting whisper in her ear amid the hard mutual effort:

"Your mind is opening like an orchid of glittering light . . . not quite yet . . . Pleasure and pain and horror . . . are you listening?"

"O . . . kay . . . yeah . . . mmm . . . please . . . bite me after . . . please . . . oh, please . . ."

"Soon. Soon."

"*God* . . . can't . . . oh, God . . ."

"I could turn into *Adrian's* wolf, right *now*. Woof, woof, woofity—"

Ellen felt her control vanish. She began to scream from the bottom of her lungs, over and over again as the scarlet mouth closed on her throat and teeth sliced.

*   *   *

"Right, we've got it all ready," Harvey said.

Adrian took a long breath and looked around. It wasn't precisely a cave, but the overhang was steep where seepage had eaten the limestone away to leave a pocket of cream-colored rock. A couple of gnarled red pines clung to the surface above; a trickle of water ran out and down the slope, still living with the last of the spring rains. The evening was warm on this south-facing slope covered in dense maquis, but the growing evening shadows hinted at a cool night.

There was an intense smell of sage and spice and pine-sap, of cool rock and cold spring water. He dipped a hand into it and drank to wet his dry mouth, tasting an intense mineral cleanness. He felt empty and light; he'd been fasting for two days with only water to drink, good preparation for prolonged night-walking. A healthy body could go without food for a week or so anyway, and in deep trance for far longer.

"It is time and past time," Adrian said grimly. "I can feel my base-link with Ellen. She is being hit . . . very hard. Particularly the last few nights since we met in Paso Robles."

"Pain?" Harvey said.

"Not so much that. My sister likes to rend and break minds more than bodies, to sculpt the *self* until it is as she desires, and she is extremely good at it. Ellen is very strong, very resilient . . . but consciously she is without hope while her memories are blocked. Much longer, and there will be permanent damage."

"Now's as good a time as any. Lucky for Ellen, Adrienne's gonna be distracted with her social obligations."

He ducked under the camouflage tarpaulin that he and Harvey had rigged. When they fastened it behind them the darkness was intense even to Shadowspawn eyes, and the older man clicked on a dim blue light. Adrian lay down on the air-mattress, and Harvey zipped up the thinfoil sleeping bag. With his body heat, that would keep him from losing too much to the earth. Then he held out his arm, and the other man arranged the saline drip.

The slight sting of the needle as Harvey taped it to the inside of his left elbow awakened him from the seductive voice of the trance. He smiled as his arm was arranged.

"Tucking me into bed again, Harv?"

The Texan chuckled. "Hell, you weren't *that* young when I pulled you out of the Brézé stable. Just into your obnoxious teenaged years as I remember. Remember *real* well."

The older man held a small tube of liquid to his lips. "Puree of Wilbur Peterson," he said. "Probably they got the DNA for replication from strands of hair or the bone marrow, considerin' how old the body was."

Adrian drank the neutral-tasting liquid. "Thank you for that thought," he said, and concentrated.

Within him mechanisms that had evolved long before the age of polished stone assimilated the paired helixes of a man who had decided that immortality was too much to bear.

"Since we're probably going to die in the next thirty-six hours . . ." he said, when he was ready.

Harvey grinned like a gargoyle. "Shit, you don't have to pay me back that twenty bucks you borrowed for beer. Forget it."

"Then just let me say that if we make it, I'm back in the war full-time. *After* my honeymoon."

Harvey froze for an instant, a blue-lit troll. "You are? Any particular reason?"

"For one thing, I don't think Ellen will stay with me if I don't, or anyway, I find I can't stand the thought of her bad opinion of me. For another, I have been infected with the delusion called hope. It is more comfortable than sanity, in the long run."

"Glad to hear you're back in."

"On my own terms."

A chuckle. "I always sorta liked approaching it that way myself. You ready?"

Adrian sighed. "I am reluctant. It is not the danger, you understand . . ."

"The danger of possibly eternal torment? Hell, that makes *me* reluctant, ol' buddy. I do it anyway, but I'm reluctant as shit."

"It is pretending to be a Shadowspawn predator. The things I must do to avoid suspicion are too hard to forget."

"Adrian, *I* don't wish to do anything much but go back to Pecan Creek, retire, go fishing and watch football and drink beer, and amble down to the crossroads for some BBQ now and then. With an occasional trip to Arles. I certainly never became much attached to blowin' people's heads off."

Softly the older man finished: "I see their faces sometimes."

"True. *Moi aussi.* Goodbye, then, old friend. Remember, she will be with Hajime of a certainty at the final ceremony, if there is no opportunity before."

"You just keep her pinned long enough for the bullet to hit." A grin. "It's going to be what you might call a target-rich environment and I've got a fair amount of ammo."

"There is only one target that really matters."

He leaned back against the softness of the sleeping bag and the air pillow. Dimly he could see Harvey take up the sniper rifle, its outline broken up by a scrim of fabric that turned it shaggy. The other man pulled down a bulbous face-mask with passive image intensifiers built into it, and clicked off the blue light.

Adrian let the Mhabrogast form in his mind, convincing his hind-brain that it did not need his physical form: *Amss-aui-*ock!

There was an instant of wrenching, ice-and-silver pain along his nerves, and he was standing and looking down at his body.

I am better, this time. Balanced and strong. Win or lose, I will not fail myself. Let's make sure I don't fail Ellie, either.

Another, and his body *flowed.* He felt duller, more constrained; Peterson had not been as purebred as he, nor as intelligent in general. The part of him that was always *him* struggled, and thought and senses gradually grew more clear. Adjusting a form was much more difficult than simply donning it, but possible, and once done could be locked in for recall. Harvey looked at him critically.

"That's Peterson at about twenty-one," he said.

"I don't have the somatic memories," Adrian replied. "It's not un-known for postcorporeals to de-age their aetheric forms, and God knows he had time."

"It'll have to do. Good luck, ol' buddy."

Adrian nodded and stepped towards the camouflage curtain. He concentrated, and to the aetheric eyes the complex fabric faded to in-visibility. The molecules of his stolen form slipped through those of the cloth, and he was naked in the early night. Around him was a web of floating energies; curtains of them crawled across the stars, still a little hurtful in the west where the sun had vanished. He raised his arms to the night, let the syllables he whispered shape what was, and *willed.*

Form flowed. Perceptions flowed and changed with it; scent dulled, but vision grew far keener than his eyes saw by day, and hearing had an unearthly sensitivity that made the rustle of a field-mouse as loud as boots on gravel and gave direction with swift precision. The sounds of the night were a roar, but after an instant each was as distinct as lines scribed with a diamond. Thought shrank, but took on a savage directness that did not seek to question itself. Broad wings five feet from tip to tip caught at the night, and a great snowy owl ghosted upward as small things skittered in panic or more wisely froze.

Exultation filled him as feathers caressed the air and danced with it, and it took the silent command of the man-mind that lurked at the back of the narrow avian brain to keep it from plunging and sporting in sheer joy. Instead he circled for height, stroking with his wings when he must, riding currents of air he could see as billowing shapes when he caught them. Land unrolled below him, not the map-image you saw with a man's eyes from an aircraft but a living tapestry as detailed as skin beneath a microscope, down to each clear-cut leaf and grass-blade. Fields, roads, buildings . . .

. . . and hovering above one a banner of energies, potentials sparkling into and out of existence.

That he saw with the eyes of the Power which never left him. A simple construct, but with the mark of his sister's savage elegance: *here*.

Ellen is there, he thought with some part of him that still remembered words. *I can feel the base-link. She is miserable, with more than mere fear.*

It was close, but he banked widely to make sure that no other night-walker rode the air. None were nearby, though their approach tickled at his senses. He folded his wings then, and dove. Speed built, and the earth swelled; he could hear the murmur of many voices, loud and ugly to the owl's hearing. Human voices, some carrying the freight of pain and fear. The building swelled, a long rectangular stable or barn of stucco-covered concrete with openings just under the peak of the tile roof at either end. For a form that could stoop on prey by sound alone it was simple to dive through, though the blaze of electric light was hurtful

The space within was divided by a fence of wire mesh. The larger part held prisoners, eighty or so men and women.

The others . . . guards, in the uniform of small-town policemen. His sister, her aura like a blow, a wave of rank salt blood and slinking menace. Another woman in elegant dress, radiating fear and a sick dread and an abject abandonment. And . . .

Ellen, he thought. *Ellen. Why did she bring you here?*

CHAPTER NINETEEN

"*Eerrk!*"

Ellen bit off the small shriek as the slim long-fingered hand fell on her shoulder while she stared at the computer screen.

God, but I hate it when she sneaks up on me like that!

"I know you hate it. That's why I do it. *Sadist*, remember? What's this?"

Adrienne's head followed the hand, looking at the arrangement of the paintings on the screen and the number-coded map of the *casa grande*.

"This is my plan for the next step in reorganization," Ellen said. "There's more than enough display space in the *casa*, you're just not using it to best advantage. We've done the basic sectional sort-and-move; now we need to get down to fine-tuning the placement of each piece."

"Excellent, *ma douce*."

The office-study of Ellen's house on Lucy Lane had had time to acquire touches of her own in the three months since she'd arrived; an orange cat that she'd half-adopted despite her resolution lounged in a corner, and a pot of coffee on a hotplate scented the air, along with the warm May flowers-and-grass scent through the open window, with a breath of coolness as the day spun down into night.

There were prints—a couple of Impressionists—and a genuine Mary Cassatt of two women drinking tea that *should* have been in the Museum of Fine Arts in Boston. It had simply appeared on the wall one day, and she'd been caught between guilt and long periods of simply staring, transported.

"*Sadist*, remember?" Adrienne chuckled. Then she trailed a finger down Ellen's neck. "You're looking lovely, by the way."

"Thanks."

"Put this on too."

Adrienne handed her a flat case, antique tooled leather with a diamond clasp. Ellen opened it and swallowed. It was a Victorian piece, a two-tiered necklace of collar and spray in gold and rubies against black velvet.

"That's lovely," she said sincerely.

"I'm glad you like it. It's been in the family for some time, as an ornament for our lucies. Note the theme of bloodred. It really needs a blond to carry it off."

The order to *dress up for evening* hadn't specified a time, so she'd lost herself in work despite the long sheath of shimmering silver-scalloped black with a cloth-of-gold shawl thrown over her chair. The first day of the house party would start tonight. She bent her head forward and held up her hair to let the Shadowspawn fasten the goldwork.

And I'm on display as the beautiful golden peach nobody else can taste. The one Adrian couldn't keep out of her hands.

"Precisely. How is your Spanish?"

Decent conversational as long as it isn't too complicated, Ellen thought. *I understand it better than I can speak it.*

"Mine's fully fluent, but European, with a bit of an accent," Adrienne said.

"What sort?"

"Occitan; I sound like a Catalan trying to be Castilian to someone from Madrid. Come along, then."

"What . . . do I have to do?"

"The last shipment of refreshments has come in, and Paco—he's a coyote by trade, but jackal would be more appropriate—didn't listen to my instructions."

"What . . . instructions?" Ellen mumbled, her mouth suddenly dry as she stood and plucked at the shawl.

I tried so hard not to think about this.

"I *told* him I wanted young adults—young, healthy, good-looking. The imbecile has saddled me with half a dozen mothers with children— all trying to get into the country to join their husbands, no doubt. Or convinced their husbands have conveniently forgotten them in this land of liberty. He probably thought I wouldn't object if he brought them just before the deadline. I want you to be reassuring so we can separate the children without a screaming scene. Reassuring is something I find oddly difficult."

"Why . . . me?" Ellen asked.

Please, God, those poor people . . .

Adrienne smiled like a cat. "Because you'll hate it, but do it any-way and feel horribly degraded and dirty afterwards, which is interesting emotionally," she said. "Third time's the charm; *sadist*, remember? *Vite!*"

God, I hate you!

Adrienne was dressed in riding gear in an English jodhpurs-and-tweed style, including a crop. The steel-cored leather landed across the seat of Ellen's skirt with a hard cracking sound. That was no braided silk; it *hurt*, hard and sudden.

"Ouch!"

"*Vite* means *quickly*. It's the imperative form of the verb, too."

She hit the *save* button and followed the Shadowspawn out to the TARDEC utility vehicles. Adrienne swung in beside the driver of the first. A rather subdued Monica was in the rear seat, dressed in a pleated skirt and a tight low-cut crimson bodice. She helped Ellen in; it wasn't the sort of transport designed for long evening-dresses. They went through the gate in the perimeter wall of the *casa grande* and around a roadway that looped towards the hills westward, along a well-kept gravel road that crunched under the wheels. The lights of the vehicles came on, as the sun sank in an orange glow behind the hills.

They stopped at a building she would have said was a well-kept large stable or medium-sized rectangular barn with plastered walls, set back among the lawns and live-oaks where the gardens turned into sweeping pastures with clumps of trees and white-board fences. Servants were lighting a trail of torches in iron holders along a brick-paved path that wound down to the main house. A half-dozen Gurkhas stood inconspicuously outside, or as inconspicuously as you could while wearing body-armor and carrying an assault rifle.

Inside, Chief Mendoza and four of his subordinates stood by a wire-mesh barricade that divided a long space floored in textured concrete. Garlands of flowers on the walls gave it a grotesquely festive feeling, and the lights were on under the high ceiling. Behind the wire were eighty or so people; she could smell their fear-sweat a little. All of them looked Mexican, half males and half females; most of the women were dressed in loose white tunics like short dresses, and the men in tunics and pants of the same cloth. Around a score were in ordinary clothes, dusty and travel-stained, and looking less frightened but more bewildered than the others.

"Paco," Adrienne began crisply to another man standing free—in his thirties, and . . .

Handsome in a sleazy way, Ellen thought. *Hairnet and all. Just what you'd think a people-smuggler would look like.*

"You are an idiot. And I am not pleased," she went on.

"*Doña*," he said, in rapid-fire Mexican Spanish. "Here they are, the last of them, delivered on time!"

Adrienne answered in the same language, but Ellen could hear the difference in dialect, the hard *k* and trilled *rr* sounds.

"I said young, healthy, good-looking, and *no children*, Paco. What part of that was too difficult for you to understand?"

The Shadowspawn pointed with her riding crop. "That one, she's forty if she's a day, five feet tall and five feet broad. And six . . . seven of the women have young! *That* one is still nursing!"

"I am very sorry—"

"No, you're not. You're just sorry I'm making a fuss about it. My guests will be arriving momentarily and we are *not ready!*"

"I will take a little less for each, perhaps—"

"You'll take nothing for the ones who don't meet my specifications."

She turned her head to Monica and Ellen: "You two get the children out . . . and that older woman. The transport for them should be here by now. *Vite!*"

Mendoza unlocked the gate; the people within surged forward, then back again as two of the policemen drew their automatics. Monica wet her lips and called out in understandable but clumsy Spanish:

"*Los niños* . . . the children should be brought out now. Nothing bad will happen to them. *Van los niños a la guardería, no se preocupen.* They will stay with good families while you are . . . are busy with the *Doña's* guests. *Please*, bring the children right now. And, you, señora. There are things . . . there are things it is not good for children to see."

There was a desperate earnestness in her voice; Ellen nodded word-lessly and beckoned. The prisoners murmured among themselves for a moment; then one of the mothers decisively pushed her six-year-old forward. The others followed suit, some crying silently, and the heavy-set middle-aged woman shepherded them through the gate, carrying the nursing infant. One was a girl who looked to be somewhere be-tween eleven and thirteen, the breasts just showing under her T-shirt. A young man who was probably her brother held her back, then shoved her forward at the last moment.

"*Vaya con Dios, carnala!*" he called. Then: "*Go!*" as she hesitated.

Mendoza stopped her at the gate.

"*Doña?*" he asked, looking at Adrienne.

Her nostrils flared for a moment, and the man who'd pushed her forward closed his eyes and crossed himself.

"A little too young for feeding," the Shadowspawn said. "Doesn't smell quite ripe yet. She can help with the other youngsters."

"Come, little ones," Ellen said, her voice trembling. "Some nice ladies will take you to a good place."

Getting the children out was like herding sobbing cats, and several of them tried to break back towards their mothers; outside SUVs driven by Monica's friends were waiting. Ellen stood, clenched her hands, and made herself turn around and walk back in.

Don't wait to be ordered or dragged. Just do it. The vicious bitch is going to make you watch anyway.

Adrienne produced an envelope that probably had high-denomination bills and tossed it to the coyote. He counted it, and flushed.

"This isn't two thousand each!"

"Hey!" someone shouted from within the pen. "*We* paid him two thousand each, lady!"

Adrienne snarled. "It's the full amount for the ones who met my request. This is your last chance to walk away, little man."

"I want my money—" he began.

The riding crop slashed across his face. He stood for a moment in shocked surprise, clutching at the bleeding weal. Then his hand darted under the tail of his shirt.

It came out with an automatic. His face showed an *ooops* reaction even before he leveled it, then a frantic determination.

"Nobody hits Paco!" he said.

There was a ringing silence. Ellen could tell that he hadn't expected Adrienne's grin, or the indifference of the policemen. The prisoners were stock-still, watching breathlessly. The Shadowspawn's smile grew wider, and she lifted the riding crop again, slowly and deliberately. Paco's lips tightened, and his grip on the pistol. Ellen's breath caught as she saw the finger close on the trigger.

Click-crink!

The gun misfired, and there was the unmistakable crinkling sound of something metallic snapping as it did. He stared at it incredulously, and tried to fire again three more times as the crop slashed at him. Then her hand blurred and he screamed with the pain of a broken finger as she snatched it away.

"Automatics have a high probability of failure," she said cheerfully.

Paco began to back up, hands in front of his face. Adrienne followed, teeth showing in a happy smile, delivering a series of cruelly precise strikes with the crop, each ending in a meaty *smack* sound.

Several of the prisoners surged forward as Paco was driven back towards the wire mesh, reaching their hands through towards him. One very dark and very pretty young woman was leaping up and down, shaking her fists in the air and shouting:

"*¡Orale y órale! ¡Dale! ¡Jodele al bruto!*"

"Meaning, *smack him, harder, fuck him up*," Ellen muttered to herself, clutching one hand against the other to control the shaking. "Oh, I guess he's not really popular in there right now. And I can guess why *she* doesn't like him in particular."

Adrienne laughed and pounced. Suddenly Paco was held helpless across her body, one of her arms pinning his, the other bending his jaw back. The shouts from the cage died away as she struck; Paco froze, and her throat moved as she fed briefly. When she released him he slumped down, dazed, and she looked up smiling with blood on her chin and lips and teeth.

One man blurted into the silence: "*Es chupacabra!*"

The goat-sucker of Hispanic legend.

Another barked harsh laughter: "*No seas güey . . . Paco no es cabra, es cabrón!*"

Ellen found her eyes prickling for the first time; the second man had managed to make a *pun*, of all things, in the middle of this, calling the coyote *cabrón*, a bastard, rather than *cabra*, a goat.

Adrienne laughed. "I completely agree," she said.

She grabbed Paco by the back of the neck. Three steps and she flung him through the door, and Mendoza clashed it shut. For a moment nobody moved, and then the young woman stepped forward, waving the others back:

"*Mío! Es mío! Y solo mío!*" she half-screamed.

She launched a vicious kick, gathering up her skirts in both hands to get a better swing, and shouting to the rhythm of the solid blows as she struck again and again. Ellen didn't have any trouble following it despite the volume and machine-gun speed; curses were the first things you picked up.

Thud.

"*¿Te sientes muy macho, ahora?*"

Feeling like a big man now?

Another *thud.*

"*¡Orale, trata de jodernos ahora!*"

Try to screw us over now!

Adrienne was laughing as she watched. Then she called out sharply:

"*Niña!*" The young woman looked up, and Adrienne shook a finger at her.

"*Puedes matarlo si quieres, pero le haces un favor enorme.*"

Kill him if you want, but you'll be doing him a big favor, Ellen translated to herself.

"What's your name?" Adrienne went on.

"Eusebia," the woman said.

"I like your spirit, little Cheba. And now . . ."

She looked up. There were open windows at both ends of the barn-prison, under the peaks of the roof. A great snowy owl swept through, turning and banking and braking to a landing, folding its five-foot wingspan. Then there was a naked man rising from one knee.

"*Efectos especiales,*" one of the Mexicans said, loudly as if to convince himself.

"*Inahualli, inahualli!*" another cried, which wasn't Spanish at all.

"It's Nahuatl. *Shapeshifter,*" Adrienne said over her shoulder to Ellen. "Absolutely *everyone* has legends about us."

The man stretched and then bowed over Adrienne's extended hand with the panache of one used to the gesture, touching only the fingertips.

"Wilbur Peterson," he said; he spoke as if his voice was slightly rusty with disuse. "We haven't met, Miss Brézé. I've been . . . very out of touch for a long time. Thank you for your invitation. My . . . baggage and servants are on the way, but . . ."

Ellen looked at him and felt an odd shock of recognition and relief.

Which is crazy. He looks a little bit like Adrian except for that browny-bronze hair, but he's just another monster.

"Then I'm honored you should choose this little affair to get back into the social circuit, cousin," Adrienne said. "You must be ravenous. Feel free to choose."

She indicated the prisoners with a gracious wave of her hand. They were stock-still now, staring huge-eyed. Several crossed themselves, and Ellen heard the murmur of prayer.

I wish I could pray. Oh, how I wish. Or that I could call to Adrian.

"Thank . . . you. That one, please."

He pointed to the girl who still stood near the semiconscious Paco. The others backed away from her as if from plague, and she looked wildly around herself.

"A good choice," Adrienne said. Then sharply: "*Ven tú*, Cheba. Come and meet your fate, the purpose for which you were born."

Mendoza opened the gate. "Better for you if you come now, *chica*," he said roughly. "Don't make them chase after you."

She did, first wiping her palms on her skirt, then walking slowly towards them. Mendoza opened the door briefly, then clashed it shut again. She slowed still more as she approached the Shadowspawn, walking step by step. The man took her by the arm and smiled; she gave a little gasp as she met the sulfur-yellow eyes.

"Feel free to feed as you will," Adrienne said. "It's . . . neater to start here, if you mean to kill your first one."

Ellen's eyes darted around. The textured concrete of the floor and lower walls, the big screened drains . . . and the neatly coiled hoses beside the large-capacity water outlets for sluicing it all down. Things like bronze showerheads shaped into the mouths of bats, with wrought taps below them. And all of it *old*, generations old, carefully maintained but at least three times as old as Ellen Tarnowski. For an instant she thought she could feel the shrieks sunken into the fabric of the place, a century of agony and death, and she gave a little whimper.

"No, I'll . . . take my time," Peterson said.

"Ah, a man of taste. My renfields are waiting to show you to your rooms in the *casa grande*. If you don't kill her, she's yours to take with you when you leave, of course."

"Very . . . hospitable of you. But I wouldn't expect anything else of a Brézé."

He bowed slightly and began to lead the girl away. She started to squirm and then try to pull free, but the grip on her upper arm was evidently like a band of steel as she was marched into the darkness.

"The early bird and the choice worm," Adrienne said absently.

Another whisper of wings, and three more birds soared into the big chamber; a golden eagle, a bald eagle, and a red-tailed hawk. They fluttered to the ground, and were Shadowspawn in human form— Dale Shadowblade, Dmitri Usov and Tōkairin Michiko. A moan went through the men and women behind the cage as the three touched fingertips with Adrienne.

"You're early, but you're not the first," she said. "Wilbur Peterson, of all people. I never expected him to actually *attend*."

"I thought he'd gone seriously hermit?" Michiko said, stretching luxuriously, rising on the balls of her feet with her fingers linked high over her head. "God, but I love flying."

"He hasn't left his nest for thirty years!" Adrienne confirmed.

"Peterson is another ancient fossil of the type we will have to deal with," Dmitri snorted. "An obstacle to the progressive forces."

"Oh, now, Dmitri Pavlovich, we have to be tolerant and inclusive," Adrienne said unctuously.

Then she laughed like a cruel girl-child and clapped her hands together. "Oh! I forgot! We don't! All we have to be is evil and ruthless, *hein?*"

"*Da,*" Dmitri said. "And I also like flying. But it leaves one with an appetite. Is all in order?"

"All according to plan so far," Adrienne said. "Have a little snack, and we'll talk later as everyone mills-and-swills, eh?"

Dale was looking at the cage. "Not bad. I always was partial to Mexican. Mind if we make a mess?"

"Of course not, within reason. Pick a pair each and go crazy. I can always have a few extras sent up from San Simeon if we run short; the place is like a perpetual revolving larder with those tour buses."

Adrienne made a flicking gesture with her hand, and Mendoza and his men left; one of them stumbled a little, and another helped him along. Michiko giggled and walked towards the unlatched door of the cage, her nude body moving cat-graceful with a mocking sway of the hips.

"Paco, Paco," she said, her voice silvery. "Adrienne says you've been *very* naughty. But I'm naughty too sometimes. Let's play a little game. It's called, *you die now.*"

The coyote was fully conscious again, but he had missed the last twenty minutes. Ellen saw his eyes bulge as Michiko let herself fall forward . . . and landed on paws. The animal was a Himalayan snow leopard, smoke-gray with black rosettes on its silky fur, even then beautiful enough to make the breath catch. The long tail swung a little as the great paws placed themselves with smooth precision, and the fangs showed bone-white as it snarled, a high-pitched half-yowl that echoed from the roof. Paco turned and ran, bounced into a wall of people who thrust him back and then faced around into the leopard's leap.

He screamed once as he went down beneath the beast, and then again, and again and again on a rising squealing note of unbearable agony. A spray of blood flicked across the faces of the other prisoners, and there were wet ripping noises. The metallic scent was suddenly, shockingly intense.

Ellen shut her eyes for an instant, but lights still flashed across her vision; her mouth was paper-dry, a ringing sounding in her ears above the rending sounds. Monica suddenly buried her face against Ellen's shoulder and clutched her, and they leaned against each other for support.

Oh, God, I'm going to lose it. I'm going to wet myself. I'm going to puke all over Jean-Charles' dress . . . God what a thing to think about . . . I want to close my eyes and I can't keep them shut.

They fluttered unwillingly open. An Amur tiger and a great black wolf were slinking forward through the gate in the wire fence, ears laid back, teeth showing as their heads swung back and forth to scent their prey. Michiko was in human form again, crouched over Paco with her face buried in the blood that welled from his torn throat, turning her pale neck and breasts crimson. It coated her face in a glistening bright-red sheet when she turned it upward, laughing.

"Let's pick one and play a bit longer, boys," she said to the two beasts; they halted on either side of her, and she rested a hand on each ruff as she crouched. "That one. She's in milk. We could have a fascinating mix of tastes."

"And now we should depart, my sweet ones," Adrienne said as the three predators stalked forward, dividing to cut the chosen victim out of the mass. "The next few will be arriving corporeally, or at least by ground."

Adrienne walked out; Ellen followed as best she could, feeling her knees buckling and helping Monica along as she staggered, gulping at the cleaner air. Theresa Villegas was outside, and nodded to Adrienne as they passed. One of the policemen began to swing the door shut behind them, and then something cannoned into it.

Ellen jerked back involuntarily. It was a woman, naked but for the panties still snagged around one ankle, red lines scored across her back. She fell forward half-out of the door, her eyes wide with agony and disbelief. Her fingers clawed into the concrete, bleeding as well where the nails tore. She shrieked and twisted to clutch at the doorframe as something grabbed her from behind; Theresa stepped forward and used the toe of her polished shoe to pry the hands loose. A savage jerk pulled her back into the room, and the policeman closed the door, standing for a moment blank-eyed with his hand on the latch.

"I will direct the guests when they are ready to come up to the *casa*, *Doña*," Theresa said with a prim smile. "Enjoy your evening."

"Thank you, Theresa. You've been invaluable."

The rhythmic pulsing screams of agony and bestial snarling and silvery laughter died away as they walked down the brick pathway between the crackling torches.

"It's natural," Monica started mumbling to herself. "We're mice. It's natural. That's what we're for. It's *always* been what we're for."

No it is fucking well not *what we are for!* Ellen screamed mentally. *No, no, no!*

"Oh, yes it is," Adrienne said, and put a hand on the small of her back.

Don't touch me! Don't touch me!

"But I will touch you," she purred. "Oh, yes, I will."

She stopped, took Ellen's chin between thumb and forefinger.

"Your mind is like a raw wound right now," she said. "Shall I feed, and make you feel better?"

"Yes, please," Ellen said tightly.

No! You made me feel this way, you keep it!

"Now there's a contradiction. Yes-yes on your lips, no-no in part of your mind. But you smell right for feeding, very right indeed."

An arm went around her bare shoulders under the shawl. Adrienne's head nuzzled her jaw up, and teeth touched her throat above the jeweled collar.

Ellen whimpered again. *I want* the bite. *But I'm . . . somehow I'm betraying them . . .*

"If it's any consolation, you have no say in this whatsoever," Adrienne said, the breath warm against her skin. "I'd have bitten you anyway after you were primed like that. Irresistible!"

The sting was slight, but it made her skin ripple all the way to her feet and back. The clamminess left her, and the twisting knot in her stomach. The horror faded; the sights and sounds and smells were still there in the eye of her mind, but now they turned to an immense soft sadness like the memory of a great tragedy long ago. That faded in turn to a feeling like reading melancholy poetry. She sighed and let her head rest against the Shadowspawn's, putting a hand to the other's throat. Feeling the burring vibration of the growl, and the pulse of the swallows as they took her blood.

A tear leaked down her face, and she seemed to be fading into a soft and welcoming darkness and yet be feeling clearheaded and more alert at the same time. The night around her turned sharp, with the rustle of wind in the oaks and jacarandas overhead and the *yap-yap* of a fox somewhere.

"Utterly marvelous." Adrienne laughed as she lifted her mouth from Ellen's neck.

Then she touched up the teardrop with a finger and put it to her crimson-coated lips.

"The mixture of flavors in your blood right now is indescribable . . . You don't mind if I touch you, *hein?*"

"No," Ellen murmured dreamily, releasing her. "But you should bite Monica too. It's been a while for her, and besides that, she's feeling bad."

"Oh, please, Adri, please, please make it better."

Poor Monica, Ellen thought; she felt immensely close to the other lucy, as if to the sister she had never had. *She sounds so wretched.*

Ellen stood and watched calmly as Adrienne bent her head to the other's inner arm.

I wonder if I looked that happy, she thought; the rigid tension of

Monica's face relaxed in the flickering flame-light, seeming to shed ten years as she smiled.

I certainly feel that way right now. I know it won't last and the memories will give me the screaming horrors, but that's . . . so far away. The feeding does look so right *now. It makes you feel so complete, so needed.*

She could walk normally again when they went on. At the archway that gave onto the rear terrace and pools, Jose and Peter were waiting for them, in formal dinner jackets and white ties. Jose's shirt had ruffles, and there was a scarlet cummerbund around his waist, a combination that usually made Anglos look ridiculous but simply gave him a dashing air. He offered Monica his arm, and Peter gave her his.

"I'll go change now," Adrienne said, smiling at the four of them. "Paco paid the appropriate penalty and we got him out of the gene pool, but he did throw me off schedule a little. Why don't you all drift on through to the main entranceway receiving hall, and I'll join you in a minute."

"Bad?" Peter asked softly when she'd gone.

The main entrance had a musician's balcony over the doorway, as well as the curling grand stair. The group there was playing something soft and ancient—Baroque, she thought. Ellen took a flute of champagne from a passing tray and drank; the great marble space was still mostly empty, glowing softly in the light of the chandeliers. Jose and Monica were chatting easily.

"Bad?" she said. "Bad doesn't begin to describe it. It was so bad my mind couldn't really take it in, though my bowels certainly believed it. But right now I know how bad without *feeling* it."

He nodded, and gave her a handkerchief. She touched it to her neck; there was only a small spot of blood, and she knew the feeding cut would be invisible except to a close look.

"*That* does make it feel better," he agreed, and sipped at his own drink, which looked to have vodka and a twist of lemon peel in it. "Rather like *this*, only much more effectively."

"It doesn't actually *make* it better," Ellen said, closing her eyes for a moment and swaying to the music. "But for the moment, feeling better will do. I wonder if you could dance to this?"

She began to turn, and then she was moving, black and silver and flying gold hair and shawl, skirts filling and flaring.

CHAPTER TWENTY

Adrian Brézé wore the shape of Wilbur Peterson easily. It was close to his own; a little taller, a little more thickly built, eyes yellow in the way most postcorporeals preferred them, hair light brown with bronze highlights. His grip carried the girl along effortlessly, despite her attempts to pull free, though she was young and strong for her size. The screams faded as they walked.

Servants showed them to the suite of rooms; it was set up for a postcorporeal. Only one room had an exterior window, and it could be closed by a light-tight steel shutter and bolted fast; there was a hidden shaft that led to the basements and sub-basements below. For that matter, in night-walker form he could simply go impalpable and drop through the floors—though that was hideously dangerous, unless you were very careful. Dropping into solid earth while impalpable left you with no way to get back *up*.

Adrian shoved the girl through and caught her arm again when the outer door shut. She was under twenty, he judged, but she'd lived someplace where hard labor started early. Despite that she was slender in the waist and long-limbed but full-breasted, rare for a villager. Her skin was the exact color of a latte, and the face framed by loosely curled black hair showed a pleasant mix: mostly Indian, probably a little Iberian and a dash of African as well in bluntly regular features and full lips. Her dark eyes flickered around the elegant entrance-chamber, with its cool white-and-gray marble floors and rugs and spindly antique furniture.

"What is your name?" he asked: "*¿Como se llama?*"

"Eusebia Cortines."

"*¿Como le dicen?*" he asked. *How are you called?*

He caught her eyes with his and held her at arm's length, making an effort to give his speech a Mexican cast; he'd traveled there often enough to do that, though he'd first learned Spanish in Europe.

"Cheba," she said, stammering a little but keeping her chin up.

"*¿Me permite?*" he said, asking permission to use the diminutive.

That ought to reassure her a little. She nodded, and he went on:

"Where are you from? Veracruz?"

"Coetzala," she said, naming a village in that coastal state he'd passed through once long ago on Brotherhood business. "Then . . . Tlacotalpan." Which was a city of some size. "Then to *el Norte*. With that bastard son of a whore Paco."

"Paco is dead, and he died very hard. Waste no regrets. He knew what he was selling you into here, or at least that there was no returning. *¿Habla Inglés?*"

"*Poquito.*"

Which meant *a little*; then she spoke in limping English:

"I say, yes, no, how much, can work, cook, clean, tend *niños*, kids."

Back into Spanish: "My mother sold baskets to tourists. I talked with them sometimes, a little, to practice."

He could sense her roiling fear, and defiance as well; her scent was healthy, clean beneath the dust and dirt of days of travel without an opportunity to wash. And her blood smelled so tempting, so tempting, even with the memory of Ellen's tormenting flower-fragrance in his nostrils. Meaty and sweet at the same time, like a skewer of honey-glazed chicken.

"You know what I am, Cheba?" he said.

"*Brujo. Vampiro,*" she said

The corner of his mouth quirked up. *She's brave*, he thought; the emotional balance was plain, even if he couldn't yet read the surface thoughts that glinted away in a mumble of firing neurons.

And she only half-believes it, despite the fact that she saw me transform from a bird to a man. Quick-witted too, when she's not stupefied with fear.

"Yes. *Shadowspawn* is the true name. In your language—*Hijos de la noche. Los indios* say it better: *Nagualli.*"

"*Nagualli,*" she repeated, in a way that confirmed his suspicion that she'd spent at least her early childhood speaking Nahuatl, the old Aztec language.

"What . . . what is happening to them?" she asked, her voice small. "The people I traveled with."

"Blood drinking. Torture, rape, death also, for many," he said; there was no point in sugar-coating it. "Control yourself, and listen to me, and you may live."

She nodded, waited until his grip on her arm slackened . . . then jerked free, turned and bolted for the door. Adrian sighed, made a movement with his left hand, called up a glyph and *pushed* with his will.

A snap behind his eyes, and a rucked-up piece of Persian carpet slithered. Her foot turned under her and she fell with a jolt of pain that made his lips curl back for an instant. When she tried to scramble to her feet one leg tripped another. After the third time she lay panting, eyes wide. She was sweating with terror, and he could smell it as well as feel it sparkling like red fire through her mind. The effort not to snarl in eagerness shook him.

"You know that there is nobody outside who will not push you right back through that door? That I can keep this up as long as you try to escape? That doing this makes me"—he let the snarl show a little—"*hungry?*"

Gradually she won a degree of mastery, enough to give him a quick nod.

"This is a . . . place of *los brujos*," he said. "I'm a guest here. You've been given to me for . . . food. For blood. That's why you and your friends were brought here. You are entirely in my power. You understand?"

Another nod.

"I won't kill or torture or violate you. You must be quiet and obedient and after three days when we all leave . . . they will probably find . . . work for you. Other work than being . . . food. Until then I will protect you from the others. That is all I promise, but what I promise I will do. Get up."

She did, cautiously after the previous three attempts. "You . . . you want to drink my blood?"

"Yes," he said. "Some. Not enough to harm you."

But I wouldn't unless I had to. I need the strength and it would ring any number of alarm bells here if I didn't. This is part of why I told Harvey I was reluctant. To be accepted, I must act as one of them in this way at least.

"I will not harm you otherwise. It's the best offer you're going to get."

She was looking skeptical, and at his crotch. He did himself, and smiled wryly: that was a reaction he couldn't help.

"I'm a man with a penis, not a penis with a man attached. I don't take unwilling women."

Which makes me, if not unique among Shadowspawn, at least highly unusual.

"The blood, for protection. Quickly!"

She nodded. He reached for her . . . and then she swung a shin up towards his groin in a hard vicious kick combined with an earnest thumb towards his eye. That showed rough-and-tumble experience; he was glad she didn't have a knife. Adrian ducked under the gouge, grabbed the ankle effortlessly—her mind had telegraphed her intention half a second in advance—and used it to fling her around, staggering as she fought not to fall. Then he had her pinned, his right arm holding both of hers against her body, his left under her jaw.

"Hold . . . *still*," he snarled, as she bucked and heaved and shrieked and tried to claw, kick and bite at the same time. "Oh, *nom d'un chien noir!*"

The body writhing against his was *far* too stimulating. He clamped her jaw upward and struck. The incisors sliced across taut skin, and the blood boiled into his mouth. She froze with the paralysis of an initial bite; not limp or stiff, simply unresisting as he held her off the ground and drank.

Oh, God, that is good, was the first thought.

Like eating a fine rare Chateaubriand when you'd been skiing all day . . .

. . . and add Madeira jus with sautéed mushrooms and a really good Côtes du Rhône . . .

. . . or like the floating feeling after sex, like the first stage of drunkenness in good company, like *triumph*. Power flowed into him; he could feel his mind uncoiling like a thing of steel and smoothly meshing gears.

Then shame. Then: *But I wish I were with Ellie. This is good, but not enough to drive me mad as I feared. I can stop . . . now.*

He did, and stepped back, licking his lips and wiping his chin, and forcing himself not to grin; the poor girl wouldn't know it was relief at his own self-control. The impulse to strip off her clothes and throw her down on the floor and take her savagely was there too . . .

But no harder to resist than the instinct to kill if I am jostled. I am not my instincts; I am a man, and my mind rules them. Feeding does not turn me into a beast. That is a choice, and I choose "no."

Cheba wobbled off and collapsed into a chair, hand to her neck.

"You . . . bit me," she said wonderingly. "You are so strong, so quick . . . you . . ."

Her voice was quiet with the artificial calm that came with a feeding attack. She took the hand away and looked at the red smudge on it.

"You bit me. I could feel you drinking."

"Yes, I bit you and drank some of your blood. I will again several times over the next few days. It will not hurt and you will be none the worse for it after a little while. What I am is not catching; you must be born so. Now don't cause me problems!"

There was a discreet knock at the door. He opened it, and his pseudo-renfields came through, with a house servant pushing a dolly with the last of the trunks on it. The servant was blankly incurious, probably a survival trait; Guha and Farmer simply carried it through to the suite's bedroom. When they came back Farmer gave him a smoldering look after his eyes flicked to Cheba. There was hate in it, though they'd discussed this necessity when they were briefing each other on the mission.

He wishes he could feed, Adrian thought. *He has enough of the genes to want, but not enough to be satisfied if he does. Poor bastard; that's the combination that makes for a Jeffrey Dahmer, if it's not spotted early, if you don't know what's happening. But he must not let it interfere with our work!*

Guha hacked him on the ankle with the toe of her boot. He screeched, cut it short as she grabbed him by the ear:

"Stay in character, Jack! Last warning! *Think* in character! Or I'll kill you myself."

He nodded, took a deep breath and bowed slightly to Adrian along with his partner.

"Lay out my dinner jacket, Farmer," he said quietly. "White tie. Guha, get the girl cleaned up. Order her a meal from the kitchens and show her where she'll sleep—there will be bedchambers for my personal attendants."

It would create a little gossip when the maids changed the sheets and realized he was sleeping alone, but not too much—Shadowspawn considered their private lives *private.*

"Find her some clothes, too. She doesn't speak much English, but

I suspect she understands more, so be cautious. And she's pretty good at trying to kick you in the crotch while gouging out your eyes, so be cautious about that, too. Get her settled in and then dress for dinner yourselves—I'll need you to lend me countenance later. Let's get going."

A couple of presentable attendants were the minimum he could sport and not be the Shadowspawn equivalent of a homeless beggar.

"Cheba," he said, switching back to Spanish.

She was coming to life again, and looked up warily.

"This is Anjali Guha, and this man is Jack Farmer. They both speak your language"—tolerably, at least—"and they are my trusted servants. They will not harm you, but you must do as they say when I am not here."

It was time to put in his appearance at the party.

"Excuse me," a voice said behind her. "You dance so beautifully."

Ellen turned and stopped her solitary drift to the music. It was the man . . . Shadowspawn . . . who'd first appeared as an owl in the killing hall, but now in a cutaway coat and white tie, trimly elegant rather than unselfconsciously naked. She met the yellow eyes . . .

Click. A feeling like rubber bands snapping inside her head. Emotion surged up as the doors in her mind opened.

"Shhh!" Adrian said—she could *feel* that it was Adrian behind the disguise.

What he calls the link. I can feel it too, now. He's happy, and afraid, and very determined. But I didn't realize he could be so fierce.

She clamped at her thoughts, and she could sense something helping her. He bowed over her hand and murmured:

"Allow me, darling. You must not spike noticeably. Use *this*. Think of it and it will help you contain. And if you are read, it will collapse your memories back to the rest state."

A shape appeared in her mind; the sense that saw it was not sight, or touch, or hearing, but it had something of all three.

Wait a minute, she thought, under the muted rush of relief; she could feel how huge it was beneath the artificial barrier.

He could *have done things to my mind when we were together. I'd never have known and he would have gotten whatever he wanted. But he didn't. He let me leave even though it hurt him. He* does *have willpower like titanium steel.*

Then he went on aloud: "But this always goes better with two. May I have this dance?"

She nodded wordlessly, biting her lip. He placed his right hand on her waist, took her left and led her into the waltz; the musicians played a little louder, and they had the floor to themselves. He smiled at her, his own expression visible behind the stranger's face and the blank golden eyes.

"Oh, thank *God*, Adrian," she said softly, swaying across the marble with him. "I feel like I want to *live* again."

"And I as if I have a reason to live again," he answered.

She swallowed. "You know what happened up there. After you left, and I had to watch some of it."

"Yes. That is how things are done at such affairs." A crook to his mouth. "You see why I am alienated from my family, Ellie."

"Thank God for *that*." Sharply: "What happened to that girl you hauled off?"

"Nothing bad." His face went stiff. "Well, nothing *very* bad . . . I'm here as an agent, Ellie, an infiltrator. I have to . . . fit in. I had to feed on her. Forgive me."

He looked miserable at her scowl, and she squeezed his hand as they moved to the music.

"Silly, I'm *jealous*, that's all. I know you wouldn't hurt her. You saved her life by getting her out of that . . . that horrible place before things started. But once we're out of here, dude, it's strictly my veins or the blood bank!"

His laugh was delighted. "You know, you are not only the most beautiful woman I've ever seen, particularly in that dress—"

Ellen snorted. "Your sister picked every stitch I've got, down to the thongs. And she's actually better looking than I am, come to that."

"If you like adolescent boys with small perfect breasts," he said, and she muffled a snort of laughter. "And I cannot fault her taste in clothes *or* in women."

"Do you *really* have a thing for Marilyn Monroe?" Ellen asked.

He looked at her blankly for a moment. "You . . . actually you *do* look a little like her, don't you? But with a better figure, and your face has more animation. You are more . . . elegant."

"Elegant? Wait until you see my new tramp stamp," she said wryly. "It's stopped itching, at least. And she thought *that* really added to my ass; so much for her taste. It's got *all* the colors the tattooist had on hand."

His eyes went a little wider. Then he smiled and let his hand shift a little backward as they turned. His face was abstracted for an instant, though the smooth grace of his movements was unaffected as they danced. Something tickled slightly over the base of her spine.

"It's actually rather pretty, if a bit loud," he said. Then a slight frown. "It's not just colored knotwork, either. There are glyphs worked into it—ideographic Mhabrogast."

That made her feel as if the skin there was still burning. Then his face cleared.

"Not active glyphs . . . not a Wreaking. Just commentary."

"What does it say?"

"Hard to translate . . . Mhabrogast concepts usually are. Something like . . . *appropriate to purpose*, or *confluence of aspects* with overtones of enjoyment-fulfillment . . ."

"*For a good time, call Ellen?*" she said dryly.

"More like, *She's a beauty*. On that, if nothing else, she and I agree. And besides being beautiful, you are the most remarkably brave person I know, as well. I do not deserve you, but I shall enjoy my good fortune nonetheless."

"So will I!"

He leaned closer and whispered in her ear:

"You are also supremely bite-able, and at last I am able to say that and not feel sorry for myself, or guilty. I was feeding on Cheba and thinking of *you*, my Ellie. Jealousy adds to my long-standing hatred for my sister."

There was something like a lick of hot wind in his voice, something that made her shiver slightly. Familiar yet not.

That's the first time a Shadowspawn's looked at me like that and it didn't scare me. Well, not really *scare me. It's sort of predatory, yes, but I can see it's Adrian in there. And . . . yeah, I really do love him, I guess. It won't be easy, but I want to try.*

"*You've* got a better butt than she does," Ellen said, just for the pleasure of seeing his smile. "And you're *here*."

The tune came to an end, and they turned and applauded the musicians. Then she heard more applause from the formal staircase. Ellen swallowed and made herself turn, smiling, as the glyph sprang into her mind.

Christ, that's strange, she thought. *It's as if my thoughts were operating on two sides of a plane of glass!*

"Be ready," Adrian murmured.

She could feel her emotions running on parallel tracks, the fear-hate-fascination-loathing-longing that Adrienne produced, and the bubbling joy at restored hope as well. The mistress of Rancho Sangre was there, gowned and jeweled now, with her parents, and the three Shadowspawn who'd flown in right after Adrian.

Dmitri Usov was in immaculate white tie and black dress coat; with his long blond hair it made him look a little like a mad, murderous conductor in a Romantic opera about an old-fashioned orchestra. Dale Shadowspawn . . . she blinked. *He* was in Apache costume, or a version thereof, complete with tunic and headband and leggings. Not tourist-ified, though the fabrics were fine dark cloth, and there was platinum on the hilt of his long knife.

And Michiko, in the full ceremonial splendor of a *Hōmongi* ki-mono, with patterns of floral roundels and birds swirling along the seams of the pale-green silk, encircled by an embroidered *fukuro obi* and topped by an elaborate hairdo held with long jade pins. Even her step in the sandals and white divided-toe socks had a mincing look.

Oh, she thought. *They're expecting this Hajime guy. He's really old-fashioned.*

"Ah, Mr. Peterson," Adrienne said. "I see you've made my Ellen's acquaintance."

"A great pleasure," Adrian said neutrally. "You are to be envied. In fact, I *do* envy you."

"I envy *you*, a little—it wouldn't be really appropriate for me to dance with her tonight; we're being very formal."

"Wilbur!" Jules Brézé said from behind her, delight in his voice. "Good God, it *is* you!"

Adrian extended his hand for an old-fashioned shake, rather than the touch of the fingertips that most younger Shadowspawn used. His shields clamped down like a surface of mirrored alloy, until his own perception dimmed.

"Good God, Wilbur, it's been . . . nearly sixty years!" his father said.

"Yes," Adrian said neutrally; he ruthlessly crushed a squib of panic. "A very long time, Jules."

And there were several unanswered letters from you to Wilbur, he thought. *Men change, even postcorporeals. Jules believes you are Wilbur, Adrian. He will interpret anything you say in that light.*

"Let's get a drink. Adrienne is stuck with the greeting tonight, until the grand entrance of our would-be mikado."

The ground floor of the *casa grande* was a series of interconnected chambers, mostly opening into each other through arched entranceways in a Moorish-Iberian style. They ducked through into a smaller room, more of a broad passageway around a courtyard, and took cocktails from a tray.

"*À votre santé,*" Jules said.

"Your health," Adrian replied.

He sipped. Then his brows rose. "A classic Deauville! Now, that does take me back."

Cognac, Coquerel Calvados, Van Gogh triple sec and lemon; the fruit flavors tingled over his tongue. It had been a popular mixture in the 1920s.

"Always one of your favorites, as I recall," Jules said.

It's the first time I've ever met my own father socially, Adrian thought. *Since I was thirteen, at least, and he is utterly unchanged. He's not a bad fellow, for a mass murderer.*

"I never thought I'd see you alive again," Jules said. "It is . . . not a good sign, when a man is as out of contact as you have been."

Adrian shrugged and smiled. "I knew I was drifting, but . . . there always seemed to be time to remedy matters later. I lived much in dreams of the past. Yet in the end, they are unsatisfying."

Which is why the real Wilbur killed himself, most probably. When the dream ends, the reality you fled is more terrible than ever.

For a Shadowspawn, it was possible to live in the interior world quite literally, shaping it to your will.

But while it feels and smells and tastes real, it isn't; and the people *are not real, unless they are captured souls.*

Jules shook his head. "I knew. Yet every time I warned you . . . well, why relive old fights? May I see it? You still carry the locket everywhere?"

Adrian let his mind relax and *chose.* His fingers went into a pocket and brought out the little gold oval; that was the path the Power saw as leading to the result he wanted. He opened it and glanced within; the face was delicate, huge-eyed. If the hand-tinting of the photograph was accurate, there had been an elfin loveliness. Adrian handed it over carefully, as a man would with a precious possession, and took it back almost immediately.

"Joan was very beautiful," Jules said. "Yet . . . my friend, it is not well to become too attached to them. Fond yes, in some cases, but not . . . attached. They die. We do not. Our natures are different. That you could not be there when she was killed and Carry her soul was a tragedy, yes, but I suspect . . . that the temptations of dreams would have been even worse if you had. Forgive me if I intrude!"

Adrian shrugged and smiled with Wilbur's face and body. "Obviously, I came to agree with you in the end," he said. "Though it was hard."

"You should acquire a few contemporary lucies on a long-term basis. An occasional kill is one thing, but . . ."

"I think I was punishing them for not being *her*," Adrian said, guessing at the psychology of a dead man.

I would feel some sympathy for him, if he had not brought so many others suffering and death.

"Some things do *not* change, though," Jules said, winking. "I noticed you dancing with my daughter's Ellen, you sly dog!"

He shrugged. "Is that her name? A glorious creature, and her blood-scent! Maddening! Trust a Brézé to find such a vision, and to torment us all with it."

A ruefully envious snap of the teeth, and Jules did the same; they laughed and raised their glasses in a brief toast before Adrian continued:

"But the mind was extremely strange, and . . . well, women spoke with more restraint when I was a young man. Except for those of the lower orders, of course, and she obviously isn't that. The mixture of sophistication and coarseness is . . . disturbing. I expected one or the other. The little *chica* I picked out of Adrienne's gift-herd is a pretty, healthy animal, and satisfying in her peasant way. I may keep her. But in our day . . ."

"Our day is not past," Jules said, giving him a brief slap on the shoulder. "Now that you are around and about again, you must come and visit us in La Jolla. Night-polo, old man! You taught me the art in daylight eighty years ago; let me return the favor. And we have a wide human acquaintance. There is much that is interesting among them."

"This is . . . a trial venture. I must learn to live in the world again. It's . . . well, it's a damned odd world now, that's all."

"Ah, and it will grow odder still, unless we take measures. You probably haven't been following Council politics?"

Adrian spread a hand out, remembering at the last moment to make the gesture palm-down and restrained. Wilbur Peterson had been American-raised, though related to the Brézés. He would be not only an Anglo-Saxon in his body language, but an antique one.

"I didn't *recognize* much of the territory I flew over to get here, except for the ocean and the mountains," he said. "God, to think that we used to drive around San Jose for the blossoms! The scent was intoxicating even for humans. I nearly reconsidered and turned around."

Jules made a grimace. "Yes. We have been negligent in caring for the greater estate. My daughter has some interesting plans for dealing with that, and I find her energy and enthusiasm quite compelling. Julianne and I never became withdrawn, but it is so easy to live from day to day. Perhaps the corporeals have a greater sense of urgency. Let me tell you about the Council meeting that's to be called. And of course Hajime will be representing us . . ."

"How did that happen?" Adrian asked; Wilbur had been well into his fugue by then.

"Oh, the usual way. Overconfidence by us, intrigue and then a swift coup by them. Hajime killed me personally, though I must say it was decent of him not to inflict Final Death. Adrienne is quite close with Tōkairin Michiko, Hajime's favorite grandchild. They negotiated the details of the peace agreement."

A Taint in the Blood

"Tell me more about this ceremony, the Prayer for Long Life," Adrian said. "And the Council meeting."

Jules smiled. "It's splendid to see you taking an interest again! Well—"

"Wilbur was quite a delightful man in his time," Julianne Brézé said. "He was something of a mentor to Jules and me after our parents died so tragically . . . Everyone was so surprised when they didn't transition successfully, given their blood-purity, but those things were not as well understood in our youth. Perhaps it was the shock of the assassination. Those Brotherhood scum were bolder then."

Several of the Shadowspawn listening hissed; Ellen felt a small crawling sensation at the sound. It wasn't contrived or deliberate, she decided; it was just the natural way for them to express . . .

Murderous hate, she thought. *Frustrated sadism.*

"I'm Carrying one of them," Julianne said; her eyes had an inward look for an instant. "The other was too quick to suicide, but we caught little Thomas. He's in a small rock chamber in my mind, feeding a very large spider. And after so many years, he's very tired of it. The spider is still extremely enthusiastic. Occasionally it becomes . . . amorous. Then it spawns in his flesh and the young eat their way out. And I'm never, ever going to let Tom die the Final Death, though he begs for that fairly continuously. Once I let him *think* he'd been given release, and then he woke up again to the spider's caress."

Oh, Christ, she means it . . .

The remark brought general laughter. Ellen sipped at her second glass of champagne and tried to ignore other comments about what could be, and gleeful recollections of what had been, done to captured Brotherhood agents. Even after the killing-hall some of them were gruesome. Peter grimaced to her as she turned away a little.

"I wonder why they let us mingle at events like this?" she said softly. "We lucies, and the renfields."

"Control rods," he replied promptly; his cheeks were a little flushed, and he was working on his third glass of the sparkling wine. "That's definitely part of it."

It's been quite a while since she fed on him, Ellen thought sympathetically. *God, that can get hard to take! Even knowing there's going to be pain doesn't make you want it less. At least not for me. I think that may be harder for him.*

"What?" she said aloud. "Rods?"

"Like the control rods in a nuclear reactor, the ones they slide in to absorb neutrons and slow down the reaction. We damp down their hyper-aggressiveness. In fact, I think it's probably the human part of their heredity that lets them cooperate as much as they do. They're solitary killers by nature, or at least the original breed were."

"Adrienne said that they don't *want* to breed themselves much more pureblood than she is."

Peter nodded. "But they pay for it," he said. "I think they have a lot of inner conflicts too."

"Too?"

"The way we do because of the dash of Shadowspawn. It . . . twists us both up in different ways."

"Speaking of which," Ellen said quietly.

Jose was talking with his aunt Theresa, looking martyred as she brushed lint off his shoulder and adjusted his tie. Monica hesitated, then approached Adrienne; she was a little haggard again. The Shadowspawn frowned, then glanced at her sidelong with a slight smile and moved away from the group around her mother. Monica followed and their heads leaned together.

"If you ask *nicely*," Ellen heard Adrienne say. "It's really Peter's turn."

"Oh, I beg," Monica said quietly. "*Please.*"

"Very well. But things will be energetic. Strenuous. Social events put me on edge."

"That's fine, Adri. Whatever you need is what I want."

"Damn," Peter said softly. "That's sad. It's also jumping her place in line, dammit!"

"I know it's hard to miss out on the bite," Ellen said.

"It's been nearly a week. Damned right it's hard. I can't *think* straight."

"Well, for you especially, lack of clarity of thought is a major downer," Ellen went on dryly. "But what part of *energetic* and *strenuous* are you so sorry to skip?"

"There is that. Though," he added, with the relentless honesty she'd noticed was one of his habits—"*parts* of that can be OK. I don't mind the actual sex much, apart from always having . . ."

His voice trailed off. Ellen guessed, and her voice went even drier:

"Apart from always having to be the girl?" she asked.

"Ah . . . well, I wouldn't have phrased it quite that way . . ."

She laughed; the sound even had some humor in it. "Peter, I am a girl, and one who's a submissive masochist at that, and *I* find it extremely wearing at times, Adrienne-style. But really . . . Monica was hit very hard by what we saw."

Something spiky flashed into the forefront of her mind for a moment . . . *a glyph*, she thought. *I wonder why?* But it calmed her, somehow.

"You *weren't* hit hard?"

"I was. *Oh*, yeah. It was grisly beyond words. But I'm better at . . . at compartmentalizing. And Adrienne took a full teeth-in-the-throat feeding from me right afterwards."

"Misery makes you taste good," he said wryly.

"Yeah. But she just *sipped* a little from Monica and it's coming back on her."

She went on:

"More . . . interaction . . . will help. You know what I mean."

I mean strenuous *and* energetic *involves a fair bit of screaming, in pain and otherwise. Been there, done that. It is distracting and distraction is just what poor Monica needs now.*

Monica fumbled something out of her handbag; her BlackBerry. She made a call on it, probably telling her mother she wouldn't be home tonight and needed her to stay with the children, then smiled tremulously and seemed to relax a little.

Peter sighed. "I don't suppose I can argue with that. I will now proceed to get gradually but thoroughly drunk. That and the hangover will distract *me* for a day or so until I get my dose. She's probably going to be feeding more than usual, with all this activity."

More guests arrived; some through the front entrance, others down the staircase, which meant they'd flown in. Some of those were corporeals too, like Adrienne's three . . .

Coconspirators? Ellen thought. *Which means their actual bodies must have been unconscious and carried in by their renfields. Maybe even in coffins . . . well, no, in padded boxes that* look *a lot like coffins, I suppose. And the postcorporeals must have something like that for safety when they're traveling . . . anyway, ewww.*

Adrienne stopped as she walked by. "I've known some of the postcorporeals to transform into a smallish creature and have themselves shipped FedEx," she said.

Peter snorted. "*Shipped?*"

"It's no hardship being boxed up if you're a comatose rodent, *hein?* And you can use a nice secure sealed container of welded steel when you can go impalpable—just walk in through the side as a gerbil or a ferret, say. Curl up, and then step out the same way when you get to your destination. But I think I'll keep my jet or whatever the equivalent is by the time I've had my Second Birth. Getting there is half the fun."

When she'd passed by, Ellen went on to Peter: "Has it struck you how dependent Shadowspawn are on renfields? They'd have to hide in caves or sewers without them."

"Yes," Peter said, running a hand through his hair. Then he took a deep breath and forced himself to stop fidgeting. "But they can *know* who's trustworthy."

"It isn't *fair*," she burst out.

Unexpectedly, he laughed. It was a little slurred, but genuine.

"No, it isn't fair. There are so few of them, and they're no smarter than we are—Adrienne is very bright, but she's well above average for them, too. Most of them are arrogant and self-indulgent and unbelievably self-centered, judging by the ones I've met. It's the damned *Power*."

By now the great room had seventy or eighty people in it not counting the house servants; milling around, talking, drinking and eating canapés off trays. Each Shadowspawn individual or couple—a few had teenage children in tow, looking sullen as you'd expect—was surrounded by an aura of their important renfields and . . .

"Show-lucies," Ellen said.

"What?" Peter said.

"That's what we are. We're show-lucies. Trophies, as well as control rods. Notice how all the lucies are extremely good-looking and *very* well dressed?"

He smiled wryly. "Touché. And thanks."

"You're a very handsome man, Peter."

"That's probably why I'm alive. No," he went on a little pedantically. "It's probably why she didn't kill me in Los Alamos. If I'd been a quarter-ton of questionable hygiene like quite a few of my colleagues, I'd have been toast. But my brains are probably why I'm *still* alive."

It might have been a cocktail party or reception anywhere, except for the odd touch—Jules disappearing into an alcove with his lucy, Mark . . . reappearing with blood on his lips and Mark looking flushed and rumpled, for example. Then Adrienne's head came up; she nodded and made an inconspicuous signal.

The Shadowspawn present moved to either side of the doors. Ellen shared a glance with Peter, and got a nod from him too; the movement was slow and ragged and Adrienne was obviously restraining a shout of *Hurry up, you idiots!* with difficulty. Theresa had the favored renfields and lucies lined up behind them much more quickly.

The great doors swung open; the air outside was a little cooler, scented with flowers and warm dust. A file of the Gurkha mercenaries marched in wearing green dress uniforms with silver buttons and little pillbox hats; they split and wheeled into two lines on either side, and brought their rifles up to *present arms* with a smart stamp and crash of boots and smack of hands on metal.

Tōkairin Hajime walked through, in a black sha-silk kimono and gray *hakama*—wide trousers like a split skirt. The *haori* jacket over it all was open at the front, and bore five *kamon*, House badges with the *mon* of his clan. His wife was behind him, in a rustling splendor of white and rose and crimson and intricate headdress; an attendant carried his swords, leaving his hands empty except for a fan, and there were several others behind him. He and his party stepped out of their sandals and a servant knelt to help them on with slippers.

Adrienne swept forward and sank in a deep curtsy—the antique form combined with a bow, but the Western gesture nonetheless. Her parents followed suit.

Ah, Ellen thought, watching his nod in return; everyone else just bowed. *That's* more *respectful, not less. I wonder what* she's *thinking?*

"*Tōkairin-sama, yoku irasshaimashita,*" Adrienne said, in formal greeting. "Lord Tōkairin! Welcome to my home."

"Sorry to be a bother," Hajime said—which made more sense in Japanese. Then he switched to English for a moment: "Thank you for going to all this trouble."

"It was the least I could do," Adrienne half-purred.

"*Tsumaranai mono desu ga . . .*" he went on; *this is a mere trifle,* or words to that effect.

The gift was a sword in a superb black-lacquered sheath, an elegant plainness. She made a small, quite genuine exclamation of pleasure as she took the silk-cord grip in her hand and drew it just enough for a sliver of the silver-worked layered steel to show, then clicked it home to keep the chill menace of the activated glyphs warded. Someone who really knew what they were doing had worked over this one. Hajime was powerful enough, but not so subtle a Wreaker.

They went through the usual *oh-I-couldn't-possibly/please-accept-this* dance that Hajime's background required.

Then Adrienne indicated a pair from those her renfields had picked from potential quarry at San Simeon over the past few months—a statuesque redheaded girl with milk-pale skin and a sandy-haired youth with a beautiful dancer's body. Both showed to advantage in the short white feeding tunics, and they had been carefully primed, mostly by a detailed and honest description of what was likely to happen to them. They had sensitive, intelligent minds, now nearly paralytic with terror but unable to stop imagining their fates in flashes of vivid imagery that came through beautifully.

It was enough to make *her* hungry, and she'd fed well today. There was nothing quite like picking out *the worst* from someone's mind and then actually *doing* it to them.

"*Nani mo gozaimasen ga, dozo meshiagatte kudasai,*" she said: "It's nothing, but please go ahead and have some."

Hajime's wife had been decorously quiet except for a murmured exchange of greetings; now her teeth clicked together slightly.

"*Oishisou,*" she said softly: *looks delicious.*

The clan-head smiled and gave Adrienne a shrewd glance, and she could feel Michiko's bubble of quickly-suppressed mirth even through her shields.

"You are courteous to a fault," he said. "Later, certainly."

Theresa and her assistants hustled the pair out; they'd be ready in the guest-suite when dawn made postcorporeals seek shelter. The formal greeting array broke down as Hajime and his retinue began to mingle.

"My only worry is that my mad brother may somehow manage to spoil things," Adrienne said to him.

The Shadowspawn overlord of the West Coast snorted. "I doubt that very much."

Michiko bowed. "I have had our best men checking carefully, Grandfather," she said. "The precautions certainly seem more than adequate."

Dale had been doing his best impassive-Indian impression, even crossing his arms over his chest. Now he smiled thinly.

"I think so too, sir," he said.

Hajime's nod was wary this time. "Ms. Brézé requested that you do so?"

"Yes. I'm not active on any Council missions right now, so I gave it a thorough going-over, and I'll be here for the full three days. It's within my remit, since you are a Council member, sir."

Dmitri nodded: "I have also reviewed the arrangements. It was the least I could do, after your patronage released me from Seversk!"

One of Hajime's brows rose with his nod this time. "You certainly seem to have taken every possible precaution," he said to Adrienne.

She spread her hands and smiled charmingly. Hajime's other brow went up; her father and mother were stepping up from behind her.

"Jules," he said. "Julianne."

The elder Brézés bowed slightly. "Haven't seen you since you killed us, Hajime-san," Jules said cheerfully.

"You're moving back here?" their murderer said with a trace of iron in his tone.

"Oh, no, just visiting with our grandchildren."

Hajime's face relaxed slightly. "One of life's great pleasures, exceeded only by great-grandchildren."

Adrienne backed out of the conversation graciously, keeping her smile to herself until she was safely facing away. Her shields were impenetrable, but Hajime hadn't survived over a century of Shadowspawn politics, and generations past his body's death, by being unable to read faces as well as minds.

Perfect, she thought. *Perfect!*

CHAPTER TWENTY-ONE

Adrian rose from the bed; he'd left the party early, by his nocturnal breed's standards. The *casa grande* was finally quiet, though some Shadowspawn lingered in the public areas, and most were still awake in their rooms. He could sense them, a prickle of the Power. Sliding through the fabric of the world, like the smooth onrush of sharks that makes the water curve just below the surface of an ocean.

And Ellen is alone.

A grimace. Close by the girl Cheba was tossing and fighting her sheets and whimpering in her sleep; the two Brotherhood agents were nearly as restless. In their line of work—his too, again—post-traumatic stress was more of a permanent condition of life than a problem to recover from.

For them this is part of the business they have chosen. Or were born into, as I was. I pity Cheba, though. All she wanted was a better way to earn her bread than selling baskets on the streets.

Those were not his only base-links, links of blood and seed. Somewhere in the great pile two children were sleeping as well; he caught a brief image of a girl curled around a flaxen-haired doll and a boy lying in the utter abandonment of childhood slumber. Adrienne was awake, but happily oblivious to everything but her own building pleasure and hunger, lost in sensation and in the mind of her partner-victim as it opened to a helpless combination of pain and orgasmic release.

He grimaced again, and clamped down on the contact until it was merely a vague consciousness of direction.

Then he walked to the outer window. The air in the rest of the suite was fresh—the system of concealed ducts was old, but well designed—yet he welcomed the cool night breeze on his naked flesh. The moon hung over the Santa Lucia Range where it divided this interior valley from the sea. It was nearly full, and the silvery light was a prickle on the skin of his aetheric form. It seemed to call to him . . .

"And I'm going to answer," he said softly. "*Amss-aui-ock!*"

The oldest Shadowspawn talent of all took him. A moment of silvery darts along his nerves, and his body flowed—to another shape as borrowed as that of Wilbur Peterson, but much more familiar. Vision grew less, color absent or muted, shades of black and white and gray predominant, though the moonlight was more than adequate. He could see movement—the twitch of a leaf, the motion of a cat leaping to a wall in the gardens below—with utter sharpness, but anything motionless blurred like the world of a short-sighted man.

Ah, but the sounds!

Nearly as keen as those of the owl, and in a different range. He could hear breathing, voices half a mile away, a frightened dog that suddenly scented an ancient enemy; the quiet night was a babble of noise now, and the wolf's mind sorted it with effortless ease.

A Taint in the Blood

And the smells! There are no words!

He snarled slightly, eager to run and hunt. It took an effort for the man-mind that lurked within to command the beast, though the wolf was his favorite. The hundred-and-eighty-pound beast sprang easily up to the sill of the window, then down a dozen feet to the ground below, landing on legs like powerful springs. He trotted through the garden, past the plashing of a fountain—*wet, wet, weeds, cool tempting flesh of a frog*—and down through steps that led through beds of azaleas—*thick-sweet-strong*—and lawns. A squeak and a snap and his jaws went *clomp* on a field-mouse, with a sweet gush of almost flowery blood. He tossed it up . . .

. . . and let it fall.

When you transform again, it would still be in your stomach, and one not intended to handle raw mouse, bones and all.

And the flush of salt savor was not really satisfying. This body was built around the DNA of a timber-wolf, but within it was Shadow-spawn still. Only human blood would do. He kept on until he reached the perimeter wall of the estate; a dash for a man was an easy trot in this shape.

Ellen's scent was strong, many trails over many days overlain on each other. He whined slightly, mixed with a growl. Part of what his nose caught said *prey*, and raised visions of rending and tearing and the hot tang of blood. The other message it carried was of an overwhelming femaleness, that arched his tail and made his gait stiff-legged. *Kill* and *mount her* warred in the sharp limited consciousness of the wolf mind, amid images that mingled pink-and-golden nakedness with something furry and four-legged.

There was another scent mixed with Ellen's; his sister's. *That* raised the fur along the beast's spine, and lips curled back to show long white fangs. His ears flattened to the massive wedge-shaped skull of the wolf in challenge-response, and he had to suppress a growl that rose from the animal's deep chest.

The man-mind within prompted, and the Mhabrogast prickled and twisted in his head. When he rose on two feet he was Adrian Brézé again. A stare, and the iron of the gate set in the estate wall turned translucent. He stepped through it, and a cold grating sensation ran along his nerves for an instant. Here he was in a courtyard garden, a tiled expanse amid raised flowerbeds and small trees, with a brick fire pit barbecue in one corner. Trellised roses gave the night a sweet-musky scent, strong to his Shadowspawn nose, dull by comparison with the wolf's but much sharper than a human's. A small trickle of water flowed from a ceramic lion's mask into a bowl, and an owl flapped through the night above.

He stiffened at that for an instant, but the Power told him it was a natural bird, off about its business.

There were two lights through the windows of the house, a pleasant Spanish-revival building with a red-tile roof that might have housed a doctor or accountant in a hundred older Californian suburbs. The glass doors showed a living-room that had a lived-in look, with bookcases and art prints on the walls, and a thick scatter of volumes on the coffee-table; those were more reproductions, from the large format. Ellen was seated on the sofa, dressed in a long peignoir of sheer white silk, with a drink by her elbow. As he watched she leaned back and pressed the heels of her hands to her eyes.

His night-walking form was imperceptible to humans, unless he wished it. Now he did, bringing it into solidity, and tapped gently on the door. Ellen started, and then shot to her feet when she saw him.

"Adrienne?" she said, when she'd slid the door open and he stepped through; the golden hibiscus-scent of her filled his nostrils. "I . . . um, I thought you were with Monica tonight."

Adrian's brows went up. He looked down at himself; unequivocally male, and *interested* male at that. Then he mentally cursed.

"Of course. She has used my aetheric form with you." *Damn her presumption!* "Remember Amalfi, Ellie . . . someday we will honeymoon there in reality."

The joy in her face and mind blazed; it warmed him even as she dulled it with the glyph he'd taught her and threw herself into his arms. Long moments later she drew back, took several deep breaths and nodded in a businesslike fashion.

"You have an extremely self-disciplined mind," he said.

"Oh, right now I'm not feeling very . . . well, yes, I wouldn't mind a little *discipline* . . ."

He groaned. "I *can't*."

Her blue eyes sparkled. "I know, but teasing you is so much fun. When we're together again, well, if you felt like punishing me for it . . . maybe in *her* form . . ."

She laughed at his expression. "Now I've shocked *you*, darling! Hey, if I'm going to have a vampiric shapeshifter for my guy, I intend to take *full* advantage of it."

"I just may take you up on that." Adrian grinned, and gave her a quick tweak that made her yelp and jump.

Then he sobered. "But now we must hurry. I need to scout the area where the ceremony is to take place, and I need you with me."

"Why?" she said. "No problem, but . . . I'm not the fem-ninja type."

"Because your blood and mind are involved with any Wreaking she's been doing lately. Shadowspawn call it *sourcing*."

"Sort of like me being fuel, right?"

"Right, but there's an element of . . . flavor involved, with repeated feedings. Now I need to see what Wreakings have been preset there. She would have done that before Hajime arrived—he's not as . . . as subtle a user of the Power as she is."

She drew a deep breath. "OK, let's get going. I'll put on something more suitable."

She looked down at her filmy garment. "Suitable for something besides being ceremoniously ripped off me like the wrapper off a chocolate truffle, that is. Or used to tie me up. Or both. I knew from popular culture that being a vamp-victim got you great lingerie and fabulous hair—"

Adrian snorted incredulous laughter at the dry humor. *That's my Ellie!*

"—but I run through these things pretty damned fast. It's a shame; they're handmade and really pretty."

She vanished for a moment, leaving him with a brief vision of stripping a silk peignoir off her that was arresting even with urgent business at hand. When she returned, it was in practical khakis.

Though she looks enchanting in anything, he thought.

"I'll carry you to the ceremonial ground," he said. At her surprise: "That will be much quicker on four feet than two. Be prepared. This is going to be, ah, startling."

"What will be startling?"

"The form. *Smilodon populator.* Big cat. Very big."

Transformation took him.

Eeek! Ellen thought, jumping back a little at the sparkling blur that didn't last quite long enough to really see.

Then aloud: "Oh, my!"

The sabertooth looked up at her. Its eyes were on a level with her chest; she didn't suppose it was more than six feet from nose to stumpy tail, not outlandishly more than a big lion—

Which is plenty long enough!

—but it was much thicker-built, giving an impression of something halfway between a cat and a bear in build, a hulking heavy-shouldered gracefulness on paws the size of dinner-plates. Art training had made her good at estimating volumes; it must weigh as much as a smallish horse or a medium grizzly. The great curved ivory daggers of its canines stretched below its lower jaw, longer than her hand from wrist to fingertip, and the tawny hide was spotted with darker circles, fading to a light cream under the throat-ruff and belly.

"That's . . . quite a critter, Adrian," she said.

She could *smell* it, too; not a bad scent, but hard and furry and dry, the breath slightly rank. Tentatively she put out a hand, running it along the long skull of the beast, over the short slightly bristly fur; it licked her hand with a rough tongue the size of a facecloth and gave a deep rumbling sound like a diesel engine trying to purr.

No, it sounds like a sabertooth the size of a small horse, purring. It's scary, but magnificent. Christ, no wonder our caveman ancestors worshipped the Shadowspawn!

Her half-adopted orange tabby Just-a-Cat had been sleeping on top of an ebony étagère she used for art-print books. It came awake, gave a look of bug-eyed horror at its distant relative, and made a flying leap that took it out the sliding door without touching ground amid a squall of:

"Eeerrrow!"

She didn't know if sabertooths could laugh, but Adrian obviously came close. Then the great fanged head butted at her and jerked over its own shoulder.

How should I do this? she wondered.

The sabertooth wasn't as tall as a horse, even if it weighed in at the heavy end of the pony scale. The back wasn't like a horse's, either, and not just because it sloped down from the massive shoulders to the rump. When she touched the skin over its spine the bone was imperceptible under the roiling coils of muscle. The beast's rumble grew a little louder; it crouched and butted her again, and she gulped.

Didn't he say once that it was hard not to . . . get lost in the beast?

Ellen gulped again and straddled the great cat, lying forward with her hands sunk in the not-quite-mane around its neck and her toes locked—firmly, she hoped—in the narrower spot just ahead of the hips. The sabertooth stood and turned, pacing out into the night; she clutched harder at the rolling foot-foot-foot-foot pace that tried to pitch her from side to side. Then the padding quickened and the hindquarters bunched, and Ellen suppressed a startled *eeep!* as it leapt effortlessly to the top of the ten-foot wall that formed the outer wall of the estate gardens about the *casa grande*. Her weight didn't seem to matter at all as it soared, a single instant of birdlike flight.

The huge paws touched the stucco-covered stone with a slight dry *scritch* sound and a *click* of claws, and then they were in the air again. The landing was so soft that the *thud* sound was startling; no matter how well the pads and paws and legs cushioned it, better than half a ton was hitting the close-cut grass. The landing turned into a bound that carried them better than twenty feet, flowerbeds and trees rushing past in a silvery night-blur. Her hands and legs clutched convulsively at the hard hot warmth beneath her, and her breath came faster as the huge cat took the hillside in a smooth reverse-cascade of leaps.

A Taint in the Blood

Past a great marble pool and fountain, soaring over a flowering hedge, past rows of cypresses beside a bridle path, an onrush like flight in a dream. At last they came to a Japanese-style garden, or the California version of one as conceived a century ago.

Which is actually pretty authentic, she thought. *Most of the gardeners in this state were Japanese then.*

The great cat reared a little, panting like a bellows as they came to the gateway with its swooping tiled roof and backdrop of tall black pines. The scent of them filled the cool night, spicy and almost incense-like. She slid to the ground and the figure was Adrian again, rising to his feet, naked and as lithely graceful as the beast he had been. His chest slowed, but he was still the slightest bit breathless as he said:

"Those things were ambush hunters. No endurance."

"That was like flying!" Ellen said, distracted into delight for an instant.

"No, flying is different . . . better. I will show you someday, Ellie."

Beyond the gate were two great stone *Koma-inu*, lionlike dogs from Japanese mythology. Ellen's mouth quirked as she looked at them.

"They're supposed to keep away evil spirits," she said.

Adrian snorted dryly as he walked past them. "Apparently they don't work," he said.

"Adrian!" He looked around, and she went on sharply: "You are *not* evil! And believe me, I now have a wide enough acquaintance with people in your family who are real-thing no-fucking-doubt-about-it *evil* to tell the difference!"

He quirked a smile at her. "Perhaps you can convince me, someday."

Beyond the gate paths wound, lined now and then with Kasuga stone lanterns, unlit, like miniature shrines on stone pillars. The low hills on either side were covered in azaleas, dim beneath the moon in white and pink—more color than was usual in a Japanese gardening scheme, but this *was* California. Rocks lined the edge of a lake, the still water reflecting moonlight and starlight. A low waterfall made music, with a half-arch bridge across the stream below it, the reflection making a circle; the sides of the bridge were carved with phoenix birds, destruction and rebirth.

"Rebirth of what?" Ellen asked, low-voiced.

"Knowing my family, I don't think there's much doubt as to *that*," Adrian said grimly.

They came to the shrine itself, stone and black-weathered beams; through it they could see the rock-garden, raked gravel and stones in their natural shapes. Slow-growing black bamboo surrounded the flagged enclosure. It soughed and rattled slightly with a breeze that ruffled the surface of the water; then that died away.

"You know, Adrian," she said slowly, "if your family could appreciate this, Shadowspawn and humans have more in common than you seem to think."

"Aesthetics, at least. Stand here, Ellie. And . . . I need a little of your blood."

She smiled at him. "Go ahead."

He took her hand and raised it to his lips. There was a slight sting, and when he held it out over the gravel a red drop welled from one fingertip to drop slowly to the ground.

Adrian made a slight hissing sound as it struck. "Yes, Wreaking sourced from you. Let me see—"

Ellen was silent while he paced the enclosure; occasionally he would pause and make a gesture with his hands held palm-down above the ground. Now and then he would speak—syllables that seemed to *twist* as she heard them, fading away before her mind could hold them.

And it gives me a chance to look at the ol' bod, she thought. *Yeah, all other things being equal, the male form really does have a lot going for it. Particularly the narrow-waisted, slim-but-broad-shouldered, really taut but not bulky types with that focused look to the butt. Like for example my fellah here. Yup, girls just don't basically compare.*

"Now that is very odd," he said at last. "The basic protectives have been renewed, yes. Here they seem to be intended to nudge minds toward harmony and cooperation, as well. But the external wards . . . the warnings of hostile intent, the twisting of paths towards ruin and disaster . . . they have not been renewed at all. Still there, still strong if old-fashioned, but they are *precisely* as the Brotherhood records indicate. Very few modifications."

"That's not in character for Adrienne," Ellen said. "She likes to give these devil-may-care vibes, but she's got a chess player's mind. Careful and she thinks ahead."

Adrian nodded. "Still, I would not care to be a human approaching this place with hostile intention."

"What would happen?" Ellen said.

"You would make noises no matter how careful you were. Your belt would snap, your equipment would break, weapons would misfire. Dogs would happen to catch your scent and bark. If you came in a group, you and your friends would quarrel with each other. And if there was the slightest chance of a heart attack or a stroke or a detached retina or a fall that twisted your ankle and then your head happened to hit a stone . . ."

She shivered, and he went on:

"But they are all directed *outward.* That is what I had to know."

He hesitated. "I am afraid I must become the beast again to take you back."

Ellen put her hands on her hips. "Why afraid?" she said.

He blinked, taken aback. "Because . . . well, it's a large predatory *animal.* Ellie, you don't even like dogs!"

"That's dogs. Who said anything about cats?"

His smile was unwilling. "You are a very brave person, Ellie."

"I hope so. But it isn't courage. That sabertooth thing is *beautiful.* And that ride . . . if I weren't scared of what's going to happen tomorrow and the day after, I'd say that was just plain *fun.*"

"I . . . well, it is sort of . . . bestial. An abandonment of myself. And . . . I thought you would find it repulsive, Ellie."

Now her smile grew into a grin. "Adrian, did you ever see *Beauty and the Beast?*"

"You mean *La Belle et la Bête* by Cocteau? Yes, of course . . . though, frankly, it bites a bit close to the bone. I liked the ending, despite knowing better."

She nodded. "Yes, that'll do. Though I had the Disney version in mind. What do you *think* of the ending? What went through your mind when you saw it?"

"It's Disney . . . so of course the ending is happy. Well, to be fair, the Cocteau isn't much different. The story always gave me a little hope."

"I'll tell you what *I* thought of it. Here I was, putting myself in Belle's place . . . and inside I'm shouting at the end: *What's with this pansy prince? I want my* Beast *back!*"

This time he laughed aloud. "But, Ellie," he said gently. "Mine is not an animated beast."

She shrugged. "Sure. If it was just a sabertooth . . . I'd be a bit nervous. But it's got *you* inside it, doesn't it?"

"Yes, certainly. But, Ellie, I am the most dangerous beast of all."

"Nah. You've got you inside you too, if you'll pardon the grammar. What you are is *strong*, Adrian. I can deal with that. I like it, actually. Women generally do—like strong, dangerous-but-safe men, you know? Bad boys who aren't really bad down deep. It's one reason I fell for you in the first place."

His laugh had something of a groan in it. "Oh, please, please, tell me I am not Heathcliff!"

"No, no . . . Mr. Rochester, maybe . . . though we don't have to remove the hand or make you blind to make you safe. Your conscience is a much more effective set of controls!"

"You flatter me," Adrian said.

"Hey, we're engaged. It's my job."

"And mine to see you safe," he said, humor fading to grimness. "Come. We must get you home before anyone notices you are gone."

"It's a house, not a home, but I know what you mean. Here, kitty, kitty!"

His smile faded into the fanged grin of the sabertooth, like a Cheshire cat in reverse.

Let's make my brave words true, she thought, and swung herself across the great animal's back. *Be what you want to seem, as the man said.*

"Hi-yo Silver, away!"

Lounging by the pool in the afternoon felt good after a swim and a late rising.

In fact, I feel good generally, Ellen thought. *Odd. Nothing's changed, but I'm . . . hopeful. Why?*

Somehow she didn't feel really curious about that either; the thought faded from her mind.

There were a number of swimming pools in the grounds of the *casa grande*. This one was a rectangle of pale-veined Vermont marble with rounded ends, a hundred feet long and sixty wide. A fountain threw water high in the center, three stone basins stacked above each other on a central shaft. There were several pieces of statuary around it, done in the smooth French *moderne* style of the 1920s.

They included a classical-themed *Leda and the Swan* that grew more disturbingly realistic the longer you looked at it. Unnervingly so, if you were a lucy, with Leda's splay-legged position and the expression of hopeless horror on her face beneath the great rampant bird that gripped her with wings and beak. That made you think about the truth behind the myth, and the mocking joke behind the statue.

Leila and Leon were playing in the shallow portion, like two lithe brown otters, with a nanny watching from the edge; Monica's children were there too. The other end had a curving semicircular colonnade, two rows of stone pillars supporting a bronze trellis with wisteria growing woven through it, the purple-white-lavender bunches of blossom hanging overhead and scenting the air with a delicate, elusive scent amid the flickering shade. Adrienne and Dale and Michiko were resting on couches grouped around a low table, close enough for conversation, which was in some sneezing-clicking guttural language. Ellen suspected it was Apache, but couldn't have been sure even if she'd been able to break the sounds down into separate words.

"I'm glad Josh and Sophie are getting to know the *Doña*'s children," Monica said to Ellen.

The lucies were lying on loungers underneath the pergola, a little aside from their Shadowspawn.

"You are?" Ellen said neutrally.

"Oh, yes. By the time Leon and Leila are old enough to need lucies, Josh and Sophie will be ready for initiation," Monica said happily.

"Ah . . . well, that's one career choice," Ellen said neutrally.

"Wouldn't it be marvelous? Well, it all depends on what Leon and Leila want, of course. I've got such bright kids, I'm sure they'll have a lot of alternatives. *They* won't have any problems with college!"

Dale's lucy Kai was wearing nothing but a black bowler hat; the rest of them had bathing suits on, albeit topless for the women. She held up a bottle of lotion-cum-sunblock.

"Anyone want a rubdown with this stuff?" she asked brightly.

"No, thanks," Monica said.

Ellen and Peter and Jose shook their heads; Wayne Jackson didn't notice the invitation. He was thinner than she remembered from San Francisco, and occasionally tears dripped from his eyes. The other lucies ignored him courteously.

Or because it's just too difficult to deal with it, Ellen thought grimly. *It could be any of us, if Adrienne decided to destroy someone. Nobody talks about whatever happened to Jamal, either. Or maybe he's destroying himself with guilt, too. Christ, I feel guilty enough, and I haven't been helping plan the destruction of the world!*

"Hell, anyone want to give *me* a rubdown?" Kai inquired.

"No, thanks," Monica said again.

Kai subsided and picked up a book of hentai manga; from a glimpse, it mostly involved tentacles and orifices. Ellen smiled a little to herself. Monica went on with a luxurious, but cautious, stretch:

"By the way, Ellen, thanks for introducing Adrienne to that delicious silk whip thing."

"Ah . . ." Ellen said. "You're welcome, I guess."

"I've always liked the smacking and spanking and smothering—well, I learned to get into that pretty quick after I came here—but I could never really enjoy being beaten with *things* before, however hard I tried. That riding crop just plain *hurts*. Adrienne chased me around with the silk whip last night after the first feeding; she used to use the riding crop for that. Those lovely silk thongs can give you a nice toasty glow, though."

"Glad you had a good time."

Monica nodded with a dreamy smile. "We were both laughing while she chased me—well, I was laughing and then squealing when she got a good swat in somewhere tender—and then she'd *catch* me and really lay into me until I sobbed and yelled for mercy and then she jumped on me and we really got down to stuff. Then more feeding, and . . . I can't think of when I've had a better time, even with the carpet burns."

What was it that Robbie Burns said? Ellen thought. *"Oh that we had the gifte gi' us/Tae see ourselves as others see us." That* does *sort of sound like fun, apart from the no-limits terror at the back of your mind. Except I think Monica was originally a straight vanilla type and would have screamed with* horror *at the thought of that sort of playing . . . even without the really weird blood-drinking Shadowspawn could-kill-you-anytime part.*

"Ummm, yeah, that sounds enjoyable," she said aloud.

"*Oh*, yes. And afterwards I was lying there thinking *I can't feel my legs anymore* and the *Doña* said, *I can always rely on you, Monica.* What do you think of it, Peter?" Monica asked brightly. "Isn't the sting it gives nice?"

The slight blond man was looking fragile today. "Ah, it's certainly less uncomfortable than the riding crop," he said politely, and Jose rolled his eyes.

A Taint in the Blood

"Lame, totally *lame*," Kai muttered, on a rising note, getting up and tossing down her book of cartoons. "What a bunch of playacting—"

Dale Shadowblade glanced up in irritation and made a gesture. Kai stopped in mid-syllable and froze, her eyes going wide. A low keening sound came from beneath her clenched teeth. Then she toppled slowly backward, head and shoulders into the pool and then the rest of her slowly sliding after. The Shadowspawn laughed. Jose and Peter jumped to their feet, looked at each other, and then leapt into the pool after her. Between them they manhandled the slim, limp form to the stone; she lay facedown with water trickling out of her mouth.

"*Doña?*" Ellen asked.

Adrienne looked over, smiled, and raised a brow at the man. He shrugged and glanced; Kai's body bucked and heaved, and she gave a whoop and coughed up more of the water. The two lucies helped her to her deck chair, and she lay quietly for a few minutes. Then she blinked, scrubbed her face, and reached for the manga. It dropped through her fingers and Ellen instinctively picked it up and handed it to her.

"Thanks," she said in a small, hoarse voice.

Adrienne raised her voice slightly. "It's really time to start getting ready for the birthday party," she said. "We wouldn't want anything to go wrong!"

CHAPTER TWENTY-TWO

A bronze bell rang through the night. The crowd walked towards the Japanese garden in chattering clumps, beneath the colorful paper lanterns. Tonight everyone *was* in Japanese costume; Adrian felt at ease in the *hakama* outfit, and it was certainly comfortable and—much more important—suited for quick action.

Plus night-walking like this I can go impalpable at any time. Convenient, if you don't mind being naked while people are trying to kill you.

These last nights and days were the longest consecutive period he'd ever been out-of-body. He was finding it subtly disturbing.

Or possibly seductive is a better word.

There was a wild freedom to it that made him understand why Mhabrogast treated existence as a dream that could be shaped by wishing it so.

In the days of the first Empire of Shadows the speakers of the lingua demonica *must have been mostly postcorporeals. For them, existence was a long fantasy of blood and lust and power.*

He licked the last of Cheba's blood off his lips with a slight grimace. She hadn't fought him this time, either. He was very glad that he'd be away or dead tonight.

"I feel as if I were in a performance of *The Mikado*, Wilbur," his father murmured, gesturing with his fan.

"Such a stuffy death," Adrian replied with a smile.

"I'd better circulate. My company is still *slightly* radioactive with Hajime's people and seeing us much together would do you no good."

They walked through the gateway; it was a little eerie to see the same place he'd come as the smilodon thronged with a laughing, chatting crowd in kimonos. The darker, restrained colors of male garb mixed with the golds and scarlets and indigos of the women. Hajime's was an exception to the men's soberness, a deep red with gold accents.

Even more colorful were the decorated *fukusa* cloths that covered the gifts on a long table; one caught his eye, embroidered on silk satin, lined with soft crepe silk. Forests of pine tossed beneath clouds; water fell down a mountainside to a river as if it were falling from the sky and was rippled to shore. A Chinese man played the *koto* among a meadow of camellias, beneath a blossoming plum tree and flying cranes.

"Lin Bu," Ellen murmured to him, seemingly casual. "A Soong-era nature poet; he used to call the plum-blossoms his wife and the cranes his children. The pines and camellias are supposed to signify longevity. That's Edo-period work."

Adrian/Wilbur nodded. His hand brushed hers, and he felt her take what he held.

Now we're totally committed, he thought. *She can't escape detection for long now. And there's only one reason for a normal human to have* that *tucked into their clothing, and no way she could have gotten it except from someone like* me. *Plus my supposed renfields have quietly decamped . . . You're back in the war, Adrian, and playing for higher stakes than mere life and death this time.*

A gong rang, and the guests grouped themselves along the long low-slung tables, with cushions to sit cross-legged on. Servants appeared, bringing sake—in square wooden boxes, the ultra-traditional form that had started out as rice-measures, each of six fluid ounces. They rested in little dishes and were filled to overflowing, for abundance and hospitality.

Adrian was on the other side of the table from Hajime, and three places down; Adrienne was on his other side, in the place of honor. That would be awkward, but he was close enough, and as a bonus he could hear the conversation.

"Ah, Yonetsuru Daiginjo sake," Hajime said. "I grew up drinking this! Though now I'm older than even the average in Yamagata. *Os-houshina!*" he added, in the dialect word for *thanks*.

"*Sasukune!*" Adrienne replied in the same local variant of Japanese, topping him neatly with *you're welcome*.

"*Kampai!*"

He laughed and lifted the box carefully to drink from one corner, smacking his lips.

"Flowery and fruity and just a bit rough," he said with satisfaction. "Enough to stand up to this *masu*, though I'm glad you haven't gone too far and used cedarwood ones. Bottoms up!"

"I liked the look of this dark oxblood red lacquer," she said, when they'd each drained theirs. "Do have a little more."

She poured for him and his wife and returned to her own.

"Ah, *longevity*," Hajime said, studying the ideogram in the bottom of the *masu*. "Very pretty calligraphy, too."

Adrian sipped; it *was* good, if you liked warm rice wine, which he did. The problem would be to drink enough to lull suspicion but not enough to fuddle himself. This sort of party would make restraint rather conspicuous.

At least the others aren't even trying *to hold back,* he thought; Adrienne was emptying hers as well—more or less obligatory, for good manners' sake.

Eat, Adrian, eat. Relax your stomach muscles . . . deep breath . . . the aetheric body needs oxygen too.

Shiizakana came next, the appetizers that went with the sake. Asazukiri Tofu, presented on a bamboo plate with a slice of Yuzu fruit, and on the side citrus-infused salt, plum-infused salt, and soy.

"Ah!" his immediate neighbor said, a Tōkairin retainer. "*Really* fresh, not that glue paste you get in the stores."

It *was* good, the bland-sweet-bitter tastes flowing through his mouth . . . and it would help sop up the alcohol. A pity that there was no rice, but that would come towards the end of the meal, if they followed the ancient pattern. The second dish to arrive was *Gindara no Saikyo Yaki*, grilled black cod marinated in Saikyo Miso sauce. The black cod was moist, but not turned into fish jelly; the Saikyo Miso taste was delicate, just short of being too salty.

If I'm going to die, at least it won't be with overcooked cod in my stomach, he thought.

Though, as he was night-walking, the contents would just fall to the ground if he disintegrated in Final Death. That made him grin; at least he could count on making a disgusting mess at his sister's party, even if he failed.

He looked over to Ellen; she was at the lucies' table, behind the principals but not too far, talking easily to the others—the striking dark-haired woman, the slight blond man and a Latino who looked like he'd stepped from a motorcycle ad but who wore the *hakama* with surprising ease. One of them made a joke, waving something in his chopsticks.

The sight line isn't good enough while everyone's seated, Adrian decided grimly. *And Hajime's between Harvey and Adrienne.*

The head table wasn't sheltered by the roof of the shrine—Harvey's shooting position above the cave would clear it. But not by *enough*; he hadn't allowed for the fact that the seating was so low, cushions on tatami-mats on the ground instead of chairs.

The surge of murderous rage that twisted at his pseudo-gut was so intense that a few of the other Shadowspawn immediately looked his way. He smiled at them and lifted the wooden *masu* again.

"Kampai!"

Wakatake Onikoroshi this time, a bit sweeter; and after all, gusts of murderous passion weren't all that uncommon among his breed. A deft servant refilled it, and he cursed her mentally with a smile still on his lips.

This is taking too long! I have to get Harvey a clear shot at her!

The next dish arrived: *Akiyasai no Tempura,* deep-fried seasonal vegetables in a light crisp batter, with green-tea-infused salt, and Japanese plum-infused salt too.

"Umejio!" his neighbor said with relish. "Really, I'm surprised. The Brézé has outdone herself! These are *Japanese* plums in the infusion, I'm sure."

"If you're going to do it, you might as well do it right," Adrian agreed.

His aetheric body was producing a slight sheen of sweat on the forehead. He took a stick of the asparagus; it was meltingly tender yet with a faint hint of crispness, and half-sweet against the salt savor of the plum; it went well with the peppers and maitake mushrooms as well.

Hajime and his wife and Adrienne and Michiko were all laughing together, looking disgustingly contented. He gritted his teeth; there was nothing quite as annoying as someone else carefree and happy when you were trying to throw yourself into combat mode. Dmitri was there too . . . and night-walking, for some reason.

"Kampai!" Adrienne called to the guests. "Bottoms up!"

Damn you! Adrian thought. *Food! Bring me food, or I'll have to make my escape in python form because wiggling on my belly like a snake will be all I can do!*

The rustling silk of the servant's kimono rescued him; this time it was rough earthenware plates with *Maitake to Yuba no Usudaki*, mushrooms wrapped in Yuba tofu with special soy, and then diced horse mackerel with green onions to make a tartare in a lettuce cup. The oil in the fish would insulate his stomach.

And damn evolutionary kludges! He wasn't even really *here*, but his hindbrain insisted on treating his aetheric form as if it were his birthbody.

More food: sashimi of Scabbard Fish, char-grilled young conger eel, deep-fried breaded fillet of Berkshire pork with katsu sauce, baby sweetfish steamed in an earthenware *donabe* pot with rice . . .

Rice at last! Adrian thought, and wielded his chopsticks; he let the Power pick an instant and poured the sake from his wooden box into the pot as well, getting it out of sight.

. . . shiitake mushrooms with burdock root, buttery Monkfish livers, free-range chicken broiled in Hoba leaves, a rice soup of red sea bream, Hirame halibut, crab and shrimp, stewed together . . .

I've got to stop going with the flow, Adrian thought desperately. *This place is too goddamned* soothing. *I can feel the Wreakings making me feel all social and disinclined to make a fuss. I've got to make something happen . . . something that* uses *the way she's set it up!*

Mhabrogast spilled through his mind. Sense the possibilities, *push here . . .*

It was surprisingly easy; the Wreakings Adrienne had soaked into the field to dampen aggression and soothe suspicious, isolate Shadowspawn natures worked in the same direction. So did his link with Ellen; he could feel it resonating as he pushed delicate lines and needles into the Wreakings sourced from her blood and pain, and he could see her shiver suddenly as if a cold touch had skimmed across her shoulder blades. Their eyes met for an instant as the yuzu-citrus-flavored sherbet was set before each guest in a champagne flute.

Now!

"A few words, Tōkairin-sama!" he called. *So Adrienne has to get up and give a reply.*

The man in the scarlet kimono looked over, surprised. Another *push*, and smiles spread down the table and to the rest; a scatter of applause grew into clapping and calls of: *Speech! Speech!*

"This is my hundredth and tenth birthday," the silver-haired man said as he stood. "I am nearly eleven-one today—"

No! Adrian thought.

Hypersensitive, the tendrils of the Power *felt* the oncoming wave of violence.

No! Not yet! Not until she replies!

Suddenly Adrienne *was* standing, or half-standing. She crouched on her feet and threw an arm around Hajime.

"Lord Hajime! I sense an attack! Your life is in danger! Dimitri, transform!"

Damn, Adrian thought with grim resignation. *Merde. Name of a black dog. My plan has met their plan and the inevitable fuckup has begun. Now to improvise faster . . .*

Aloud: "*Amss-aui-*ock!"

Change flowed through him, effortless, the unbearable complexity of human thought slipping away into the simple focus of the saber-tooth's incarnate purpose.

Kill.

The guests on either side of him tumbled away, yelling, as the great beast crouched on the discarded tumble of Adrian's kimono. He *felt* Hajime decide not to go impalpable—and felt the push behind it, the sudden taste of his sister's Power, like a razor across the tongue. He screamed and leapt.

Power hummed through the air, twisted at the fabric of existence as dozens of Shadowspawn minds reacted with instinctive fear and rage to the sudden shocking threat. World-lines writhed and tangled.

Hajime snarled and whipped out the curved *tanto*-dagger that had been hidden in his sash. Then the lined face turned towards the smilodon went rubbery with shock—physical shock, a rippling idiot's grin as the massive high-velocity .338 sniper round punched into his skull behind the left ear and blasted out most of the front of his head. Almost in the same instant the dying mind lost control of its pseudo-body; to Shadowspawn senses there was a silent scream, as the personality and the others it Carried within dissolved into entropy. A brief glimmer, as if seen from the corner of the eye, and the scarlet kimono and the knife fell to the ground amid the harsh unpleasant smell of stomach contents.

She was holding him, the remote human portion of his mind knew. *Holding him in palpable form.*

The rest of him was outstretched paws with claws like giant fish-hooks, mouth open a hundred and eighty degrees to bare the ivory daggers for the killing strike.

Adrienne leapt backward herself. That put her in view of the waiting marksman . . . but just then another form erupted upwards, in the shape of a Ruwenzori gorilla, a giant silverback male. One of its great black hairy-spider hands *happened* to throw a plate into the air. At precisely the angle needed to deflect the bullet that would have smashed her spine. Fragments of it hummed through the air, and he jinked aside as he landed.

The gorilla threw itself forward and came down with both bent, immensely powerful legs between his shoulder blades. Five hundred pounds of bone and muscle hammered the sabertooth's belly to the ground, and the gorilla's bunched fists hit him in the back of the head with all the strength of the tree-thick arms. A fang splintered agonizingly on the rock pavement as his head was driven downwards.

"Alive!" he heard his sister snap. "Alive, Dmitri!"

I am not afraid, Ellen knew, as the ceremonial dinner dissolved in chaos. *I may be about to die, but I'm not* afraid. *For the first time in months.*

Peter was down on one knee, looking around . . . curiously. Jose had grabbed Monica and thrown her to the floor, pitching his body over hers protectively and swearing in English and Spanish.

Ellen's head turned, to where Adrienne sprawled backward a yard away from two great battling animal forms.

"Alive!" she heard the Shadowspawn woman say. "Alive, Dmitri!"

Ellen pulled the lead foil tube out of her obi, took a deep breath and whipped it down on Adrienne's half-bare sandaled foot with all the strength of a forehand smash. The Shadowspawn doubled over with a—literally—inhuman screech as the hypodermic within slammed through bone and tendon, pumping its load of silver-solution and radioactive waste into her tissues.

"Hey, bitch, I'm not your bitch anymore!" Ellen shrieked, in an abandonment of rage. *"And* fuck *your fancy lingerie and* stupid *sadistic head games!"*

Adrienne's head came down, her teeth bared in a killing lunge. The flask of hot *Honjōzō-shu* sake in Ellen's other hand splashed out and took her full in the eyes; she went over backward in a flailing heap, the barest instant before another of the heavy .338 bullets cracked through the space her head had occupied.

Adrian-smilodon's forepaws gripped the flagstones and flung him upward despite the weight on his back, the taste of blood and pain in his mouth, the whirling in his head. He turned as it left him in a blur almost as fast as the double strike of his talons; flesh and hair ripped as one scored across the gorilla's belly. It screamed and rolled backwards, wrenched a board loose from the table and took stance—kendo modified for the giant ape's form. Behind it Adrienne shrieked in mingled pain and rage herself, sprattling in the confining silk lengths of her kimono.

"Adrian!"

The voice cut through his rage, and he stopped the strike that would have disemboweled her.

"Adrian, the soldiers are coming. We have to *go.* I got the hypo into her. Go, go!"

Her weight landed on his back. He launched himself forward in the same instant, high above the gorilla's strike. His foreclaws caught at the wooden beams of the shrine's roof, then his hind-legs sank into the wood and launched him forward. Ellen clung desperately, and the night rushed by them.

Harvey Ledbetter let the sniper rifle drop on its bipod, patting it affectionately.

"Said I'd go for Hajime if you gave him up," he chuckled softly. "Didn't say nothin' to your little friend Michiko about not killing *you* next if I got the chance, did I?"

He rose and stepped through the camouflage screen and onto the edge of the steep almost-cliff. A ripple went down his spine, the Power speaking, and ancient human fear; a night-walker was coming.

The smilodon was staggering as it approached, and Ellen Tarnowski slipped to the ground, struggling out of the remnants of her kimono.

"Th-th-that was *wild*," she wheezed, and then astonished him by grinning.

"You and Adrian may pull it off yet," he said, as the great cat slipped past.

Adrian had a hand to his jaw as he walked out of the cave in his birth-body; the other held his Glock. His fatigue-clad form moved with a slight stiffness, three days of inaction telling even on one so fit.

"I still *feel* as if I have broken a tooth," he said; then he looked at Ellen and smiled a long slow smile. "It feels *good*. You were magnificent, and I love you utterly!"

"Hey, the feeling's mutual, Big Cat Guy—"

"Let's go," Harvey said. "Save the mushy stuff for later."

"The rifle?" Adrian asked, all business.

S. M. STIRLING

"Leave it, too heavy. Monster Truck gun here will do; she's my main squeeze anyway. The Hummer's still two miles thataway and we ain't clear yet. Vamoose!"

"This is the weapon," the Tōkairin retainer said.

"Yep," Dale Shadowblade said, handling it gingerly.

Even with protective gloves the silver was painful, and the glyphs were a menace. Though not to a user who pointed it at a Shadowspawn with ill intent.

Crack.

The flash strobed through the night, a dazzling T-shape from the muzzle-brake and the muzzle itself. The bullet punched the Tōkairin in the center of his black-clad body and hurled it backward in the wake of fragments of heart and lungs and spine, and Dale worked the bolt to chamber another.

Click. Click-click-click-click.

The assault rifles of Captain Bates' squad misfired as one, all aimed at the second Tōkairin.

"Pretty impressive Wreaking." Dale nodded, grinning.

Crack.

This time he had the leisure for a head-shot, and the back of the other Shadowspawn's head struck the rock wall of the cliff as the bullet *peeenned* off into the darkness.

Bates was sweating as Dale closed his eyes and concentrated.

"Don't worry," the Apache Shadowspawn said easily, wiping off the weapon before he set it down again. "Looks like those Brotherhood terrorists killed another couple were-Japs and made their escape. How fucking tragic. Still, we tried, hey?"

*   *   *

"Gun it, ol' buddy," Harvey said.

He grinned like a shark. Adrian's smile matched his. Ellen looked between them with a slight frown.

"Sorry, Ellie," Adrian said. "We were reliving old times."

He put the heavy vehicle in gear and stamped on the gas pedal; the wheels spun, and they began to lurch faster and faster down the rough forest track.

"Ah . . . don't you need the headlights?" she asked.

"No, in fact," Adrian said.

He could *still* feel the lance of pain in his upper jaw, where the equivalent of the sabertooth's canine was. His laugh was joyous nonetheless.

"Next stop, Amalfi."

"Yeah," Harvey said, as Ellen smiled back at him. "And then, Tiflis."

EPILOGUE

Adrian sat in the deep stone windowsill, barefoot and naked to the waist in his loose cotton pants, a cigarette in the hand that rested on his raised right knee. Ellen leaned back against the pillows and the headboard of the bed, watching his face as he looked down from the *alberghetto* towards the Mediterranean, squinting a little into the setting sun. The summer day was cooling towards evening, and there was a slight smell of lemon from the grove around the inn; more distantly the town-scents, and underneath it all pine and sea.

I could look at him forever, she thought.

He turned his head and looked at her. "And how are you feeling, Mrs. Brézé?"

She writhed deliberately in the tumbled sheets. "Sore. Tired. Otherwise fine. You go back to your deep thoughts. You look prettier than Rodin's *Thinker* in that position anyway."

"I was not thinking . . . just enjoying being alive. It is not a sensation I had much of, until we met."

Sleep came easily; there was plenty of time for a nap before they wandered down into the city for dinner. Her eyelids drooped.

Hallo, chérie, a voice said, and gold-flecked eyes looked at her. *Have you missed me?*

Ellen darted upright, gasping, feeling the sweat sheen on her face. It was darker, and the last of Adrian's cigarette made a red coal-star in the night as he turned.

"Ellie?" he said.

She put her hand to her head as the images slid away into a confused jumble. "I—I think I had a bad dream. About . . . you know. I . . . it's gone."

He came over to the bed, leaned down and kissed her gently. "That will pass."

"Yeah."

She took a deep breath. "Feel like a shower before dinner?"

A long slow smile. "But certainly. It *is* our honeymoon!"